Something Small
That Saved Us All

Samantha Narelle Kirkland

 www.trafford.com
North America & international
toll-free: 1 888 232 4444 (USA & Canada)
fax: 812 355 4082

DEDICATION

On January 20, 1961 E. B. White espoused how he felt as he sat in front of his television and watched the newly inaugurated President Kennedy take the oath of office:

> "One of the excitements of American citizenship is a man's feeling of identity with his elected leader. The man spoke with such verve, the lectern seemed to catch fire!" [1]

This book is dedicated to the many millions of Americans who were sentient, eager, and hopeful citizens on one fateful November day when our collective national faith in the future was shattered.

We were fortunate to have had John Fitzgerald (Francis) Kennedy as our inspiration, albeit too briefly. This tribute is intended to return, if only for a whimsical moment, to a time when Camelot was ours.

Notes

[1]   Schlesinger, *A Thousand Days*, pp. 731-732.

CONTENTS

TRIBUTE TO A FALLEN LEADER

He was flawed, both physically and morally,
Perhaps even more so than prior presidents.
But this very mortality enhanced the clarity
Of his thinking, vision, and understanding.
While holding this highly consequential, stressful job,
He proved to be a natural chief executive.
His character enabled him to select the correct
Solution when those near him were bent on
The pursuit of war as a hotly violent panacea.
We saw him as leading our nation to a better future,
One that extolled the virtue of the Everyman,
A land where all of us would have the opportunity
To earn and keep the fruits of our sweat and labor.
He would lead us to the sunny side of our possibilities.[1]
During two fateful weeks in his second October,
When the survival of the entire world wavered,
Our President chose a course that saved us all.
Yet not very long thereafter, we lost him forever.
What follows is what we wished had happened.

---

1   Bishop, p. 302

Dear Reader, please note:

Out of respect for those in the spotlight of history, key people herein have the spelling of their names slightly altered throughout this book.

After all, a storyline such as you hold in your hands is but a fantasy which, to this day, remains unfulfilled...

SOMETHING SMALL
THAT SAVED US ALL

PREFACE

Once you loved and respected John Fitzhugh Kennerly, you never got over him.

Although he was young as elected presidents go, this man was unusually astute when he became the leader of our nation. With many years of thought-provoking study of influential men such as Winston Churchill behind him, he assumed office with a clear concept of how he could make America a better place in which to live. More importantly, he had the inner fortitude required to take us there.

Elected as our President while in his mid-forties, he was tall, charmingly handsome, and possessed a smile that captivated women while expressing self-assurance to men. He embodied a buoyant attitude and a ready intellectual wit which enabled him to inspire Americans to achieve wondrous things. The key was to get everyone working toward such goals. This would require, accordingly, that each of us be empowered to participate and—even better—to benefit from such achievements.

This magnificent president desired to be remembered as a leader of high purpose and firm resolution. He was at his best when he was inspired, and thus far ahead of the people he governed. He'd beckon to us over his shoulder as if to say: "Get your hearts and minds ready, and then follow me!" Like a track star imbued with fleetness of foot, his mind raced ahead, striving to achieve the best for everyone.

Will we ever catch up?

SOMETHING SMALL

THAT SAVED US ALL

CHAPTER ONE

Meeting My Parents

I was sired on the back stairs of a hotel somewhere on the chilly plains of North Dakota. My mother was a comely gal who was employed as a housemaid. However, being young and unattached, she didn't want me. Moreover, Washburn, near Fargo, was a lonely place isolated by some of the most frigid weather in the country. As soon as she was freed of me, my mother headed for warmer climes. Thus, shortly after my birth on the 4th of January, 1932, I was immediately placed with an adoption agency and, when no takers came forward, I was sent far away to the Boston Atworthy Home in Massachusetts. I stayed at BAH in relative obscurity until just after my twelfth birthday.

As I grew old enough to be a young teen, what I came to value was freedom: to call my hours my own, to say what I thought, and to do what I wanted. The rules for behavior at the orphanage had encouraged me in this regard. The standards for molding behavior were not merely lax, they barely existed at all. They didn't have to be strong; the nuns saw to it that temptations within the orphanage walls were nonexistent. Even the jars containing the highly prized chocolate-chip cookies were kept locked in cabinets behind solid oaken doors. Towels and wash cloths were given out only on a one-for-one exchange basis. "If you lose it, you go without!" went the saying. When a boy asked for the loan of a volume from the small library, he had to sign his name on the Book Registry and return it undamaged within one week. If he failed to do this, he suffered the worst punishment that could be meted out: no cookies for a month.

We had very few personal possessions. A hair brush, two sets of pajamas, one pair of leather and one pair of canvas shoes, underwear, socks, winter coats and summer shorts, and a toothbrush were the only things that an individual kid could call his own. Even the uniforms we wore during the day were the property of the orphanage. Fun things, like soccer balls or kites, had to be checked out like a library book and then returned that same day. Looking back, I can remember thinking that the system was designed to stultify independent action and thinking.

One cold day in 1944, I got a real surprise. Sister Penelope came to my room and told me to follow her. At BAH, when one of the nuns summoned you, you followed without even a murmur of protest. "Management," as I had come to call the Sisters, was very strict on that point.

I was ushered into the inner sanctum of the Queen Bee, as we called Mother Agatha. She ran the place. As I entered, she gestured to the straight-backed chair in the center of the room. Once I was seated, she seemed to glide from behind her wide desk and then to hover over me. The nuns wore such long gowns or robes that you couldn't ever see their legs moving; hence, they appeared to float along the hollow, stone corridors of the refectory building.

Mother Agatha had some significant news, apparently. She placed a finger pointedly on my shoulder and then pressed her finger to her lips. That motion indicated, "Silence!"

"I have important news for you, Clint. You have been chosen by a young couple to join their family, we have met with them, and their application has been approved. You will be leaving us this afternoon, so take a few minutes to say goodbye to your friends here and then prepare yourself to become a member of the Brill family."

On that otherwise cold and dreary winter day, my life took a step toward genuine significance. I was surprised that anyone would want a spindly, dark-haired, green-eyed boy with pale skin. I'll bet that the Mother Superior neglected to tell my prospective parents anything about the pranks I pulled off while sheltered in the orphanage. The most notable one had taken place about two summers earlier. At the wise age of ten, I began to experiment with mankind's first significant invention: fire.

There was a thick stand of white pine and various other trees behind the dormitory that served as a kind of windbreak protecting the large windows of the dining hall from storm damage. In addition, it marked the property line divide on the grounds of BAH. A kid could go into this area during his free time without risk of being lost because a split-rail fence ran along the actual dividing line. All of us had been taught the honor system early on, so an individual was trusted never to scale that fence. Thus, you couldn't go very far into the woods; it was easy to remain on the grounds proper. Fortunately, this also meant that you would be within hearing if the supper bell rang or the call to worship sounded.

One Wednesday, with my classes over for the day but before having to sweep—yet again—that darn hallway in our dorm, I popped outdoors and found myself wondering what to do with this ever so sweet, but unavoidably short, personal time. It was the kind of summer afternoon when the warm air is still, the crickets are chirping, and the cicadas are droning their impossibly long buzzing. In short, it was a kind of special azure time when you feel glad to be alive but don't yet know how to express your happiness.

A thought gradually drifted into my young head. This would be the opportunity I'd been thinking about for a week. I'd dig a small pit and build a tepee with sticks and start a real campfire, just like the Indians used to do! I'd seen drawings of the chiefs adorned with their feathered headdresses sitting around what was called a "council fire" in my history books. I had matches stolen from the sacristy where I used to prepare the candelabra for Sunday services. I was reputed to be such a well-behaved boy that I had been serving as an acolyte for some months by then.

This was going to be fun! I'd get my fire going, enjoy it for a few treasured moments, and then blow it out and cover it with pine needles so there'd be no trace of what I'd been doing.

I prepared a mound of leaves and built a pyramid of sticks over them, leaving a small air opening into which I could insert the match. The thought of rubbing two sticks together and starting a fire with friction never occurred to me. Didn't the pioneers and natives have matches? As a ten-year-old, I figured they'd been around forever as one of God's gifts to enable Mankind to survive and thrive.

When I struck my match and inserted it into the bed of leaves, my disappointment was extreme. The match lit the leaves all right, but they promptly flamed together and withered to mere bright red glows along their stems. I would need kindling, tiny chips, and twigs to serve as a base to fire up my stick tepee. By the time all this had been figured out, I was pressed for time because I knew I should be cleaning that hallway. If that wasn't finished before the dinner gong sounded, I would be punished by having to sit at my place at the long table watching my mates eat while my meal was withheld.

I collapsed my sticks into a pile and carefully covered my once artful tepee over with pine needles so no one would know what I'd been doing. As I left the woods, I glanced back; the ground looked undisturbed with the ubiquitous needles evenly covering everything.

I remember thinking to myself: "What a pretty wooded setting! I'll be back to try again later."

Smiling a rueful grin—as though I had gotten away with something—I plodded over to the dorm, finished my sweeping, and then headed for a seat at the table as the dinner hour arrived. I was sitting munching and joking with my buddies when I looked ahead. I could see directly through the windows to where I had been experimenting earlier that afternoon. I stood straight up, horrified yet stunned: the little forest was smoking like mad and, down on the ground, I could see flames at least a foot high!

What had I done? I raced for the exit, thus causing everyone in the room to ignore their plates and watch my wild, sudden departure. As I dashed through the door, I heard someone command me to come back to my seat, but she was immediately drowned out by a chorus of voices saying, "Fire, fire! Let's go see it!"

I was already on my way to doing just that. I picked up two buckets and was filling them with water as others crowded around me to help. The grounds-keeper was summoned. He wisely poured dirt on the blaze, suffocating its oxygen supply faster than my dumping endless buckets of water would have.

My quick response saved the forest, but not my hide. When the Queen Bee discovered who had started this calamity, I was whaled well beyond mere reddening of the skin. Her punishment made my bottom feel like it was on fire itself for some three days.

As a result, I became known to all the nuns as a handful. I never sank to the level of a destructive prankster, but I was thereafter regarded as a kid possessing a restless mind. This made me develop my own kind of inward self-assurance. Everywhere I went for the rest of that summer, the other kids—including my own friends—would stare at me, muttering softly to each other as I passed by. For their part, the proctoring nuns never let me out of their sight. Even if I asked to go to the bathroom to relieve myself, a sister would accompany me and wait outside the door until I finished and returned to whatever I had been doing.

With all this attention, I developed a defensive sort of stare. My gaze became steady, even piercing. As the months passed, this trait discomfited many prospective adoptive parents. Thus, I'd been hanging around for some time and was fully twelve years old when the Brills first introduced themselves to the Queen Bee. Without a doubt, she knew just the kid whom she wanted to place with this innocent couple. I was about to be adopted sight unseen, but apparently fully described. I quickly deduced that Mr. and Mrs. Brill must be folks with firm backbones to want to take on someone with my reputation.

Upon my first encounter with newly-weds Lloyd L. Brill and his wife Ellie, probably I was more shocked by their appearance than they were by mine. He was only 22 while she was 20, far too young for the "standard-issue" adoptive parents. Apparently, they wanted to do something meaningful in the face of a world-wide conflict that had claimed the youth of so many nations. Then, when the war in Europe appeared to be winding down following the June 6 landings in France, they decided to adopt a male youngster who was in need of doting parents. They felt this would allow them to express their mutual love by requiring sacrifice for the benefit of another human being.

Since my adoption was to occur before they had children of their own, this plan made them an unusual couple by anyone's standards. For me, however, they were to prove absolutely key to my weathering the rough years of maturation.

* * *

I would come to love the Brills as if I had been born to them. The development of my strong feelings began the very first time I sat down to a meal with them.

"Clint, will you help me set the table for dinner?" Ellie's invitation sounded more like a command than a request.

"Gosh, Mrs. Brill, why? It's only 12:30." My response sounded more like a protest than a simple question.

"I'm sure the nuns taught you that the Sabbath is a special day of celebrating with worship. On Sunday, we always have dinner as a noonday meal; supper is a light soup and sandwich affair."

She looked commandingly at me while moving forward to place the various settings—mats, napkins, utensils—in my still unsuspecting hands. Clearly, this woman was not going to be cowed by my direct stare. No escape now; I had met my match and was hooked.

She sweetly smiled my way as she turned to fetch plates and glasses. Instinctively, I perceived that protest was useless. I was their child now, and I would have to learn, and then become a part of, their routines. Above all, I did not want to be sent back to the long hollow halls of the Home! I was lucky to have escaped that stultifying place. Here I was, being welcomed into the shiny warm lives of a loving couple: I wanted to become loved! At that moment, I left my troublesome nature behind forever.

"By the way," Ellie observed, "You might think about calling us 'Mom and Dad' when you're ready."

I could clearly see where my best chance to become happy lay. I behaved, and thus I stayed.

When I moved in with them just shy of becoming a teenager, I already held rigid prejudices about the value of parents and something the nuns at the orphanage wistfully referred to as a "secure home." As an abandoned youngster, such a place—and a person's longing for same—had always struck me as rubbish.

Back at BAH, anyone five years or older would be assigned daily tasks commensurate with his age. These were to be performed at the same hour each day, between 9:00 and 10:00 in the morning, and again for an hour in the evening. Fortunately, you would rotate through the tasks each week. For example, if you were assigned to help the kitchen staff scrub the floors and tables, you did that each day for one week, then you rotated to the next task such as sweeping the gymnasium's wood floor during the following week. You never got in a rut, and you were always trained how to complete a task correctly. Nevertheless, you were always watched as though you were expected to fail. Most definitely, you never were praised for doing a good job. Doing so was simply expected. Going unappreciated can be wearing.

Worse, the Mother Superior would make unannounced appearances to see how you were doing as you pushed, rubbed, and polished. Neither me, nor my roommates, could figure out how she could suddenly appear, as though emerging from within the very walls, and ominously loom over us with her hands clasped as though in stern judgment. If any one of the three failed to perform his task in an acceptable manner, then he as well as his roommates got only breakfast the following Saturday. Now that's tough on a growing boy!

I had to hand it to them. The nuns knew how to use peer-pressure to elicit correct behavior far better than even a willow stick laid across your bottom could.

On the other hand, if all three performed up to standard, each occupant was treated to half a dozen cookies at the end of the week. You were allowed to select which jar you wanted to raid. Since I vacillated between chocolate chip, oatmeal, and ginger snaps, the choice was important. I usually took two of each: I had a lot of cravings to satisfy. The older I got, the more intense these cravings seemed to become.

There was one huge benefit to this system: it instilled in me the value of teamwork.

The nuns were savvy enough to realize that a boy aged six was not going to be as ravenous as one who was twelve years old. Fortunately, once you reached the age of nine, every year thereafter entitled you to another three cookies in your allowable reward total. By the time I went to live in the Brill household, I was accustomed to receiving 15 cookies every Saturday; that is, if I had behaved properly. Such large caches of pleasure required that I own a sealable cookie jar of my own. When I passed my tenth birthday, I undertook some extra leaf-raking work to earn sufficient credits for just such a storage jar. I kept it in a cool, dark corner and frequently retreated to it in order to devour part of its contents. Consuming any one, or three, of these hard-earned treats always lifted my spirits considerably.

It required a few weeks, and some inspired hinting, before Ellie got smart enough to start providing similar stimulants for me.

It's much easier to go about completing a task if you know you will be rewarded. Simply being ordered to do it would often be enough, of course, but then I'd become grumpy and sullen. My descent into such a state would render me unfit to be around, no matter how clean the house would appear to be. So, a system of rewards similar to the one I'd been accustomed to was put in place by Lloyd, but on a grander scale—meaning hard cash—because, as he would reiterate, I was a young man now. His method proved to be very effective; his "carrots" soon enabled me to reach the point where, when Ellie would ask me to clean my room or tidy up the garage, I could smile with satisfaction and say:

"Gosh, Mom, it's already done!"

In this way, my time with Lloyd and Ellie Brill passed in nurtured security until about seven years later. In 1951, I graduated from high school at nineteen and began to make my own way in society. I was fortunate to have learned lessons in bravery and thoughtfulness regarding other people.

Looking back, I think the long persistence of the Great Depression sapped our nation's moral code. That dreadful period changed everyone. The behavior of people toward one another was governed by the simple need to survive from one day to the next. Respect for your own neighbor could quickly deteriorate if you could gain an advantage, no matter how fleeting, for yourself. Even folk who would, as faithful churchgoers, be supportive of persons in need were capable of stealing during the 1930's. "Help thy neighbor" was subordinated to the more pervasive: "I will help myself, thank you."

CHAPTER TWO

A Day of Infamy

One beautiful Sunday morning in December 1941, the Japanese attacked our Pacific outpost and harbor, badly crippling warships and air squadrons. We went to war with the Japs immediately and, shortly thereafter, Adolf Hitler's Third Reich declared war on America. Thus, an adult got out of bed one day and prepared to go to work on December 5th, but within a few days he was getting out of a bunk and training for war at sea, in the air, or—for those who liked hiking with blisters, dust up your nose, bug bites, and uncomfortable temperatures—as a foot soldier.

Of course, this world conflict didn't consume only those who wanted to shoot; it required support personnel as well. In this way, hundreds of thousands of young Americans were transported to foreign lands and exposed to standards of behavior that severely undermined the civility they had been brought up to respect. If captured by the enemy, this translated into abusive, demeaning cruelty as well as incarceration and, often as not, summary execution.

It must be remembered that, while America entered the fray in late 1941, we citizens were being required to make sacrifices well before then. These might be staple foods like sugar and flour, fuel for heating or travel, or even a new pair of socks. With the outbreak of war, we Americans found it difficult to retain friendships with ethnic groups within our own population. Germans and Italians were obviously suspect, the long-suffering Jews were to be pitied, and the far eastern "slant-eyes" were to be avoided or even placed in fenced pens.

As for Canadians or Aussies, well, they would have to be evaluated on a case-by-case basis. A common language would be insufficient, by itself, for American parents to permit fraternization with their daughters. Perhaps that explains why so many American women volunteered to become nurses overseas; once abroad, they would be subject to military regulations, but not to those of their parents.

Here is a recap of various events that will set the stage for what you are about to read.

1940: In October, Secretary of War Henry Stimson pulled from a glass bowl the Serial No. 2748 for a student at Stanford University Business School, John F. Kennerly. Rather than be drafted, he enlists in the Navy and eventually is assigned to command PT-109.

1944: At the Yalta Conference, Franklin Roosevelt, old and doddering, acts on the advice of General George Marshall, the esteemed WWII hero. Roosevelt gives away the farm to Stilan, including most of Eastern Europe as well as the Kuril Islands off the eastern coast of Siberia. The Communist takeover in Eastern Europe begins without being challenged by us, while Truman relegates the pro-West regime of Chang Kai Shek to insignificance as the Communist movement grows in China. This proves that even truly great people can make truly huge mistakes.

The oldest Kennerly brother, Joe Jr., is killed along with his copilot while flying a heavily bomb-laden plane on a daring classified mission against the suspected position of Hitler's "supergun" emplacements on the coast of France. The plan was for the men to bail out just prior to reaching the coast whereupon the plane would then be remotely guided to the target by a fighter plane piloted by none other than President Roosevelt's son, Elliott, who was flying alongside. Something shorted the electric trigger fuses and the massive load of explosives detonated with the two men still aboard. No bodies were ever found. Jack assembles a memorial book in his honor, *As We Remember Joe,* penning a chapter himself expressing his great love and admiration for his older brother: *He accomplished so much in the very short time in which he lived.* He could not know that historians would be writing much the same about him well into succeeding decades.

1945: We bomb Japan August 6 and 9; Emperor Hirohito surrenders his nation on August 14th. World War II is over.

1946: John Fitzhugh Kennerly from Boston, Massachusetts runs for a seat in the House of Representatives. Since he was a war hero and a descendant of "Fitzhoney" Kennerly, he wins.

1948: Jack's oldest sister Kik dies in a plane crash. Greatly loved, her death hits JFK hard. He decides to enter politics and devotes himself to becoming electable. Representative Kennerly even takes on the American Legion as archaic and out of tune with the needs of veterans. Kenneth McDonald is hired to manage JFK's political campaigns; he had been a roommate of Robert Kennerly while at Harvard, the football captain, a WWII bombardier, and a Nazi prison camp escapee. He can't help being impressed by JFK's inspired oratory and resulting crowd appeal, so he finds himself becoming devoted to his friend.

CHAPTER THREE

Learning to React like Dad

When I was around eight years old, I was tall and sturdy enough for the priests at the Boston Atworthy Home to let me try out for their baseball team. At this time, there were many fabulous professional players whom we kids idolized; however, I couldn't belt one like the Babe used to, nor run fast like Ty Cobb. I quickly determined that my physique and strength would never earn widespread acclaim.

What I did to compensate was to use a little mathematics to devise my stratagem. There are nine players on a team and nine innings unless the teams are tied in the bottom of the ninth. In that event, the ballgame continues until the tie is broken during the bottom of an inning. If a pitcher had a great day and threw a perfect game, this meant that the minimum number of times a player would come to bat was three. Since such perfection was rarely achieved, a typical game might see the batting order rotate four, and even six times through the lineup. My goal was to strive for three base hits. I figured I'd have between four and six chances each time and that sort of pressure I could handle. Since I never tried hitting for the fence, my swings were far more controlled and my hits more consistent. By the time I left BAH, I had earned the moniker of: "Mr. Reliable."

I had achieved a modicum of success; consequently, I loved the game.

During the early forties, even before our country's entry into the war, conditions got so bad that, for quite a while, we could not go to the parks, like Fenway Field, and gaze in wonder at our heroes playing baseball. To replace the many empty slots that opened as the professionals joined military units and left to train and then to fight abroad, the owners brought in girls as substitutes.

Girls? Ugh! When I became an older teen, I realized that females could be highly desirable. They could even be worth pursuing: they did indeed have unique attributes. However, even such special attributes had nothing to do with the world of baseball!

Being an orphan in an institution had left me with few alternatives for developing outside interests. Thus, by the time I went to live with the Brill family, I had become not merely strongly self-reliant, but also insular. What I needed as a teenager was the chance to develop some real abilities, as well as friendships.

When Mr. and Mrs. Brill showed up to adopt me, their timing could not have been better. Ellie had been in love with Lloyd since meeting him at Henderson State College in Arkansas; she didn't mind sharing him with me; she was sure she was pregnant and would thus need another hand to help with a newborn baby.

Ellie and Lloyd provided shelter, food, clothing, and—almost immediately—love. In retrospect, they did far more than serve as parents. They offered friendship. As an only child, Lloyd had felt the pangs of loneliness and boredom all his life. He wanted companionship as much as he wanted sex, so having both a spouse and a "child" suited him just fine.

First of all, my "father" was only ten years older than I was. He sported a thick crop of blondish hair and a jovial smile that seemed to be so broad you couldn't help being reminded of Jonah the Whale. Thus, he became more like an older brother as well as my dad. He had not yet served in the military, but Lloyd was already aware that he would probably do so in the near future. What he was looking for in me was, perhaps, the younger, adoring brother he had never had while a boy.

As a young man starting a family in 1944 and facing the world on his own, he needed someone with whom he could share the exciting lessons of life. He had begun accumulating these a few years earlier when he was employed as a counselor at a summer camp. It was situated in the mountains of New Hampshire and provided training in survival skills such as axe handling, canoeing, marksmanship, and weather forecasting. As he would relate fondly during quiet moments of reflection with me, those two summers in East Hebron at Camp Mowglis had revealed how fulfilling it is to nurture the sense of discovery in a bright-eyed boy. As a counselor, patiently coaching a lad in how to right a canoe or steadying his aim as the camper fought with the intricacies of a rifle sling, Lloyd learned to love being a teacher. He enjoyed the role of dispensing knowledge to eager young minds. He viewed young boys as a sort of sponge on two legs who could soak up his pearls of wisdom and then proudly run off to demonstrate their new-found skills to all the other boys.

I was the lucky one. As his son, I could have access to his accumulated wisdom anytime I wanted, all without charge. It was my dad's code of honor rubbing off on me that started my maturation. I witnessed numerous occasions where he would become embroiled in a situation and react reflexively with correct action. In the blink of an eye, he could reverse some danger into a thrilling adventure. I'll give you this example since, if it had not been for my father, I probably would not be alive to relate how exemplary his behavior could be.

Typically, a young teenager is just coming into his own as an athlete, yet struggling hard with conflicting, even overwhelming desires produced by his abundant, surging hormones. This certainly applied to me but, with my being adopted, I had an older "sister" as well as an older "brother" from whom I could learn much while sharing in nearly all their activities, discussions, and adventures. With this frame of mind, I traded a supervised but impersonal institution for a close-knit, interdependent family requiring commitment and shared responsibility. This structured form of living came in the nick of time. Not only did I thrive, but I learned how to have a sense of duty and to perform my assigned tasks diligently and faithfully.

To prove how comfortably secure I was in their home, I can attest that, even upon the arrival of a new sibling, I never became jealous of her. My little sister simply became one more person to love.

The main attribute that my new father embodied, and which he thus imparted to me by a kind of osmosis, was accountability. I found I was granted broad freedom so long as I shouldered the responsibility for the consequences resulting from my actions. More importantly, I developed a strong sense that, *when faced with danger, a man must react quickly, as though by instinct.* At such a moment, the typical delays inherent in thinking a problem through must be discarded.

I developed this skill without having to mull it over; all that was required was for me to emulate my father.

Our family of three was driving down a long straight country road in New Hampshire. We were moving at a responsible speed of 45 mph or so in a 50 mph speed limit zone. Out of nowhere, a sports car zoomed past, and I mean zoomed! It used the oncoming lane to speed by us at more than 80 mph, I'm certain. It seemed to disappear down the long straightaway in an instant. Even I, riding in the back seat, had felt the force of the wind as that car rushed by us.

After the speedster disappeared from view, we three relaxed and Ellie resumed telling the tale we had been enjoying before the scary interruption. We were merely thankful that the madman driver had not sideswiped our car. Whoever he was, he was now out of sight and, presumably, out of our lives.

Then my Dad drove around a blind bend in the road. To our horror, that very same car was sitting in our lane, idling a mere thirty yards ahead. Apparently, the driver had come to a full stop to await an oncoming car before he executed a left-hand turn onto a side road. There was absolutely no time in which to apply the brakes. If Dad had done so, he would have lost control and swerved sideways, causing us to roll or flip. If I had been old enough to be at the wheel, I would have frozen with fright, causing our car to smash straight into the stationary vehicle and kill everyone involved.

Swerving to the left was out due to the oncoming vehicle. Close by on the right, the roadway dropped down sharply into a deep drainage ditch. Careering to the right would surely have overturned the car, perhaps causing it to explode. Mother pressed her legs forward against the dash and braced her arms for the rear-end crash. I saw the inevitable as well and quickly stretched both my hands across the back rest while pushing my feet forward against the rear of the front seat.

My Dad made no such preparatory moves; however, neither did his concentration falter. I watched him as he simply looked straight ahead and gripped the steering wheel more firmly. Without braking at all, he guided our car astride the sports car with not more than one inch separating the two cars. I dared not budge, but I was sure our right-side wheels were spinning in empty air. I assumed he was hoping our momentum would keep our car upright long enough so he could steer to the left after passing alongside, thereby returning all four wheels onto the paved roadway once again.

As we flew past with unabated speed, I had just an instant where I glanced across to the face of the passenger in the right seat of the speedster. He was looking our way with terrified, wide eyes and a face screwed up tight, bracing for death.

It took less than a second for us to be past the danger and sailing smoothly down the road. My dad never twitched a muscle in hesitation. It was as if there had never been a problem. I had never witnessed such cool concentration and nerve when death was a mere breath away.

I averted my eyes from my Mother, however. I was sure she had wet herself while looking into the cavernous drainage ditch. I could picture her pretty blue eyes wide as saucers as she stared hard at the chilled stream coursing through the small gully formed from the adjacent upslope. The soft skin of her face bore a whitish appearance naturally, but today it had probably blanched translucent.

If she had looked in the mirror after returning home that night, she might even have noticed her first gray hairs.

Dad had been faced with several choices, either one of which would have ensured the death of his family, yet he had found the one opening which would bring us through the challenge. He had nary a doubt as to what to do.

I learned a very significant lesson that day: Immediate response, rather than freezing to consider alternatives, was the key to surviving in today's modern world of speed. React, take action without thinking, commit yourself to the course you have selected, and reflect on the possibilities only after the danger is safely past. Life was sure to present hazards where there would be no time for second thought. If you vacillate between alternatives, only sorrow—or worse—shall follow.

I might add that, to this day, I am grateful the scared passenger didn't open his door and try to make a run for it. Doing so would have forced calamity on us all.

* * *

I had no idea back then that all the lessons learned at my father's side would become imbued in my psyche. The example of behavior which my dad set enabled me, down the road, to perform well when faced with a crisis myself. For example, I was 19 and a senior in high school when some careless teen tossed a still-smoking cigarette into a barrel of trash which the janitor had not emptied. Maybe the kid wasn't being careless; perhaps he had done it on a dare just to see what would happen. If so, that would be a strange sort of curiosity for a person to possess. In the space of less than an hour, not just the trash, but the length of the hallway, was ablaze!

At the time, the entire student body was in the auditorium listening to some behavioral lecture being delivered by our principal. As he droned on, my buddy Hank Louis smelled smoke, opened the double doors, and promptly turned to shout for all to hear: "FIRE!"

In all the drills we had performed and practiced for clearing the building, none had ever been conducted as one student body. Certainly no drill had been executed by students from this very large room. Typically we would dutifully file from our individual classroom and then all the grades would assemble outside the building as the various rooms emptied. Today, however, we were all packed side-by-side in one huge group.

The teachers were not present; they were all taking it easy in the Faculty Lounge during the lecture. Thus, they were an entire floor removed from us students.

I heard Hank's warning and instantly sprinted from my seat. Propping the double doors fully open, I directed my friend to stand by the head of the emergency side door. His job would be to shepherd the group of pupils in the very front rows toward him.

"Hank, you take charge of that stairwell. Make everyone go single-file in an orderly fashion. Don't let them panic and start shoving each other."

As he dutifully headed off to the side exit, I collared Jason Henry and commanded: "Jason, keep these doors wide open and maintain calm as you guide students through. Don't let them pile up in a logjam."

"Don't worry, Clint. I've got this covered." His voice was controlled and steady: I knew he'd be rock-solid. He proved this by calling out to Pete Curry to go to the bottom of the stairwell and hold open the doors leading to the parking lot so everyone could escape into fresh air.

Then I turned to the student body. Even in the immensity of this auditorium, I could see they were showing signs of panicking as the smell of acrid smoke began drifting up toward the tall ceiling. I could sense the situation was about to slide out of control. Even Principal Edgars had been so surprised by this calamity that he remained standing next to the podium with lines of fear and bewilderment beginning to crease his expression. The surprise of the situation held him suspended from reality. He seemed to be gripped by so much fear that his mouth remained clamped shut.

Without considering what I was doing, I ignored him completely and stood at the end of the last row. These students were the closest to the rear double doors. I scanned along the eyes of the obviously terrified students. Each seemed to be riveted to his or her seat with dread, but I held my arms out to my sides and said, "Rise together on my command!"

They each looked toward me and fixated on my arms as though they were angels' wings of deliverance. As I commanded: "Rise," I lifted my wings up and ordered: "File toward me and leave through the rear doors."

I wasn't thinking. I was just doing. My taking charge inspired them to dutifully file from this row and head for Jason standing by the double doors. Thereupon, I moved to the next row and guided those students to stand and file out in the same manner.

Every so often, I'd intone: "That's good. Move calmly and quickly. Keep your spacing and we'll all get out safely!"

Thankfully, I noticed that Principal Edgars had come down from the lectern and had positioned himself on the end of the row opposite me. As I would raise my arms, he would draw students at the other end toward him and then send them to where Jason was positioned. He moved in sync with my commands.

Suddenly, several students a couple of rows to the front stood all on their own. I lowered my right hand toward them, saying, "Stay seated. We will all get out alive if everyone follows my lead!"

I don't know whether it was the assurance in my voice or my confident bearing, but they listened and sat back down together.

Hank was not so lucky. A few enterprising students in the very front rushed his fire escape door and tried to crowd through but this caused them to start pushing and shoving with the pupils already filing down those stairs. A couple of younger kids tripped and fell, causing a bottleneck, so I grabbed Big Bill Bixby's arm and told him to help Hank regain control. As a large, imposing guard on our football team, Big Bill had little trouble getting the feckless fliers under control.

No one who followed my lead was hurt, and we escaped ahead of the life-threatening smoke. When the faculty members emerged from the lounge, they counted heads and found that everyone had safely gotten outside. I was written up in the school news for this; there was even a mention of my name in the local newspaper when it was published the following day. I simply shrugged it off as doing what was required at the time.

During the interview, I stated: "I just did what my dad would have expected me to do."

I must be forthcoming. On that day, I was not only among the oldest students in the school, but everyone knew me since I headed up our Safety Patrol. Its members were responsible for getting students safely across the two-way street which fronted the main building. This meant my team members had to be early to arrive in the morning, but they would be the last to leave as well, so I purposely rotated assignments so no one would become bummed out by an overly burdensome responsibility.

The advantage, of course, was the adoring adulation the girls would shower upon us. Perhaps that was due to the distinctive badges and hats we would wear while on duty. Frankly, I didn't care what the reason was; I simply enjoyed their attentions.

The fellas didn't tease us, not one bit. All my team had been chosen from the guys who were part of the football squad. Besides, something that was never mentioned, but was clearly understood, was our status: we could be late to class, or leave the day's last class early, and the teacher at the time would simply nod his head as if to say: "Okay, go ahead." Once a student had experienced such a privilege, he would be loath to lose it by being disobedient in some other manner.

I had no idea that my behavior during that fire emergency had been reported beyond our local Boston area. Apparently, some newspaper article on it appeared in papers 100's of miles away. It was noticed and cut out by a man named Kenneth McDonald. He was the Assistant for Domestic Affairs to some young, rising star in the U.S. Congress whose name was John Fitzhugh Kennerly. That man was serving as my parents' representative from "Bean Town."

Mr. McDonald, or perhaps the congressman he served, must have had connections with the Secret Service because, when I applied for a position with this organization after my graduation in June, a man named James J. Rowley responded to my letter of inquiry. He asked me to come to Washington for an interview. Since he claimed to be the chief of this government agency and had even enclosed a train ticket in his reply, I went.

I was tested on my physical coordination, eyesight, intelligence, and even my reaction time to a couple of staged situations. I can remember one of these tests vividly. At the time, it seemed simple—more like a prank than a test—so I didn't realize that it was part of their evaluation scheme. Only with later reflection did I realize my interviewer wanted to check on my reflexes.

He was pretending to reach across his desk to hand me a manual of some sort but, as his hand neared mine, he let the book slip from his grasp. With a quick, straightforward move, my outstretched hand caught it in mid-fall. Nothing would have been broken or spilled. Regardless, Agent Rowley, as chief of the Secret Service, must have been impressed. The agency asked me to return for a second round of interviews to be conducted with various members of the service whom I had not yet met.

Toward mid-afternoon of this second go-round, I completed meetings with several different men, as well as one woman. She in fact reminded me of our mousy librarian back at high school; that was not someone whom I could ever have imagined working as an Agent!

When I returned to the waiting room and resumed a seat, I still didn't have a feel for where I stood, so I merely occupied myself with the various magazines, as well as a pretty receptionist, located close at hand. I was miles away, absorbed in some adventure story about men in rowboats plying the Colorado River, when a man I had met earlier, Agent Gerald A. Bean, came in. He had the appearance of the successful football coach whom one reads about winning the latest state championship. Sporting dramatically broad shoulders, thick torso, crew-cut hair, and an expansive personality, I momentarily lost confidence in my application. I certainly wasn't the football hero type.

Therefore, he caught me by surprise when he reached out his capacious hand in a welcome-aboard. With surprise wreathing my face, I stood up.

"As the ASAIC here, I am pleased to say: Congratulations, Mr. Brill, we want you to be part of the Service. You're to report for your first day of training at..." (I'm sorry: this is a classified place which I am not permitted to divulge at this time).

CHAPTER FOUR

Leaving Home

As you can imagine, I entered the Secret Service as a raw beginner in late summer of 1951. However, that was not all. My dad had joined the army as a reservist a couple of years earlier. Life is filled with weird coincidences. Just as I was entering the Secret Service, Dad's unit was activated. In one brief period of just a few days, my mom Ellie was left alone at home with a newborn baby. Our writing letters to her would now be the only link to keep her connected with those whom she loved most dearly.

With my suitcase safely stowed aboard the train, I watched as my home town receded from view. For just a moment, I imagined my past being left behind as well, but then it suddenly dawned on me that Mom was about to become very lonely. On Tuesday of this week, she had been frenetically trying to keep up with a house stuffed with activity and chores and a nursing child as well as two male bodies. Suddenly, with the simple snapping of some suitcase clasps, her everyday world had come to an abrupt halt. Both her men had been removed from her daily life. In the morning, there'd be no need to rise and prepare a hearty breakfast; in the afternoons, no one to shepherd through schoolwork; and, as evening settled like a quiet cloying coverlet around her home, no one with whom to share the day's gossip. Could she get used to peace and quiet, with only a baby boy crying for milk, as her companion?

I'd never once given a thought to my mother's status while living with her and Lloyd. I'd merely accepted life as it then was. My being adopted had transformed my lonely world to one of happiness. I was loved every day. Those associations which work so wondrously when you are bonded with others by duty, honor, respect, and sharing make the closeness of family life uniquely satisfying. Regrettably, these very same bonds can really tug at your heart strings when forced separations arise.

As my rail car swayed gently from side-to-side and its trucks beneath clicked rhythmically over each passing bolt junction, I started to daydream about the household I was now leaving. My thoughts drifted to Ellie. It gradually occurred to me how hard life can be for the woman of the house. As I went about my daily affairs, having breakfast and attending school and returning home for a hot dinner, I always presumed my mother would be ever-present.

Look at her situation now. She gives her all to her men, but in a twinkling, they are plucked from her life. It has been my experience that women are more adaptable than men. Regardless, Ellie must have had to make quite an adjustment. Of course, numerous families in our community had suffered the wrenching pain of similar partings, so the women had managed by forming bonds amongst themselves without hesitation.

Over the next few years, there would be many who would have to fall back on the friendships formed during those desperate times. Simply getting through one day to the next would try many a woman's soul.

In 1951, the weekly casualty lists started getting very long.

CHAPTER FIVE

Cold Hell in Korea

These events are relevant to the time-line of this tale:

1949: After separating from the Navy, young Jack Kennerly is made aware that the daily pain from his Addison's disease, leukemia, and wartime maladies will never be cured. In fact, there is a real risk that these may cause his life to terminate early; consequently, he adopts a "live-for-today" attitude whereby he embraces a life-style where risk-taking is a constant companion. He turns to female companionship to alleviate his suffering, but upon meeting Jacquelean Bouffant, he decides she is the person with whom he wishes to sire children. His womanizing continues without letup despite having found his perfect wife.

Truman vacillates as Mao Tse Tung seizes China in a communist coup and sets about tightening his control over more than a billion residents.

1950: Alger Hiss, our ambassador to the United Nations, is jailed as a Russian spy. Julius Rosenberg sells atom bomb secrets to Russians. Late in the year, Chinese Communists invade N. Korea after NKPA forces are repulsed and then chased north by UN forces.

After eight weeks of active training stateside, my dad's division was shipped to the Pacific Theatre in the latter part of 1951. As he would relate almost two years later, these "civilian soldiers" ranged widely in age: from seventeen to forty-eight. As a group, their advantage was having known one another "socially," as they used to joke about their experience in the army reserves, for many months; thus, there was no adaptation when they were deployed. They arrived ready to fight as a team, already familiar with one another's personality quirks and theoretically sound fighting skills.

A few months before his company had been called up, Lt. Brill had participated in a company-side, and subsequently battalion-wide, competition during summer training at Ft. Bragg, North Carolina. Each man had been evaluated on appearance, conduct, knowledge of the twelve Standing Orders, manual of arms, as well as subjected to expository questions. Lloyd L. Brill had stood before the panel of testing officers and been asked a fire-and-maneuver question.

"Lt. Brill, your platoon has been notified that a German artillery battery has emplaced a half-mile from your position and is wreaking havoc on our boys landing on Omaha Beach. There are four 88's guarded by two machine-gun emplacements and a platoon of entrenched soldiers. You are unable to locate their forward observers. Your platoon must take these guns out. Explain your conduct of fire & maneuver."

"Yes, Sir! I would position each of my machine-guns opposite its German counterpart, and a three-man team would be assigned to outflank each nest and take the machine gun out with a triple grenade throw once the gunner's attention had been committed."

The examining officer nodded for him to continue.

"I would position pairs of riflemen as snipers to take out the crews servicing each gun, with orders to shoot once I gave the 'attack' signal." Second Lieutenant Brill's expression turned steely. He had read about this form of assault made famous by First Lieutenant Dave Winters back in the Second World War; subsequently, the method had been rendered as American doctrine. He could recite these maneuvers in his sleep.

"Then, Sir, I would take a small group with me and start at one end of the German defensive position until we had killed or captured everyone within the breastworks."

The officers glanced at each other as the interrogating officer gave an almost imperceptible smile.

My dad knew from his studies that the four German cannons had been spiked after their crews had been killed. The American side lost one man to a trip-wire snare, and several were wounded, but the mission was 100% successful. That lieutenant had been promoted to captain shortly thereafter. However, his fast rise did not go to his head. For the duration of the war, this officer continued to lead paratrooper units sensibly and without fanfare. Having been wounded three times during his active duty, the then Major Winters remarked to the throngs of reporters who greeted him upon his return to America that, indeed, his greatest triumph had been to live through the war.

That was the kind of leadership my dad wanted to exemplify. He admired the valor required of those committed, whether under orders or by heroic voluntary action, to gaining a strategic objective in wartime.

During the completion of the exam process, he was asked whether there was anything he wanted to add. His natural response was to launch into a theory which he had discussed with me when I had reached my senior year at high school. My history teacher had sent me home with an assignment regarding a place in Italy called Monte Casino. This was an elegant monastery atop an enormous hill in northern Italy. The Germans had positioned cannon atop this hill and zeroed their sights on the surrounding roadways. As a result, the Americans could not move trucks, supplies, or even tanks past this place without being blasted to smithereens.

Dad stated that the Allies' decision to bomb the religious monument to rubble, thereby providing the Nazis soldiers with hundreds of new places in which to hide and kill attackers, was an absurd waste of resources. The hill should have simply been bypassed and left to surrender when hostilities ceased. Alternatively, redeploy our troops further north via amphibious landings. Finally, rather than bomb the bastion, the American planes should have dropped smoke sufficient to enshroud the forward observers, brought speaker trucks in at night and broadcast sounds of tanks moving, and then shelled the German positions given away as their cannon fired at the bogus convoys.

In my ignorance, I had suggested the use of paratrooper commando units to land on the hilltop and root out the gunners. Dad had simply smiled; no one wants to be shot at while descending at the mercy of where the wind can take you. Moreover, as wide as the monastery appeared to dogfaces crouching down behind boulders in the valley, to a paratrooper descending from 3,000 feet or so, it would be an impossible target to land within. In reality, the hill was taken by brave Scottish units sneaking up at night despite the constant risk of being slaughtered where they stood.

We became so consumed by our discussion that day that I forgot to ask Dad how he eventually made out in the competition. The answer became self-evident a few months later.

As the result of his grasp of tactical maneuver, Dad was promoted to First Lieutenant and was assigned command of his company's Headquarters Platoon. The Korean War had started slightly more than a year earlier, during June 1950, and was to last until a cease-fire was arranged three years later, whereupon all the parties returned to the demarcation line on the 38th Parallel. Thus, after four bloody years of fighting, everyone was back at the starting point. If I'd been stationed over there, July 1953 would have seemed like a lifetime away. My dad simply took it in stride. As I said earlier, he had been expecting such an assignment for some time.

Initially, my dad's unit was ordered to deploy to Japan where the unit would undergo further combat training, receive clothing necessary for the coming harsh winter, and ascertain that those who held command positions could function effectively. Promotions were no longer peacetime honorariums; holding rank now meant you had to deliver the goods when danger threatened.

By October, the HQ platoon and the four other platoons in Company G of the 5th Cavalry Regiment, 1st Cavalry Division, were stationed in the "hotbed" of frozen Korea. As everyone was soon to learn, the region above the 38th Parallel could be one of the coldest spots on earth. They would also quickly learn that staying alive depended on the buddies who were dug in only ten yards from your foxhole. Company G was immediately committed in action against elements of the NKPA. Facing units made up of only North Koreans would not last very long. In short order, my dad and his men would face, surprisingly, combat divisions from China.

No one, including President Truman, had said anything about going to war with Red China. At the time, that single nation comprised one-fifth of the population of the entire world! American rules of combat would soon be rewritten. Daylight would see engulfing masses charging, charging, and still charging in unending hordes; the darkness of the night would provide cover for close-in attacks on individual foxholes without letup. Surrendering would sentence American dough-boys to being beheaded in front of assembled ranks of jeering chinks, or to torture in cold, dank cells without reprieve.

That was the new trait of this particular war. The bad never seemed to stop. As word spread, American dog-faces dug in and fought to the last. Doing so would be better than shamefully being beheaded.

On this embattled wasteland, you fired your weapon until you were carted off with wounds or you died. Word soon came down that capture, and its agonizingly endless torture, would be worse than death. The Chinese and North Koreans couldn't have cared less about the rules of the Geneva Convention. Their civilization and culture may have been richly embellished and preserved over several thousand years, but they behaved as though all rules of decency were abrogated in their drive to remove the forces of the United Nations from the Korean Peninsula.

This was waging war on a different footing from what the textbooks taught.

When the initial incursion was made in June of 1950, soldiers of the North Korean People's Army executed various surprise attacks. They launched their campaign for total dominance of the peninsula with unstoppable commitment. Neither the South Korean nor the advisors in the United States Army were prepared. Their campaign was executed very capably. It was so complete that the NKPA was able to occupy not merely Seoul, but almost the entire peninsula in very short order.

This conflict was brutal in its lack of compassion. An American or South Korean soldier could lose his life in any number of ways, beginning with getting caught in perimeter barbed wire or executed after surrendering. During the initial stages of the invasion by the NKPA, they didn't even take prisoners. If captured, a soldier was shot or beheaded as soon as he was disarmed, or marched away for torture in some encampment, lined up thereafter astride a foxhole he and his fellow prisoners had just dug, shot, conveniently pushed into the trench regardless of whether he had expired, and then buried without decency.

This encroachment by North Korea and the cruelty of their troops caused serious concern in the United Nations. Forces from India, Australia, England, Turkey, the Philippines, Canada, Greece, and even the Netherlands joined with us as the United Nations Forces. These allied soldiers battled the NKPA to a stalemate but, in September, General MacArthur added to his already prestigious reputation by staging a surprise landing behind the enemy lines at Inch'on Bay. He monitored the success of this "end run" while aboard the *USS Mt. McKinley,* and shortly thereafter he proudly returned the capital, Seoul, to the South Koreans on September 29, 1950.

Having received the surrender of Japan back in August 1945, this general was now riding high, almost as though he was sitting on the left hand of the Father, since the right hand was already spoken for.

Over the course of 1950-51, the NKPA was pushed north of the 38th Parallel. Victory sometimes goes to one's head, and now the allies, unfortunately, discarded wisdom and decided to charge beyond the demilitarized zone into enemy territory. The generals reasoned that the North Koreans would not be satisfied with such a quick repulse, so they would probably try again when the weather became favorable. The Red Chinese government specifically warned against any such encroachments, but their protests were ignored as being mere rhetoric.

Truman and MacArthur should have listened.

Toward the end of October 1951, on the 28th to be exact, my dad got into the thick of the action. He had a day's pass to Seoul, the first in some weeks. A deuce-and-a-half pulled up prepared to transport him there, but as my father stepped up into the cab, he noticed his unit suddenly stand as though someone was shouting at them. Being so close to the truck's diesel motor as it throbbed and rattled, Lt. Brill couldn't hear what was being said, but clearly something was causing them real concern. He could see his sergeants and corporals shouting orders and gesticulating as all his men started checking their ammo pouches and loading their rifles.

The United Nations forces were about to pay for having pushed well north of the 38th Parallel while chasing the retreating NKPA. Dad alighted and quickly learned that elements of the enemy were conducting a delayed, and therefore surprise, counterattack in order to retake Hill 673. That site was vital to the control of Heartbreak Ridge. Lt. Brill's men had taken it while attacking in concert with the 2nd Infantry as those soldiers attacked Hill 749. It had been very rough. Success had been achieved at considerable cost mere days before. No allied soldier wanted to give it back.

His leave was over before it began. He told the driver to shut down the motor and prepare for action, and then he stepped back through the still open swing door and waded into the confusion. He quickly organized his squads in staggered defensive positions.

As he went down the lines checking on their equipment and readiness, he noticed movement 100 yards off to the left and a little below their position. In the shimmering smoky air, it looked like a long, weaving snake, but dun-colored. My dad grabbed a private who had just finished loading a fifty-round magazine into his submachine gun, and together they crept across to intercept the ambush line.

It was no snake, but rather some 100 enemy troops threading their way up the hill to try and outflank his boys. Brill became angered; these sons of bitches were interrupting his long-delayed leave.

They would pay for this transgression.

Private Logan and Lt. Brill checked their weapon loads, released the safeties, and crept astride a dirt mound. The communists were close to the other side. Rising as one, Logan aimed down the right and his lieutenant down the left flank of the line, firing and killing as though at a carnival gallery. A group of three tried setting up a machine gun, but they were mowed down before completing its assemblage. When about half of them had been shot, dog-faces dug in further up the hill came charging down to support their lieutenant. The entire commie snake was mowed down. There was no sense in taking prisoners when counterattack had become an inevitable concomitant of any momentary triumph.

Two mortar crews were included in the carnage; they would have killed Brill's entire platoon and put the company at risk if they had been able to set up launching pads. Shells were still tied to the backs of some of the nearby North Koreans. These men were lying inert with their bodies in the skewed contortions of sudden death. My father's heroism had prevented these mortar shells being unpacked and sent on their evil mission.

Several months later, 1st Lt. Lloyd L. Brill and Private (now Corporal) "Lefty" Logan were awarded Medals of Honor for their intrepidity. The citation lauded their "Disregard for their own safety in order to save others." Both men had courageously forsaken the protection of a foxhole and acted beyond the call of duty to subdue some 100 enemy soldiers as well as prevent the operation of mortars and machine guns which could have put numerous allied soldiers in mortal danger. They exemplified the heights of bravery by summoning a degree of courage that stirred wonder and respect in their fellow man.

My dad was a hero to his fellow soldiers as well as to the American people. The newspapers back home reported on the award ceremony.

Lloyd remarked that the moment which had been most important to him was when he felt his buddies come alongside to back him up. Yes, of course, he was their commanding officer but, in this war, American soldiers could be counted on to protect a comrade no matter his rank, skin color, or hometown.

"Having their unbidden support when the going was the toughest gave Logan and me the greatest feeling of comradeship we have ever felt! When you're fighting in the trenches, whether you or your comrade gets shot is often simply a matter of chance. You can both be well-trained and equipped, but if one of you raises his head for a look-see, or to take a leak, and the enemy gets you in his sights—then *wham*: You're fried! This is what I call 'by the grace of luck.' Today, both Logan and I will remain ever grateful to the men in our platoon! But for them, we'd be layin' out there, sunny side down and cursin' our fate!"

I didn't need to take his award to heart; my father had been a hero to me for almost eight years already. Nevertheless, I was impressed. By the early 1950's, counting all branches of the military, there had been fewer than 3500 Medals of Honor bestowed in our nation's history, and only 5% of those had been awarded to living persons. A recipient is entitled to a small life stipend and can be buried at Arlington National Cemetery if he so wishes. Naturally, he has earned the gratitude of his countrymen. It can be won by a citizen in peacetime, as well, so 3500 is a pretty small number when one considers that a total of half-a-billion people have lived and/or died in our nation since the time of the Civil War.

Despite these heroics, they weren't sufficient to cause the Korean War to stop.

CHAPTER SIX

Change of Command

Colonel Homer L. Lautenberg would, in only a decade, be a general in a presidential war cabinet, but in 1951 he was stationed on the front lines in Korea. Looking over our defensive lines, he became highly concerned that the UN forces had become not merely overextended, but had also riled the Red Chinese into fomenting what he warned would be the next world war.

Apparently, President Truman had been advised that it was a good time to unite Korea. If the allied forces delayed, he was warned, China might complete its development of the atom bomb. In that event, the entire battle scene would revert in favor of the communists.

Unfortunately, the Chinese—even without that ultimate weapon—didn't care for encroachments being made so close to their borders, so even as "victory" seemed within reach to MacArthur, the Chinese began crossing the Yalu River on the night of November 2nd, thereby proving Colonel Lautenberg right. However, his warnings had gone unheeded. The next morning, ominous rumors began trickling into MacArthur's headquarters, with the trickle-down result that my dad would be assigned to reconnoiter the border with China in the northwestern part of Korea. My father had not been part of the decision-making process to continue beyond the 38th Parallel, but now he was about to bear the brunt of such foolish generalship.

Colonel Lautenberg had sent word down that a speedy reconnoitering was required ASAP. The order eventually was passed to Lt. Brill's commanding officer. Captain Horace Feingold called my dad into his tent to assign him the mission.

"Listen, Lloyd," Captain Feingold began. "The dinks have come at us for six days straight but have now backed off. I don't think it's the usual resupply and replacement of their missing soldiers; I surmise they are being supplanted by the Chinese. If those forces come over, not only will we be unprepared, but it will be an entirely new war. We don't have the weapons, supplies, or even fresh troops for such attacks. This is a vital undertaking. If you don't get us on-the-spot intelligence, we could literally be wiped out in a matter of days. It's my opinion that MacArthur is still fighting a desk war; he's lost touch with the real war occurring in these forlorn, frozen hills.

"I'm giving you two trusted South Koreans as guides. Select two of your own men and then proceed in full stealth mode: camouflage, night maneuvering, cold rations but no cans. Deaden your canteen chains. Hood the lenses of your binoculars. For security, you will not have a radio. You are authorized to fire for effect only if you are fired upon and your lives become endangered. This is not a search and destroy mission. Your sole job is to observe and then to immediately report back here, alive!"

As the captain finished, Lt. Brill took a step back, saluted, and did an about-face in order to find his First Sergeant and prepare for this assignment. What had gone unstated was that this was a horribly dangerous assignment. The Red Chinese soldiers were fighting on terrain similar to their homeland; as a consequence, they would be adept at cover and concealment during daylight, so using an airplane to scout the border area would prove useless. If the Chinese were indeed deploying into Korea, this would spell certain defeat for MacArthur's troops. Nobody was prepared to stop the onrush of scores of trained and well-equipped divisions fighting a border incursion by the UN forces. The relatively over-extended and, by now battle-weary, troops from the allied countries needed accurate information, and their commanders needed it fast!

My father was psychologically attuned to this sort of stealth mission. He had proved to be a reliable fighter and was conversant with all the current techniques for staying undetected in the field. His small team would be armed with a scoped sniper's rifle as well as two submachine guns made popular during the heyday of the Chicago liquor gangs. The ROK guides had proven themselves on numerous occasions to stand strong when under fire. Nevertheless, with only 300 rounds between the five of them, they wouldn't stand a chance if discovered by armed enemy units. Accordingly, they moved in single-man relays using cover and concealment to the fullest extent possible, but always under-the-gun to actually observe the Chinese incursions before they could undertake their return.

The lieutenant would have carefully studied the route they needed to take, but still one man had to precede the others, feeling for mines or alarmed barbed wire. Belly crawling made for slow progress. Even with spelling one another, civilians have no idea how exhausting it is, both mentally and physically, to crawl along frozen, snow-covered ground while feeling for booby traps with your bare hands in very chilled conditions. Lt. Brill consoled their flagging spirits with the limited objective: all they had to do was reach a promontory overlooking the Yalu River as it flowed past China's eastern border. According to the map, this would provide a good view of the presumed point of crossing.

Upon attaining their objective, they were utterly awestruck by the hordes coming across. Obviously, the North Koreans were indeed being supplanted by Chinese brigades. There was still time for this to be reported with sufficient leeway for the UN allies to withdraw in an orderly manner without casualties. The trick would be returning via the way they had come, but now more quickly.

As events were to turn out, the massive Chinese buildup and crossing of the Yalu River in the area of Chong-Dong was made in extraordinarily short order. My father's team was lucky to get so close without being discovered. It would have been suicide to engage any of the advance elements, so his five-man team had simply observed. The assemblage of attack forces they saw appeared to be so massively overwhelming that it was clear the entire U.N. contingent would be overrun should they be surprised by these troops.

Corporal Chung and Sergeant Kwan were armed with M-1 rifles. These were heavy with only a five round clip, but very accurate at distance. My dad carried the sniper rifle while Private Edgars and Corporal Harris had the submachine guns. The team had returned close to their Line of Departure, perhaps four hundred yards short, when they came around the west side of a small rise and suddenly ducked for cover: there was a squad of Chinese ahead digging entrenchments preparatory to bedding down for a rest. No doubt they were part of a larger detachment setting up for a nighttime incursion that was pegged to begin in mere hours.

Lt. Brill directed the riflemen to stay abreast of him as the three of them crawled carefully to the crest of the rise. Edgars and Harris crouched behind, staying low. Locked and loaded, the men in prone position opened up with single shots, firing for effect, and a few seconds later the other Americans rose and sprayed the position until their magazines had emptied. Then all five rose and sprinted with their smoking weapons as fast as their feet could go toward the American defensive line.

Running out in the open, they were soon spotted by a forward observer of the 5th Cavalry Regiment who relayed the word for the American batteries to open up on the ground behind them to provide a screen. They made it safely, winded but alive. My dad delivered his report, but all this excitement and risk proved to be in vain. To the regret of the many allied troops who were soon to die, not one of the top U.N. generals believed the reports of these scouts. My father's reputation for veracity was brushed aside and his reports simply discounted by even the top dog himself, MacArthur.

When word was telephoned up channels to the famous general, the formerly victorious hero adamantly refused to fathom that the Chinese could be offended by such a parochial war, even if it was the allied forces who were winning. The high command sniffed that, if my dad's reports were to be believed, Macarthur would have to promptly order a massive retreat of all UN forces to below the 38th Parallel "effective yesterday."

Such a move would overturn MacArthur's heady dash north, casting adverse publicity upon this hero's awesome acclaim. After all, when this dispute was over, this reputed "second Napoleon" would opt to run for the office of President of the United States. With the arrogance of pride, he could not abide such a pull back, so he retained the men deployed throughout North Korea in static locations. The famous general mistakenly believed that the success of the UN troops would force the NKPA to sue for peace. With consummate misjudgment, MacArthur failed to understand that the United Nations forces were now exposed with poor defenses.

Worse, their actions had stirred up a ferociously angry hornet's nest of Chinamen.

Toward the end of November, a hot Thanksgiving meal was served to the front-line troops; four days later, not one of them remained alive in their foxholes. The retreat of the UN forces after November 25 became precipitous. Over 300,000 Red Chinese rolled over the allies as though those soldiers were firing nothing bigger than BB guns.

The allies didn't know it, but the Chinese commanders were so incensed that even a rapid retreat by the allies would not satisfy them. Driving the foreigners completely off the peninsula became their sole focus. Possession of Seoul would change hands several times over the course of the next two years as the UN forces strove to hang on under the massive onslaughts.

My father told me later that it took some months for his men, and the other American soldiers, to come to grips with the mindset of the communist fighters. Each individual Chinese soldier's goal was to kill as many of the foreigners as possible before dying. Every man was ready to sacrifice his life to the focused goal of killing the opposition. As for an American, he wanted to shoot enough enemy soldiers to stop their attacks, but he also wanted to stay alive even as he did so. The Chinese did not have to cope with such baggage. On they would come in endless, seemingly mindless waves.

Theirs was an entirely different sort of culture whose combat tactics bamboozled our generals and politicians. To the Chinese, gaining the objective and sacrificing yourself in that effort brought a soldier respect and glory. His individual life did not matter; the government's goal did.

To us, losing your life in the struggle was important only if your sacrifice allowed your compatriots to escape to battle another day. You were expected to resist and hold your assigned position, but—above all else—to stay alive and continue to fight as part of a coherent force.

The commanding general's disbelief in my father's reports quickly led to a dreadful, overwhelming rout as the Chinese forces surged across North Korea, chewing up, killing, or capturing for later torture every allied soldier in their path. The festive Thanksgiving turkey dinner was soon forgotten. The Reds possessed numbers that simply overwhelmed, regardless of training, *esprit de corps*, or skill with weapons. Many a brave allied soldier was lost to hand-to-hand fighting as he'd prevail over one, two, even three Chinese at close quarters, but there was always yet another who could shoot or bayonet him on his blind side.

The allies, who had been so close to victory in October, were ignominiously sent reeling back in late November, like waves withdrawing from a beach in forlorn embarrassment. In the face of the onslaught, MacArthur failed to comprehend the realities of the developing situation. President Truman was forced to replace him with Lieutenant General Matthew B. Ridgeway.

Unlike MacArthur, the new commander's first action was to get up to the front lines where his battalions were positioned rather than direct a paper-defined war from Japan. His quick grasp of the essentials in this combat theatre impressed his subordinate commanders. They in turn rallied the Australian, American, Indian, Turkish troops and so forth to stand fast south of the 38th Parallel. In this manner, the all-out rout which, prior to the general's arrival had appeared imminent, was stemmed and, by January, the conflict had degraded into skirmishes and probing attacks.

General Ridgeway adhered to several principles regarding "changing of the guard," which was essentially the purpose of his replacing MacArthur. He wanted to be at the front for a sufficient period whereby he could understand the threats to a current commander and how the situation was being handled. Understanding not just that person's tactics, but also how confident he was as a commander, was important. Did he know the terrain, names of the features and water bodies, the slopes and the attendant opportunities for enemy use of armor and artillery, their supply chain weaknesses, the weaponry they faced, as well as the morale and capabilities of his men? If a commander was found wanting, the final factor for Ridgeway was: What would be the effect on the men if Ridgeway replaced him? Occasionally, sub-par performance wasn't due to poor leadership at the top; the subordinate officers might be the ones who needed transfers out.

Conversely, when he would learn of an officer who had demonstrated extraordinary leadership, clear thinking under stress, bravery, and/or initiative, he would promote that man and then promptly take him aside, I imagined, for this kind of private talk:

"I am aware (e.g., Major X) that you have filled your responsibilities well and demonstrated sound principles of leadership in front of your men. I am informed that you have exposed yourself to high risk while displaying initiative to both conclude the mission and extricate your unit successfully. You have demonstrated that you can plan for the big picture yet attend to the myriad little details that preserve the well-being and fighting ability of your men. You even visit your soldiers who have been evacuated to hospital. I can assure you that you enjoy a well-deserved reputation.

"Listen to me carefully: you must now change your natural instincts. You have become far too valuable to me to risk your life by leading at the front. I am ordering you to search your unit for noncoms who can fill the shoes you once wore. From this day forward, you will continue to experience the conditions of battle alongside your men as usual. Command certainly requires that you are at the center of crisis should it happen; only in this way can you appreciate the threats, pressures, and requirements to deal effectively with the enemy.

"However, you will no longer be out front with your sword held high as though you were leading a charge in person. Concurrently, you will retain a squad in your immediate vicinity and direct their sergeant that his unit— should it come down to it—shall fight to the last man to protect your life. Am I getting through to you?"

I imagined a short stunned silence would follow his hearing such orders, but that was the nature of command during wartime. A good leader observed, developed, but also husbanded his best assets. Fate was such that an errant artillery round could land close enough to take a cherished leader out, requiring that one of his junior officers step forward to replace him. If all those junior to him had been killed by leading from the front, that unit would be in a world of hurt.

In short, his guiding rule was that the troops must have confidence in their leader. Such a man would be able to devise coherent plans of attack, marshal reserves, and have the words at his fingertips which would inspire men to risk their lives in the face of death. My father was just such a man. Sometime in the future, I would have the responsibility for protecting the life of a dearly beloved American. As it would turn out, I would perform my job in a manner that would make my parents very proud to have adopted me.

Lloyd had learned a lesson fairly early in his deployment as a platoon commander. The plan of attack of these mongrel, but savagely motivated, units is to come at you with overwhelming, seemingly unstoppable numbers for six days, including counterattacks. Then the enemy backs off for a bit to regroup and resupply. These thrusts and pullbacks became as regular as a train schedule.

During one of their massive onslaughts, well before the sixth day, Lt. Brill saw three Australian enlisted men lying in various positions in their foxhole. The troops were below and about thirty feet to the left of my dad's position. Neither of the three was holding a rifle or even looking forward; they seemed to be dazed and uncomprehending.

First Sergeant Bledsoe also saw them and remarked sardonically: "Those guys must be shell-shocked from that commie shell we heard hit a few minutes ago. They're goners, for sure!"

As the tale was told to me, my dad then pointed his finger down toward the base of the defile.

"Look there." he directed.

His First Sergeant, Hiram Bledsoe, could make out six Chinese riflemen inching up the slope a mere thirty yards below. They were taking advantage of the smoky haze persisting over the battlefield and had approached dangerously close without being spotted. As soon as my dad saw them, I'm told that he leapt from his protective foxhole, cocked an M-1 on the fly, and drew his sidearm Colt-45 pistol from its holster all in one smooth move.

"Cover me!" was all he said to Bledsoe as he made a headlong rush for the stricken allies.

"Cover him!" repeated the first sergeant to the rest of the platoon.

The Reds saw him storming toward them and momentarily straightened up in surprise. There were **eight** of them! Lloyd had 13 or 14 rounds to use. He let loose with the full load from his automatic and then turned his rifle on the startled Reds. As his magazines ran out, he dropped into the foxhole astride the dazed Australians.

There was a momentary lull before the three gooks left alive collected themselves and charged the remaining distance to the foxhole. As they came up the hill, each of them began howling some sort of fearful, hoarse curse, but my dad suddenly popped up from the shelter of the foxhole and sprayed them with bullets chambered in one of the Australian rifles. One fast Red made it all the way to the lower edge and thrust at Lt. Brill with his bayonet, but the American shifted right and, pushing the rifle-mounted blade out to the side, plunged his service knife deep in the commie's throat, then twisted his hand hard so his weapon turned, thereby creating a large hole in the man's windpipe. The Red recruit never even choked; he died instantly.

Lt. Brill promptly yelled for assistance to haul the three Australians up to his platoon's backup position. Once they were there, they were treated by a First Aid noncom and brought around to being combat-ready once more. However, they chose to remain in protective ditching close by the Americans from there on.

Meantime, Lloyd had dropped into one of his unit's foxholes and taken a long, long drink from the proffered canteen his sergeant had uncorked. A few moments of silence ensued, but then the whole company began to applaud my dad and shout praises toward his foxhole.

He did not stand up to acknowledge the accolades. Rather, he faced downhill in the direction of the enemy. He was still breathing hard and needed some time to collect himself, which meant he had to stand up and take a wicked piss. However, First Sergeant Bledsoe did notice that the lieutenant had a broad smile on his face while he sprayed his hot stream on that cold ground. The sodden earth seemed to smoke for an hour after he finished.

CHAPTER SEVEN

Friendship from Adversity

Time-line:

1950: JFK wins a third term in Congress. He begins to be convinced that the seat of action is not in the House. However, the Senate seat is occupied by Henry Cabot Lodge, a person of long-standing repute and power. JFK devises a new campaign strategy to unseat his rival.

1952: JFK dislodges Henry Cabot Lodge as a Massachusetts Senator. He is reelected in 1958 and thus is a sitting senator when he enters the 1960 presidential race.

Republicans Dwight D. Eisenhower, the esteemed hero of the Normandy invasion in 1944, and Richard Millhouse Nixy are elected as President and Vice-President, and then they are reelected in 1956.

The terrifying film *Psycho* by Alfred Hitchcock knifes its way into movie theaters across the country: Americans stop taking showers for weeks.

Dawn was just beginning to color her palate of pale oranges and Petunia pinks across the eastern sky as Arthur Walinsky yawned, took one last deep breath beneath the cozy warmth of his bed sheets, and then looked over at the alarm set for 6:00 AM on his night table. The luminous numbers held fast to their position as the minute hand crept relentlessly toward an erect position above the hour hand. Very soon the alarm-clock would start clanging.

"Close enough," he thought. "I may as well go ahead and get up."

Today would find him yet again driving the 7:00 AM route from Dallas, Texas through Shreveport and on to Jackson, Mississippi, before heading south and terminating in New Orleans, Louisiana. He didn't have a problem with that. He'd done the round trip for several years by now and was known as a driver who "kept to the schedule" by management at the Greyhound Bus Lines company. What made today different was the date: it was December 23, 1952, and he knew the bus would be filled with Korean servicemen anxious to return to their homes in time for Christmas.

He made a full-length stretch after inserting his feet into his slippers, raised his arms toward the ceiling as he savored one last, cavernous yawn, then it was off to the toilet to enjoy the complete release of his bladder. The birds would not be chirping outside the bathroom window today—it was too cold—but relieving himself provided a pleasant interlude. Doing so permitted a man to relax in complete privacy. Not even his Labrador, Alfie, would disturb him at this time, although the dog would surely dip his head into the bowl once his master had flushed.

After shaving, Art donned his light chocolate-toned uniform, fitted his black-brimmed cap, slipped his gloves on, and was out the door with Alfie in tow. At the start of each work week, he would board his treasured "best friend" with his sister Eunice who, conveniently, lived next door. This had proved to be suitable for both households; Eunice enjoyed pampering Alfie, and of course Art loved being licked all over with affection after returning home from yet another long drive.

Arriving at the terminal, he could see the bright lights for the loading platform had not yet been extinguished for the day. Though the pinks and oranges of the dawn had been replaced by the glory of a full Texas morning, it was wintertime and, even this far south, it took several hours for the sun to rise to its full brilliance. Nevertheless, the platform was a swarm of military uniforms: olive green, navy, light tan, dark brown: something for just about any taste, as long as it was sea or earth-toned. A few civilians, looking like sleepy refugees, were present, but he guessed even those men were veterans from the First World War. This would be a rowdy passenger load, for sure.

He reported in, received his route ticket, and gave his bus No. 70 the once over. He could rely on his employer to keep the craft in tiptop shape, but he always gave his assigned vehicle a personal inspection. Tank was fueled, lights and wipers worked, brakes hissed with full pressure, tires looked properly inflated, no trash or belongings in the passenger area: his craft was all set.

Art positioned himself astride the opened wing door and checked each man's ticket as he prepared to board. No women traveled this early in the day during the winter months; this meant he wouldn't have to put up with infants crying during the run. He gave a quick glance to The Man upstairs and murmured his personal "thank you." This trip should be uneventful.

He stepped aboard, pulled the door to, and checked the big clock beneath the platform roof: 0700 exactly. He fired up the thirsty diesel motor, checked the mirrors so he could spot the back-up guide clearly, and proceeded to clear the terminal. Soon his craft would be free of the city and out on the open road. He loved the rush this gave him. Today must be the hundredth time he'd driven this route, but even so he was exhilarated by the sense of command the elevated, cushioned black seat provided. The large knurled steering wheel rested level and securely in his hands, the double rear tires gave him stability for his load, and the wide view through the large windows gave him a clear line for oncoming traffic.

Motorists cutting in front of him were irritants, but as for passing a semi-trailer, well, that was where the risk lay. Every driver, regardless of his personal driving habits, knew all about the bus that had nearly killed the famous golfer, Ben Hogan, while passing a tractor-trailer in the fog some years back. Such an accident would finish a motorman's career.

At this time, the sitting President, Dwight D. Eisenhower, had not yet begun the extensive interstate highway construction that would characterize his administration, so Art would constantly be adjusting his speed to accommodate the myriad rural restrictions as his bus passed across the various county lines.

That was okay. He liked variation—it kept him awake. It was the boys in the back of the bus who concerned him today. The first few hours were fine. The constant whirr from the tires, combined with the gentle sway of the cabin area, would lull the passengers to sleep or to quiet reading. But always, as the noon hour approached, appetites would become strong, general restlessness and movement about the cabin would increase, and jeers about his driving would become loud enough to be heard, so stopping for a bite would become imperative.

At last, the bus closed on Madge's Café. As he had done for the past few months, he pulled his vehicle astride the eatery and disembarked all his passengers. After refueling, he went inside himself.

As he had stood outside cranking the fuel pump, the air seemed to be particularly crisp, but the sky was still cloudless. However, once seated at the counter, he listened in to the radio broadcasting atop the pastry shelves and learned that a strong low-pressure system was sweeping southeast across Oklahoma. The forecaster was announcing that it would be spreading heavy snow across the panhandle. It was due to start blanketing his route later that afternoon.

He telephoned Greyhound but was told to continue. "The snow is expected to amount to under two inches and shouldn't be a problem," the dispatcher had confidently told him. He decided to pack up most of his lunch for later; no telling when his next meal might be.

At the table over near the window, two men in blue uniforms were conversing with a pair of similarly-aged khaki-clad lads. Their talk focused on dames until one of them happened to mention something about the fighting that had occurred proximate to the storied Green Duck River crossing over to Antung (now Dandong) from South Korea.

One of the dough-boys was particularly animated: "Man, now there was some real fighting! That was the first time I've felt genuine fear. The Chinese seemed to be everywhere at once. After firing and fighting for two hours, I yelled to my sergeant that I was running out of ammo, but he shouted back that everyone was. The three of us in my foxhole fixed bayonets; soon, these knives would be all we had, which meant sure death. The enemy had far too many troops for us to take them on in hand-to-hand combat."

"We never had any relief, either," his buddy Roy Chesboro added. "At night, the chinks would shell us at irregular times, making rest impossible. Your nerves can take only so much stress at that kind of fever pitch before they fray and give out."

The two twenty-five-year-olds in blue uniforms leaned forward. The guy doing the talking riveted them, despite his being a Negro. They knew the area he was talking about. One day, right around

November 23 when they should have been at home observing Thanksgiving Day with their families, they had been ordered to sortie their sapphire-painted, snub-nosed Sabre jets over the very area that Corporal Chesboro was going on about. At this time, Harry Ruskin and Jim Root were wing men and had just finished the required number of missions for their tours of duty. Unless they decided to extend, they could muster out after the close of the year.

They leaned forward together, eager to hear what these "dog-faces" had to say about combat conditions on the ground.

"Yeah, I mean, it was real bad," continued Roy. "My buddies and me, we punched fists. If we was goin' to die, we'd go fightin' to the end! Our howitzers was out of rounds and we could see them, all these gray uniforms with yellow faces comin' across that bridge like columns of fire ants, nonstop and lethal. Now jus' when I thinks we're done for, here come these jets, screamin' in from the east as though there's no tomorrow."

The story-teller simulated the two planes with his hands, swooping and banking them across the shiny table-top just above their glasses of Coca-Cola and Hires root beer, and then he brought his palms down to his sides and stared dreamily up at the ceiling. In his mind, he was vividly recalling the deafening roar of their afterburners as the two jets had thundered past his foxhole like avenging angels sent from Heaven above.

"Yeah, like they didn't have a care in the world," he continued. We could see anti-aircraft guns firing, but these planes was so low, not more than 200 feet above our position, that the Chinks didn't seem able to zero on them. Two at a time, side-by-side and steady like they was on a wire, they'd scream in and let fly with the most wonderful sight I ever did see! Bright red flashes and huge booms and that bridge was a goner. We quickly engulfed the troops on our side of the river and slaughtered every one—we knew they'd simply decapitate us if it had been us who were surrendering, so we gave them no quarter."

Roy sat back and sighed, then punched his fellow grunt in the side. Reminiscing together, they each produced wide smiles. They had lived through the cacophony of Hell in concert, and were glad to be home on leave, at last. Their tours would resume following New Year's Day but, for the moment, they could relax while devouring large plates of grits, griddle cakes, and ham.

The two men in blue sat back and folded their arms like side-by-side sphinxes.

Roy noticed and asked, "Why is you-all boys smilin' like that? You look like the cat that just swallowed the canary!"

Harry and Jim looked at one another and then couldn't contain themselves. They both laughed heartily and thereupon stood up, extending their hands to Roy and his mate Justin. The two dough-boys looked confused, but they also stood.

As they grasped the Negroes' hands, Harry stated, "Boys, you're looking at two of them-there screamin' pilots!" Wide smiles of satisfaction wreathed his and Jim's faces.

Roy couldn't believe it. Standing right in front of him were two of the very same guys who had saved his unit's ass! After a moment's disbelief, he found his voice.

"Well, shake my hand, fellas. Thank the good Lord for you! Justin and me wouldn't be here, enjoyin' these fine vittles, if you guys hadn't showed up. Just in the nick of time, for dang sure!"

These men exchanged handshakes amongst themselves, and then each in turn resumed his seat. Jim was the first to speak.

"Where are you guys headed? Our tours are up and we're going on to Mississippi. I live in Biloxi, and Harry here lives over in Philadelphia."

"All the way up in Pennsylvania? What are you doin' on this ride?" queried Justin.

"No, no, right down here in the 'ole South, boys. Philadelphia, Mississippi, is a bit less than 300 miles from Shreveport in Louisiana. Ya'll have to come visit, when the weather is warmer. We've got some sights to show ya, for dang sure!"

Jim sat back, satisfied that he and Harry had found some new friends. Saving another comrade in combat makes men buddies for life. In battle, variations between men in color or race or religion had no more relevance than differences in age or accent. Having the courage to stick by your chum—even when confronted with charging, screaming enemy soldiers—that was what counted between soldiers.

Art came along the row of booths stating: "Okay you guys, it's time to board!"

With everyone accounted for, all the bills paid, and the waitresses amply tipped, Art pulled the door closed and started up the motor. In a cloud of black exhaust, his bus found a gap in the traffic flow and they were on their way. In fairly short order, the passengers fell asleep one by one as the heaviness of lunch overtook them. That explained why Art had an apple, a soda, and a bar of candy wedged in a dashboard nook. He kept to light meals, relying on frequent snacking to carry him along while remaining alert.

He was driving for less than an hour when he began to experience buffeting. While the vehicle was broad of beam and incorporated little in the way of streamlining, its weight typically allowed him to forge right through side winds with little trouble. Today was different. Obviously, some sort of powerful front was forcing its way across the easternmost part of Texas. As he crossed over into Louisiana, the snow began. Just a lazy flake here and there, then a few more, then quite suddenly the bus was enveloped in swirling sheets of a blizzard.

Art reached down and opened the salt chute a little, then a bit more as the snow became thicker. He could feel the tandem rear tires retaining their traction.

As he turned the defroster up to "full" on the windshield, he shouted over the whir of the tires to say, "Well guys, looks like we're gonna get caught by this storm. Everybody better don your jackets and put your shoes back on; it's gonna get a bit chilly in here due to all our heat going to the defrost mode. Sorry, but I want to keep you safe!"

That was going to be his last exhortation to the passengers for a while. From here on, the road was getting slippery and he had to stay focused on controlling the wheels. He had just passed the sign welcoming visitors to Monroe when he decided the weather was just too dangerous. At the first motel he came across, he pulled into the parking lot and, telling everyone to stay seated, he left the motor running so the heat would stay on, and then he went into the office to confer with whoever was manning the desk.

"Good Morning!" he began. "It's getting pretty bad outside. Have you rooms for thirty-two servicemen? It'd be better if I waited out the storm before trying to continue." He smiled toward the desk clerk.

She returned his smile and stated, "At present, we have six rooms available. How many did you say you needed?"

"Well, that's a bit tight. I'd say fifteen rooms would be easier on everybody."

"Oh, goodness gracious! That would be far too difficult for us. Would you consider just parking in our lot while staying aboard the bus? That way, you could rent one room and thus have bath facilities, and you could use the diner on premises as well!"

"I'm sorry, ma'am, but I can feel it in my bones: this storm is going to be a humdinger and I really want to be off the road until it lets up a bit."

She stood her ground, so Art returned to the bus and took up a commanding position facing down the aisle.

"Gentlemen, the weather is putting us in a pickle here. This place cannot handle all of us, but I don't want to have anyone sitting out here if the storm really socks us in. I could pull up right next to the fuel pump and leave the motor idling; that way, the heater would continue working and we could simply remain on-board. But to have access to bathrooms, we have to take a room. Any volunteers?"

He had forgotten: these were servicemen. The first thing recruits learn in the military is not to volunteer for anything. If an officer selected you, well, that was how the cookie crumbled, but there was no reason to go sticking your neck out just asking for trouble.

This put Art in a bind. Acting contrary to an inner voice urging him to simply stay put, he put the bus in gear and returned to the roadway. Everything was becoming swathed in white, but at least the traffic had dwindled to only an occasional tractor-trailer.

As he motored along, Art couldn't help thinking, "Man! This is getting really bad. There must be some lake-effect with moisture coming up from the Gulf of Mexico! I am definitely pulling over at the very next place we come to."

They almost never made it. Rounding a curve, the road suddenly dipped down. Art knew the route in dry conditions, but now with the snow creating a white-out where neither roadway nor horizon nor the sky could be distinguished, he over-steered and the bus started to slide. Slowly at first, but instead of letting up off the gas pedal and turning the front wheels with the spin, the driver panicked and abruptly pressed the brake pedal while turning the wheels against the spin. This caused the front tires to lose any traction. With the downward right-curving roadway, the bus started swaying dangerously toward careering on just the left tires. It was now under the control of the heaviest part—the rear.

Although he considered himself to be a lowly noncom, Roy sensed the coming rollover and acted like a genius, shouting: "Everyone to the right side of the bus!"

Being military, most of them responded as though a grenade was going off. In the nick of time, everyone shifted as one body. The bus stayed upright, but of course it continued descending. Art used all his skill to gently keep the vehicle heading along the roadway. As the pitch leveled out, he began pumping the air brakes and gradually brought his bus under control. The passengers returned to their original seats, gave Art a round of applause, but then chorused together.

"Okay, you've made your point. Let's stop and wait this storm out!"

Now Art was on a roll, however, and he pressed on. He figured the closer they got to 'Ole Creole" the better would be their chance of outrunning this snow squall. As luck would have it, he was proved right and he pulled No. 70 into the New Orleans terminal a mere two hours behind schedule. As he passed the supervisor and saw him glance at his pocket watch, Art remarked, "Hey, the return to Shreveport will have to wait. I got us here, didn't I? In that storm, it's better to be safe than stranded!"

The supervisor smiled as he nodded his head. Art had always been a reliable employee. His judgment to truncate his assigned route on this unusually dangerous day would not go down as a black mark on his record.

For their part, Jim and Harry shook hands with Roy and Justin. The latter would be heading back to Korea after Christmas leave, but the pilots were about to be free as birds and didn't have immediate plans beyond hanging around friends from their old neighborhood.

"Thanks again for saving our ass!" remarked Roy, to which his new-found buddy rejoined:

"Just remember, the two of us are staying stateside from here on. Don't go sticking your neck out any more than necessary when you return from leave!"

Then they were gone, catching a ride into Mississippi. In the very short time typical of wartime meetings, these men had forged a bond of friends-for-life. But, would they ever see one another again?

CHAPTER EIGHT

The Agency

You will recall that I, like my father, had been inducted into a governmental service, but for me, that meant the Secret Service rather than the military. One benefit I appreciated very quickly was my boss, Special Agent in Charge James Rowley (code-named *Domino*). This man enjoyed access to military bulletins that found their way to the Department of Defense. The syndicated news reporters always operated at a disadvantage; they wanted to report what was going on, but the military needed to keep a lid on what was going on. The Defense Department saw the real, unedited after-action reports.

During one special day during my training, I was privileged to be called into Agent Rowley's office during March 1952. He showed me the accounts of what my dad had accomplished during the preceding months. Once again, I learned a valuable lesson. Never stop pushing. When you have an advantage, press it. If you're trapped, do the unexpected and get free.

He was quite a man, my dad Lloyd Brill. I was proud to bear his name.

The training of an agent called for assignment to desk duty for the first 6 or so months and then posting to a field office somewhere to gain practical experience. That "secret" location which I demurred discussing earlier was to delude the innocent into thinking there was such a place. Sure, there's a training school, but everyone knows its location. It's called the Treasury Building, and it's located on Pennsylvania Avenue in Washington, D.C., right across from the White House.

Not much of a secret there. Sorry to disappoint you, my dear reader. It's what goes on inside that building that makes all the difference in preparing a member of the Secret Service to put his life on the line. That's where the secrets lie. Boiled down to its essence, the training I underwent was primarily designed to supplant my innate sense for self-preservation with that of protecting the individual to whom I was assigned. Carrying out such assignment does not come naturally, yet it often must be accomplished without thinking, as though it is an instantaneous, even instinctive response in time of danger.

The Secret Service is different from that of members of the Federal Bureau of Investigation. We're both attuned to seeing that laws are obeyed, but Hoover's men bear the appearance of not knowing enough about something which the rest of us would prefer not knowing anything. For our part, we foster the look that says: "Don't mess with me!"

The novice agent has to understand the procedural detail and learn law enforcement techniques, such as preserving incident scenes and executing warrants. He becomes an experienced pistol marksman; he might even qualify on Thompson submachine guns and 12-gauge shotguns. The amount of time required for a trainee to be considered "worthy of trust and confidence" varies greatly, depending on the individual, the experience of those training him, and the kind of man, such as the person occupying the White House, whom he will be protecting.

Thus, it might be some six years before an agent would be offered Presidential Protective Detail assignment. On the other hand, it might be six days. Circumstances varied, depending primarily on the availability of trained personnel. When the chance arose for me, I grabbed it immediately. The year was now 1959, so I'd been with the Service for eight years. Moreover, the very man whose assistant had, no doubt, greased the path for me to become a member of the Secret Service in the first place was now vying for the presidency of the United States. What a thrilling honor it would be if I were to be tasked with one of his entourages! Should I be assigned protective detail for the President of the United States, my father would be very proud of me.

Surely, carrying out such a task would make any man honored to be a citizen of this great country.

These protective details had come later in the agency's existence. President Lincoln had signed the law bringing the secret service into existence; initially, their mission was to stop the proliferation of counterfeit currency which was rife throughout the country as the Civil War came to a close. At the time, individual states printed their version of the currency; no one could keep track of all the variations. By the end of the century, however, counterfeiting had become much less of a societal problem, so in 1894 agents began assuming other duties such as accompanying the chief executive on trips and encircling the White House with protective details.

Presidential Protection Detail might sound glamorous: "Wow! Imagine all those foreign, exotic lands an agent gets to see, the luxurious hotels, the fancy meals he gets to enjoy."

Let me disabuse the person who is inclined to think that way. The hours are not merely long—double shifts are standard—but also tedious and mind-numbingly filled with peril. When on duty, you must always be on edge, ever alert to the scores of people surrounding he person you are protecting. Wherever your detail is headed, or wherever your charge is located, you must always be conscious of avenues of escape should you be confronted with a dangerous threat. You may be walking, loping, or perhaps at a full run for distances of six miles or so if posted on a motorcade. In Texas, these can be as long as thirty miles! Sideboards are supplied on the secret service cars to give the accompanying agents both a rest, as well as an elevated vision perch, but these nevertheless remain aft of the presidential limousine. As a result, an agent's ability to handle a threat could be severely compromised should he be distanced from his assigned official.

Such duty, with its endless hours of nonstop mental alertness, is obviously not for everyone. I haven't even covered the sacrifices that are required daily. A man's home life must virtually be put on hold should the assigned person travel outside of the Capitol. You never eat regular meals—you are on duty. You can watch your man eat his meals, but you can't participate. Sleep—well, you better catch that any which way you can. Even when you're given a full eight hours off, likely as not you will be aroused from the depths of your peaceful repose because some emergency has arisen to which you must respond.

If it's Jacquelean Kennerly herself that you are guarding, God help you! Her style is to let her moods be her guide. A passing curiosity or a sudden inspiration would determine her schedule: an agent had to be prepared to serve at any hour. Some visit to an ornate temple simply because it was all aglow from the clear moonlight might be all the motivation this lady would need to sally forth!

Protected persons are important people, or they wouldn't be deserving of your close attention. Like as not, such persons will have strong egos, larger-than-life personalities, or otherwise harbor a need to be on display beyond what would seem prudent. Or the assignment could involve a mere child with all the wide-eyed spontaneity that comes with growing up and innocently exploring the world. An agent has to be tactful, possess kindness yet toughness, and be able to adjust quickly to unexpected situations.

Regardless, ensuring the physical safety of the President of the United States had to be the penultimate assignment.

Initially, of course, I was on President Eisenhower's detail during 1960. I accompanied him to Seoul, Korea where the crowds revered him as having helped end the war there. That trip was special to me since my father had fought so bravely for the right of those people to govern themselves.

My days of such deceptively easygoing duty would not last long.

CHAPTER NINE

Leadership Renders Frailties Irrelevant

Events of note at this time include:

1953: On September 12, Jack Kennerly marries Jacquelean Lee Bouffant at St. Mary's Roman Catholic Church in Newport, Rhode Island.

1960: Cassius Clay (later, Muhammad Ali) wins Olympic Gold for boxing in Rome; his success as a professional boxer and limerick poet endears him to many formerly alienated Americans.

The first Playboy Club opens in Chicago, forever loosening the 1950s' taboos on sex.

Four neatly dressed and decent college students stage a sit-in protesting segregation practices in Woolworth Department stores; the Civil Rights movement is launched.

In November, JFK wins the presidential race by 118,000 votes against Nixy; it is the closest margin since 1884. In December, he confers privately with the outgoing president, and afterward the two walk out arm-in-arm. Ike emotes that Jack is keen of mind and grasps the intricacies of the world's problems clearly.

Joy Adamson publishes *"Born Free,"* a book about the plight of African lions, not civil rights.

"Astro Turf" is invented for all-weather contests on athletic fields, thereby allowing attendance to rise but bills for cleaning uniforms to decline.

1961: JFK asks the Interstate Commerce Commission to prevent bus companies from servicing those terminals that operate segregated facilities.

The U.S. breaks diplomatic ties with Cuba.

The Peace Corps, with Sargent Shriver at its head, is created to help foreign countries with farm and health-care techniques. This promotes goodwill; the response by young Americans overwhelms the agency's rolls, creating ill will.

Cosmonaut Yuri Gagarin orbits the planet Earth. Alan Shepard makes the first American manned spaceflight, but only goes straight up and then comes right back down. High altitude test pilots deride his voyage: "He was only Spam in a can," affirmed Chuck Yeager. Regardless, he is the first American to enter Outer Space and is feted with an enormous parade in New York City. At the award ceremony on the steps of Congress, President Kennerly drops the medal as he prepares to pin it on the astronaut-hero, but he immediately quips, "This medal, which has gone from the ground up, is awarded for your historic accomplishment!"

During August, the Berlin Wall is constructed in some four days to block exit by residents to the West. On the one hand, it does achieve its purpose of restricting travel, but this backfires as "The Wall" becomes a hated symbol of the suppression of freedom for people under the thumb of communism the world over.

JFK sends over helicopters and support crews to Vietnam in direct support of efforts to resist unification by guerrilla insurgents from the north. Together, the number of "advisors" in-country thus rises to about 16,000 troops. Shortly, however, the President begins to have second thoughts about his having done so and begins to explore avenues for justifying our country's withdrawal from the region.

Electric toothbrushes are introduced, saving time with a daily routine; Legos are introduced, providing a distraction for all our newborns. The Beach Boys debut on the West Coast while in Greenwich, Bob Dylan captures the mood of the people with *The Times, They Are A-Changin'* and a young British foursome debuts at the Cavern Club in Liverpool; in a few years, they will invade America unopposed.

The peaceful interlude engendered by President Eisenhower's administration continued into 1960, and then 1961 rolled around. Everything changed with President Kennerly's inauguration. And I mean *everything.*

Where we traveled, how frequently we did so, the number of individual stops we made, even the hours we stayed awake: all of these vastly accelerated with the arrival of John F. Kennerly as President (code-named *Lancer* by the S.S., which I would come to think was quite appropriate). The man was born to be at ease with his fellow citizens, and that meant getting out on the street and shaking their hands even when he wasn't "politicking," as he called it.

To everyone's surprise, this man came with additional security risks that had heretofore never been considered. His wife Jacquelean became the focus of the kind of attention usually accorded to famous movie stars. Who would want the job of protecting **her**! The trappings of status would go to the agent charged with protecting the president, not his wife.

The Secret Service had become a full-fledged government body following the assassination attempt on Harry Truman in 1950. Security duty nowadays required detailed planning, keeping abreast of current events, learning how to anticipate each other's actions and reactions, staying fit, and foreseeing potential threats wherever the president might be traveling.

To those agents assigned to President Kennerly's detail, the man was extraordinary because he had ailments that, taken together, certainly rivaled Woodrow Wilson's 1920 problems and Franklin Roosevelt's paralysis for rendering a person debilitated. By the time he was inaugurated, Kennerly still suffered from malaria and jaundice left over from his tour in the Pacific.

This was the reason he maintained a bronzed public façade. In fact, he once curtly reminded me: "Never let me miss a tanning session because they allow me to hide the yellowing of my skin. If the public ever saw my real coloring, I'd be finished overnight."

He could be very matter-of-fact when the circumstances warranted his doing so.

His Addison's disease probably began in childhood, but by the time he had reached adulthood, it was forcing him to take a steady diet of steroids to prevent further degeneration of his body. The cortisone administered during his presidency caused his cheeks to look as full as a chipmunk stuffed with acorns to store, but at least he did not have to deal with actually being overweight. He had some mysterious form of leukemia, adrenal insufficiency, prostatitis, colitis, intense back pain due to congenital weakness (and one leg shorter than the other) which forced him to wear a corset as a back-brace, ongoing intestinal disorders, and other ailments that only his doctor, Admiral George Burkley, could understand.

The public never saw Janet Travell's hard work to ease his back pain with reading stands and special seats. The famous rocking chair in the Oval Office, with its cushioned armrests, seat, and back-stay, was far more than a prop to lend an air of relaxation to the setting. It allowed Mr. Kennerly to minimize the discomfort which his ever-present back brace caused. If he had found a way whereby he could have taken that chair with him wherever he went, he certainly would have done so. None of us, regrettably, came up with a believable answer should the overeager reporters start inquiring about such a behavior. The chair remained in front of the Oval Office fireplace.

Then there were the painkillers that Max Jacobson administered on a daily basis. When asked whether the localized use of Novocain could be replaced by a shot to stifle all his pain, Jack was told that yes, there was such a treatment, but it would eliminate all feeling below the waist. It was never administered.

It's a wonder that the man could appear in public at all, much less as tanned, radiating health, and projecting a smile that was bright enough to light the moon.

A person has to stand back and marvel: each of these three men became president and served—capably—despite physical handicaps.

Enormous help was provided to President Kennerly by his wife, of course. Jacquelean was determined not to let her husband's responsibilities interfere with their children's "home life." She had decorated the family quarters in much the same way she had furnished their former home in Georgetown. This section of the White House was closed to the public. The use of subtle wall tones, graceful furniture, and porcelain or sculpted vases from China and Belgium were designed to make these quarters soothing and comfortable. French armchairs rested their exquisitely toned and shaped legs on a thick, cream-colored rug while chandeliers sparkled overhead. The First Lady (a title she abhorred) had even secured one from the Capitol Building itself for installation in the ceiling of the Treaty Room, courtesy of Senators Dirksen and Mansfield.

Well-known American artists such as John Singer Sargent and Winslow Homer were displayed near the richly-mantled fireplace, and these canvases were balanced by a desk and small harpsichord from the court of French aristocrats. Wall space was found on which to hang Cézanne and Auguste Renoir as well. The books lining the walls would have, most likely, already been devoured by the President well before he had taken up residence here—Winston Churchill's multi-volume history of the world wars comes to mind—but their jackets lent hints of color to the nooks they occupied.

In short, this ambiance of culture and good taste allowed the leader of the free world to feel as relaxed as though he was in the private study of his personal home. Clearly, Jacquelean wanted him to draw not just inspiration, but also comfort and peace of mind from their private quarters.

In a rare moment of intimacy, Mrs. Kennerly cornered Kenneth and me to relate her guiding principle regarding doors. When she had been growing fond of the President's father, Joe Kennerly, the old man had drawn her into his study and related how ten-year-old Jack had gotten angry at some directive by his father and kicked in a pane of glass contained in the French Doors separating the main house from the front door. After the shards were cleaned from the frame, there was some delay in replacing the splintered pane. Jack found that he could crawl through the opening, and thereafter he proceeded to show off this feat to his parents every day until he outgrew the 8" X 14" opening.

"Thus, I know that my husband is not afraid to maneuver in a tight situation," she explained. Then she added: "However, I don't want my son to be tempted to imitate his father while we are living here in the Chief Executive's mansion."

She thought of every eventuality. She was very impressive!

One day, when the President's back pain was less harsh than usual, no countries were being invaded, and no governors were defying federal law (so it must have been a winter's day!), Jack eased back in his rocking chair, took a long drag on his cigar, and then shared with Kenny and me a genuine *faux pas* he had made. He had dined with former First Lady Eleanor Roosevelt shortly after he had assumed office. After finishing, the two of them were leaving the room when the President stepped aside to allow the Grand Dame of American Politics to pass through first. He was, after all, a gentleman.

But Mrs. Roosevelt didn't budge. Standing aside, she said, "No, Mr. Kennerly, it is not for me to go first. As President, you must always take precedence."

He had smiled a sheepish grin and said, "Oh. For a moment there, I forgot who I am."

"But you must never forget!" she had quietly chided him.

That meant that while he was in office, the pressure to make decisions, to lead, and even to inspire would never be alleviated. Despite everyone's efforts, the president's back pain eventually became so severe that Jacquelean herself stepped in and convinced Admiral Burkley to bring in Dr. Hans Kraus as a consulting physician. As an orthopedic surgeon, Kraus insisted that exercise and massage therapy be initiated immediately. Although he had never been a devotee of exercise, the President was fearful of becoming confined to a wheelchair by this latest ailment. Accordingly, he undertook the Krause regimen and, within weeks, he was pronounced to be in the most robust health of his presidency. Regardless, he still needed to be encased in his back brace when riding in an automobile for longer than a few minutes.

I've always been close to my wife, Gail. If ever I'm unsure about some decision, I attempt to enlist her for a consultation. Even when I'm absolutely certain about a decision, she will often bring my entire line of reasoning to a halt with some penetrating question which I had not thought about—or worse, had thought of but had chosen to ignore.

For Jack Kennerly to rely on his wife for help in making decisions would be something new. She had enlarged his horizons about art and style, and they shared a mutual love of history, but he'd never considered consulting her regarding the management of his health.

She told me, "I never realized that his having his office in the same building as our home would allow me to see him so many times every day. I am so happy for my husband! His entire life has prepared him for the very job in which he is now engaged, but the configuration of the White House provides a proximity that will make the years spent here the happiest of my life." [1]

Despite his physical suffering, he would not permit his workday to be truncated by pain. His schedule would not be limited to a short speech, a pleasant walk, a chat midst easy chairs for an hour, and then a leisurely lunch. Rather, his trips involved a stopover here, another there, then over to some other place, make a quick visit at yet another town, zip back to his hotel for a change of clothes and a luncheon speech, then do it all over again until perhaps midnight.

We agents, of course, always had to be right there with him. Even if he was sitting down and enjoying lunch, this did not mean that we could; often, an agent's rations consisted of a bag of peanuts which he kept in reserve in his coat pocket.

When Kennerly was elected, and our group started riding protective detail for him, the difference from Ike's detail was like night and day. Dwight Eisenhower had been a major war hero, along with Winston Churchill and General George Patton, but his residence in the White House had been relatively uneventful. He entered office in his sixties. The greatest danger during his tenure was that some innocent bystander could get bonked on the head by an errant golf ball and storm onto the course demanding an apology. Such were "the risks of the game" the president would remark, smiling as he handed over yet another freshly autographed ball.

John F. Kennerly admired the game of golf but played it infrequently. The condition of his back would not permit his pursuing more than a few holes. Besides, it was hard to get a pal to partner with him.

"There would always be these serious-faced men dressed in suits and toting golf bags with shotguns hidden inside," his friend Ben Bradlee would complain.

Jack's links and traps were oriented more to the pursuit of female escapades. This man loved having a variety of women. There was only one whom he sought to make his wife and with whom he would sire children. His marital status didn't matter. Whether he was a bachelor, or married to Jacquelean Lee Bouffant, he would often fill his free moments by summoning some girl that Ken had discretely readied for him.

In marriage, he simply continued habits that were leftovers from his bachelor days. After all, he was in his early thirties when he married Miss Bouffant. This behavior continued for every month of his tenure in 1961 and 1962. Then in 1963, their newborn son Patrick died shortly after birth. That tragic event brought the two parents very close together emotionally; Jacquelean would be unable to bear any more babies. The infant's father may have suffered from some venereal disease which could have caused the premature birth and death of Patrick. The lad had been named after the great grandfather who had left Ireland to found the Kennerly clan. Jack's probable part in his son's death would weigh heavily on his conscience from there on and create a formative difference in his relationship with Jacquelean.

Up until that loss, however, when Mrs. Kennerly was away on a trip, Mr. Kennerly would have his support staff—the Irish Mafia, as they were affectionately known—summon someone from the stable of White House staffers or from a long roster of outsiders furnished by friends. The sheer variety that crossed into his bed or joined him in the heated pool or accompanied him on trips involving AF-1 boggles the mind. These gals provided him with release during days packed with stress, anxiety, commitments, deal-making, and family tragedies.

As I came to know my President well, however, I discovered what I deemed to be the real motivation behind all his womanizing. He had a deep need that arose from his youthful stays in a sick bed. Some of these, such as while he was attending Canterbury School, and again while initially enrolled at Princeton, had lasted months. He had come to eschew loneliness in favor of constant company. In particular, he learned how to enjoy himself fully as he was experiencing something; that is, to be fully in the moment, whether it was a biography, escapade, or intimate conversation.

He had his books, of course; I doubt if any lad in America had read Churchill's accounts of the campaigns waged during the Great War as thoroughly as had Kennerly.[2] Historical accountings and his absorption in them could take him only so far. Interestingly, while he became adept at retaining facts and events portrayed in books, he could not lose himself in such adventures as most boys did. However, not once did I ever consider that this man wished he could be somewhere other than where he actually was, although his meetings with Russian Premier Crushchev could be most trying on his patience.

As for myself, when I finished an exciting novel, I could fully explain where my mind had been and the details of my imagined adventure. On the other hand, if you asked me the name of the main character's dog or what state the story took place in, or even why the author had penned his work in the first place, I'd draw a blank. I don't think Mr. Kennerly's mind took flight, as mine did, when he concentrated on a tome; rather, he was more like a sponge absorbing the words as they were presented rather than using them to springboard into flights of fancy.

His mind and how he used it fascinated me. That part of his makeup was not what impressed his contemporaries, however. What did impress them were his many exploits with women. His amorous encounters even became known as "Jack's sexploits!" It was through knowing fresh female faces that he could lose himself in imagined adventures that, for him, became real with some girl lying next to him. These moments made him feel alive. An apt phrase catches his relationships accurately: *short-lived, but long savored.* [3]

Here is a defining blurb that a buddy of his remembered and proceeded to entertain me with. While at Harvard one day, he asked his friend Billings to: "Get something that likes loving, like that model Georgia Carrol—she was really something. While with her, I'll also need some other good stuff!"

Kirk Billings would often joke that his best friend's frenzied forays into the world of sex made him feel like a short-order chef, serving up tasty dishes that were quickly sampled but then tossed aside with a curt call for: "Next!"

One of his older brother's friends said of him at Stanford: "I think he had a much better time there than he deserved to have." [4]

What is the descriptive word I am searching for here? Jealousy, that's it!

Jack pursued danger as well as sensory pleasure in many of his liaisons. His taking on risk—yet escaping it readily—provided satisfying, emotional thrills for him. Perhaps that was why, as he matured into a full adult who also happened to be President of the United States, he could so readily keep his head while others all about him were losing theirs.

The shapely Marilyn Monroe was rumored to have serviced both the older Kennerly brothers. She would travel wearing a brown wig and sunglasses when aboard AF-1. Regardless of who she was married to at the time, she was so well known that Jack's having a tryst with her conferred on him the dual titles of conquering hero as well as that of magician who could dodge the risk of exposure. Marilyn thus provided double the excitement level of most women.

Inga Arvad ("Inga Binga," Jack playfully called her) was considered a security risk during WWII due to her association with high-level Nazi Party officials. Jack began this affair while barely of voting age. Their liaison was stormy from the start politically, as well as in the eyes of the Catholic Church, since she was already once divorced and then remarried.

According to eyewitnesses, she was a perfect example of a Nordic beauty who could stupefy men with her allure. They were introduced by Jack's sister, Kik. They hit it off because they both held jobs as news reporters, although Jack's assignment on a naval base provided little in the way of exciting tidbits, whereas Inga's interviews with the stars of the social scene ensured her a steady job at the *Times-Herald*. However, her links to Nazi Germany led the Navy to reassign Jack far away. Thereafter, his father probably stepped in to get her to end the affair after accepting a substantial payoff.

Judith Campbell was known to be the mistress of Sam Giancana, the Chicago underworld boss, and therefore personified the label *femme fatale*. Due to this connection, Herbert Hoover had been keeping a file on her, and when he let Mr. Kennerly know that he had tapes of their White House conversations, this affair was broken off immediately.

Gunilla von Post, a Swede, captured Jack's attentions longer than most—between 1953 and 1959—after their chance meeting on the Riviera. She was enjoyed despite his marrying Jacquelean during this period. The presidential campaign, however, dropped her by the wayside. He had become too important a man.

Once ensconced in the White House, he dabbled with staffers and even their assistants. This was sticky business: these gals were, of course, on the government's payroll. Of ongoing interest were "Piddle" and "Diddle" who worked for members of the White House staff and who would work the president over either in the heated pool or aboard Air Force One.

During overnight trips, Pamela Turnure would be part of the presidential entourage. She was a dark-haired beauty reminiscent of Jacquelean's appeal but with a different approach to sex. Since she served as Mrs. Kennerly's press secretary, she was omnipresent and could carry on with Jack when Mrs. Kennerly was away visiting friends.

Playing fast and loose but close to home, he enjoyed the attentions of Mary Pinchot Meyer, the former sister-in-law of his good friend and journalist Ben Bradlee. As so many had been before him, Jack was captivated by her physical beauty but couldn't help observing to his friend: "She'd be difficult to live with." But then, he didn't have to. [5]

That wasn't enough, however. His friends supplied him with outsiders as well, whether showgirls from Las Vegas, entertainers from nearby barrooms, or wives of other men in government who were conveniently out of town for a few days. One of his earliest conquests later wrote of how he liked to have the girl on top "so she could do all the work. This saved him from being embarrassed, or possibly incapacitated, by his bad back. He didn't like to cuddle, but he sure was fun to be around. His sense of humor and broad-toothed laugh could just dazzle a girl!" [6]

To be sure, the man had failings, but what human being didn't? In his case, the gifts of oratory and inspirational leadership made him the man of the hour. He would be just the person to lead our country forward into the space-age. I would come to stand faithfully by his side, albeit down the line after his father Joe, brothers Robert and Ted, close buddy Kenneth McDonald, reliable and savvy Leonard O'Brien, his vice-president Lyndon Jensen, his fabulous speech writer Ted Sorensen, a long train of friends from Charlie Bartlett, Red Fay, and Torbert MacDonald to relatives by marriage such as Sarge Shriver, and—of course—his wife Jacquelean. After all, at their wedding, they each had a dozen bridesmaids and ushers, but that number doesn't include their blood relatives!

I must single out groomsman Kirk Billings, the President's best pal from their days as tenth graders at the Choate School. This jocular man had real affection for Jack; in fact, at a time when the family was idolizing older brother Joe, Kirk furnished a confidence-building, single-minded adoration of his classmate. He provided the solid link with the values and attitudes which grounded the young Kennerly. As someone who knew Jack inside-and-out, he was a calming influence who could reassure the President that his instincts were sound. This buddy even maintained his own room in the Executive Mansion so his levity, and ability to be a sounding-board, would always be close-at-hand. He was an advertising bigwig. He'd even briefly held fame in the 1950's as the inventor of Fizzies, but his real mission was to keep Mr. Kennerly amused during tense days, to listen with an independent mind, and to provide the President room to vent without fear of consequence. If Jack needed to unwind, Kirk would be the one he'd find.[7]

As I've previously described, this president had the amazing faculty of living life in compartments. Personal friends kept him bucked up with jokes and pranks, political backslappers kept to problems with society or the "other" party, and women existed to idolize him as a swain. At Stanford, his dating would be shunted aside while he was discussing the possible involvement of America in the European theatre. His conviction was so strong it even changed the mind of an erudite professor, Harry Muheim who, before listening to the Harvard grad expostulate about world affairs, had held to the isolationist view. [8]

When he assumed the office of President, his friends, advisors, staff, cabinet members, international associates, even his wife all had their own niche. When he was with one set, he was with them fully and unreservedly. However, this meant that a member of any other compartment would be blocked from his mind for that period.

On the other hand, even though he was running the most important country in the world, he still made time for his two children. Nevertheless, they could distract him for only so long; when it came time for him to move on to serious matters, the kids would have to play elsewhere.

His longtime friend Dave Powers would import women from outside the White House as something new and fresh. These women were his opiate to take his mind off his constant pain. "Happening babes" included airline stewardesses, campaign workers, burlesque queens, Las Vegas showgirls, Palm Beach socialites, Hollywood starlets, even perfect strangers who entered the White House surreptitiously through the service entrance as friends of aides. The boss's hobby resulted from his childhood depriving him of a genuinely intimate connection with his parents. This left him as a sort of make-out artist who couldn't be reached emotionally.

One girl said sagely, "You wouldn't share dreams or longings with him. He was a probe, enter, perform, then get out sort of guy. No post-coitus cuddly pillow talk for him." [9]

The man liked women. He needed them. Notably, even after meeting and subsequently marrying Jacquelean, he still didn't feel committed to a relationship. [10]

Such trysts rarely involved emotion; the president would be serviced and then he'd move on to resume the demands of being the leader of the free world without dawdling over the expression of emotions. These women, no matter their status, merely provided a diversion from our leader's constant, and often excruciatingly debilitating, pain that had been a part of his life from childhood.

No one ever talked about his suffering; accordingly, those close to him never talked about his pursuit of pleasure. Everyone simply looked the other way and kept their mouths sealed shut. Given the pressures of his office, we in the Secret Service believed he deserved the chance to embrace momentary bliss wherever he could find it. More importantly, he was our man to protect, so we would keep both his physical person, as well as his image, safe from prying, gossiping eyes.

As a younger man, his attitude toward women was demeaning. Could this behavior be related back to a desire to put down his mother? On the surface, he did appear to consider women to be mere playthings who existed merely for his entertainment. Some, like Marilyn, were in the business of entertaining, but surely there must have been many who fell for him, serviced him, and then were discarded in favor of a new fresh face. One of them confided to me that Jack was not a cuddly sort of guy who wanted to share or get close emotionally. It was important to his independent, Irish manhood that he never allow himself to become dependent on them; women were objects to enjoy and then leave. This allowed him to remain freewheeling. The fact that these forays went on even after he was married seemed of no import to him, nor indeed to anyone else.

Kennerly once ruminated that happiness for him was not so much achieving some status or reaching a goal, but rather coming around to perceiving his environment in a fresh light. This would allow him to take comfort from a position that was simultaneously placid as well as intellectually invigorating. Such a place would unify both the head and the heart together, similar to what James Hilton envisioned when he wrote the book *Lost Horizon*. It portrayed survivors from a plane crash discovering a remote Himalayan dell of idyllic and long-lived harmony. This concept was pursued by former president Franklin Roosevelt when he named today's Camp David as "Shangri La." What I choose to dub "Swiss Bliss" defines a state of mind wherein one is joyfully satisfied. The only thing missing is the endless urge to constantly grasp for more! Thus, happiness means fulfillment and satisfaction with what life serves up. Ergo, contentment means that one is able to control greedily grasping for more as his expectations elevate. Fortunately for Mr. Kennerly, while he constantly pursued conquests, his desire to possess women was limited to his wife Jacquelean. [11]

Of course, such ruminating is beyond my ken, as well as far above my pay grade.

Extraordinarily, the Press left this part of his life alone. After all, he had briefly been a newspaperman (covering the founding of the United Nations in 1945 for Randolph Hearst) and he liked the kind of men who made reporting their profession. As a senator, he had often invited them into his "inner sanctum" to share jokes and bourbon. I could see it for myself when I wasn't actively protecting Mrs. Kennerly. He was a fresh change from the scowling annoyance which most public officials exhibited when confronted with reporters. When the media approached him, Jack thrived on the repartee; their questioning stimulated the clarity of his rational thinking.

One time he was questioned for what the press considered to be exaggerated crowd estimates at one of his speeches, but the President smiled and said, "Well, Plucky simply counts the nuns present and then multiplies by 100. He's always right!" Then he laughed with them even as they hurriedly jotted in their notepads. [12]

Closer to home, where he didn't need to couch his language or expectations in lofty ideals, he seemed less forgiving toward women and staff members who failed to measure up to expectations. As to these underlings, integrity was a vestigial or useless accoutrement. As a Congressman, Jack's demeaning attitude extended to women in the workforce as well. If they were mere employees in an office, he believed girls were to be kept at a low level of compensation; in fact, they'd never be worth more than $60/week as far as he was concerned. If they'd ask for $6000 per year, as one long-time, valued staffer did, they were fired. This was his approach, despite his father being so wealthy he could have paid them $20,000 and no one would have believed the budget had suffered.

Every man, even a very great one, has his blind side. It would require several years having his two children at his side, and the sudden death of his newborn son Patrick, before this Man-among-Men would come to truly love and value the woman he had originally married merely as a stepping-stone to the highest office in the land.

Notes

1   Schlesinger, pp. 126-7 and 141.
2   Much the same could be said of his six-volume set regarding World War II!
3   Matthews, pp. 22-23.
4   Hamilton, Nigel, p. 350.
5   Matthews, p. 357.
6   Hamilton, Nigel, p. 349.
7   Pitts, pp. 25-26, 197, 209, and 216.
8   Hamilton, Nigel, p. 355.
9   See Klein, pp. 166-170 to probe for more detail.
10 Hamilton, Nigel, p. 358.
11 See Weiner, pp. 39, 50.
12 Bradlee, pp. 20, 56-57, 73. No doubt smiling to himself, Ben related how "Plucky" Pierre Salinger, Mr. Kennerly's Press Secretary, had gotten his name. During a routine briefing one day, Pierre was asked by reporters whether he was going to join the Kennerlys on one of their macho, healthy 50-mile hikes. Disregarding this tongue-in-cheek ribbing of his rather rotund figure, Pierre had replied: "I may be plucky, but I'm not stupid!" The President was so comfortable around reporters that he actually sought to have men such as Tom Wicker, "a straightforward, luculent writer," assigned to the White House beat. The prevailing attitude at the time was: if a public official's private behavior does not impinge on the performance of his public duties, reporters will abstain from reporting on it.

CHAPTER TEN

A Most Inspiring Leader

This historical time-line has significance for the survival of America as well as the world:

1962: John Glenn orbits the earth three times, but the Russians have already had a man stay up for an entire day. Accordingly, our President issues this challenge: *I believe this nation should commit itself to achieving the goal, before this decade is out, of landing a man on the moon and returning him safely to earth. While we cannot guarantee that we shall one day be first, we can guarantee that our failure to make this effort will make us last.*

In October, American U-2 surveillance planes discover Russian offensive missiles which are being assembled on the island of Cuba. Our President secures resolutions from Congress and the Organ of Consultation of the American Republics and, duly empowered, demands the immediate removal of the missiles. Wisely, he invokes a naval quarantine (invoking a blockade means all vessels will be stopped, which can be interpreted as an act of war) to interdict shipments of offensive weapons while the world nervously awaits the outcome. To facilitate acquiescence by the Russian Premier, the Americans privately promise to dismantle missiles on NATO bases in Turkey; this allows the Russian Premier "to save face" with his politburo. The removal of the Soviet missiles proceeds. This withdrawal sets the stage for arms reduction agreements (such as the S.A.L.T. treaty whereby Russia, Great Britain, and the United

States end certain types of nuclear weapons testing) to be concluded in the near future.

Subsequently, the C.I.A. learned that nuclear warheads had in fact been delivered to this beleaguered island **before** the launch pad construction ever began. On the 22nd, therefore, some missiles had nuclear warheads already mounted, but these had been so well concealed that our flyovers had not discovered their existence.

There but for Mr. Kennerly's clear thinking, and Mr. Crushchev's red-faced rationality once his country was caught with its "hand in the cookie jar," you might not be reading this.

Thinking back to those ten tense days in October, President Kennerly had remarked privately to Ken that, "In our country, we try to sidestep the need to compromise. Our very cars have separate climate controls for front and rear, as do our mattresses and blankets. Compromise is a skill, and like all skills, it atrophies from lack of use. I'm thankful I had the wherewithal to find the middle ground and avoid catastrophe back then.[1]

Shortly you will learn that after I moved from protective to advisor detail, I was fortunate to win the confidence of Ken O'Donald because he could share intimate tidbits such as the foregoing with me. In fact, as I proceeded to serve in close association with Mr. Kennerly on a daily basis, I came to see that this very public figure enjoyed taking risks. Pranks, kidding, and particularly his sexploits, as they came to be known, transported him out of an endless world of physical pain, but he also got a kick out of risking exposure. Probably such need was a holdover from having to be perfect while living under his father's roof.

These musings, of course, are mere side notes to the inner drive and charisma of the man himself. Wow! His self-confidence, knowledge of history and men of stature, and ability to assimilate complex facts were singular. His desire to lead was exemplary. In fact, he bore a force field around his persona that was alive with electricity. In his presence, one felt that here is a man who is fully embracing all life has to offer. He presented himself as blessed with vitality, youthfulness, energy, and—for the ladies—sex appeal. That's right, even I could feel it! In fact, a blind man would have been able to sense it; the man fairly warmed the air with his humorous wit and exuberance.

Life Magazine reported on: "The blissful fog of feminine adoration that surrounds Jack Kennerly. Being in his presence provides one with a whiff of romance and adventure; here is a man who values honor and duty but who pursues life with joy and indulgence."

At this time the Press was famous for taking what it wanted from an embarrassing situation in order to print a scoop. *We bring other peoples' business to our readers!* was generally accepted as the standard on which to pillar and hang whoever made lurid copy. Prior to Mr. Kennerly, politicians would joke that newsmen couldn't even spell the word "gratitude," much less abide by its good graces. All of this seemed to simply drop by the wayside when Jacquelean and Jack moved into the White House. As time on the campaign trail thundered on, even savvy and hard-boiled journalists would become all excited if they were assigned to cover the Kennerly election campaigns. If these reporters were lucky, they might even be asked to comment on his proposed ideas for a speech. He liked to make them feel—if only momentarily—within the inner circle of policy making. As a gaggle, they would sometimes follow Mr. Kennerly into his bedroom so they didn't miss even a single inspired thought.[2] Former presidents politely addressed journalists as a group in a stately setting but, with this man, they were *included,* occasionally even *consulted* for advice. He provided entrée to an exciting, privileged world, and they loved him for it. That made covering him a "top-drawer" assignment.

His lanky, six-foot frame led a person to focus immediately on his face, and once you looked at him, you didn't look away. His features, tanned and smiling beneath thick, well-groomed hair were pleasant to look upon, but what captivated you were his eyes. They scooped you into his universe. You had the feeling that you—and only you—mattered to him at that moment. No wonder women fell for him like a ton of bricks tumbling off a truck. During those events when I stood close to him as he greeted citizens accompanied by his wife, I occasionally imagined that I could hear bodies thudding to the ground as women swooned at his mere approach.

A Secret Service Agent needs to have an active imagination. A lot of his time is spent standing around looking at wallpaper as he waits for his assigned charge to emerge and go somewhere. During the period of time that I was assigned to cover Jacquelean, I actually found myself being jealous of those agents assigned to the President; I was certain that his adventures provided vivid fantasies for those men to occupy themselves with during quiet interludes.

Most people I have discussed the President's perambulations with say they had no effect on his ongoing ability to administer and to perform his official duties. With his mind calm and refreshed, his ramblings would allow him to express what he sincerely believed to be important to Americans and to convey this sincerity to the public's satisfaction. Unique to his administration was his vision for a fairer distribution of America's prosperity as well as the benefits accruing from a more peaceful world. His "sexploits" probably enabled him to perform heroically while in office. They served as his opiate to deaden his ongoing physical suffering.

To survive the daily grind of life, most people use liquor, some rely on gambling or tobacco, but he relied on female companionship.

In the grand scheme of things, his peccadilloes were trivial. Everyone I met during Mr. Kennerly's presidency believed him to be a visionary: with his leadership, the world could be a better place in which to live. Radiating humor with funny quips emanating from a most attractive smile, he would initially attract attention, but soon his words of motivation and challenge would inspire everyone listening to follow his lead. This man had experienced the slings and arrows of war, he'd known deep, personal suffering due to the loss of beloved family members, and he had survived election to Congress not once, but a total of five times! In short, he had known pain, and could thus feel ours. He identified with everyday Americans and was able to embolden us to believe society could genuinely be improved. All we had to do was to act in concert.

One of his advisors at Harvard University had perused his articles for the school newspaper, *The Crimson*, and had subsequently been his advisor while the college senior wrote the perceptive, heavily researched book, W*hile England Slept*.

After it was published, he wrote this accolade to the young man's father:

> *Mr. Kennerly, your son is not a crusader. He is not committed to an idea which thereby controls his behavior. He is much deeper than that. He is a realist who is interested*

> *in ideas. What he responds to is not the exercise of power in an institution, but the process by which it functions; he wants to ensure that it functions capably, and this requires that the persons managing it are themselves capable. Men who understand ideas, rather than mere politics, are rare, and I am proud to congratulate you: you have raised your son to be just such a man.*[3]

As a candidate for the presidency, Mr. Kennerly went beyond what he had required of his fellow Democrats while in Congress: "The time has come for us Democrats to embrace new ideas, policies, and even new faces; we must become unafraid of controversial issues and learn to benefit from candid critics."

Indeed, he held fast to such precepts.

McDonald told me of the time that the President took him aside for a moment to confide an observation which he had made during a lifetime of studying human motivation. The words had carried such import for Kenneth that he copied them down for posterity. He showed me his memo:

> *Too often we hold fast to the clichés of our forebears. We subject all facts to a prefabricated set of interpretations. We enjoy the comfort of opinion because this allows us to avoid the discomfort of thought. I have learned from my study of history that men often fall into the trap of creating conflict, rather than accommodation, by words and actions that have not been well thought out.*

He was a thinker, no doubt about it. Throughout his life, he immersed himself in reading biographies of famous and astute leaders, but his ability to understand pressure situations developed more from personal exposure to situations far beyond the realm of the typical teenager. Part stemmed from his being the progeny of an ambassador, but primarily it was due to young Jack's insatiable need to know and understand what motivated men.

He saw fear and anger firsthand when he helped repatriate the American survivors of the *Athenia* sinking. Additionally, as the son of the United States Ambassador to England, he saw how the British government had been blindsided by isolationism and failure to keep their military forces up-to-snuff subsequent to the Armistice of 1919. Ultimately, that led to his writing the senior thesis and eventually the book, *While England Slept.*

A personal confrontation on the border of France had even more impact. He and Kirk visited France in 1937. Their passports forbade their entry into Spain, but they traveled right to the border and talked with refugees of Franco's viciously inhuman aerial-bombing of his own countrymen. One man told of how he had been starved in prison for seven days, then he was given some meat—which he devoured hungrily—and thereafter the guards escorted him to his son's body prior to its internment. He looked down at where a chunk of the boy's flesh had been excised. It was exactly the size of what the man had just consumed. The man tearfully declared to Kirk and Jack that he did not know how he would be able to continue living with such guilt.

Franco's suppression of the civil war so devastated Spain that it remained neutral during the Second World War. This meant that Franco was still in power when, twenty-five years later, the now matured Kennerly was elected President. Thus, he had first-hand exposure to the ruthlessness of this particular foreign leader. He would deal with him at arm's length.

Of far greater pleasure was the boys' visit to Italy where they met up with fellow Choate alumnus Al Lerner. They saw Michelangelo's *David,* "the most beautiful statue I've ever seen or hope to see," Kirk would effuse, and they also toured Venice. Over two decades later, one of Alan Jay Lerner's musicals, *Camelot,* would become a favorite of the President and his wife.

Kirk and Jack finished their European tour in Germany where they saw the fabulous concrete autobahns stretching to and fro across this country. "I suspect Adolf Hitler has something up his sleeve and is planning to use them for fast transport of his military forces," Kirk surmised in his diary. "He claims they provide a means for his countrymen to visit Austrians and relatives in the Sudetenland, but we disliked the whole setup and left with a very bad taste in our mouths." [4]

Time would shortly prove his conclusions to be prescient.

During Jack's time at Choate and Harvard, it was his sense of humor and relish for pranks that had won people to his side. As he matured, his listeners could see beyond the jovial exterior to a man of true substance who could think both globally and wisely. Throughout his life, Jack's laugh was so contagious that everyone within hearing would poke his head in the door, anxious to join in the fun. Jack's personality was winning but not serene. In fact, it sometimes seemed to me that he loved to savor the adrenaline rush of coping with danger. He was always taking risks! Whether his romantic trysts would be found out was an obvious example of this. This was his way of *living* life due to all the physical maladies with which he dealt daily. Each of these harbored the power to undo him without warning.

When his PT boat had been split in half by a Japanese destroyer patrolling the South Pacific, he had heroically rescued his surviving crewmen. Later, during recovery in a navy hospital, Jack found time to write to his gal-pal Inga: "The feeling I used to have—that no matter what, I'll pull through—is gone now, but I knew that should anything happen to end my life, I've already lived a full one. If I live to be a hundred, I could only increase the quantity, but not the quality, of my life."

He had met the fear of death head on and acted to survive. Later, while serving as President, though the stakes would be far greater, the players and principles would be much the same. His wartime heroics had given him a platform of confidence from which he derived the ability to remain cool-headed.

Fortunately for the world, as he grew in maturity he solidified the ability to think his way out of a crisis situation rather than react from gut instinct.

When you stand back and think about it, one realizes that this man had endured an extraordinary rite of passage; now, he possessed a kinship with Churchill's escape from the Boer prison as well as Hemingway who had been wounded driving an ambulance for the Italians in the Spanish Civil War.[5]

Jim Reed, a friend from his days in the South Pacific, said of Jack: "There was an aura around him that I've never seen duplicated in anybody else. He had a light touch and yet a serious side."[6]

During one of his many buddy-bull-talks, as he called a gathering of longtime friends, he heard about Jim's opinion and gave this riposte: "It's not your origins that count; rather, it's what people perceive you to be that's important. I may be the son of a rich father who sent me to top schools but, at heart, I'm an average guy who likes to laugh and balance a little fun with a bit of adventure. And, on the side, I know a lot about issues that bother people; thus, their concerns become important to me, and people listen when I discuss their resolution."

If only a reporter had been present, the line "an average guy who likes to laugh" would have been blazed across the front page as, "How to understand your Senator!"

He loved sitting around talking with a bunch of guys while in school; later, he carried this comfort zone with him when surrounded by high level cabinet members. He'd come out with these remarks that would be startlingly accurate which, in the general flow of the everyday hubbub, would have been totally lost on assistants like me. He'd take a briefing report from an important agency, such as the Atomic Energy Commission, and speed read through it, occasionally making an observation or asking a question, and then four days later I'd watch as he would raise a point of discrepancy in that day's briefing from the report he'd read earlier. His retention of detail was impressive, but his ability to clearly discern and then deduce that something was important or relevant astounded all of us.

He had a way of picking the brain of someone he was conversing with, especially if that person knew something that he didn't.[7] When he found himself involved in a discussion or debate about which he knew little, he would soak up sufficient knowledge until he had found his footing and would thereafter stride purposefully forward.

He was always educating himself, whether by books or conversation, without consciously trying to do so. That's rare in any man.

Others saw his potential early on. While still a student studying at Harvard University, he was included in the hearing regarding the British passenger ship *Athenia* which had been sunk by Germans the day after the Second World War started. In Glasgow, he handled the stories and recovery of the Americans onboard who had survived.

Of course, his father was our country's ambassador to Great Britain; perhaps that had something to do with the young man's appointment, but not with his adroit handling of the raucous survivors.

Later, his father Joe spoke of how he saw his second son at the time: "I thought his older brother Joe would run for the presidency. Comfortably sociable, without pretense, and outgoing, he was totally different from my son Jack who was bookish, always ready with a joke, and aggressive only when trying to find some girl to date; that is, unless we were playing touch football out on the lawn. Then, he could be quite competitive!"[8]

As he matured, Jack Kennerly developed an inner drive to fix institutions, even when as cumbersome as the House of Representatives! His goal was to make such places operate better and with greater renown. He was not one to promote a cause about which he was fanatical; it was more the machinery and methodology of existing institutions that intrigued him. To function effectively, he observed, a Congressman had to be able to compromise; without that ability, he'd never accomplish anything.[9]

He had taught himself to think this way by all his reading and subsequent writing the biography, *Profiles in Courage* about career politicians who paid a high political price for maintaining unpopular stances. To him, it was more challenging to possess political courage—to act as your conscience dictates rather than toadying to the weight of public opinion—than to have bravery in battle.[10]

As for himself, it was as though he had been preparing for a leadership role all his life. When his dad was America's Ambassador to England, an over-eager German submarine *Capitan* had mistakenly targeted and sunk a British commercial ship (the *Athenia*) early in the Second World War. Among the British passenger victims were two dozen Americans who drowned as well as hundreds who were left burned, scared, and seething with anger.

No one at the embassy was available to attend to the survivors, so the eighteen-year-old Jack was sent to Glasgow to cope. Initially out of his depth, he quickly adjusted and filed a report with recommendations which were largely followed by the State Department. This occurred "not because he was Ambassador Kennedy's son, but because he was himself bright, able, and helpful. Moreover, he was interesting to converse with and kept the Americans assured that our government would be attending to their safety."[11]

The surviving Americans returned home safely under a flag of neutrality even without a naval escort. From such encounters, the young Kennerly gained insight into the real-life dramas that often lurk behind the stately mask of international law. Professor Wild at Harvard graded Jack's senior paper debating the rights of submarines to attack ships of neutral nations which reportedly were carrying munitions to an enemy power. Little did he imagine that this same student would someday avoid a nuclear holocaust by ordering a naval quarantine, rather than a blockade (which can be construed as an act of war).

In 1941, his *Athenia* experience gave young Kennerly entry into the military despite his physical failings. A naval captain, Alan Kirk, had chaired the hearing regarding the *Athenia* and he remembered how effective the young man had been. He brought him aboard in the Department of Naval Intelligence. Thus, John F. Kennerly, who couldn't obtain life insurance due to his medical history, entered the United States Navy. Based on his education and broad list of acquaintances, the lad was sent to Kirk's agency as an ensign. Eventual assignment to the Pacific and thereafter as skipper of PT-109 would bring him to national prominence, and this would carry him through his first political fight for a seat in Congress. [12]

Years later, during his first term in the Senate, he remarked to his campaign manager McDonald how, if one is a politician, the number of temptations and pressures to take the primrose path of never-ending compromise is perhaps greater than in any other profession. Torn between obligations to one's constituency, concern for the welfare of family, gratitude to supporters, loyalty to his political party, as well as a sense of public duty regarding right and wrong, it's difficult to call it a day and go home at night to sleep soundly. This tumult takes no account of personal ambitions. The poor put-upon politician must stumble along, ever prepared to weather the next onslaught of his critics who can be counted on to never speak to him in a disinterested fashion.

If someone were to naively ask, "Well, wouldn't the best course be to bring an attitude of humility to political office," Mr. Kennerly's response would be made with electrified feeling.

"Good grief! Heaven's no. If you don't feel a sense of pride in what you are doing—and feel it strongly—then what kind of satisfaction can you derive from serving the public interest so devotedly? No, you can't be humble in public office; it in fact takes a person who believes in himself and feels great pride in utilizing his best talents to execute the duties of his office as effectively as he can for the benefit of his constituents."

Then, smiling as he remembered some long-forgotten moment, he told me about a story that President Lincoln used to tell on himself.

As he stood before his assembled Cabinet one day, Lincoln had asked for all those in favor of some measure to vote *aye* and the entire cabinet voted *aye*. President Lincoln added, "All opposed, vote *no*" and then he alone voted *no*! Thereupon, he stated flatly: "The vote is no!"

"You see, Clint," Kennerly continued knowledgeably, "The Constitution states that there are some decisions that only the President can make. Ike had warned me that there would be no easy decisions in this office. If the problem was easy to solve, the decision would never reach my desk. It would be settled at a lower level. Decisions that come to me are always going to be difficult. This places quite a burden on this office which I must daily shoulder!"

He sat stroking the side of his face with the backs of his fingertips for a bit, and then smiled as he said:

"At this point in time, I can fondly recall a vote some years back that I was fortunate to lose. In 1956, before you were on President Eisenhower's detail, I was surprised to be nominated as the Democratic candidate for vice-president under Adlai Stevenson. As the balloting progressed, I gained a lead but was still about 10% short of the required delegate support, whereupon the mood of the convention turned on a dime and went for Senator Kefauver. I saw his victory coming and went straight to the podium to ask the participants to vote for him by acclamation. This loss was one of the luckiest events I ever experienced because it meant that, throughout my life, I would never be 'vice' anything! If you're going to lead, you have to be the person everyone perceives as the leader rather than merely his backup. Kefauver's running with Adlai Stevenson meant that duo would lose to Eisenhower in the November election and neither ever ran for high office thereafter."

Later, when he was seeking the presidency, he began to broaden his exhortations from mere electioneering and to urge his listeners to work toward what became esteemed goals. In order to do that, substantial changes would have to take place in society's general attitude that, while our Constitution was, verily, a supreme achievement, our nation's early history had implied that its precepts and guarantees applied only to white males. To the contrary, this fresh-faced leader believed that, as citizens of the same country, each one of us must be empowered with an equal chance to participate and contribute.

He had laid his thinking out for the entire world to see way back in 1960 when he accepted the Democratic nomination for president:

> "Some would say that our struggles in the world are over. Presently, there is peace throughout the world. They might go so far as to claim that there is no longer a frontier in America.

I would respond that they are looking only at physical borders. We cannot allow ourselves to be limited to such narrow, pedestrian thinking. The New Frontier is here for each of us to embrace. I see it clearly stretching into uncharted areas of science such as surviving in space, plumbing the depths of the oceans, even conquering the vast unknowns of debilitating disease.

"As vital as each of these areas is to our continuing success as a competitive country on the world stage, of far greater importance is the overriding need to relieve our nation's imbalance of shortages and surplus. If I am elected, we will adopt a new maxim in government. To relieve the suffering of poverty in America, my administration will provide a 'hand up' rather than just a hand-out. Yes, I am the scion of wealth, but I have traveled this country and met with people from all walks of life and backgrounds. Even as I stand here on this podium, I can see you. I empathize with what your life is like. I pledge to those who are feeling deprived and disadvantaged that my administration will exist to empower you to write your own life story! From that day forward, your President will undertake to make America a place in which no one is invisible, where everyone has the chance to realize his or her potential, and where neither skin nor ethnicity nor sex will be a presumptive bar to success.

"Now the harsh reality of the threat of Communism forces us to fortify our beliefs and to make a stand, a stand for freedom of choice and the sanctioning of opportunity limited by only the inventiveness of one's mind rather than by strict rules of state. Heed the clarion call and rise to accept the challenge. As I stand before you today, I offer myself ready and able to lead our nation into this New Frontier!"

I wasn't there; I was still assigned to Ike. But I wish I had been. It would not have mattered whether I was a spectator or on assignment. Reading these lines in a newspaper was a poor substitute for having been present in that convention hall, where one single man was completely surrounded by scores of citizens wanting him to succeed in making their circumstances better than what had existed in the past. No doubt the hall thundered with resounding applause for this handsome new leader. Now that I have been at his side for a year, I can appreciate why. His effect on citizens is mesmerizing. He makes us believe that the future beckons with the glowing prospect of improving our lives. Working toward a better future together will provide all of us with an opportunity that is too good to forego.

* * *

Having been his longtime political assistant, Kenneth knew the newly elected president had joked that, upon initially assuming the office, he kept worrying that some tall, broad-shouldered police officer would suddenly appear from behind a hallway door and stop him in midstride with a firmly outstretched arm.

"Whoa, there, sonny boy, and just where do you think you're going!" he would say, turning the new president around in his tracks.

Of course, that didn't happen. In fact, he took on the demands of the highest office in the land with aplomb and certitude, if you can ignore his gaff with the Bay of Pigs invasion. As time-in-office made him more sagacious, even sedulous in analyzing what his advisors were suggesting, he often found their proposed courses of action jejune.

One newspaper editor—who also happened to be a personal friend and thus knew about his human failings—went so far as to alert his readers that: "Here is a remarkable man who lights the skies of this land bright with hope and promise!" [13]

He developed an unusual ability: Approach a crisis discussion with *engaged detachment*.[14] His critical thinking and clear-headed analysis would be there at the table, but knee-jerk emotional responses and prejudiced assumptions would have been left back home resting atop his night table.

At heart, he desired to be remembered as a leader of high purpose and firm resolution. He was at his best when he sought to instill such nobility in his audience. Beckoning to us over his shoulder, he would step forward, as though walking in God's light, and inspire us to follow where he was leading. Like a track star imbued with fleetness of foot, his mind raced ahead of us, striving to achieve the best for everyone. An example of this was his speech to a Ft. Worth crowd during a future trip to Texas. With his wife Jacquelean standing at his side, he opened with:

"Two years ago I introduced myself in Paris by saying that I was the man who had accompanied the tastefully dressed Mrs. Jacquelean Kennerly to Paris. I am getting somewhat that same sensation as I travel around Texas and speak to you today in Fort Worth."

Then, pausing for effect, he added, "I've noticed that nobody is wondering what Lyndon and I are wearing."

His assembled audience roared warmly and profusely with laughter.

Then the President continued: "If our country is to fulfill its obligations around the world, every resident adult should become a participant in the obligations of citizenship. If each of us shoulders this burden, we will move forward economically together, with no one being left behind in the drive for improved prosperity."

He went on to say that our nation needed to be economically strong in two technologically new environments: under the sea and in outer space. To further our goals, our country would have to maintain existing alliances but at the same time forge new pacts with additional foreign nations. We would have to faithfully maintain both sets of endeavors."

Further expanding on this idea, he explained: "Our strength depends upon strength from within. As citizens of this great nation, each of you here today must be ready to step forward and assume the burdens of leadership and example so we may all strive for improvement together. The burdens of leadership must be undertaken and borne willingly by you, my fellow citizens."

As he spoke, his earnest tone confirmed that he was not merely mouthing politically correct phrases; he sincerely believed in what he was espousing. The President's hands would alternatively point outward toward his listeners, then upward, and then a single forefinger would pound down on the rostrum to punctuate his message. He was never unsure of his words. He spoke with steadfast assurance and conviction. An attribute that was unique to him was his ability to seemingly speak directly to every individual there, as though personally urging each person to embrace a sense of national purpose.

"Working together, we can generate a momentum whereby our combined forces will pursue morality in our country. We can exercise our civic duties, such as voting and paying taxes, with extra pride. We can use our freedom of choice to pursue our own destinies in a manner that enhances our nation's future. In this manner, we can engage in the pursuit of happiness for all our peoples; such an endeavor will be strenuous and exciting, but also heroically exalted."

It would be clear to everyone present, as well as to those watching on various television broadcasts, that here was a man who could confidently take us as a nation in a better direction. The big difference from other politicians was that he would be in the forefront. He would undertake the task of leading us to become a nation of better people: such would be the right thing to do. He already held the most powerful post in the land; thus, he had no hidden agenda of personal gain. Improving our lives, and thereby our nation, would be his guiding ambition.

He concluded this address as follows:

"What we are trying to do in this country and around the world is quite simple: to build a military structure which will defend the vital interests of our people. I am confident that our chances for security and peace are better than they were in the past. The dedicated efforts of men who are free to choose will meet these goals without fail. The reason is that we are stronger, and with that strength is a determination to maintain the peace which has been so dearly paid for in blood. To that cause, Texas and the United States are committed."

Everyone within hearing stood as they applauded this vital, visionary leader. *If it's to be, it'll be up to me.* I felt this famous quip surely reflected the inner workings of John Kennerly's mind. However, he never evinced a holier-than-thou attitude, either to his advisers or the citizens he represented. Right out of the starting gate, he let us know that, if conditions in our nation were going to improve, we ourselves would be the generation to shoulder that burden.

In 1962 he had the opportunity to appoint a replacement judge to the Supreme Court. After focusing on two candidates, with particular emphasis on how each would fit in with the Court's current composition, he chose Byron White, a man nicknamed "Whizzer White" as an All-American running-back turned Rhodes Scholar.

When Ken inquired about this selection, President Kennerly replied, "It came down to a question of who was needed at the time. Whizzer is the kind of guy I want to see on the bench. He understands America, what we are about, and where we need to go. He has wide experience and has good judgment, which is unusual for an intellectual. I respect him and think he will make fair and sound decisions for the good of all Americans." [15]

Here follows an excerpt from his inaugural address back on January 20, 1961. Many of you are old enough to recall these stirring, luculent words about the direction our President wanted to take our country:

> "My fellow citizens, in your hands you hold the success or failure of our future course. Since this country was founded, each generation of Americans has been summoned to give testimony to its national loyalty. The world in which we live is not yet a safe haven in which mankind can thrive. It must be made so by our achieving peace through strength. Only when our arms are sufficient beyond doubt can we be certain beyond doubt that they will never be employed.
>
> "Our primary goal is the control of force, not the pursuit of force. Our preparations for war are intended to preserve the peace. Not every nation around the world esteems the constitutional precepts of our form of government, but the governments of such nations must understand that their use of modern weaponry will lead not to their victory, but to their total destruction.
>
> "Today, the trumpet summons us as well to unite against the enemy common to each one of us here at home: poverty, disease, and prejudice itself. **If a free society cannot help the many who are poor, it cannot save the few who are rich.** Americans must be defined by their potential, not their shortcomings. Here on earth, God's work must truly be our own. Let us never compromise the principles upon which this great country was founded.
>
> "And so, my fellow Americans, ask not what your country can do for you—ask what you can do for your country!"

During the Inaugural Address, I was posted in the wings, watching over the First Lady. Nevertheless, when he walked up the stairs into the Capitol after concluding this address, everyone there could sense that a new vigor and strength had taken hold of our form of government. We now had a president who not only understood democracy and embraced all of its advantages, but also stood ready to defend it to the last. More significantly, this leader was stimulating Americans to embrace a newfound sense of national purpose.

When ill as a youngster, this great leader had developed a love of reading history. By the time he had graduated from college, Jack Kennerly was writing history. By the age of forty-four, he was making history. Only two years into his presidency, he would be called upon to preserve history by saving the world from destruction.

Notes

[1] See Weiner, p. 87.

[2] See Bishop, p. 281 and Kunhardt, pp. 6, 7.

[3] Lieberson, p. 174, describing Professor Arthur Holcombe's impression. See also: Hamilton, Nigel, pp. 322f discussing the Harvard student's obtaining years of British periodicals on the subject. Studying these let him conclude that British public opinion was controlled by pacifist sentiments. The danger lay in the fact that Americans were now clinging to those same false isolationist hopes, and politicians who valued their political positions were being irresistibly forced to accede to public opinion. Without American help, Britain would most assuredly have been strangled by the Nazi juggernaut of submarines and elite battleships interdicting all supplies.

[4] Pitts, pp. 61-65.

[5] Matthews, p. 59.

[6] Matthews, p. 49.

[7] Matthews, p. 50.

[8] See Lieberson, p. 39.

[9] See Lieberson, p. 50.

[10] Amplified by Pitts, pp. 144-146.

[11] See Hamilton, Nigel, p. 286 citing an article in *The Boston Globe*.

[12] Hamilton, pp. 406-8.

[13] Bradlee, p. 10.

[14] Hamilton, p. 300.

[15] See Bradlee, p. 66.

CHAPTER ELEVEN

Jacquelean

1963: The office worker and the plant employee benefited from government-mandated increases to the $1.25/hour minimum wage. At the time, a Big Mac cost 15¢, gasoline was 19¢/gallon, and a six-pack of beer cost just $1.00. A two-bedroom apartment would rent for approximately $150/month unless it was located in New York City, Hollywood, or Darien, Connecticut.

Lucille Ball, Ed Sullivan, and Johnny Carson enlivened our TV sets. *The Twilight Zone* stretched our beliefs while The Beatles were mere months away from invading America and altering the sound of pop music. Alfred Hitchcock's *The Birds* made us afraid to ever open a door again; that is, unless Jayne Mansfield should be behind it lying on a bed. She created quite a stir by appearing nude, from the waist up, in *Playboy Magazine*.

Newsweek Magazine publishes the Surgeon General's report regarding the genuine risks to one's health of smoking cigarettes; this was counterbalanced by the realities of major revenue losses for the tobacco producing states.

Despite all the attention and adoration that Mr. Kennerly enjoyed wherever his meetings and negotiations took him, no one in the secret service's presidential detail was luckier than me. In 1961, I was assigned to look after the president's wife, the vivacious and exemplary Jacquelean Lee Bouffant Kennerly. Jacquelean's birthday was July 28, so she was only thirty years old when we first were introduced. Regardless, providing protection for her shifted my career into high gear.

Initially, I worked with Jim Jeffries as my shift replacement. He was just under six feet tall, as I am, early thirties, with bright reddish hair that made his head look like kindling already aflame every time he stepped from the shadows. For my first meeting with Mrs. Kennerly, he introduced us.

As soon as he said, "Mrs. Kennerly, this is Clint Brill," she turned fully toward me and extended her right hand charmingly. When Jeffries intoned, "Clint, meet Mrs. Kennerly," my hand moved forward shakily, as though it was about to enter a newly discovered dimension of experience. And yet, when her hand slipped inside mine, like a graceful foot hiding in a warm slipper, I could immediately see her demeanor soften.

Her limpid brown eyes pierced right through my veil of stern fortitude as she said, "Well, Mr. Brill, it appears that I am the lucky one. I can tell we are going to get along very nicely. Kindly tell your boss, Mr. Rowley, that he has chosen wisely."

"I'm very pleased to meet you, Mrs. Kennerly." It was all I could do to keep my tongue from twisting as it groped amongst respect, politeness, and awe all at the same time.

"Oh, Mr. Brill. The pleasure is all mine! After all, from now on, you will be responsible for my staying out of harm's way. I hope I won't prove to be too much trouble," she said while still looking directly at me. However, I sensed that this elegant woman possessed a bit of devilish humor with which I would have to cope. As she would be my assigned person to protect, it was important that I remain on good terms with her.

"Well, Ma'am," I responded authoritatively, "my primary assignment will be to simply shadow you wherever you go and to step forward should any suspicious threat arise." My voice now had a bit of confidence in its tone. After all, I knew my job and had performed it well during Ike's last year in office. Then I added, "I will be at your call as needed, Ma'am."

This claim brought a laugh from the First Lady. It was melodious, like the tinkling of wind chimes on a soft Cape Cod breeze.

She warmly replied, "Thank you. I do appreciate everything the Agency will be doing to keep my family safe while my husband occupies the White House." Then, flashing that wide-mouthed smile that so snowed her admirers, she added: "I will have Miss Tish Baldrige furnish you with my daily itinerary, but don't be too surprised if I deviate from the schedule. I do hate being bound to a slate of appearances and meetings. I much prefer to go where my mood dictates, even if that means a midnight foray to some moonlit marble façade or blossoming festival of hyacinths."

Then, pausing for a moment while an additional thought occurred to her, she spoke to me with a bright new twinkle in her eyes. "Be prepared to soak up so much knowledge about art from the Federal Period and furniture created by French artisans that you'll want to sit for your advanced-degree exams!"

She was only kidding, of course, for by now it was obvious that good taste, as well as humor, coursed through her veins as though it was a necessary ingredient to her breathing in and out. Her social secretary Tish once summed up Jacquelean's effect by saying she changed the White House from a plastic to a cut-crystal bowl. I couldn't wait to get home and celebrate my new assignment with Gail. The next half-dozen or so years were going to be fun!

On the spot, I had to admit it: I loved my job!

There was no denying the impression Jacquelean Kennerly could make upon merely entering a room. As the First Lady had confidently glided into my life that day, my immediate reaction was: Everything that had been written about her attractive beauty was mere tripe. In person, she is the loveliest woman any of us in the Service were ever to meet. She possesses an erect elegance that catches one's eye as she moves about a room; a man's attention becomes instantly riveted on her alone. She exudes an air of quiet but regal confidence, as though she had been born to be exactly who she now is. The visitor senses that she is comfortably in her element.

Her attire is gently flattering but without a hint of being ostentatious. Her manner is the epitome of thoughtfulness. She puts visitors at ease, as though her being with them is the most natural and desirable activity she could imagine.

I indulged myself in the thought that, on the Seventh Day, God had only pretended to rest; actually, he was off in the workroom somewhere creating Jacquelean Kennerly. For my money, she bore a lovely radiance, perhaps the best that Nature had yet created. Later, I came to see that she could pout and sulk as well as any mortal woman, but on that first day, and for many in the future, she epitomized the wonder of being female. Her presence would grace any room; men simply became stupefied as they felt her meet their gaze and converse warmly with them.

"I have a gift for communicating," I once heard her demurely admit after wowing yet another foreign diplomat with her grasp of his native tongue.

As my own bride once pointed out to me, everyone recognized that Jacquelean was the best woman at any gathering, but she assumed no airs of pretense or superiority, so everyone found themselves welcoming the opportunity to be around her.

"If truth be told, Clint," she murmured low to me, "when I first saw her in person, I was immediately entranced and found myself wanting to copy her outfit, demeanor, accessories, even her voice! She's just delightful to behold."

Coming from my wife, who likes to be decorous and informed, this was high praise.

Photo by Robert Knudsen

What astounded me the most was, despite her demure, soft-voiced manner, this woman exuded control over her environs. As for everyday life in the White House, she knew exactly how it should be managed. Her family life was not going to be on display for people to gawk at like some showpiece. She wanted to maintain this magnificent structure as an edifice which proudly proclaimed to the world that: "Here is the centerpiece of American leadership!" With only one child to attend to at the time, she could devote her energies to refurbishing the White House as America's repository of treasured memories through its portraits, period furniture, and table settings.

More importantly, she wanted this home to offer comfort and relaxation for her husband. She wanted the President to have a means to shunt aside the everyday pressures of leading the Free World in the era of the Cold War, so she set about providing a home filled with affection and intriguing dinner guests as well as children who were groomed and playful. [1]

"The White House belongs to all Americans," she declared to the CBS television audience glued-to-the-tube one chilly Valentine's Day in 1962. Her tour of the Executive Mansion was conducted in the company of Charles Collingwood as host of the "Jacquelean Kennerly Show" as reporters would soon dub it. She held the TV audience transfixed as she breathlessly told us: "It should be a living museum of our nation's history, a house of which all Americans are proud because important decisions were made and momentous events took place therein. Indeed, we must make it a place which everybody will want to visit!"

As they walked along the corridors, Mr. Collingwood was moved to observe: "The past is so very important to the future, isn't it?"

Mrs. Kennerly had simply beamed that broadly captivating smile of hers while she graciously completed the tour of our chief executive's home. In short, simply by her demeanor, elegance had arrived at the White House. She intended to keep it there.

Moreover, this nation-wide broadcast transformed her into a valuable political asset.

Her devotion to antiques and fine furniture with silk cushions and tasseled drapery made me wonder about all the animals that were, bit by bit, taking up residence on the grounds of the White House. The First Lady's horse, "Bit of Irish," was the largest. However, Carolyn's pony, the pair of ducks, various dogs, cats, varieties of birds, and no doubt a host of hamsters and such that I never saw made for quite a menagerie. Naturally, all this was a great pleasure for Carolyn and, apparently, even her parents.

One summer evening, Mrs. Kennerly and I were strolling among the fragrant blooms of the Rose Garden. We sat on a raised stone border hovering protectively around a small fountain-pond and gazed across the broad expanse of the South Lawn. Except for the backdrop of the falling water droplets, the scene was peaceful, even ataractic, which is saying something given how close Dulles International Airport is to the President's residence.

Jacquelean was clearly deep in thought. Eventually, she turned toward me and asked, "Did you know, Agent Brill, that there used to be extensive horse stables where we are now sitting? That's right! Where the President's Cabinet now meets, horses used to paw the ground neighing for more hay. Where the Oval Office sits, manure was stored. These facts from our nation's illustrious past I am sharing with you today so we can have a little secret between ourselves. It is not something *The Saturday Evening Post* is going to ask Norman Rockwell to evoke for next month's cover!"

Frankly, I was stunned. When one lives in the present, he hardly ever stops to consider how the spot on which he sits might have been put to an entirely different use by prior generations.

"No, Mrs. Kennerly, I confess I sure didn't!"

"Why yes, it's true. Being an equestrian myself, I can almost smell the scent of freshly lain straw and hear the swish of the mares' tails as they swipe away insects. This makes me love this place all the more!" Her breathy voice was alive with feelings and emotions for things she just adored.

I had a good comeback. "Carolyn must love it as well. She gets to ride Macaroni amidst all these crabapple trees and tulips, primrose, and honeysuckle. It's a veritable smörgåsbord of fragrances!"

"Oh yes, you're so right!" she observed in her breathy voice. She smiled at her next thought. "Carolyn loves that little pony so. Even when I helped redesign the Rose Garden with extensive replanting in 1962, that didn't deter my daughter and Macaroni from trotting all about it to inspect that everything had been laid out correctly!"

"Ma'am, you are so knowledgeable about the history of the White House and its place in American history. I hope the President appreciates how you grace his tenure."

Her head tiled back as she laughed at my remark. *"Au contraire, mon ami!"* she responded. "I know very little about politics, and care even less. In fact, my ignorance on that subject is advantageous; it leaves more room for the topics and interests that are most important to me. If you need me to encapsulate my passions in a single word, it would be *culture*. Art, music, well-designed menus, elegant dancing, all these are what captivate my heart! I have a gift for languages, but these other areas require me to apply myself diligently in order to appreciate them."

"That diligence has resulted in you making exemplary contributions to the quality of American civilization." Not too erudite, perhaps, but certainly my honest opinion.

"Not me, Clint. It's my wide circle of friends and acquaintances that should be thanked. I simply use my ability to make them aware of how good they will feel by contributing an Andrew Wyeth or John Singer Sargent to the art of the White House. Nobody has ever raised an objection. When I suggest, they always agree that their donation would be timely and significant. I'm... no, *we're* all so lucky to be Americans!"

With that, we wended our way back from our idyllic musings.

* * *

On November 14, 1962, Mrs. Eleanor Roosevelt passed away. A strong sense of personal loss was felt by millions. She had come to be regarded as a permanent guidepost, even a blessing for Americans. She possessed tough common sense and had no hesitation in speaking out when she perceived injustice. For anyone committed to excellence in government, she provided counsel and example. Even if your politics were adverse to hers, you couldn't help admiring her courage and spirit.

* * *

Despite being the wife of a president, Jacquelean evinced no interest in the machinations with which her husband dealt on a daily basis. She frankly eschewed politics. Beautifying America with museums was a sometime pursuit; however, bringing grace and taste to our country's foremost residence, through furnishings such as a

Louis XVI escritoire donated by her friends, was to be her focus as First Lady. As far as she was concerned, this came second behind her primary duty: to be a good mother.

She, in fact, was a very devoted parent. She told Jeffries and me that, on a daily basis, she would set aside "Carolyn time" so, regardless of the demands of her official role, she would have moments to enjoy her daughter's active and inquisitive mind. Her daughter thrived in the White House. There were so many secret places to be explored, so many new sights which could titillate her imagination!

What the little girl needed most, of course, was a younger brother whom she could dominate and bend to her will; Mrs. Kennerly soon obliged, producing a baby boy, Jon-Jon, whom all the world could admire. He would quickly become a dream photo-op for the White House photographers and, after he learned to walk and explore, would provide levity and joy to his father during serious moments of crisis in the Oval Office.

For her part, Mrs. Kennerly enjoyed her lack of knowledge about politics; doing so kept her sane, she once told me. She quietly possessed her own orbit of expertise; should the conversation turn to art, music, and language, her responses would show she was well informed. She was gifted in the latter area, possessing *sprachgefühl*, or facility with languages according to the German Embassy officials who met her during the President's stop in West Berlin. She wowed a Latin American audience when she addressed it using Spanish. She became the envy of the Foreign Service staff for the way she won over the haughty Frenchman and war-hero Charles De Gaulle when she spoke to him in French during a presidential visit to Paris.

I still marvel at her ability to convince the world-renowned authority, Monsieur Malraux, France's Minister of Culture, to loan the fabulous *Mona Lisa* to the United States so that many millions of Americans might spend a few lovely moments with that lady's alluring smile. This was cultural diplomacy at its best!

Even her adept handling of Frenchmen didn't stop the President from grousing about our ally's low unemployment rate resulting from high annual increases in their gross national product. When her husband mentioned his jealousies to Jacquelean at dinner, she merely laughed: "Oh, Jack, the French have been succeeding at whatever they try for centuries. We're just the new kid on the block. Don't worry, we'll catch up!"

However, he did take her up on the suggestion to hire a French artist, Bernard Lamott, to paint murals on three sides of the heated indoor-swimming pool which Jack used to alleviate his back pain. Upon its completion with floor-to-ceiling mirrors on the fourth side, this space became a highly desired, restorative retreat from his pressure-packed day solving international and domestic problems. I accompanied the President to enjoy its ambiance only a few times, but I can attest that health spas would be well-advised to imitate its uniquely designed properties.

Regarding the interior decorations of the White House, somehow the First Lady managed to solicit suggestions from the great restoration expert Stéphane Boudin. "We wouldn't be here if the Marquis de Lafayette hadn't helped General Washington win our revolution!" she liked to point out when people questioned her use of a Frenchman. She also relied on David Finley—who chaired the U.S. Commission of Fine Arts—so her approach balanced foreign with domestic talent.

"The White House is a powerful symbol of our democracy," she would say about her soliciting gifts of American paintings and furniture for its decoration. "The past is a source of pride for people throughout the world. The President's residence should be shown at its best to visitors wherever they are from, even if they live just down the street."

Everyday citizens, as well as the fabulously rich, responded to her entreaties. Employees of the Sears, Roebuck Company pooled sufficient funds to donate four canvases by Charles Bird King; his paintings of American Indians are as highly prized as those of the better known Frederick Remington.

"See," she would observe, "we Americans have homegrown talent that can be the envy of the world!" She would then lightly hold her hands down in front of her and just beam. She was so happy being First Lady, although she never used that title herself, and we were so pleased with the way she filled us citizens with pride in being American!

Her sense of the decorous seeped into the consciousness of her beleaguered husband who was trying to shoulder the heavy burden of running America's government. On quiet nighttime walks along Pennsylvania Avenue, Jacquelean would hold her husband's hand as she pointed out the tawdry shops that lined what French architect L'Enfant and then President Thomas Jefferson had designed to be a grand ceremonial mile connecting the Chief Executive Mansion with the Domed Capitol Building. Jack established a commission to rebuild this grand mile and followed the progress of redevelopment with feeling. [2]

Due to her sense of elegance, she became the focus of couture designers for her taste in clothes; in fact, she engendered an entirely new mode of dress for women. We men enjoyed the benefit of her good taste: our wives never looked more elegant than during the 1960's!

Despite her being raised amidst wealth and the upper crust of society, she surprised me with how down-to-earth she was. When we would take walks at Glen Ora, an estate outside Washington leased by the Kennerlys, she would be very aware of our surroundings. Whether it was the silken flow of a stream or a lark's melody in the springtime blossoms, she'd appreciate the sound: "Isn't that just lovely!" she would exclaim, jolting me back from my constant surveillance fore and aft to ensure her safety.

Her awareness of the aesthetics of her location struck me as though she lived in some masterful work of art, ever conscious of how the colors and textures about her worked in harmony to stitch and hold her everyday world together.

Her excellent sense of what would be in good taste came from her bloodline as well as her private schooling prior to entering Vassar College. However, the main drive behind her exquisite sense of decorum and decoration derived from her endless quest to know. Her husband loved reading history as it pertained to the formation, governance, and decline of nations, but she focused on what people had done and said in social settings. Her "need to know what has been done before" kept me hopping. Her mind dictated her daily activities, and spontaneity nourished that mind.

The only difficulty lay in the fact that her sallying forth had to be satisfied within the purviews of the Service. Wherever she went, Jeffries and I had to go also. We moved well together, as though we were a team: I never once heard her complain that Jeffries and I were slowing her down. And I say that with respect, for there was many a time when he and I were roused from sleep in order to accompany the First Lady on some foray to the light of a moon-drenched scene or a garden setting with katydids all a-buzz at 2:00 AM!

Fortunately, when she finally met my wife, I had been on the detail so long that my Gail had forgiven my being dominated by Mrs. Kennerly's perambulations.

Jack freely admitted that, though his wife was apolitical, she gave him tactful, and thus tactical, advantage when dealing with international leaders. Socially, the Kennerlys brought taste and elegance to the White House. "Art, whether in music, poetry, or culture must become, and forever remain, a part of the American way of life," Mrs. Kennerly was fond of stating whenever a reporter was close by, which was pretty much all the time.

The arts, according to the First Lady, encompassed culture as well, and that led to the Kennerlys honoring winners of the Nobel Prize by hosting a dinner for them. The 49 recipients were accompanied by writers, scientists, and educators who, after the President had stood and surveyed the assembled guests, led him to observe: "I think this is the most extraordinary collection of talent, of human knowledge, that has ever graced the White House, with the possible exception of when Thomas Jefferson dined here alone." [3]

The remark brought the house down.

If my memory serves me right, it was about a year later when the couple celebrated their tenth wedding anniversary. It was a pleasant September twelfth evening. Gail and I were invited along with the McDonalds and Mr. and Mrs. Jeffries. We admired the solid-gold Egyptian snake bracelet which Jack had given to his wife, and we also effused over the silver cigar humidor inscribed by all the cabinet members.

Jacquelean had secretly enlisted Tish Baldrige to round up the signatures for the engraver to imitate. Even I hadn't noticed this lengthy project as it proceeded along the heart of the White House corridors during August.

It was at this celebration that we met Jack's longtime pal, Kirk Billings. This man was such a close friend of the President that he maintained a room on the third floor of the White House. That was a rare privilege for a nongovernmental employee! But it was also fun for us since we had heard so much about this man's ability to "keep it light" for his longtime buddy, a friend who now headed the government of the United States.

As Billings would say with a bright smile, "The reason the President and I are so close is that Jack can tell me anything, but I tell no one!"

* * *

96

When it came to political events and appearances, Mrs. Kennerly was often at odds with the wishes of the President. If the wind was blowing during a motorcade, she preferred riding beneath the plastic bubble top. That's, in fact, all it was: a shield against the wind and rain. Such limited protection didn't bother me; I thought that if a bullet or bomb were aimed at the occupants in the president's car, anything bouncing off or even penetrating the bubble would instantly alert us agents to danger, even if streets were so crowded with vocal well-wishers that our hearing was compromised. Eyes are better than ears: you take in more information more accurately, so you can react more quickly. In my world, seeing was more important than hearing.

If the bubble top were on, a bullet that cracks or deforms it would be immediately noticed by everyone—agents, bystanders, and the people under the bubble. Taking evasive action in response could be instantaneous! People wouldn't crane their necks asking, vacantly, "Gee, what was that? Sounded like a rifle shot..." We would instantly see it happen and quickly cover and whisk the president to safety. Significantly, simply having it between a sniper and the president would provide a certain amount of uncertainty. Reflection and distortion would create confusion even if a marksman had a telescopic sight.

Jacquelean, however, was not serving as the president. Jack Kennerly was, and he loved being close to the people whom he served. "I want to appear to be available to them," was his rationale. He wanted to be seen as one of them despite being their leader. As his motorcade would pass by, having a bubble top would interfere with the view. The smiling charm that clearly captivated everyone would be quashed.

In short, he wanted to be out there, greeting, meeting, even being touched by the people. Doing so provided him with great pleasure.

And, he wanted his wife with him. She was now an important asset. Whether she was politically savvy or not, her popularity transcended politics.

For those of us in the Secret Service, any decision to forego the bubble top would, most assuredly, put us under hellish pressure.

Notes

1 Schlesinger, *Journals*, p. xxv.
2 Schlesinger, *Journals*, p. xxv.
3 Pitts, p. 239.

CHAPTER TWELVE

Just in Time?

During a luncheon in early November 1963, the President was sitting around the dining table when he looked across at his wife, and then steadily at Kenny, Larry, and even me standing off to the side. He paused for a moment, reflecting on the worst moment Mankind had yet known: the Cuban Missile Crisis.

"Do you remember the words I used back in October of last year? I tried to encapsulate the problem in clear, realistic terms. I said, 'When our over-flights revealed the threat of missile construction and launch pads in Cuba, we as a nation were forced to embark on a difficult and dangerous course, but the greatest danger of all would have been to do nothing. The choice we have made for the present is full of hazards, but it is the one most consistent with our character and courage as a nation, as well as our commitments around the world.'"

The man had demonstrated grace under pressure as well as faith in his own clear thinking. That event had been reminiscent of Abraham Lincoln's declaring "the vote is no!" when his entire cabinet had voted "aye."

Clearing his throat, he had continued with this stirring challenge: "The cost of freedom is always high—but Americans have always been willing to pay it. One path we shall never choose, and that is the path of surrender. Our goal is not the victory of might, but the vindication of right—not peace at the expense of freedom, but both peace and freedom in harmony."

He expanded on his point. "My generals were urging warlike responses which would have led to the thermonuclear destruction of mankind. They wanted to act on the basis of what the overhead flight reconnaissance was showing, but they did not understand that the warheads had been brought onto the island well before the missiles—since these were so much easier to hide—and could be placed on the launch vehicles in short order. Moreover, there were far more sites than we had discovered. These had been camouflaged successfully. Russia had one-upped us badly. Their missiles flying from ninety miles off our coast would have wiped out half of America before our retaliatory birds had even gotten out of their silos. Crushchev had gambled on our sitting on our hands even when we'd been put in a really alarming position; I am fortunate that he was swayed by the light of reason. Let me repeat that: by the light of reason."

During the crisis, John A. McCone, Ray S. Cline, McGeorge Bundy and the President met to review the over-flight photos of the missile sites. Initially, Carolyn skipped about the room, playing with her dad. As she hopped away, the men were reminded that the fate of future generations—as well as their own—depended on the decisions they were about to make. Over the next few days, they would collectively ponder not merely some of the most dramatic intelligence of the century but, more importantly, the meaning of life itself. [1]

Those of us in the room breathed in and out in unison as we contemplated the life-altering consequences if Soviet leader Crushchev had remained bellicose. Although the luncheon was over, the President was still fuming as he thought back on those cliff-hanger days when his military advisors had been so uniformly in favor of violent action. They forced him to wrestle with adherence to bilateral diplomacy versus disregarding diplomacy altogether in favor of unilateral response. After a moment's reflection, the President continued.

"In my position, I often have to be both conciliator as well as firm in my adherence to principle. I cannot afford to appease the aggressor, as did Chamberlain back in 1939 when, clutching a piece of paper signed by Hitler, he proclaimed he had achieved 'peace in our time.' Give me facts, not advice; information that is accurate, rather than counsel. Then I can form a logical course and make a sound decision. On this basis, if you hear me standing firm, it is because I have thought through the arguments and taken a position aligned with humanistic principles regarding right and wrong, rather than merely bellowing out of desperate prejudice."

Then, his face reddened a bit as he reiterated the inner drive that kept him level-headed in a crisis. "Nobody is going to force me to do anything I don't think is in the best interest of this country. National reason will never succumb to national pride on my watch!"

That wasn't just his navy-training talking. Kenneth and I looked at one another, each knowing how lucky our country was to have this rational, level-headed man as its president. His decisive and effective handling of the threat that Premier Crushchev had fomented exemplified his complete control of the enormous powers of the office of President. If it hadn't been for him, I doubt any of us sitting around the table would be alive today to reflect on this.

Now, with the election campaign in 1964 looming ever closer, the President had decided to foray into Texas with Mr. Jensen in order to firm up his southern support. Due to harsh feelings of betrayal over the segregation question, his brother Bobby advised against doing so. But fellow Democrat John Connolly had arranged for a big dinner in Austin and, as the current governor, deserved Mr. Kennerly's support. Moreover, Representative Albert Thomas would be applauded at a testimonial in Houston. This man had been instrumental in raising support for the launch of our country's space program and therefore simply had to be acknowledged for enabling the President to lead this country toward the technological age of the coming century.[2]

For this trip, Winston G. Lawson was the Secret Service agent in charge of the White House detail. He had flown down earlier and filed the Preliminary Survey Report assessing the dangers inherent in conducting motorcades in the Lone Star state. In early November, the president ordered this agent to direct Kitterman, in charge of the Texas motorcade, that the bubble top would not be used unless it was raining. Kitterman relayed this directive to agents Sam Kinney and Harold Goodbody. These men obediently removed the bubble top and stored it in the trunk; thus, it would be readily available should the weather become ominous in Dallas.

The result would thus be a Third Degree Exposure for this motorcade. If a person, whether he is our man or a foreign dignitary, wants to stand on the ground and work the crowd, that constitutes First Degree, whereas if that person stands to smile and wave as his motorcade moves along, that is Second Degree Exposure. Sitting exposes a smaller mass, to be sure, but the important parts—upper torso and head—remain revealed for all to see. An outsider would reason that the higher the number, the easier the protective mission; however, the risks inherent in our job never take the easier path. The

President wanted to enjoy maximum exposure; this, he felt, would assure everyone who had come out to cheer, wave, and shake his hand that he was available and ready to satisfy their needs.

Politics and security do not mix any better than do oil and water. In Texas, the value of exposing the President trumped our concerns for his safety. America is the land of his birth, for god's sake, plus it's Lyndon's home state. What could possibly go wrong?

For the trip through Dallas, the president would put us through the wringer, adopting all three degrees of exposure on any given day. We would have an advance detail awaiting his arrival at each airport and, of course, he'd have an eight-man detail traveling with him. You get the picture: we were working double shifts during this Texas trip. Even when you are conditioned, highly trained, and working with an elite bunch of cohorts, things can go awry when fatigue sets in.

Jerry Blaine had related a typical end-of-day story when he had met up with his wife Joyce following his standard midnight-to-8:00 AM tour. As she drove him home, he started to nod off even as she was detailing what she and the kids had been doing the day before. She realized her words were simply drifting through one ear and out the other without registering.

She had asked herself, "What do they do to these guys during their duty hours? Even when Jerry gets a day off and comes home, he's no good to me!"

All the other wives she talked with reported the same result: when their husbands got off shift, they were useless, good only for lying down and falling instantly asleep. There was no way these women could be made to understand; a person had to actually pull the duty hours, with all the accompanying, <u>relentless</u> pressure, to appreciate what an agent endured every day.

Regardless of how tough it would be for us, our President preferred, wherever possible, to be completely visible to the cheering crowds. That was how he liked it: "These are voters!" he would exclaim in response to our suggestions for better security. Clearly, here was a man who was in his element. He obviously loved being close enough to the people he represented so they could touch him or shake his hand. In short, so close that people could express themselves in a brief moment of intimacy.

After all, that encapsulated the whole reason for this swing through Texas. Polls were suggesting that his challenger, Barry Coldwater, was closing fast and might take the state, which would put garnering enough Electoral College votes in next year's November election at risk. The Democrats needed Texas to swing their way. Despite it being the vice-president's home state, the chief executive's stance on civil rights had turned many of that state's residents against the party in the White House.

When anyone pointed this fact out to him, he was quick to respond: "We cannot ever let our past ignorance regarding the enslavement of certain people shame us into pretending that we were right in doing so. There are some in Congress who advise against enacting laws before the problems which they are designed to address are fully understood. I agree with that, but I do not think it inappropriate to say that, at this point in time, we in government are fully aware of what depriving citizens of their rights means."

This trip, showcasing Mr. Kennerly's broad smile and inspirational speech-making, with his radiant wife standing attractively at his side, was meant to mend a lot of fences. Television was his ally, but Leonard and Kenneth knew that nothing worked as much magic as the President himself encountering voters face-to-face and shaking their hand. People would remember the moment when the president's eyes had met theirs all the way to the voting booth.

No Democrat had ever gained the presidency without taking Texas' 25 electoral votes. That made the state, and this visit, vitally important.

When Air Force One touched down in Dallas, the portable staircase was rolled astride the fuselage. As the exit door was opened, the President wisely suggested that Jacquelean precede him down the steps. Her face was alight with appreciation for the receptive and large crowds who were cheering and waving their welcome. The president had been prescient; while he would be the one to make the speeches, most likely all these citizens had come to see and be near Jacquelean.

As I stayed unobtrusively close to the First Lady, I could hear the crowd cooing with delight.

"Isn't she just lovely?"

"Don't you just adore the color of her pink suit with matching pillbox hat? I want to get just that outfit for myself!"

"Look at the way she walks; she's simply gliding on air!"

I never did hear anyone comment on the clothes the President was wearing.

As a couple, they exuded elegance as well as pleasure at being amongst their citizenry. The people loved seeing them, catching their hands during a walk-through, lapping them up like kittens confronted with a bowl of succulent cream. I could see for myself: merely being in the presence of such lovely, attractive people lifted everyone's spirit and made them prideful.

I could almost hear the unspoken boast: "Look, people of the world, these are <u>our</u> American leaders, and we love them!"

The President was elated at the warmth of the greetings he and Jacquelean were receiving throughout Texas. The two of them visiting together—for once—riveted the attention of the crowds during the entire route of each motorcade. Their youthful appearance, their tasteful clothes, and their broad flashing smiles captivated everyone. The faces of those in the crowds were approving, adoring, even rejoicing!

Before the motorcade got underway, Jack took a moment to turn to Larry O'Brien and ask: "Well, how do you think the size of this turnout compares to my solo trip to Houston last year?"

Larry didn't miss a beat. "Well, Mr. President, I'd say it was about the same. But there are around 100,000 more that came to see Jacquelean!"

Jack smiled. He knew Larry was right.

It didn't matter how a citizen had voted in 1960; we Americans now had people of taste and decorum in the White House. Mr. and Mrs. Kennerly would be the closest thing to royalty that we would ever possess. During this trip, it seemed as though each person wanted to taste, or at least smell, the fine bouquet that was the wine of the Kennerly personality. All the people along the motorcade route appeared to need to reach out and touch either one or the other. Clearly, getting in a handshake or smiling word would improve the rest of their lives.

Mr. and Mrs. John Fitzhugh Kennerly had become the American drug of choice.

As he no doubt confided to Kenneth McDonald last night at the hotel, these strong outpourings of approval were earning the President plaudits regardless of party allegiances. It was evident to me that this man was single-handedly removing Americans from partisan politics and fusing us as a nation.

Larry O'Brien was Mr. Kennerly's political guru, but McDonald was Jack's political guardian. His days as a well-built football hero had stayed with Ken. He still sported broad shoulders and a muscled physique which, together with his thick crop of black hair and ruddy complexion, lent him a hearty persona. Like his boss, when he spoke it was from his heart, and that heart was fashioned from sincerity. Reminiscent of the famous Rock of Gibraltar in the Prudential Insurance Company ads, he was always there for Mr. Kennerly—solid and reliable.

These voluble, surprise endorsements were gratifying to them as a team. With these in hand, next year's campaign would be that much easier. Not even the prescient press secretary, Pierre Salinger, had anticipated such strong showings of approval.

The result was that the President of the United States wanted to be "out there" as I called it, fully exposed but being able thereby to shake hands, flash his magnificent smile, and actually speak to people as his motorcade moved along. Apparently, Ken raised some concern, given the enormous crowds some eight people deep, but Jack merely stated that it was not the president's job to worry about his life. It was our job. If he had to do our job too, he'd never be able to focus on the important demands of his office, so he'd put staying alive out of his mind and was relying on the Secret Service to take care of him.

All this adoration made our lives sheer hell, however. Of course, the Secret Service would never admit to that. Providing protection regardless of circumstances was our job. Besides, what if everyone hated the person we were guarding; would that not be a far more difficult environment in which to operate?

I was in no position to disagree with the President's directive about the bubble-top being removed. I wasn't even responsible for him; my duty was to Mrs. Kennerly, after all. She was expected to be sitting to the left of the president. The same rule applies to military officers: subordinate rank sits to the left of the higher. Thus, her position didn't trouble me at all. I was stationed at the forward end of the left runner on the support vehicle assigned to travel just behind SS100X, the President's car.

By November of 1963, I'd been on presidential details for some five years. Usually, we walked astride the president's vehicle; agents had done that during the June tour of Cork, Ireland, as well as his recent jaunt out to Billings, Montana. If speeds were expected to exceed

10mph, we would ride on specially constructed platforms astride the spare tire hood as we held onto raised bars secured to the trunk cover of SS100X. Such position was, of course, our preferred position. We would be very close by if we needed to react, and our bodies would block line-of-sight from the rear to any passenger occupying the back seat.

These procedures were clearly defined. Such proximal positions had been utilized without incident ever since the elongated black Lincoln had been added to inventory. Most telling, we would be a mere five feet from the leader of the free world should anything untoward occur. We could react with the speed of lightning to cover his body protectively. If some projectile cracked or deformed the bubble, we would instantly see it happen and quickly provide cover to the president.

None of this applied today to the Dallas motorcade. All of us detailed to the president's entourage were either seated within the secret service car, dubbed "Halfback," or else standing on the running boards of such following vehicle. Four motorcycles were assigned to local policemen; these would be just aft of the president's vehicle, providing a sort of interference screen if a person was standing at ground level. Agent Ron Pontius had been responsible for getting everything in place for the motorcade, but even this agent—strongly built stud that he was—had been surprised when he'd heard about: "no bubble-top" and "no agents aboard SS100X."

"The Boss doesn't want our agents crowding him," was the phrase carried down the hierarchical line of command all the way from Washington, D.C.

The President had snidely remarked: "My motorcade should not be a sort of tennis court dedans where the people are screened off to the side."

His directive was too much for some of the agents. "What the hell is the point of our standing around close to, but not in the line of fire, for the President?" Pontius had asked no one in particular when he'd been informed of the President's desires. "With these crowds, eight to ten people deep, there's no way we can do our job in such circumstances!"

His complaints reached my ears; they sent chills of apprehension up and down my spine. I would be on the front lines of this protective detail. Would I have the wherewithal to handle a sudden, perhaps mortal, threat?

Unbeknownst to those of us assigned to protect our President and the First Lady that day, there was a scheming twit awaiting us in a tall structure astride Elm Street. Six stories up in the Texas State School Book Depository building, secreted amidst stacked cardboard boxes, squatted a man on a mission to achieve the renown he believed had long been denied him. Since dishonorably separating from the U.S Marine Corps, he had emigrated from the United States to the Soviet Union seeking asylum as a defector. There, he had been held at arm's length until he revealed that he had been employed by the American C.I.A.; he then produced documents detailing the capabilities of America's primary international monitoring tool, the U-2 spy plane. These revealing plans were so important that the Soviets immediately granted him protected status, enabling him to take up residence in Minsk. The turncoat's documents also allowed the Russians to track and shoot down the high-flying plane of Gary Powers, causing intense embarrassment for the Eisenhower Administration and emboldening Premier Crushchev to crow: "See what the Americans are doing! Now no one can doubt that they intend evil things for Mother Russia!"

Over time, the defector became disillusioned with the tight restraints of Communist life, but his stay in the U.S.S.R. enabled him to meet and marry a young Russian. In a far-reaching gaff by our State Department, second only to Ethel and Julius Rosenberg's handing over secrets to the atom bomb a decade or so earlier, this former marine's dishonorable discharge was waived and the newlyweds were permitted to enter this country and gain citizenship. After reaching our shores, he apparently took a boat to Cuba and, upon returning from that trip, joined a pro-Casstra group and successfully infiltrated a stateside bunch bent on removing Fidel Casstra from power. After some months pursuing this deception, his behavior became erratic. He told his now worried wife that he would someday kill the vice-president of this country. Since she knew he had already shot at a famous general but missed, and had heard him boast that he would have killed Dwight Eisenhower if he'd had the chance, she took his boasts very seriously. But she was an East European: Russian wives did not openly question their husbands. More importantly, any concern she raised with her spouse always resulted in his severely beating her. She kept her mouth shut.

By his own admission, this sharpshooter had run away from several chances for notoriety already; he was not about to do so on this, the 22nd day of November 1963. Like a secretive, starving spider that has woven its web and is awaiting a victim, any victim, this brooding, pitifully psychotic "patsy," as he would call himself later that day, sat and festered.

As we motored along, I heard over Channel 2 that Deputy Chief Lumpkin had stopped his car in front of a tall brick building to alert a policemen working traffic that the motorcade was less than 2 minutes behind. As I learned later, several people at the time could have approached Officer Lumpkin to ask about figures they had seen passing behind the sixth-floor windows of the Texas School Book Depositary Building. Apparently, several people had spotted a man leaning out the right-hand one while brandishing a rifle. Sadly, everyone thought he was a marksman assigned to that perch by the Secret Service to protect the approaching motorcade. Several citizens, including Messrs. Howard L. Brennan, Robert Edwards, Ronald Fischer, and Mrs. Carol Walthers had all seen the man in the sixth floor window. Some thought he was standing, some that he was lying prone, but they all saw him pointing a rifle out the window on the right-hand corner of the building.

Additionally, Mr. and Mrs. Arnold Rowland noticed a man in the sixth-floor east window hanging out of it, as though looking for oncoming cars. However, this man had nothing in his hands when they saw him.

Richard Carr was working up high on the new Courts Building at the corner of Main and Houston Streets; his position gave him a view directly into the sixth-floor windows where he noticed a heavy-set man in the company of two other men. He was too far away to shout down to anyone, let alone the police officers. Besides, what would be the significance of him seeing men behind windows? Obviously, the TSBD Building was occupied and being used that day.

None of them notified either of the policemen. Most of them had the same thought, "Well! Isn't the Secret Service being thorough posting anti-sniper details along the motorcade route today?" This singular chance passed them—as well as our nation—by.[3]

Chief Curry's car turned right off Main Street: the motorcade had arrived!

As the lead car approached Dealey Plaza, I could see it turn right off Main Street onto Houston Avenue preparatory to making the overly sharp left turn onto Elm Street. That would mark the completion of our motorcade route in Dallas because, almost immediately, we'd take the Stemmons Freeway and head out for the luncheon at the Trade Mart.

As the President's car closed on the turn to Elm Street, it slowed down to walking speed, 3 or 4 miles an hour, completed this severe left turn, and began its final leg toward the underpass. The large clock mounted on a nearby county building showed 12:30 PM.

I suddenly had misgivings.

Why had we taken a route requiring such a severe turn? Hadn't anyone vetted the route? Someone could easily be concealed behind that wall atop the grassy knoll, or possibly perched up high behind one of the underpass walls. There were several offices and public buildings towering over our route. A shot at a car that had slowed to four miles per hour could score a hit even if a clueless assassin possessed little skill as a marksman.

Someone should have set up this route differently! We could have simply ended the public motorcade at the intersection of Main and Houston and thereafter negotiated the various twisting turns to the freeway unencumbered by either further onlookers or a pace ratcheted down to that of snails.

If that had been the case, then Win Lawson could have directed that all windows in the area of the grassy knoll be shut tight and locked. I know that he was supposed to have done a good job, in the company of Agent Sorrels, in vetting this route, but my intestines were unexpectedly twisting into tight knots as we approached Dealey Plaza. The sensation would not leave me alone.

The hairs standing on the back of my neck told me that something was wrong, but what, I couldn't pinpoint. I'd been doing motorcades for nigh on five years, yet I'd never had such a feeling of dread as I did now.

Significantly, the driver—Agent Bill Green—though very experienced in handling this particular vehicle, had never rehearsed negotiating such a severe left turn on any route, much less this one.

The customary ten miles per hour speed for a motorcade was slow for a car, but these low speeds provided an ideal opportunity for Mr. Kennerly to smile and wave and, perhaps, hold a bystander's eye momentarily. In this manner, our president could communicate with his fellow citizens even if pausing for a visit was not possible.

A speed of only four miles an hour, on the other hand, made this supremely valuable man a sitting duck for conspirators. Today, however, the bystanders seemed more buoyant than if they had been invited to a Texas barbecue. They were waving and shouting support as they extended welcoming hands to this esteemed guest. The exuberance confirmed that he was well loved; surely, I reasoned, the members of this emotionally charged crowd were there to express gratitude and admiration rather than hostility.

Despite my murmured self-assurances, I could not afford to relax. Like all agents, I was equipped with a handgun, a set of handcuffs, a pair of sunglasses, and a neatly-knotted tie. If someone appeared intent on harming Mrs. Kennerly, or anyone in our entourage for that matter, all I had to offer was my body to absorb the bullet or knife thrust. True, I was wearing a protective vest, but what good is that if an assailant thrusts at my assigned person's head?

In high school, I had read that Abraham Lincoln's security man had accompanied the President and Mary Lincoln to the Reserved Box at Ford's Theatre. Then, thinking his charge would be safe while merely watching a play, bodyguard John F. Parker went off for a drink at a nearby saloon, leaving the revered president exposed to being murdered by J. W. Booth.

Nowadays, whether an attacker is a foreign spy or a furry guard dog, it had been my experience that a surprise attack was best executed during a period of apparent peace that would lull a victim's mind into somnolence. That would make a fast response delayed, at best.

Such behavior would not be the sort of protective action expected of an agent assigned to Presidential Detail. Jerry Bean's last words to me before I had left on this Texas trip had been: "Stay loose."

"Duplex" couldn't have expressed himself more clearly. However, he had chosen this week to take his first vacation in four years. Until the day he had left for this respite, he had always been right by the President's side from the day Mr. Kennerly had beaten Richard Nixy for the presidency.

Since Duplex had overseen our training, we were well prepared. "Expect to be confronted with the unexpected and be ready to adjust as the situation demands," was practically a mantra for his trainees. Succinctly put. An agent could never be sure what was around the next blind corner.

On this particular day, however, he would not be providing protection for our President. For this motorcade, his place would be taken by Agent Kitterman riding in the front seat of the President's limousine alongside today's driver, Agent Green.

This car had finished its left turn and was proceeding along Elm Street. As for us agents aboard Halfback, we were momentarily blinded by sunlight bouncing off the nearby Reflecting Pool. My eyes readjusted as our car completed its own excessive 120-degree turn. Immediately, I noticed a man to the left of me pointing upward at the bricked building to our right. I knew that was the Texas School Book Depository building. He appeared to be transfixed, even horrified!

With all the cheering, I couldn't hear what he was yelling, but the man—later identified as James R. Worthy—looked to me as though he was trying to shout a warning.

As the president's car completed its turn onto Elm Street, this slow move would give the sniveling spider the chance for which he had been waiting. Fame would soon be his.

Saints preserve us! As I stared at Mr. Worthy's face, it suddenly dawned on me the word he was mouthing: "GUN!"

I'm my father's son, by training even if not by blood. I neither turned my head to where the bystander's arm was pointing nor did I hesitate. I was off the running board and streaking to the president's car in a flash! I leapt the five-foot gap onto the foot stand as the Lincoln passed beneath overhanging tree limbs. Even as it did so, I could swear that I heard the report of a rifle. Apparently, a bullet had been fired but was deflected by the branches. It hit the sidewalk and sprayed several bystanders, including Virginia Baker and James Tague, with particles of cement. Unfortunately, none of my fellow agents saw these bystanders react; each one remained immobile at his post as though he was carved from stone. Why none of them responded to support me as I leapt toward the President would have to remain a mystery for some weeks. That's not for the record, by the way.

Somewhere off to the side, I heard a woman scream, and immediately thereafter I recognized the voice of Agent Youngblood back in the Vice-President's car yelling for everyone to: "Get down!" All of this happened as though in another world outside mine. I remained intently focused on getting to and covering the President and his wife.

Just in Time?

Retaining my momentum, I sprang forward off the jump platform as I pulled hard on the hold bar. I sailed speedily across the trunk cover. It was made of metal that was in a state of high polish; this enabled me to slide spread-eagled across the surface and smother Kennerly's torso with my chest in one smooth move. From the time I saw Mr. Worthy, to my spreading across our President, totaled perhaps four, maybe five seconds.

I couldn't have moved faster with a month of rehearsals, but had I been quick enough?

President Kennerly was wearing the stiff brace that supported his back. This prevented bending him forward out of the line of fire, so I yanked him sideways into the First Lady's lap. I made the correct choice. That brave woman didn't start crying or flutter about with uncertainty; she immediately bent her own slender torso directly over her husband's head, thereby insulating him completely from an assassin's view. She was uniquely courageous.

Of course, this meant she was now in the apparent line of fire. A thought flashed quickly across my brain: *They broke the mold when they made this one!*

Even as I pulled Kennerly to the left, I felt something slam powerfully into my backside. That's when my protective vest paid for itself; it absorbed the bullet so I could keep on working. I made a quick estimate and realized that the round hitting my vest had been mere fractions of a second from penetrating the president's neck or shoulders. I was a pretty fair shot myself, and I knew that a marksman allowed a ghost image of his target to sit on his retina long enough that, were he to close his eyes prior to squeezing the trigger, his aim would remain correct.

Obviously, the assassin had not perceived my protective approach. Even as I covered the Presidents torso, the shooter still had Kennerly's shoulders in his mental sight-picture; in effect, he had fired at a ghost image.

As for me, I had saved the real thing.

Piercing the cheers and calls of the lines of onlookers, I heard Agent Youngblood repeat his order for everyone to "get down!" In the midst of all the resultant noise and confusion, Agent Green slowed the car almost to a stop so he could ascertain what was happening. He had been trained by the White House police force before being hired by the Secret Service to be a driver. I suppose his natural curiosity, left over from his days as a gate guard, still made him suspicious about any untoward event.

During his training to be a driver, his instructor should have taught him to stay focused on his job rather than try to satisfy his curiosity. He never should have paused, let alone slowed to a stop, while in this motorcade. He almost got me killed.

I glanced behind me and saw that Agents Jack Ready and Paul Landis were looking upward trying to discern whether there was a sniper(s?) perched above the motorcade route. Landis had been on Eisenhower's detail with me, but I wasn't yet confident in his abilities to spot assassins. He had worked the Kiddies Detail for Ike and then spent the next few years with me as we traipsed around protecting the First Lady. Motorcades were new to him; in fact, this was his first one. Coincidentally, his code-name was *Debut*. Both he and Ready were canvassing the buildings, so neither one was rushing forward to assist my covering the President.

Standing in the rear of Halfback was Agent Harold Goodbody, a driver like Green pulled from the ranks of the White House police force. His sidekick that day was Glen Bennett who was actually a

PSR analyst rather than an armed agent accustomed to protective detail. Goodbody had stood erect in Halfback in reaction to Agent Youngblood's warnings. Now, he held an AR-15 loaded with explosive bullets resting on his hip. Bennett was no doubt nervously clutching the 12-gauge pump shotgun. This detail was proving to be far removed from his bending over some Preliminary Survey Report as he analyzed possible risks while seated in the quiet safety of his office.

My friend, Presidential Assistant Ken McDonald, was perched on the jump seat in front of these agents. At some point during the commotion, he turned his shoulders to try to see what was going on; as he did so, he jostled the hip of Agent Goodbody, causing him to become unbalanced. Harry started to fall forward. At this very instant, Agent Kinney, driving the car they were standing in, braked abruptly to avoid hitting SS100X in the rear as Agent Green slowed it to a stop.

Harold Goodbody must be credited with possessing great agility during this unexpected gaff by Agent Green. Despite his inexperience with any protective detail, he possessed quick reactions. Harry reached forward to recover his balance but, in doing so, he allowed the muzzle of his rifle to lower and point at my position in the car ahead. His trigger finger twitched involuntarily when Kinney braked. The AR-15 jerked, cracking the air with its report as a bullet rushed straight ahead, zipping through the sinewy flesh of my right triceps as I pressed down against the President's back. It missed the humerus but nipped my brachial artery as it plunged through my arm and continued into Governor Cummings's torso. My flesh burned and the searing pain almost overwhelmed me. Gritting my teeth and suppressing the vociferous swear words jockeying for room on my tongue, I stayed focused on shielding the President.

This was a fungible bullet, designed to shatter when impacting something hard and thereby causing shock and immediate immobilization. When it broke apart in a man's body, that victim would suffer multiple wounds. When it entered the governor's rib cage, he felt pain in several places, causing him to cry out, "We're all going to die!"

In my position protecting Kennerly, I could do nothing to assist that man. Even as his body convulsed from pain and fright, Nellie Cummings bent to her right to take her husband into the comfort of her arms.

At the moment Agent Green had slowed the president's car, a shooter would have had a clear and relatively stationary target with Governor Cummings. He could have quickly ejected the spent round, chambered a fresh one, and finished the governor off, thereby making quite a name for himself despite missing his primary target. No one can say for sure, but probably he was preparing to fire a third time when he heard a rifle shot crack below his perch. He must have been confused and ducked back into the protective alcove he had framed from the building's window ledge, cardboard boxes, and brick walls.

Up to that time, the assassin appears to have acted flawlessly in preparing to kill the president—patient, steady, and unemotional. The fact that his plans had gone awry is due largely to my being positioned on the front of Halfback, which itself was kept at a close five feet from SS100X by our driver, Sam Kinney, as the motorcade moved along.

I can picture the assassin looking forlornly at the three spent shell casings abjectly lying on the floor of his ambush nest. He would have momentarily stared at them, and then cursed himself. Three? In the excited anticipation of today, he had forgotten to eject the last spent shell after his prior practice session at the Sports Dome Rifle Range. Now he understood why his very first shot had seemed to misfire. He had heard a simple "click" as he squeezed the trigger, causing him to angrily reject that shell; thus, he had become rushed by the time he proceeded to aim the second. As he panned the muzzle, he had squeezed off his first real shot with a good sight picture, but he'd totally screwed up. This round was deflected by intruding tree limbs as the car motored along, making the bullet strike the pavement and thereby spraying bystanders with bits of concrete.

Then some person had unexpectedly slid across his sight picture to block the target just as he had squeezed off his next round. As far as he could tell, he had caused a lot of excitement on the sidewalks below, but had he ever actually hit anybody with his rounds? Most likely he had not. Was this yet another failure? As his brain filled with embarrassment, shame, and chagrin, he tended the three shells into a neat row, removed his gloves, and then rose and strode across the floor to a spot where he could hide the rifle behind a separate stack of boxes. By this time, he was thirsty, so he forlornly trudged slowly down the stairs to the canteen. He purchased a can of soda from the vending machine and was sitting there morosely when he saw Superintendent Roy Truly and some police officer fly by the portal and rush up the stairs. Still holding his soda, he rose to leave the building but encountered an excited patrolman blocking the exit. He identified himself as an employee, thereby bluffing his way past. The officer had merely stepped aside after confirming that this slender, sad-looking man worked in the Depository Building.

He wasn't certain about the extent of the damage he had created, but he was proud of himself. Surely now he would become famous; he had taken on the Establishment. Should he start boasting of his achievement to everyone he encountered? "Look at me, see how important I really am!" he wanted to shout. But he couldn't, not yet. Many people were running madly about; the entire scene was confused. No one would believe he was a man of serious purpose. Worse, what if they pointed out that he had not hit anybody; that, in fact, he had failed yet again? Would he ever get the fame he longed to have? Presumably, the best thing for him to do now was to skedaddle and worry about getting his picture in the newspaper after things had calmed down.

I didn't care about him, whoever he was. In fact, I couldn't care about any such twit. He had just tried to assassinate a man whom God had provided to deliver us Americans from poverty, inhumanity, and life-threatening destruction. I was damned sure the shooter wasn't going to get another chance.

At the scene of the bloodbath, I shouted to Kitterman sitting up front. We suddenly had two injured men so Kitterman, riding "shotgun" in the front seat, turned and took one quick look at the perilously exposed people in the rear of the car.

He immediately ordered the driver to "get the hell out of here!" Green floored it. We detoured from the Trade Mart to Parkland Memorial Hospital, reaching a speed in excess of 80 mph along the way. Straddled between the seats and lying across the trunk cover, I remained positioned over the president's chest while Mrs. Cummings held tightly to my sleeve as Kitterman supported the governor. President Kennerly tried to continue breathing while squashed beneath my body and his wife's torso. Blood was spurting over him as the puncture in my artery gushed. Regardless, this meant his safety was assured, at least for the moment.

When we reached the hospital, Green shut the vehicle's siren off and various men who had been alerted to receive us reached across the trunk to extricate me from atop the president. The bullet which went through the fleshy part of my upper arm had missed the humerus. If it hadn't, the bone would have shattered so completely that I might have died on the spot from shock. However, it had opened my right brachial artery. I'd had no time in which to apply a tourniquet; even if I had, I would have failed miserably because I was close to passing out. Fortunately, even as I was grieving over whether I'd survive this horror, strong arms lifted me off the president and then placed me on a wheeled gurney. Along with Governor Cummings, I was rushed through the emergency entrance, whereupon we were trundled into separately prepared operating rooms.

Once I was placed on the gurney, I lost track of the president. However, as I had been lifted off him and out of the car, Mrs. Jacquelean Kennerly had looked straight at me. I held her eyes for just a moment, but the depth of feeling her face conveyed will stay with me for all my days. I was simply doing my job, but the gratitude her face expressed was heartfelt and strong. Her emotion couldn't have been better expressed in a ten-page letter of thanks.

They say: "A picture is worth a thousand words," but they should add, "Glance of gratitude" as a deserved corollary.

When a surgeon approached me with the needle to put me under, he said, "Just relax. This won't be much." He smiled down at me briefly, and I was out. My last thought was of my father. He would have been proud that his boy had done a good job, and done it well, despite life-threatening danger.

It's a strange world when a human is under ether. It's more than simply blank. The world is black, with no sound or perception of light; fortunately, there's no pain either. While I'm no astronaut, I bet the experience would be similar to a voyager being able to float in space without the need for a suit and an oxygen cord. You hover between life and death without any input or feedback, yet you most definitely still exist.

I'm not proposing that taking a bullet is worth having to undergo an operation, but I can darn well attest that when the intensive-care nurse gently tickled the sole of my right foot and said, "Okay Clint, it's time to wake up!" I experienced what it was like to be born; only this time, I was fully cognitive. Apparently, the surgical team had stopped the bleeding from my brachial artery in time and thus spared my life.

The first thing I did was to ask: "Is the President okay?"

"Yes, he's doing fine. He should be in to see you shortly. He sent the vice-president on ahead to be his stand-in and deliver a speech at the Trade Mart. Lyndon readily accepted. It's his home state, after all."

The surgeon stepped aside to allow my boss, Agent Kitterman, to come forward and bend over my prostrate form: "Today, you exemplified our motto: *To be worthy of trust and confidence.* Mr. McDonald asked me to alert him when you would be able to receive visitors; I have a feeling you're about to get one from an important man who is very grateful to you!"

"What about the governor?" Obviously, I was not in a position to assist that man, but it would be helpful to know whether he would live to recover.

Now a staff person in the hospital whom I did not know came from the alcove he had been standing in and leaned over my platform-on-wheels. Looking me in the eyes as he held my wrist in a warm, comforting way, he stated, "Don't you bother your head about him; I'm told by his attending physicians that he will survive. Recovery will probably be tedious, requiring several months, but he'll be able to assume the duties of his office again in time. By the way, we are all very grateful for your bravery."

I weakly mumbled something about just doing my job, but I was beginning to fade; the effects of the sodium pentothal were not finished with me.

About then I was wheeled to my hospital suite. I called it that because it already was filled with flowers and well-wishers and, regrettably, reporters.

In the midst of them stood Jack Fitzhugh Kennerly, smiling that fabulous broad grin and sporting all those white teeth. As best I could, I smiled right back, but weakly. The sedative was taking hold. As I slipped back into the dark clutches of the Pentothal, I heard him say: "The decision to use you today was something small, but it saved us all. Thank you, Agent Brill!" then I returned to the comforting arms of Madame Sleep.

My codename was *Dazzle*, so I suppose great things had been expected of me when I joined the Secret Service. But still, what a day it had been!

Notes

1   Andrews, p. 287.
2   O'Donnell, pp. 11-12.
3   See generally Tague, pp. 69-75 and 363-368.

CHAPTER THIRTEEN

Reassigned

The gentle dusk of a late November evening was darkening the view out my window when I awoke from my slumber. Everyone, save the President and the head of his Dallas detail, had been cleared from the room. Kitterman rose from his chair and stood close by my bed as soon as he saw me open my eyes and blink from the overhead glare of the hospital lights. Agent Kitterman (appropriately code-named *Digest*) spoke first.

"Well, you certainly acquitted yourself well, Clint! I was sitting perhaps three feet in front of the President, but I wasn't aware of any threat, let alone an actual shooting until the governor got hit." He shook his head in wonderment. "Yet you had already covered our President with protection. You're more than a testament to our training; you vindicated the Secret Service today!"

He rested one of his hands on my left shoulder, the good one, and then he turned toward his boss, John F. Kennerly. It was obvious that man had something he wanted to say.

My President stepped forward and sat on the edge of my hospital bed. He enjoyed conversing with people when sitting close by them in a relaxed, attentive way. It wasn't at all like Lyndon's famous "Jensen treatment." The vice-president, when in the throes of trying to win a senator or colleague over to his point of view, would bend forward and get his towering frame so close to his victim that there would be no escaping the onslaught of his domineering manner.

Kennerly, on the other hand, liked to sit comfortably while allowing either opponent or close friend plenty of space. He was basically impartial. What he was interested in was the quality of the conversation. Pulling rank to embarrass or belittle someone didn't appeal to him; he simply enjoyed an intelligent, informative repartee, especially if it permitted him to learn something new.

In fact, this was the principle which guided him in the organization of his presidential staff. Ike had been the supreme allied commander during the Normandy invasion, so he had set up his operations with a chief-of-staff through whom everyone went before they could reach Mr. Eisenhower proper. Jack, in contrast, wanted a direct conduit to each of his appointees; therefore, he established himself as the axle who maintained a direct spoke from his wheel of command to every individual cabinet member. However, he kept two doors to his office: one manned by Ken—who was difficult to get past—and the other by his appointments secretary, Lynne, who freely let chums and buddies pass. In this way, he could always be assured of company to prevent his being left alone.

It was obvious to me that Mr. Kennerly loved the office of being President. It is the locus of power with men committed to action. He admired those who could perceive available alternatives with unblinking realism. He enjoyed immersing himself in a stew of restless minds trying to cope with solutions to difficulties that were so new that neither guidance from textbooks nor prior experience could be had. Standing so close to him, I could almost feel how politics provided him with the opportunity to participate in the solution of seemingly intractable problems. His absorption allowed him to achieve the Greek definition of happiness: the full use of his powers along lines of excellence.[1]

It was almost as though he could put up with all the pain and physical discomfort of his medical problems, but he could not stand one minute of boredom. He liked keeping his mind in gear, whereas I couldn't wait for the chance to unwind and let my mind simply drift peacefully on a sea of idle thoughts. However, I wasn't president.

"Breathing room," his clear-eyed friend Ken McDonald called it. Ken had been a he-man sort at Harvard, captain of the football team as well as being roommates with the young Bobby Kennerly. Though this aide was responsible for keeping the president's house in order, while I shared responsibility for keeping him alive, we got along as well as two men bearing adjacent but overlapping duties could manage.

One day, when the president was giving a speech and was thus out of earshot, Ken had leaned over to me and confided: "Jack wants to enjoy talking with whoever is sitting across from him. Whether it's a foreign diplomat, a young military officer, or the local school janitor, it doesn't matter to him. When he is with someone, he wants to be <u>with</u> him, fully and at ease. He genuinely likes people; I've never heard him say he wished he had been somewhere else after meeting with someone, although he did once say that General MacArthur had been a bit difficult to take. Apparently, that former commander had asked Kennerly for permission to develop hand-carried nuclear bullets which could take out entire squads with a single shot. The President had merely laughed. He feels that even a man such as Casstra or Crushchev has a human, innately good side, albeit well disguised. One time, before the race for Senator had concluded, he had postulated that, if someone were to split Stilan down the middle, he'd probably find a large hole where the heart was supposed to reside. Such a person was driven by bile alone. But, for the record, Jack admitted that he had never actually sat down with the man for a heart-to-heart talk, as they say."

Both of us had sat back and roared at this story.

Today, however, Kennerly himself was all heart. One thing I already knew about this man was that he admired courage. It didn't matter whether such fortitude was exhibited on the gridiron, the battlefield, standing behind a rostrum, or seated in front of a congressional grilling. If a man demonstrated courage "in the face of fire," he readily won this President's admiration.

He bent over my prostrate form and murmured sincerely, "I want to thank you personally, from the very core of my soul, for what you did today. While you were sleeping, everyone that I queried stated that your reactions were guided by the Hand of God. They were simply amazed at how prescient you were. Among the tens of thousands of people overflowing the streets of Dallas today, not a single one seemed to perceive an incident was even possible, much less appreciate the threat this sniper posed when the shooting began."

My President paused for a bit, giving me time to digest the import of what he was saying. I must say, in my relatively groggy state, his message was getting through even my addled brain. I began to appreciate the immensity of what I had pulled off. My adoptive parents were still very much alive, whereas my "real" parents were total unknowns to me. Nevertheless, I could appreciate that when a youngster lost his birth parents, his past would largely be lost to him. We never seem able to formulate questions we want to ask our parents while they are still with us: "What was it like driving a horse and wagon versus a car? How did you keep the house from burning down with all those whale-oil lanterns? How did you keep vegetables preserved in the absence of pressure cookers? Was math this hard for you, too?"

I'm sure you've had the same feeling, dear reader, in your own life. A chance to ask your folks about the past, once missed, cannot be recalled. In contrast, if we had lost John Kennerly to a dumb bullet, we would have lost the incalculable benefit of a better future for everyone in our nation.

I motioned that I wanted to speak, and the President and Agent Kitterman both leaned forward. I made my point fast: "If we'd lost you, a piece of each one of us would have died with you, sir." Then I lay back, exhausted by this simple utterance.

The President sat forward a bit more on my bed, got my attention, and took the lead.

"Do you remember hearing about that day outside the Kennerly compound in Florida when Mr. Pavlick, 'the human bomb' as he called himself, was arrested? That had been scary. I never even told the First Lady about it. Today, however, was an even more narrow escape. My wife and I, and very likely everyone in our nation, are very grateful to you."

There was a pause as he obviously prepared to say something additional. What could it be? He'd just thanked me for saving his life; nothing could be more important than my having reacted as I was trained. He turned away to clear his throat, and then he turned his attention back to me.

"What I'm leading up to, Agent Brill, and by the way, I've already cleared this idea through your boss Kitterman here, is for you to remain with the Service while you recover. At the end of December, when you've healed, you are to resign honorably. This will leave you free to come to work for me as my Assistant Undersecretary for Internal Affairs.

"My plan is for you to be near my side for consultation regarding domestic problems and their concomitant legislative considerations. Your assignment will include assisting Vice-President Jensen when coordination is required. The goal is for you to be the conduit between our offices as I bring him into closer coordination and execution of my domestic agenda. I'm sure you've heard that he's unusually skilled at bringing key leaders, even men as self-important as senators, around to his point of view. It will be our high purpose to begin making substantive improvements in the lives and relationships of our own countrymen. There will be many in Congress with whom we will have to parry if we are to succeed. I've set a tall order for our team, and I want you to be a part of it!

"If my programs meet with success, the effectiveness of our country internally, as well as internationally, will be improved. For the remainder of this term, and indeed during a second one if I survive reelection, the Vice-President and I will work more closely, perhaps even in tandem on crucial domestic matters such as civil rights, rather than as two separate individuals whose only common bond is their political party. The objective of making laws is to meet and satisfy the desires, needs, aspirations, and even the dreams of the American public. That is an area in which Vice-President Jensen excels, so I have decided to give him a chance to run with it rather than be left sitting in a corner waiting for me to become incapacitated.

"If nothing else, today has shown how easily that can happen. Like most men, I've experienced tragedy in my life. My adored sister Kik, as well as my well-regarded brother Joe, are dead. My father has become largely incapacitated; moreover, I lost buddies in the war. If it hadn't been for your professionalism, I'd be gone as well. The time which we are allotted on this earth is far too short. I have pursued pleasure and jocularity because doing so eased my physical suffering, but going forward, I pledge to devote my Presidency to achieving good for my fellow citizens with a determination to brook no delay and tolerate no hesitancy. Tomorrow could all too easily be my last day on earth, and I am determined that my life will be judged as having been spent improving the lives of my fellow man.

"Clint, if you come to work for me, then Ken McDonald, whom I understand is already a friend of yours, will be your immediate boss. In this way, you will be exposed to all the policy debates we have regarding domestic affairs. As you get up to speed regarding the various factions and interests involved, you'll be at my side to hand me briefings regarding the NAACP, CORE, AFL-CIO, F.B.I., VFW, B.S.A. (scouts), SOAR (Revolution), National Association of Manufacturers, and a host of other acronyms too numerous to mention.

"Department of the Treasury investigations will continue to be handled as they are currently, so you will not be involved after

December. I've heard that you have experience in that area dating from your early years with the Service; don't fret—you have simply moved on. Immigration violations, governmental contracts, the CIA, and oversight of the military will be beyond your purview as well. I have no doubt you will be kept very busy despite these limitations.

"On the other hand, the international stage and affairs of state are what I plan to focus on as soon as Vice-President Jensen and I have a little tête-a-tête. Meet with Ted Sorensen after you are up and about; get him to bring you up-to-speed with the myriad problems we face on that stage.

"Going on the assumption that you accept my request to redirect your career, you will have to prepare yourself more thoroughly than anything you ever tackled in high school. Don't be concerned about your lack of higher education. There are plenty of books for you to read that can bring you up to speed on any matter new to you. That doesn't even include all the people in Washington who believe they know more about practically anything you can mention than I do. I doubt any of them will refrain from the chance to show you how erudite they are, so brace yourself. I haven't yet met a politician who shuns the opportunity to display his superior wisdom regarding my areas of interest!"

He paused, letting this career-altering, or should I say life-changing, event sink in. Strangely, I found that my right arm was not nearly so stiff and painful as it had been when I had awakened some minutes earlier.

"Naturally," he continued, "you'll want to check these ideas out with your wife, Gail. If you decide to remain in your present line of work, I'll understand, but that won't prevent me from being disappointed. I could use a person who thinks as deductively as you do. When I'm surrounded by Russian two-tongued diplomats who perceive our offers to ban the weapons of war as a failure of will rather than as an example of our good will, or by argumentative Southern gentlemen striving to maintain the status quo by denying full and equal rights to certain Americans, I would be far more comfortable having a quick-thinker by my side."

For a moment, I considered asking my President: "What about Larry O'Brien?" As the President's congressional liaison chief, I imagined he already filled the role the president was outlining for me. I stayed quiet; that question could be answered later.

The President then surprised me.

"There's another reason all this has come about, Clint, quite apart from today's events. As we flew down today, Jacquelean took hold of my arm and firmly told me to take you on as a member of my staff. Her words were: 'Do it, Jack. You'll love it!' Apparently, you've made quite a good impression on her. Congratulations! That's a hard thing to do!"

This man would come to secure the Nuclear Test Ban Treaty, initiated the Peace Corps that sent unselfish young people throughout the world to help less fortunate societies develop their agricultural and industrial base, saved the world from annihilation by his adept statesmanship during the Cuban Missile Crisis, and brought nations in our southern hemisphere into cooperative partnerships through the Alliance for Progress.

"Just think about this," he observed as he sat on my bedside. "We have more than one million Americans serving abroad, but to help educate and uplift, not to carry out conquest. We have undertaken burdens around the world which no nation in history has ever shouldered. With our population representing but 6% of that of the world, I hope our example will inspire other countries to come forward and do their part. Of course, such programs rely on appropriations being passed by our Congress, and therein is the problem. My proposals can become hostage to an obstructionist Congress. If our foreign policies are to work, Congress must be supportive. I intend on significantly altering the active relationship of the President and Vice-President in the future to get around this problem. You can play an instrumental role in my doing this."

Now here he was asking me to serve at his side. If I hadn't already been lying prone on a bed, I probably would have fainted from surprise right there in front of him.

My President rose and looked me straight in the eye. "I'll return to Washington now. Given the circumstances, we'll terminate our trip and let Vice-President Jensen take my place in Austin this afternoon." He rose from my bedside and stood to his full, commanding height and ended by saying: "As for you, take your time, think it over, and talk with whomever you think could help you make a decision. In particular, consult that fine father of yours. Perhaps I should ask him to leave that steel mill of his to come and work with us as well! I found myself parting ways with my own father when it came time for me to enter politics, but that has been my own particular cross to bear."

As he finished, he made his right index finger outline the sign of the cross to punctuate his point, as if from habit even in the absence of an awestruck audience. We all three laughed at this, but I realized that President Kennerly might not be kidding. I'd have to lay all this out and discuss it with both Lloyd and Ellie.

And, there was another person: my Gail. I've kept her hidden from your view because she is uniquely special to me. Now might be a good time to bring you up to date on the love of my life.

Notes

[1] Widmer, pp. 12-13.

CHAPTER FOURTEEN

Falling in Love

My marrying Gail was the hand of Fate at work. It was no big secret. In fact, I was following up on a problem the Treasury Department was having. I still wasn't considered a full-fledged agent yet. My status was more like a plebe who was sorting out the administrative ins-and-outs of the Secret Service, but then I caught a lucky break: to check up on a new printing of $50 banknotes that were due to begin circulating in January 1956.

Many of you will recall that Ike had been reelected to a second term that year. As a nation, we had begun to worry. Spies were popping up with alarming frequency. Our very own ambassador to the United Nations had hissed secrets to the Russian bear. Congress held hearings to determine how the Russians got the atom bomb so soon after 1945. In connection with that, two Americans by the name of Rosenfeld kept surfacing.

Almost as sad, the family automobile sold by Ford, Buick, and Chrysler had grown to be an enormously wide, long, gasoline-guzzling monster. This vividly portrayed our society as spendthrifts. We were practically unconscious that there even was an environment! Long ago we had carelessly cast aside the alternative—the electric car. For Americans, gasoline was king. We didn't know it yet, but our dependence on this single kind of energy was to grab us by the throat and practically strangle us in the next decade.

There was a Congressman named Stuart Udall serving as a member of the House of Representatives. He was destined to thrive in the future post of Secretary of the Interior in Kennerly's administration. Hailing from Arizona, he embraced the concept of clean air and protecting the environment but, at this time, no one was tuned in to what he was espousing.

In the mid-1950's, Mr. Kennerly was toiling with intransigence as he butted heads in the halls of the Senate. The only war the nation was engaged in was the cold one with Russia and its apparent goal of spreading communism abroad. Peter I. Stilan, and then Nikita Crushchev's government merrily disregarded our plaintive objections. In the mid-1950's, the Berlin wall had not yet been conceived. Yuri Gagarin was still training for being launched into space to chase a pair of sputniks. Most dramatically, we maintained cordial relations with Cuba and its then dictator, Battista. Americans had not yet heard the name "Fidel Casstra." His followers constituted just a small guerrilla army hidden in the mountainous bush country.

All these conditions would be altered dramatically as the decade came to a close but, in 1956, the Treasury Department merely wanted me to ascertain that these $50 notes were being well received. America was reasonably prosperous; after all, Eisenhower, who is one of the best logisticians and organizers to have ever lived, had been president for four years. His shooting under 80 on the golf course was about as hard a challenge we had faced during his presidency. He had launched the U-2 spy plane program to monitor Russia; the Defense Department was certain these flights would keep them abreast of any aggressive moves by the Kremlin. Other than the agonizing surprise of the Korean War, which as I have related my father had heroically helped keep in check, peace was now both pleasant and pervasive. Nonetheless, I believed that a nation's influence in the world rested on the certainty of value in its currency, and acceptance of such depended on that country maintaining a strong balance of payments; i.e., its reserves of gold bullion. Lack of international trust in its currency could quickly drain such reserves.

The problem concerning the Treasury Department involved counterfeit notes which had begun appearing shortly after Thanksgiving. They apparently were circulating in the mid-Atlantic and Midwest federal districts. Would the public receive the new printings without flinching, or would these notes present the problem of "Dead Paper Money" that had long been dreaded, but so far not realized. It's so acceptable for Americans to exchange mere paper, bearing black and green doodling and faces of dead presidents, that we never pay our currency any mind. It states right on the front of each bill that it is "redeemable for gold." Of course, that never happens; we basically accept them as payment because we have confidence in "the full faith and credit" of our government.

Two new features had been added in 1955 to differentiate these new notes which would facilitate their being tracked in 1956 and beyond. First, the threads in the official paper used by the Treasury Department on which to print the various denominations were varied in color and orientation. Second, the background of the famous single eye-in-the-pyramid was altered. These were not noticeable by the average American user of currency, but they would be spotted immediately by trained Secret Service agents and highly motivated bank tellers.

I was sent to the Philadelphia office initially; if the situation looked worrisome, then I'd head out to Chicago for deeper probing. I arrived in Philadelphia by fast train from Washington. Having been founded by William Penn, a Quaker by faith, before the American Revolution, this metropolis was known affectionately as the "City of Brotherly Love." If the assignment that had brought me here resulted in area banks becoming incensed over being stuck with confusing bank notes that failed to circulate, I'd need all the "love" that the imposing William Penn standing atop City Hall could offer.

It was now 4:30 PM on a Tuesday. The hour was too late to undertake a brand-new project, so I headed to the Bellevue-Stratford Hotel on Broad Street where I found a room and turned in for the night. I expected the next day would be a long one. This hotel was across the street from the Land Title Building where, on the 14th floor in unassuming quarters, our mid-Atlantic office overlooked the length of Broad Street from City Hall to past the Fidelity Bank Building. These blocks were the nerve center for mid-Atlantic currency trading. I could also see the long-standing, red brick of the Union League, the bastion of Republicanism for over a century. Only a mile directly to the east, down Chestnut near Second Street, stood the Federal Reserve Building for the Atlantic District.

My week would be spent scurrying between these two locations until I had resolved everyone's issues. At least, that was my assignment. The next few days would surely involve a lot of voices being raised in anger, perhaps accompanied by vociferous finger-pointing as well. When I awoke the next morning, I would have to summon all my bravery simply to get out of bed.

But that was tomorrow. Right now, as I looked over at the phone astride my bed, I realized there was still time to place a call to an old friend of my parents. They had trained me not to bother people with telephone calls after 9:00 at night, but I would not be impolite by calling at this hour.

I leaned forward and picked up the ear piece which simultaneously alerted the operator that someone wanted to place a call. Just as I was about to give her the number for Mary Meade, who lived west of the city in a town called Bryn Mawr (sorry, it's Welsh), the big gong atop the John Wanamaker Department Store interrupted my call with its slow, deep tolling. I had to shout over the reverberations of the bell. Between the gong strikes, when the air would momentarily become quiet, I must have sounded like I was yelling to report a fire.

My stay here began to look more promising when the operator rang me back to say Mrs. Meade was on the line. I found myself flopping across the luxurious cream-and-wine-colored quilt atop the double bed. I lay back against the pillows plumped against the wide walnut headboard and felt my body relaxing. The scent of freshly-laundered linen and cut flowers placed atop the bureau wafted over me. The security of occupying a room in one of the city's most renowned hotels created a cocoon of ease. My mind began to idly drift upon a gentle sea of daydreams. All of the tension and weariness of travel began to flow out of me. I don't know where this negative force went, but I was soon feeling in sparkling shape.

Reaching out to communicate with close friends by telephone is almost akin to reaching out and touching them. Conversing with a loved one while stretched out on a comfy bed can make a person feel better fast!

I'd known Mrs. Meade for a little over five years. She enjoyed a standing-invitation to stop by my parents' home anytime she was up north visiting relatives in Boston. When I was a senior in high school, she was invited one night for dinner while she and her daughter, Gail, were visiting Boston over the Christmas holidays. The place was famous for sparkling displays on the Commons. City employees tied colored lights around many of the leafless oaks and elms in late fall. Then, between Thanksgiving and New Year's Day, these would be illuminated starting at 5:00 PM. People would come from all over to tour the pretty sight, get hungry, dine in one of the area restaurants, and then catch the late train for home. It was a great marketing gimmick that had been going on ever since the war ended.

Since I grew up nearby, the display had become fairly ho-hum by the time I was nineteen years old, but there was nothing ho-hum about my dinner with Mary Meade and her daughter on that December Saturday back in 1950. As a longtime family friend, Mary had visited the Brills a few times while I was living with Lloyd and Ellie, but that year was the first time that she had brought her daughter.

As New Englanders know, Massachusetts winters are accompanied by early darkness. The shortest day of the year may not come until December 21, but even early in the month, it is utterly black outside by 5:00 PM. All the neighbors have their outside house lights on so friends can see and navigate walking stones, sidewalks, or steps as they approach a front door.

Even though I was accustomed to these conditions, I was not prepared for what happened this particular night. I was in the kitchen helping mom prepare the roast beef, baked potatoes, and succotash swathed in butter that her treasured guests would warrant. Having dinner tonight with a longtime friend would be fun for Ellie and Lloyd: Mrs. Meade was well traveled and an accomplished conversationalist.

When the doorbell rang, I still had no idea that this night was about to be just about the most important of my young life. Dad was in the living room, so he rose to answer the bell. I could hear his pleasant greeting to Mary as mom and I walked through the dining room to "meet and greet!" as our family called it. Mrs. Meade was inside, shaking some snow from her galoshes in what was called the "boot room" since that's where everyone stored outdoor coats, galoshes, and such.

Behind my parents' familiar friend, there stood a slim, tall, long-haired girl of seventeen. What's so unusual about that? It's a perfectly valid question. I answer the question thusly: the porch light shown fully on that long chestnut hair, making it fairly glow. It was obvious that this girl knew how to take care of herself. Hmm, if she knew how to do that, maybe she'd know how to take care of me as well. With that first look, I mentally began transference. I loved my mom, but here was someone with whom I could share a life devoted to pleasing her. I didn't know whether I stood a chance, but if there would ever be an opportunity to show this angel that I was a worthwhile prospect, it would be right now. It was time for me to step up to the plate and take a few swings.

The girl's face was creamy smooth, and her cheekbones were heightened by the shadows from the overhead lamp. I was accustomed to my mom's face with her very attractive smile, but this girl had lips that were softly parted from having to breathe so much cold air: they looked as though they needed kissing. Furthermore, it seemed to me that any man who would undertake to satisfy that mouth would surely be sent into orbits of pleasure. She lifted her face slightly to look straight at me. I was a goner; her hazel eyes drew me in, sucking all conceit and resistance from me. She hadn't spoken a word, but she'd already won not just my interest, but my complete surrender as well.

If she'd snapped her fingers my way, I would have turned somersaults just like an excited dog about to receive crunchy chews. I'll say it straight out: I know a good thing when I see it, and it's a bad thing to let her go unclaimed.

From there on, while I was gracious to Mrs. Meade and my parents, the only person in the room that night was Gail. I ignored the fact that I was two years older than her but still attending high school, while she was already a junior. Anomalies such as that happened back in those days.

I must say, I was startled when, during the course of the evening, I got a few moments alone with her and learned that she was hoping to apply to a few colleges next year. "Geez!" I thought to myself. I had no interest in such plans for myself. Her ideas intrigued me, so I gently inquired whether she was considering a school up near Boston. Stupid idea because, within a year, I would be spending my first months with the Secret Service at that unspoken location referred to earlier. She had a forthright personality and spoke openly about attending Bryn Mawr College. Our guidance counselor at school had mentioned it in passing when he was attempting to sign me up for Haverford College, a small men's school nearby. I was thus aware that the school Gail was considering enjoyed the highest of academic standards.

I forgot to mention what happened to me when she got fully inside the hallway and Dad helped remove her coat. I have no idea whether she knew what she was doing, but as she slipped her arms from the sleeves, she thrust her chest forward. I was riveted. Her breasts were small, just barely mounding the Faire Isle sweater she was wearing. Unconsciously, I licked my lips. I'm a dyed-in-the-wool leg man, and her gams were both long and oh, so slim! This meant she was narrow hipped as well. Pretty, slender, and small-breasted, like Jacquelean Kennerly: just my kind of woman.

When I finally got up enough nerve to say "hello" to her, her reply just floored me. Her voice was most definitely feminine, but its timbre held a far lower pitch than the cheer-leading teens I was used to in high school. Her husky tone was music to my ears.

Basically, I spent that entire night falling for this girl. I'd had warm feelings, even crushes, on a few gals as I aged from 15 to 18, but Gail represented something entirely different. Head-over-heels would aptly apply to my state of mind tonight.

I did not like having to say "good-bye" to her after dinner was finished, but there was no fighting reality. Her mother was spending the night someplace in the heart of Boston so they could visit the Christmas light display. The very next day, the two of them were taking the train back to Philadelphia and catching the Paoli Local to their home in Bryn Mawr.

So **that's** why she wanted to go to that college! Gail could live at home and thereby cut way down on the expense! Infatuation does that to a young man's brain; he gets so addled, he can't think of even the most obvious connection.

My course of action became clear. Graduate from high school, get accepted into the Secret Service, ask Gail for her hand in marriage, start having children, and then get promoted to presidential detail. With such an assignment, my earnings would improve markedly. But I would apply for that only after our kids were out of diapers and walking; that way, Gail could care for them alone while I was escorting the president who knows where. Things didn't work out exactly that way—reality rarely matches imagination—but the future came close enough.

After all this talk about her figure and sex appeal, I realized that this budding young woman would be taking on quite a load if she were to marry me. Despite my attentions over the course of this evening, she had probably spent the entire dinner regarding me as yet another swain who couldn't help drooling over her.

That wasn't the worst of it. If she did marry me two or three years down the road, what about her college degree? What if I got hurt in the line of duty? The government had a realistic attitude about this and plans existed to provide for widows who lost their husbands in the line of duty, but who wants money if it means an empty bedside? I'd have to be very clear with her regarding the risks, and this meant I would have to become much more familiar with the potential dangers myself. Since I had not yet applied, but was only contemplating being a part of the Secret Service, I was still pretty naïve about the all-too-real chance of being killed while serving with that agency.

Oh, youth! When we're teens, how much we want to grow up and be capable of earning our keep, but then how we yearn to be young again once we're over forty years old! Perhaps that's why couples are so tuned to having children. Kids give parents a chance to relive their youth; the only problem is, while one's children are growing up, parents may get so wrinkled and grayed that they become unable to recapture the fleeting youth which they had once enjoyed, but which they had failed to fully value.

The conclusions to be made from this sort of erudition were unimportant for now. Such concerns lay well in the future. What I presently needed to do was to get Gail's mailing address and start a long-distance romance. More to the point, the following Monday I had an English composition paper due, and on Tuesday the math teacher had promised to give us a "preparatory final" exam just to get us set for the real final in early January. I went upstairs and hit the books, but I also did a lot of dreaming when I fell into bed that night.

CHAPTER FIFTEEN

Marriage

You've now learned how we met; however, wooing this pretty girl would take far longer than I had initially imagined. What with the heavy pressures of my initial training and textbook work at the Secret Service training facility, and her finishing high school, I managed to see Gail only one time: I joined her parents in attending her graduation. She beamed with a sense of fulfillment that day. She had indeed been accepted at Bryn Mawr College. She spent the summer of 1957 boning up on her academic knowledge, and upon her matriculation in September, she became even more studious, if you'll pardon the pedestrian quip.

We saw each other fleetingly between 1956 and 1958: a weekend here, a summer break there, and one cotillion at the 1957 Christmas Ball held for debutantes at the Bellevue-Stratford Hotel in Philadelphia. She was fortunate to have been asked. Since the average age for debs was 19, at 20 she was pushing it a little, but her mother had wangled her invitation to be delayed a year so her studies would not be interrupted. I always thought the fact that her father had perished in the Second World War carried more weight with the matrons who ran the gala than the nature of her education. If she'd worn summer shorts, probably no one would have raised an eyebrow. For the girls, naturally, this event was their big chance to get all dressed up in a floor length gown and sport some fancy hairdo.

Gail was not going to let her chance slide. Thus, it ended up that I also had to get all gussied up in white tie and tails. I was even required to wear spotless kid gloves! Having had the experience of looking like a stuffed penguin, as well as coping with the awkward stiffness that all these starched bibs and cuffs and cummerbunds demanded, I never once chaffed about dress codes once I joined the Secret Service.

I didn't bother boasting about this event to anyone in the Service; they would have never stopped ribbing me about my going "High Class" ala Cary Grant for a night!

The long and short of what I've been relating is that, on that night in 1956 when I arrived in Philadelphia, I had decided that I was finally going to take firm action regarding the young lady who had been occupying my fantasies for the past four years.

When the operator put through my call, Mrs. Meade came on the line. I cheerfully exclaimed, "Hello! Guess who's in town tonight?"

"Clint, is that you? Why, where are you, my boy? What are you doing in town?"

"The Service has me here on a week-long project. I thought I'd call to see what Gail was up to, now that I'm so close by."

"Why, I'm sorry, Clint, but it's Tuesday. She has a lab in her chemistry course on Tuesdays, so I don't expect her home for another hour or so. Perhaps you can see her tomorrow."

"Oh, heavens, don't be concerned, Mrs. Meade. May I resurrect some shred of joy by coming out and taking you to dinner? Maybe my timing will be better later this week, but I don't want to miss a chance to see you, too!"

I know my voice sounded disingenuous but, actually, I liked Gail's mom. If inviting her to dinner was the only way I could be close to a member of that family, I'd jump at the chance.

"That is really thoughtful of you, Clint, but...Wait a minute. I think I hear the front door opening." There was a pause, and then I heard Mrs. Meade calling "hello!" to her daughter.

Soon, the girl who occupied a significant portion of my everyday thoughts was on the phone. "Clint, is that really you?"

"Hi, Gail, I just got into town. I'm down here at the Bellevue for a few days."

"Gee, that's just swell! Look, my classes tomorrow are over by 3:00 PM tomorrow. Would you be able to come out and meet me? I know there's a Paoli Local scheduled to get in at 3:30, but you'd have to find out when it leaves Suburban Station. Can you do that?"

She was asking whether I could approach the desk clerk downstairs and inquire when a train departs on Wednesday afternoon for Bryn Mawr. I stated with assurance, "Of course, I can manage that. I'm running my own show on this one. I'll meet you tomorrow at the Bryn Mawr station at close to 3:30. We can go to Parvin's Pharmacy for an ice cream soda if you like!"

"That'd be just super, Clint. Thanks so much for calling. I'll see you tomorrow!"

As soon as my call ended, I dialed the lobby, learned when a convenient train departed the next afternoon, brushed my teeth, put on my pajamas, and immediately crawled beneath the sheets. I was not hungry, at least not for food. My dreams were wildly romantic that night, and I awoke with a broad smile on my face. I told myself that the boys down at the Federal Reserve better look sharp today! I was primed and in top form; moreover, nothing was going to delay my catching that 2:50 PM local.

After meeting with the printers and resolving the problems with the fifty-denominated notes, I successfully caught the train out to Bryn Mawr. After 6 or 7 stops, the train pulled into Bryn Mawr Station. The cross-hatched red bricks forming its platforms looked as though they had been laid during the Middle Ages, while the waiting room, constructed from large irregular stones of granitic schist, could have been the façade of William Shakespeare's boyhood abode. In other words, the place looked older than our nation. But I was immediately cheered as I descended from the passenger car. Gail was already there, waiting for me with an expectant smile and an adorable soft hat perched atop her head. Her face looked exquisite despite her having rushed over from some fact-filled history class.

"Well, what are you in the mood for? Would Parvin's satisfy you?"

I carefully sidestepped the double-entendre she offered with a devilish sparkle in her eyes. She suspected I wanted to surround her in my arms, lift her from the platform, and kiss her deeply, but she also deduced that I had arrived famished. On this occasion, an ice-cream sundae or strawberry malt would definitely take precedence over intimacy. I took her hand and we went swinging up to the drugstore about a block away. This walk provided my opening.

"Gail, I've got something very important to ask you."

As a hardened agent, I may have been trained to respond quickly in dire emergencies, but this occasion would trump anything to which I had yet been exposed. My heart was racing as I studied her invitingly expectant eyes.

Demurely, she stopped in mid-stride and turned to look me straight in the face. "Yes?"

I still held her hand but now was squeezing it a bit too hard. I saw her bite her lower lip and immediately let go her hand and got down on one knee.

"Gail, I've been in love with you from the first moment I saw you back in 1950. I now have a full-time job and am making my way in my chosen profession. I can provide for you and any children we would want to have. Will you marry me?"

There you have, it, plain and direct. What would she say? "Yes!" was what I yearned to hear. Her answer did more than surprise me. It rocked me!

"Lord bless me, it's about time you asked! Why do you think I attended Bryn Mawr—to be near my Mother? It was to keep me at an all-women's college so I could reserve myself for you, silly. I can't think of anything I'd ever want more than to be your wife. Yes, Clint, yes! I am yours!"

And so, in about five months our life together began. We were married in the magnificent Church of the Redeemer about 1000 yards from where I had asked for her hand. We had sealed that special occasion by going to Parvin's for an ice-cream soda immediately after the reception, dragging all our ushers and bridesmaids with us. Gail knew each of the druggists by name and had arranged for the owner to close early when we got married on May 18, 1958 (her grandmother, Elise Metzger's birthday) so our wedding party could celebrate in style amidst lots of delicious frozen treats.

I took her to the Costa Brava in Spain for a week of honeymooning. Sorry, but I can't tell you much about the places or scenery there. The weather was crystal clear beneath a fabulous dark blue sapphire sky, but I spent most of my time looking either down or up, but always with delight, at Gail; she and the love expressed by her face are all I recall clearly from that week.

If I survive my stint with the Secret Service, I plan to surprise my wife with a trip to the same spot for a second go-round, if you know what I mean. First, I'd have to find a reliable babysitter for the young children who were sure to come, and that might prove a more severe challenge than simply finding the time for us to get away. That was way in the future, however, so who could tell what was in store for us?

CHAPTER SIXTEEN

Unexpected Ceremony

During the years I served on motorcades with the Secret Service, the agents were made to feel as though they were part of the President's inner circle. His persona defined a sort of gravitational field that surrounded him; being a planet in that universe would be an enriching experience. In this manner, he drew even seasoned professionals into a close, even though brief, orbit. Such men imagined that their own lives would acquire richer meaning merely by tumbling into the gravitational sphere of this magical man.

There were five who had to come back to earth following the debacle of November 22, 1963. When I returned in late December to relive that painfully horrible day with my buddies, these particular agents revealed that they had gone drinking at the Fort Worth Press Club the night before the Dallas motorcade. Then, a few had moved onto the Cellar Coffee House where liquor was not the problem. All the waitresses prancing around in scanty underwear were. It had been difficult to tear themselves away to hit the sack. They'd gotten very few hours of sleep. They had been undernourished, both as to quantity and quality. The direct result of this unprofessional behavior would have been sluggish reactions on the 22nd. It was possible that they had mistakenly considered the Dallas motorcade as the tail end of a party rather than as an ongoing, important duty assignment.

This helped explain why I felt all alone when I rushed to cover the President and First Lady as fast as I had. I had gone to bed promptly at 10:00 PM and woken on the 22nd feeling fresh and ready to go. Probably, some of the others had their senses dulled which caused them to stand still, as they scanned for possible exposed rifle barrels, rather than run to cover the First Couple.

If you're assigned to protective detail, **you must act first to cover and protect** before you have the luxury to scan for threat sources. Of course, the ideal would be for men on the running boards to scan for sources of danger while the proximate men on the rear hand-holds immediately obscure the target by blanketing him with their bodies. Don't tell me I'm Monday-morning-quarterbacking here. We did not work properly as a smoothly functioning team on the 22nd, so it was my hope that Agent Rowley had taken steps to upgrade the service's ability to perform in future emergencies.

I didn't reveal any of this, of course; not even to Rowley. As far as I was concerned, the event was over. After all, it had been one of my cohorts who shot me. In the future, however, should I be close by the side of a president, I would check on these men to ensure each one was in top form as they undertook their shifts. There'd be no more careless or loose behavior when the President was in my company. Of course, if I'd been a blackbird perched on some telephone wire, I would have seen that my thinking was exactly why President Kennerly had made me a permanent part of his entourage. It was only later that I connected these dots and realized how important a role I had assumed in the Kennerly presidency.

I was no longer assigned to an outside agency tasked with providing protection to some important person. I was about to be part of the inside team and standing right next to that very same important person every day.

Nevertheless, the second most meaningful thing I did during December was to retain the respect and friendship of my fellow agents. They each had to take a poke at my healing arm, but that was simply their way of ascertaining that I was not faking. Men are like that the world over, I'm sure. They can't accept on faith; they have to see, or even poke, for themselves. Over time, my howls and complaints grew softer as the healing process proceeded, so they gradually lost interest in provoking me. Thank god!

As my time with the Secret Service drew to a close, I was surprised to receive a summons from SAIC Gerald Bean. I was directed to appear at the Treasury Building on the 20th of December to meet with Secretary of the Treasury Douglas Dillon. I innocently surmised that some farewell was planned, with the obligatory toast, and perhaps a "heartfelt medal of conduct" bearing the likeness of a goat that someone such as Paul Landis would have cut from cardboard with the intention of pinning it on my back when I wasn't looking.

As events would soon show, I had missed the mark completely.

Having been in this office several times previously, I expected to see the two tall windows adorned with the customary opaque black drapes and the forbidding mahogany desk starkly facing the two stiff wooden chairs. I knew their discomfort well, having occupied one or the other during Gerald's famously demanding, after-action reports. When I presented myself to my boss at the appointed hour on this day, however, I was pleasantly surprised to see Gail and my two sons sitting in Agent Bean's office. This in itself was a treat, inasmuch as anytime we agents were summoned to this august office, we simply stood at attention and stared straight ahead until told to sit down.

Today was to be altogether different, apparently. The sunlight was pouring through the floor-to-ceiling windows and each was adorned with forest-green velvet drapes fringed with gold tassels. The all-important symbol of his authority—his paper-strewn desk—had its lion paws feet gleaming and its surface neatly covered with navy-blue velvet. In its center rested an attractive box large enough to contain some sort of service decoration, perhaps a medal.

Apparently, this was a stage set for some award ceremony, so I relaxed. I had worn my best dark-navy three-piece suit, so I was confident I was presentable for whatever was planned. I even took this opportunity to marvel at the room's noble furnishings as well as Agent Bean's academic and service awards, ornately framed items which I had never dared glance at before.

Sitting next to my wife was none other than Jacquelean Kennerly. Each woman was wearing a nubby wool, two-piece tailored suit. Jacquelean's was ivory-colored sporting tiny gold buttons down the front, while Gail's was powder-blue with a low-cut neckline which showed off a white silk blouse which I'd never seen her wear before. I didn't know who was copying whom. Neither of the women paid any attention to my entrance, however; they were deeply absorbed in their own world discussing Grecian statuary flanking the path to the Acropolis somewhere in Athens.

Standing next to Gerald Bean was Douglas Dillon. He was holding himself tightly erect, as though he himself was about to be inspected from head-to-foot. Much to my surprise, standing next to him was my father, Lloyd, and my mother, Ellie. They did not seem surprised to see me. I immediately became suspicious that whatever was up might be about me. Nevertheless, we all hugged with affection. If this was meant to be an end-of-service going-away party, I surely had been caught by surprise!

As I entered, I noticed Gerald reach for his phone and speak briefly into the mouthpiece, then put it down and come forward with his hand extended.

"Clint, I'm so glad to see you! Thank you for coming. I believe you know everyone here," he said expansively as he rounded up the occupants in the room with a swing of his right arm.

Before I could answer, everyone who was not already standing rose from their seats and we all looked respectfully toward the doorway as President Kennerly entered. To my surprise, he did not stop to shake anyone's hand; instead, he proceeded forward until he faced me. I couldn't salute, shake hands, or even wave a greeting: my entire right arm was still immobilized in protective bandages.

"Agent Brill, thank you so much for coming. Jacquelean, Gail, I hope I'm not interrupting something important." He paused, and then a broad smile revealing all those glamorous white teeth of his crept across his tanned face as he enjoyed this little ribbing. Then he turned back to Agent Bean and asked: "Has anyone informed Clint about what's going on today?"

Looking over first at Gerald, and then at his Treasury Secretary, he saw that they had not done so. Picking up the slack, the President stated:

"Well, it looks like I must take charge then." The President reached over to Mr. Dillon and was handed that dark maroon box I had noticed. Now, he stepped toward me as he opened it to reveal a cream-colored satin interior. Resting comfortably within the velour folds was an attractive blue and red ribbon attached to a beautifully embossed medal.

The President removed the decoration from its housing and allowed the medal to fall from its handsome ribbon; it was obviously designed to go over a person's head and hang proudly suspended down a person's chest.

Mr. Kennerly looked straight at me as he extended the ribbon between his two hands.

At that moment, someone I hadn't noticed flashed a camera bulb as President Kennerly announced:

"To Secret Service Agent Clinton Brill, for conspicuous bravery at great personal risk on November 22, 1963. His fast reactions, which were executed with complete disregard for his own personal safety, displayed the very best attributes of the members of our Secret Service. His unselfish execution of duty reflects great credit on the United States of America. I am so glad to be here today to present the Treasury Department's highest award, The Presidential Medal of Freedom, to him."

Reaching forward to place the ribbon around my neck, Mr. Kennerly adroitly avoided my healing right arm, stepped backward a bit, and then grasped me by both shoulders in an unspoken "Congratulations!"

Flashbulbs were flashing all around our little group. Someone had organized quite a surprise!

I looked over at Agent Bean and then several of my buddies who had crowded into the room during the President's statement. Where had everyone come from? How did they all find out when I knew nothing? None of that mattered, of course. I was being hugged by my wife as well as my son Chris and three-year-old Corey crowding close against my legs. Mrs. Kennerly stood to the side looking pleased, beautiful, and grateful. The President beamed upon all of us.

Usually, when a member of the Secret Service is surprised, he quickly frowns deeply and immediately undertakes a responsive action. Today, I just stood in the midst of all these appreciative people and smiled broadly. I glanced down at the engraving of the famous eagle of the United States holding the arrows of war and the scroll of peace. There, on the perimeter in raised letters, were the words: "Worthy of Trust and Confidence."

My father came forward and shook my left hand while holding onto my forearm with his right hand. His eyes sparkled with pride as he said, "Congratulations, son, we are very proud of you!"

Then Ellie stepped forward and folded me in one of her all-encompassing bear hugs. When I was a young teenager, this used to make the world and any troubles I had go away, but today she simply said "Thank God you made it through alive. We love you so dearly."

Then she took a step back and declared to everyone present: "Clint, it's time you found a job that is less stressful!"

The entire room broke up in laughter. Then, as things quieted down, they all began clapping. The President came over to stand next to me as flashbulbs popped once again.

At last, Gail was allowed to step forward so I could embrace her, and only her. She looked up at me with those wondrously deep hazel eyes of hers and murmured, "Surprised?"

"You can say that again!" I responded unabashedly.

Yes, I had been surprised, but this would be a day I would always recall fondly.

CHAPTER SEVENTEEN

Private Conversation

The most important thing now was to return to my hometown and spend my final Christmas as a member of the Secret Service with my two young boys Chris and Corey, my wife Gail, my ever-growing sister Alice, and of course my parents, Ellie and Lloyd. My folks were looking well, considering that dad had taken on a job as a production foreman at the local steel plant ever since he had returned as a decorated Korean War veteran. He also held an important position with the local VFW Post. When these activities were combined with the love for competitive, duplicate bridge that he and my mother shared, one could say my parents were leading a "full life." I can't stand that form of card playing. If a person is going to sit down at a table, it should be with beers and chips by your side and inscrutable opponents bent on one-upping you at poker rather than smirking when they "trumped" you or made all their "tricks." If I lost, I wanted to kick my own butt, rather than take it out on an unfortunate partner.

All of us got along jovially as we sat at my parents' house opening gifts before a cozy fire during the Christmas holidays. Even Alice, now approaching double-figures, was no longer a whining basket-case-of-a-sister demanding attention. In fact, soon she would be old enough to babysit **my** boys! When our group became surrounded by colorful papers and ribbons being strewn about, Ellie rose to restore some order to the living room. At that point, Lloyd took me aside and confided that he had been awestruck that my job had required so much of me.

"I'm far more than proud of you, son. I also have exposed myself to the terror and certainty of death in risky situations. There are few who can better empathize with what you had to overcome than me, your own dad. God bless me, son, I'm glad you stayed alive!"

"Thanks, Dad. You make a good case, but you know probably as well as I do that when the actual circumstances present themselves, you don't have time to consider your personal risk. When it's your job, you've got to execute as best you know how."

My father was nodding his head in agreement.

"Frankly," I continued, "my situation was an instantaneous reaction to a sign of danger. I never did try to spot the sniper's position. If I hadn't noticed Mr. Worthy when I did, I probably would have been caught with my pants down, looking just as foolish as my colleagues staring vacantly up into space while our world turned topsy-turvy beneath our very noses."

"Oh, I doubt that," Dad asserted. I then took a deep breath and looked him straight in the eye.

"You, on the other hand, experienced far worse mental challenges while posted abroad. That night reconnaissance which you and those four others pulled back in Korea, now that was really something!"

Lloyd looked as though he was about to protest, but I held up my hand. "You guys were crawling through dirt or snow at night, causing you to be uncertain about your course. At any time, you could be discovered and exposed to withering fire from hordes concealed in trenches or hilltop bunkers. Even worse, after reaching your objective, you had to retrace your steps to reach the safety of your own lines. Now that's **real** pressure! I never worried about food, noise discipline, low light conditions, or bone-chilling, constant cold."

Dad looked ready to raise still another protest, so I forged ahead. "I'm sorry dad, but your bravery beats mine hands down! While I appreciate your concern and compliments, there's no one in the world of whom I'm prouder than you!"

Dad beamed. At this point, he couldn't help himself. He motioned as though to wipe a corner of an eye, but instead observed, "Like father, like son, eh?"

I laughed as I expressed my affirmation. Then he stood and, taking me by my good elbow, guided me to a quiet nook. On the way, he yelled to Ellie, "Hon, let me have a few minutes alone with Clint, will you? We're gonna have a man-to-man before he returns to duty at the President's side."

"Okay by us girls and boys; we're doing just fine here by the fire!" Her melodic sing-song voice filtered pleasantly down the hallway.

Lloyd had a smile wreathing his face as he turned toward me. "May you and Gail always be as lucky as we are, Clint. Ellie means the absolute world to me!"

"No kidding? Geesh, Dad, I see your love shared in the long glances you give one another. It's clear to everyone that, after all these years, you still can't get enough of each other."

My dad warmed to his subject. "I'll tell you, son, when I retire, it won't be to spend time fishing or starting a photographic hobby. What I look forward to is the day when I wake up in the morning with Ellie lying softly and contentedly beside me, so our only challenge will be: after breakfast, what shall we do together for the rest of the day? If she wants to travel, I'll take her wherever she wants to go; but, if she wants to stroll down to the end of the driveway and see how far our mood takes us on some balmy spring afternoon, that will be just fine, too. My only requirement will be that I have the opportunity to spend my days in her company."

"I love you, Dad. Pure and simple."

There I was, a few weeks from turning thirty-two years old, and gushing like a pubescent schoolgirl. I didn't care; expressing these feelings made me feel truly great.

Nevertheless, despite the intimacy of this Christmas get-together, I couldn't have been less prepared for what he imparted next.

"I wanted to take this moment to share with you an experience I had after I returned to the states from Korea. There was no shooting, no massed attacks, no one sacrificing himself in the name of some ideology, yet the experience has stayed with me more clearly than any of my frightening assignments abroad. I want to share it with you because you are about to embark on an entirely new dimension in your life, serving at the president's side not for protection, but as a resource. For god's sake, son, you are about to become an oracle of information, do you understand?"

"Well, that's the goal, but it's just a distant goal at present. I'm going to have to be beholden to various assistants who may not have my reactive and physical training, but their education and sheer breadth of knowledge will remain beyond me no matter how long I serve."

"I won't argue that point, not at all," replied my father as his mouth turned up at the corners, crinkling his cheeks at the thought.

"Hey! I thought you were on my side!" I exclaimed.

"Of course, of course, son," my dad said reassuringly. "I'm simply looking at your situation realistically. You will see firsthand why President Kennerly is so effective. He enters into a discussion with his head free of emotional prejudices. His goal is to ask penetrating questions until he is assured that he understands the core of the problem under discussion: i.e., what the conflicting pressures and forces are, and then—most importantly— what the consequences of choosing a particular outcome are. Your associates will bear names like 'Sorensen,' an incredibly able and educated thinker, and 'Shriver' who has more organizational skill lodged between his ears than a city planner. Then there's 'McNamara,' a sharp cookie who can reel off statistics and numerical relationships from memory faster than you could read them on a blackboard. Pay attention to him, because he speaks with clarity and makes workable recommendations and, once a decision has been made, sees that the job gets done."

Pausing, he formed his fingers together in a steeple and then rested his chin on his fingertips. Lost in speculative thought, he whispered to himself more than me, "There he is: head of the Defense Department. If only we could crank out junior-officer clones of him, we'd field the best outfit in the world!"

Returning to our discussion, he resumed. "I will also tell you about something I heard through the grapevine after I came off active duty. McNamara is unique. Should someone ask whether he has anything to say regarding a matter under discussion, he is able to say: 'No, I don't,' if he has nothing to contribute. Thus, he never wastes anybody's time.

"Then there's Robert Kennerly, a smart and upright man if there ever was one. For all we know, he might run for office as president himself in the future. As his brother's appointee in charge of the attorney general's office, he has a lot to prove, given his lack of experience and youth. However, no one can question his absolute commitment to and devotion to his older brother's success. Be careful not to put yourself in a position where you appear to stand in the way of that bond. Am I getting through to you?"

"Loud and clear, Dad. Simply seeing them together makes me jealous that I grew up without a brother, older or younger, but then I step back and think about most sibling relationships I know, and this allows me to realize that what you're saying is correct. Their camaraderie is uniquely strong."

As I finished speaking and inhaled, the pause gave Dad his chance to dive into the topic which had been so dark and esoteric that he had closed the door on his beloved wife. His hunching forward made the distance between us close and intimate, as though we were confiding state secrets. Should I live to be 100 years old, what he began to relate will be the strangest story I will ever hear.

"Do you recall what I did when my unit returned from Japan following the Korean Armistice?"

He paused for my answer, and when I gave it, he responded, "That's correct; I assumed a posting as captain in charge of training some 200 new inductees into the army. Under such circumstances, my duties were largely administrative; I essentially rode herd on four or five lieutenants who ran their own platoons. Every so often, we'd have competitions between companies for bragging rights over softball prowess or rifle qualification scores, but in the main, I trained my commanders to act autonomously. So long as my men reached the required levels of proficiency in the areas designated by the Army, such as marksmanship and physical conditioning, how I got them there was up to me. In my company, that meant allowing my officers to have a free rein in managing their platoons.

"In the job you're about to undertake, you won't have that sort of leeway. I mostly shuffled paperwork and resolved disputes and enforced discipline when required. If we marched on review in some parade, I was in front, but the everyday job of training was left to the hard-bitten, experienced sergeants. They had more experience than I did, understood the inductees intellectually, and could lend an ear when one of them had a problem that needed airing.

"On the other hand, their world was what the Army had said it always should be. They held their positions of responsibility because they followed Army doctrine implicitly, without hedging or debating. Should they ever have a problem which they couldn't immediately resolve, they always had their lieutenants to whom they could turn as backup. This system has worked because, while a lieutenant is less experienced regarding military tactics than his platoon sergeants, he's usually more experienced via schooling or studious thinking and can provide leadership based on his wider-picture thinking.

"No one in the history of the army was prepared for what confronted me one snowy day where the temperature was low enough that all of us were keeping the training restricted to indoors wherever possible. I'll keep this anonymous, but the details will be eye-popping nonetheless.

"I was sitting at my desk when my sergeant-major came huffing into my office with his face beet red. His eyes were nearly popping out of his head. I immediately stood up and, as he tried to ready himself to salute, told him to skip it and get right to the point. He looked to be in that much of a state. He asked me to please let him sit down; he just didn't think he could tell me the problem without doing so. When I got him seated, he began to relax a little and then told me the following tale.

"The platoon sergeant was conducting a standard inspection one day when he paused in front of a particular trainee. This man had a very clean complexion with no noticeable beard, which was unusual for an eighteen-year-old recruit, thin bones, and features that appeared to be remarkably delicate. Up to that point, no one had bothered him more than the usual bickering and kidding around that goes on in a barracks; everyone is under the same pressure to survive and conform. The men in his platoon assumed he was some long-distance runner or something similar where a lean build is an advantage. After all, no one knew when the next conflict might erupt that would cause the men to hunker down in the same foxhole while trying to survive artillery or enemy assault. A trainee is well-advised to get along with his mates during training.

"Well, the reason the sergeant had paused in front of this man was that the trainees had now entered their seventh week, their performance levels were right on target, and their morale was high. As a reward, their lieutenant told his platoon sergeant that the men could now take the upper right-hand slot in their foot locker and replace the required three pairs of rolled-up sox with a personal item. In other words, the well-ordered partitions—with a place for everything Army and everything in its place—could now have one single, personal item in that slot. This boon was against regulations, to be sure, but it was that officer's way of rewarding the ongoing diligence of his men. I don't know whether you've ever had to go without mayonnaise or razor blades for a month, but I can tell you that there are times when a man has to have his individual items close if he's to remain productive.

"The idea was to give the men a small chance of self-expression in a world otherwise tightly controlled for the sake of uniformity. When the lieutenant responded to his sergeant's call for help, he saw that this compartment contained a pair of ladies' underpants. The officer, gesturing toward the slot, asked the soldier 'What were those?' The answer—'a trophy, sir'—made the lieutenant take out his pistol and nudge the muzzle into the silk and hold the panties aloft for all to see. The lieutenant exclaimed that everyone better buckle down and spruce themselves up because they had an accomplished stud in their midst and his trophies were going to be tough to compete with!"

"What's the big deal, Dad? We raided the cheerleaders' lockers whenever we won a football game back in high school. Girls' undies are cute and can be sexy, but they're generally just a hindrance to our main objective rather than a trophy."

My father's eyebrows rose up as high as they could go. "So you would think, my boy! But not in this case!"

It suddenly occurred to me that dad had only just begun to tell this story. He was far from the punch line. I began to understand why he had closed the door. This was not merely private; it was about to become juicy!

He continued. "It turns out that the sergeant and lieutenant got together after the inspection and compared their reactions. Both of them had been appalled, but the officer had been quicker on the uptake and been able to make a positive out of something that appeared weird as hell. Having handled the situation in front of his men, this First Lieutenant, who was 24 years old and himself battle-hardened, remained rather mystified and went to my unit's Sergeant Major, who promptly came to me for advice. That's how I got involved in one of the most unique experiences a man in the military has ever had.

"I heard the rundown by my subordinates in person because, as I mentioned, what they had witnessed was simply over their heads, so I decided to speak to the enlisted man alone. Let's call him: "Connors." So he appeared as ordered and after just a few minutes with him, I realized that here was one recruit whom I had overlooked. In the general tumult of running 200 some men, ensuring their physical development, skills with weapons, fire and maneuver tactics, *et cetera*, this individual had escaped my notice.

"Yet when I sat alone with him in the room, I couldn't help but be struck by what an effeminate appeal he possessed. I cut our interview short and told him to come back the next afternoon for a further talk. After dismissing him, he had no sooner closed the door when I dove for the phone and ordered my clerk to get Major Alice Brummell on the line. She was the psychologist on the base. She is considered ahead of her time for her thinking and insights into human motivation. Ellie had met her at church one Sunday and introduced me, so I knew her socially, but when I mentioned I had met Major Brummell to my battalion commander, Major Hoskins, his eyes had widened and he stated I was a lucky man. Apparently, she is known nationally for her incisive theories of human behavior. He told me to listen whenever I was in her presence; she understood more about people than I would ever learn. Additionally, he asked me to treat her most respectively; we were lucky as hell to have her assigned to the Ft. Devens Military Base. According to Hoskins, she should have been posted to the Pentagon.

"With this knowledge in hand, I called her and informed her about Private Connors. She immediately told me to put down the phone, whereupon she appeared in my office in person twenty minutes later. She ordered me to go through the entire litany of inspection, discovery, boast, interview, and then she announced that she wanted to be present the next day when the soldier reported back.

"She ordered me to keep my talk very relaxed, almost informal, if such a thing is possible in a military setting. Above all, she said, do not let any negative or disciplinary overtone creep into my talk with this man. Her plan was for her to sit next to him and should I stumble, or if the soldier needed reassurance, she would then step in. Her manner was crisp and assured. I had done the right thing to bring her into the picture.

"I thanked the woman and assured her I would be most respectful and discreet during the interview. Well, 1500 hours rolled around and the soldier reported to my office. I introduced Major Brummell whereupon Private Connors turned toward her and smartly saluted. Then she did a most extraordinary thing. I'd only witnessed such informality after men had shared battle engagements together. After returning the salute, she stood up and extended her hand, saying how pleased she was to have the opportunity to meet such a fine-looking soldier.

"The major asked only one question: To what extent did he feel assimilated with the men in his platoon? He assured her he was very comfortable and even held the temporary post of cadet corporal in his squad. Then the major lapsed into silence as she took a seat next to him and let me do the talking.

"I'll tell you, son, this is where I actually began to sweat beneath my T-shirt. Before I posed my first question, I had a moment where I actually wished I was back in Chong-Dong crawling along in the snow.

"I laid the ground rules and explained that absolutely nothing was wrong. His behavior had been sufficiently unusual that I was simply taking the step of giving him the opportunity to come clean if there was something troubling him. I'm no prude. But I never imagined anything like the scene that quickly erupted.

"Private," I had said, "I am under some real pressure here. I am responsible for not only the training but also the well-being of all my men. This applies to both their physical, mental, and spiritual welfare. Therefore, I must ask—and your response will be kept confidential to the major and me unless you approve its wider dissemination—do you enjoy men?"

"Why, certainly I do, sir! I seem to be well liked by them. They're always jovial around me, so I'm always comfortable being around them, as well. By the way, sir, if I may, what does that d-word mean?"

"Oh! You mean, 'dissemination.' No, there's no sexual implication there. It simply means to tell others, to spread the news around. Understand?"

"Yes, sir, thank you. Now I do. So, if that's what it signifies, then no, I don't mind you're spreading around that I like being in the company of men. It won't be news to any of my pals."

"No, no, I'm sorry. I wasn't clear. I am asking whether you prefer the attention of men, for sex, as opposed to women."

"Clint, I'm telling you, I've killed I don't know how many enemy soldiers whose faces were not more than three feet from mine, but I've never seen a look of such horror, of utter revulsion as crossed the face of that private that afternoon. You'd have thought I had just approached his naked body with a red-hot branding iron attached to an electric cord. He shivered and rose up and proceeded to stand behind his chair as though it offered protection from my question. He stuttered. He shook visibly. His actions clearly conveyed that he was very uncomfortable with my asking him such a question.

"I tried to soothe him and get him to return to his seat, but he remained adamantly erect while gripping the back of his chair. Fortunately, this was where Major Brummell intervened.

"Calling him by his first name, she reached over and lightly touched his forearm and asked softly, 'Conrad, you really would like to be called *Connie*, isn't that it? And those panties were not some trophy you plucked off a woman, but rather they are your own, to keep you in touch with your dream and vision of your true self, am I not right?'

"The private's eyes widened to dark soup bowls as he turned fully to face the major. I could sense that he was listening with every hair follicle in his eardrums pointing her way. No one had ever spoken such words to him. He stood stock still, mute as a button.

"'And, if you could,' she had continued, 'what you really want to be, what you have desperately wanted all your life, but have never understood how it could be achieved, is to be physically female. This would comport with how you see yourself in your mind. If you were whole, that is, female, your dream would be to fall in love with a woman and cohabit with her for the rest of your life...'

"The major had hardly gotten out that last word when Private Connors flung himself toward her, wrapping his arms around her shoulders and sobbing soulfully: 'Oh ma'am, good god, oh thank you! No one has ever understood, ever broached such words of hope to me. I love my parents; they gave me life! But I have never been able to explain myself to them. They simply had resolved themselves to rearing a frail, short son who avoided any kind of physical danger. I hoped my entering the Army would make them so proud that they'd look beyond my physical build and simply love me as their child. I'm so ashamed, I'm so sorry, and I'm so stupid. You'll have to get rid of me as being 4-F or whatever and my hope of ever getting a job will be ruined. My life will be over. What's to become of me?'

"By now, he was sobbing. I was so dumbstruck that I simply sat there with my mouth closed, but my eyes wide as saucers!"

"'Hey, chin up there, Connie, the world is not nearly as bleak as prejudice and ignorance would lead you to believe.' The major looked directly at Private Connors. 'Now, get back in that chair and listen, listen real close to what I have to say. Here, dry your eyes with this while I huddle with Captain Brill for a second.'

"Thereupon the major, leaving the sobbing, despairing lump in the chair, drew me aside to a corner and spoke in low tones.

"'Captain,' she said, 'I checked your security clearance before stopping by today, and you are permitted to stay and hear what is to follow. However, you must look me in the eye and give me your word that what I am about to say will never be revealed to anyone after this conversation concludes. No, not even to your own wife, Ellie! And, you must abide by this pledge for a minimum of five years from today's date. Do you agree?'

"Clint, it's now well past five years since this happened. Thus, I can tell it to you in the confidential manner we agreed to at the start." He caught my eye and looked hard and straight at me.

"Yes, sir! No problem," I merely replied. I wanted to shake my father and yell that he must not stop here. This was **such** an incredible tale!

"Good," said Dad as he settled into regaling me further. "The major stunned me, I must say. She said there was a program underway right then and there, as we were talking, to develop potential assassins in our country, presumably from the ranks of the military, who could prove useful in the clandestine war of espionage in communistic satellite countries. In the late 1950's, there was one city above all others in the world where tension and secrecy were most acute, and that was Berlin, Germany. East or West, they were both part of the same cauldron of kill-or-be-killed while the spies of both sides sent coded messages to their handlers. The Central Intelligence Agency desperately needed people who could be trusted to carry out their necessary programs, but who could not be blackmailed, impregnated, or otherwise compromised while on a mission.

"Major Brummell stated, 'I'm going, with your acquiescence, to offer such a posting to this private. She has the fortitude, drive, and pleasant disposition that would make her a favorable candidate.'

"Clint, I was reeling. I noticed her use of the feminine pronoun regarding Private Connors right away. This was heavy, blood-curdling stuff from spy thrillers, the sort of stories that Richard Burton excelled in as an actor in fog-shrouded, London mysteries. Heavier even than Alfred Hitchcock. I merely nodded to the major, and she then addressed Private Connors again."

"'Connie,' she began smoothly, taking hold of the private's left hand and retaining it in her own. When their eyes met, she could see that Connors was beginning to relax, so she continued.

"'Connie, there is a program run by the C.I.A. that is in need of recruits. Have you heard of that agency?'

"He said he had, but his voice was quavering with fear and uncertainty.

"The major continued by saying, 'Connie, and you don't mind my calling you by what should be your real name, do you?'

"Private Connors looked at her with such joyous relief filling his face that I almost thought he was going to kiss her. It would have been my first experience with lesbians making out in front of me, except one was still a male, and the other was my superior officer. I nevertheless held my breath.

"To my relief, Connors only looked grateful while nodding his head. Major Brummell then continued."

"'If you are accepted, and I can assure you there are some rigorous tests you will have to endure, both as to your mental acuity and loyalty to your citizenship and, most prominently, your suitability as a candidate physically. From their standpoint, the evaluators will want to determine that you need to be female. They want to perceive that, should you spend another year as a male, you might well commit suicide. Otherwise, this process is so severe and trying that, before they can undertake to shepherd you along the path to achieving outwardly what you inwardly hold yourself to be, they have to be assured that this is truly your last option for survival. Make no mistake: once accepted, and the physical process is undertaken, there is no going back. Let me repeat that. Connie, once you start down this path, there is no turning back, no changing your mind, no having second thoughts.'

"'I'm not privy to the goings-on at the C.I. A. headquarters,' she continued to explain, 'but it wouldn't surprise me that they have a rule such as: *once in, always in*. Any indecision, any wavering once you're in their program, and they will assign someone to terminate you. You would be considered to be at high risk of exposing the entire program. So, let me hear from you. Have you clearly understood what I have set forth and the risks inherent in such a course?'

"Acting-Corporal Conrad Connors took a deep breath, placed both hands on his knees, sat straight up, and looked from one of us to the other. He then responded in the gentler voice which, apparently, he wished to use but heretofore had been unable to: '*Ma'am, Sir, I am prepared to enter this program and perform as instructed and ordered. For the very first time in my life, I am sure of something!*' I was amazed, Clint, at the change from fearful to assured. It had transformed the face, even the demeanor, of this young recruit.

"Major Brummell stood up, saying: 'That's good enough for me. I'll contact the agency, give my approval, and your orders should arrive by the end of the week. In the meantime, don't let anything crude happen to you.' Then she turned to me and remarked, 'Captain, you now have a potentially high-value asset in your care. I direct you to ensure this soldier's safety during all your training exercises while this soldier remains on base here.'

"She let her right hand stretch forward, Conrad shook it, and then he stepped slightly back and smartly saluted her. Since she ranked me, I simply rose and stood as a mute witness. My shirt was now soaked through with perspiration, plus I needed a shower, and badly!"

"When Connors left the base that Friday, I did not see or hear anything further about his person. Nearly six years had gone by when, just two months ago, Ellie and I were downtown shopping. We had paused to stare into an illuminated shop window. In the reflection of the large pane, I could see a slender, tastefully-attired lady walking up to stand alongside us. She paused for a bit, but when my wife and I turned to walk elsewhere, this person held an arm across our path, faced us, and said, 'Excuse me, Mrs. Brill, but I must say something privately to your husband.'

"Ellie turned to look at me for a quizzical moment, but she could immediately see that I had no idea who this person was, so she gave way: 'Certainly,' my wife had said, 'I'll wait right over here.'

"As Ellie stood off to the side, this delicately-faced, bewitching female, who looked to be in her mid-twenties, said, 'Thank you so much, Major Brill, for giving me the chance to be who I have always been inside. I have a secure job, I'm very good at it, and I get to travel frequently to places one usually just reads about in magazines. Please remind your wife, on those days when you seem less of a treasure to her, that you are a good, wise, and fair man.'

"I started to respond that I am in fact always the apple of my wife's eye, but the only thing I could say was: 'Who are you?'

"The pretty, svelte, woman looked up into my eyes as she replied, 'Why, I'm Connie, Connie Connors, Major Brill!' and she pirouetted to walk out of my life, I assumed, forever.

"Your mother, standing off to the side but within earshot, was transfixed. 'Who the hell was that!' was written all over her face, but she could see that I was perplexed, as well as a bit stunned and momentarily at a loss for words, so she said nothing, at first. For one thing, I was on a public street in civilian clothes. I worked at the nearby steel mill as a plant foreman. My hair was neatly cropped, but it was certainly longer than when I had been in the service. My promotion to major had come through the reservist lists a mere three days earlier. How had this person known all about me? When the hell had I ever done anything for her?

"I was still thrashing about in this stew of my own making when Ellie approached me. Taking hold of my forearm, she gently inquired, 'Dear, have you something to tell me, perhaps some incident from your active-duty days?'

"Then it hit me, like a wall of bricks that comes rushing at you as your car skids on ice and goes out of control into the side of a building. *This was the delicate soldier who had displayed a pair of panties in his foot locker back at Ft. Bragg!* Now Conrad was this tempting slip of a girl who worked as an assassin for the C.I.A. Of course, she hadn't said any such thing, but the conclusion was obvious. Such would have been the reason for her recruitment in the first place.

"She had mentioned, matter-of-factly, that she was *good* at her job. Jezzus! I sure didn't want to get mixed up in her world. Chinese soldiers massed and screaming as they charge my position are something I know how to handle, but this agent probably lives in a world of subtlety where the mere arching of an eyebrow conveys all sorts of covert messages.

"My breathing began to return to normal as all this swept across my consciousness, and then I realized that your mother was squeezing my arm.

"'Yes, dear, what was that you asked?' I turned toward Ellie with a look of innocence on my face, but she saw right through my mask and pressed her inquisition.

"'Lloyd, who was that woman? Was she a secretary from your command days back at Fort Devens?' As Ellie pressed herself close in against my side, she breathlessly added, 'Well! What have you to say for yourself, Lloyd Brill? That was just about the sexiest, most demure woman I have lived to see. Who was she?'

"I responded as best I could. 'I'm sorry, honey. I love you totally, as the dearest part of the life which God has bestowed upon me, but verily, I say unto you now that you will never know everything there is to know about me!'

"Clint, that was the best I could muster, taking a high-toned, sermon-like tone. I'd made my excuse, but possibly stepped into deep doo-doo as a result.

"Your mother, ever the quick wit, came right back: 'Nor will you ever know all **my** secrets, Mr. Big Army Officer!' At this point, she revealed her teeth in a momentary grimace, but then she immediately relaxed into a wide smile.

"I scooped her into my arms and caressed her lips and nuzzled her cheeks and held her close during the entire taxi ride home. The cabby probably figured we were simply elderly teens whose libidos had been penned up for too long."

After my father finished his tale, we both remained silent, breathing slowly in, then out in parallel rhythms. When at last I rose to find my way back home, we briefly stood together in a bear hug and, when we parted, we exchanged a long look into each other's eyes. Not a word was spoken. Something had been shared between us that would never again be referred to, but it had deepened our already solid bond.

I was reminded of a perceptive lyric I'd heard on the radio:

> *Life is just a game we play;*
> *But no matter how long we stay,*
> *All of us must lose it someday.*

Jack had once remarked to me that poetry nourished his soul, rather than confounding his brain. As for me, I sure was happy to have been alive this day. What a wild ride it had been!

I had learned about an entirely new aspect of my father's unusually fantastic life. Was he ever my hero! I was a lucky fellow. I had a wife whom I treasured, a sister who I had learned to tolerate, and parents whom I loved more than I'd ever be able to convey. I decided, right there and then, that Gail and I had done well to produce grandchildren for them.

At the time of this Christmas in 1963, it never occurred to me that I could come to regard President Kennerly with the same degree of esteem as I did my father. However, indeed I would. As I worked at his side over the ensuing months, John F. Kennerly would come to mean more to me than even Jacquelean herself. He would command my total loyalty and commitment for this reason: his entire presidency was devoted to bettering the lives of his fellow Americans first, and after them, the peoples of the free world.

CHAPTER EIGHTEEN

Correcting a Mistake

Way back in 1951, during his third term in the House of Representatives, John Kennerly had decided to run for the Senate seat occupied by the wealthy and influential Henry Cabot Lodge. The story ran that the Lodges were so well-connected that they asked only God Himself for advice. Thus, this election was one for higher stakes, so Joe Kennerly advised his son to learn more about the Far East and, in particular, Thailand, Burma, Laos, Cambodia, and Vietnam. Doing so would permit him to sound more erudite about this region of the world should Senator Lodge ever question him about international politics. Since he'd already shown insight into England's self-delusion regarding the coming of the Second World War (*While England Slept*), the candidate agreed. He set off to tour Indochina with his younger brother Robert who had recently graduated from Harvard University.

They made a good pair: the older brother was well-read and a deep thinker, while the younger one's sound and clear-headed judgment served to rein in any impetuosity of his older sibling. Indeed, they not only valued, but also depended upon one another. Jack was well known for always giving it his all at whatever he undertook—whether athletics, dating, or backing a bill in Congress—while Bobby was more serious and intense, but their devotion to one another could never be cleaved.[1]

The young duo formed the unbiased opinion that countries in the region were developing strong nationalistic fervor. During this time, Mr. Kennerly shaped the political view that would become his guiding beacon: *you can't lead a country anywhere unless you have the hearts and minds of its peoples in your hip pocket.*

The French couldn't see it yet, but Mr. Kennerly was certain that the willingness of these Far Eastern countries to submit to foreign colonialism was coming to an end. Even his beloved Churchill retained anachronistic views on this subject. Early in his first term as a Senator, he blasted imperialism, stating that nationalistic fervor would sweep aside the days of empire and become the most important factor in international affairs during the 1960's.[2]

Thirteen years later as President, he would pay close attention to such countries as Africa, the Middle East, India, China, and Indonesia. This latter country, loaded with resources but held back by roiling internal conflict, particularly fascinated him.

"We've got to become friends with that charismatic man Sukarno if we're to have any influence in that region," he stated out loud, probably voicing his own inner turmoil over how best to work with these areas that were so foreign to our own culture.

When the administration was having difficulty coping with Fidel Casstra's resentment at being embarrassed during the Cuban blockade, I asked the President, "How do you find the inner courage to proceed in the face of such adversity?"

His prescient answer took my breath away. "Always remember that the highest form of appreciation for what someone does for you is not to merely utter words such as 'thanks,' but to live by them as well. By embracing the art of politics, I intend to strive to make our world better for the peoples of the nations that have, and renewed for those that have not." [3]

"For example, ever since I read Crushchev's speech where he adroitly disavowed conventional war while strongly endorsing guerrilla warfare to so-call liberate oppressed countries, I've paid attention to both the tactics our ground forces use as well as the tools of their trade. I had the generals institute the Green Berets as a counter-guerrilla specialty force. To instill pride for their dangerous work, I insisted on distinctive attire being authorized for them. More importantly, I sought to improve their weaponry and field guides, both of which were absurdly ill-suited to these missions. Their prime weapon was designed for long distance, open terrain, so we developed a high rate-of-fire bullet with tremendous velocity for the jungles; their footwear was solid leather for prickly or rocky terrain, so we had the Army design a breathable boot with steel plates in the sole to prevent injury from sharpened bamboo stakes; and, the noisy heavy helmet was replaced by a tough but light man-made fiber we had previously developed for the skin of the U-2 airplane.

"In other words, I didn't merely send these guys on dangerous missions: I saw to it that they were outfitted with equipment properly designed to enable them to do their job. I pay attention to what a soldier is asked to do and then insure that he has the tools and training to accomplish the mission."

He was their commander-in-chief and, though he no longer wore a uniform, was beloved by the everyday soldier serving on active duty because they knew he paid attention to equipping them to perform assigned missions.

Ruminating on some facts long withheld from the public, the President sadly shook his head. Integrity when dealing with other nations was an important attribute for Mr. Kennerly to promote. The lessons learned from mistakes made early in his administration at the Bay of Pigs, a place only ninety miles from our shores, now enabled him to deal with problems brewing half-way around the world.

He revealed: "Some months after the failed invasion at the Bay of Pigs, Bobby learned that Director Bissell had concealed from me the assessment by the C.I.A. that the invasion was doomed to fail. Essentially, he and that agency made me look like a fool who had pulled the rug out from under the feet of heroic men who wanted to take back the island and stop Communism in its tracks. Nothing could be more infantile. The Agency misjudged me. That is an extremely important arm of our government which is vital to protecting our interests in national security, but I have learned a hard lesson: never simply follow their advice without careful, reflective analysis on my own. As I affirmed to Art Schlesinger, I will never again allow my judgment to be overawed by professional military advice as long as I am in this office." [4]

Apparently, Dulles and Bissell and the generals and admirals in on the plot reasoned that the exiles would quickly fail, so the president would be pressured into calling in the armed forces of America, thereby essentially declaring outright war which would then annihilate the communist forces under Casstra. Thus, the exiles were to be used as mere cannon fodder to light a fuse which would trigger our overwhelming invasion.

Now that plot had been thwarted and their hard-liner, Cold War logic was on the way out in favor of more enlightened leadership.

Government bureaucrats such as Allen and John Dulles would no longer be running the government as a family franchise deceiving and manipulating a president with threats of cold war communism.

In the international theater, he had learned to become his own man and to rely on his cadre of advisors and close associates before acting on suggestions put forth by governmental bodies which seemed more interested in their own prestige and survival than that of the nation. To the new president, keeping the United States out of any war would be paramount.

"I will not let this country be plunged into an irresponsible action just because a fanatical fringe in the C.I.A. or the military or the manufacturers of war materiel put national pride or personal profit above national reason."

In accordance with this belief, he promoted Curtis Lemay as Chairman of the Joint Chiefs of Staff in order to prevent his retirement and subsequent recruitment into the ranks of politically connected and vocal men who advocated striking first rather than thinking through the problem. Indeed, during 1961 the president was pressured to strike preemptively at the Soviet Union because we enjoyed, at the time, significant advantage rather than parity; such superiority would diminish as the U.S.S.R. caught up due to their highly effective spy network delivering our closest secrets to them without the need for testing and development.

Fortunately, Mr. Kennerly was able to convince former General Maxwell Taylor to come out of retirement in order to serve as his military advisor. This relegated the Joint Chiefs to the sidelines.

He paid attention to the countries of South America, Central America, and the Caribbean as had no president before him.

The OAS was an important attribute of the Western Hemisphere. His First Lady spoke Spanish and could rally crowds to pay attention and consider America's role in Latin American affairs with more equanimity. The First Lady communicated to the leaders in Spanish, while the President appealed to the "new generation" of Americans born in this century; he used the stick of economic aid to bend the leaders toward reforming their repressive social policies. These included schooling for those denied it and land for those without it.

The President hired Richard Goodwin, a graduate of Harvard Law School with a curly-headed, incisive intellect and endless ideas about how the government can support the aesthetics of American society through support of the arts. While in the Justice Department, he had gained notoriety by uncovering the hoax behind a popular television quiz show. When he joined the State Department, his views on our Latin neighbors—based on realistic assessments—so impressed Kennerly that he appointed the young man to head up the Alliance for Progress. In August 1961, this program had been designed to shift support from the reigning oligarchies and dictators to governments aligned more with "power to the people," and to end the decades of United Fruit Company dictating policy for the region. The goal was to encourage member nations to work toward regionalization of their markets, price stabilization, and development of technical research facilities. For example, in Uruguay the prevalence of poverty contrasted with the vast potential of the greatest untapped reserves of oil in the world. True, the young man caused ferment, but he was supported by the President: "Without ferment, there can be little useful progress!" Mr. Kennerly would retort to naysayers objecting to Goodwin's appointment.

Prior American leaders had paid scant attention to our neighbors "south of the border," but now that Cuba and Fidel Casstra's cow-towing to Moscow had shown how vulnerable these resource-rich countries were, Mr. Kennerly decided that it was time for the United States to step up to the plate and do something for—and with—countries in our own hemisphere. What would be the point of carrying a big stick ala Teddy Roosevelt in far flung regions such as Laos and Latvia if we couldn't help neighbors in our own backyard?

The first challenge was to convince residents that democratic reform was preferable to armed revolution. In truth, many of the current governments were in power via just such an approach. Often ignoring his hosts' use of violence to rise to power, Goodwin—and ultimately President Kennerly himself—journeyed to these countries to assure the people that the rule of law through the application of democratic principles could improve the lives of everyone in society without the violence and repression to which they had become familiar.

Unfortunately, Bobby was still too young to have gained control over his hotheaded suspicions of the WASP establishment as being allied against his father. He convinced Jack to reassign Goodwin to the Peace Corps; this caused resentment which led this towering intellect to opt for serving as a special consultant on the arts. Thereby, the administration lost a level-headed, insightful intellectual. Even a magnificent leader such as President Kennerly could make mistakes of judgment.[5]

We were, in fact, becoming far more cognizant of events in the Far East. The Philippines, Taiwan, South Korea, and Malaysia had once been important for strategic reasons during military conflicts, but the productivity of these emerging nations was becoming a global force to be reckoned with when forming trade alliances with Japan and her neighbors.

Ever the expert diplomat on international concerns, our esteemed President stated to his close advisors: "When the Russians are bellicose, remember this salient fact: our two countries have never gone to war against each other. Despite their form of government being repugnant to all our precepts, negating as it does personal freedom and dignity, they have achieved much in this past century, emerging as they have from a form of autocracy."

This background led him to initiate an important call for world sanity. Speaking to the graduating class at American University on June 10, 1963, he stated:

> "On this beautiful Monday, and before this accomplished audience here today, I affirm publicly that our nation is committed to the maintenance of peace, not just within our shores, but around the world. To that end, I call on Premier Crushchev to commit his country to a ban on testing nuclear weapons in the atmosphere or beneath the seas. Such activity threatens the survival of mankind as a species on this earth. Our two nations should pursue peaceful relations together.
>
> "This is not the peace of the grave or the absence of hope for the slave. Genuine peace makes life on earth worth living, the kind that enables nations to thrive, to grow, and to build toward a better future for their peoples.
>
> "Some will say there is no need to so limit ourselves. The world is at peace, so why should we constrain it? I answer that the time to fix the roof is when the sun is shining. As I look about this proud and happy gathering here, I see that the sun is, indeed, shining."

He then issued one of the most memorable calls to action our nation has ever heard:

"The concept of peace of which I speak does not merely apply to the peoples of our two nations. Rather, it transcends generations to be observed by all nations, and for all time to come. Our two nations must commit to an enduring peace not just for the citizens of America and Russia, but to a peace for all men; not merely peace in our time, but peace for all time. We must conduct our affairs in such a way that it becomes in the Communists' interests to agree on a genuine peace. As we work to end our differences, we must also work to make the world safe for diversity, a world of peace where the weak are safe and the strong are just. In the final analysis, our most common basic link is the fact that we all inhabit this planet. We all breathe the same air. We all cherish our children's future. And, we are all mortal. In this regard, **we must put an end to war—or war will put an end to us.**"

He thanked his audience before leaving the podium and returning to his seat. He always liked to give a respectful parting after delivering a formal address.

Later, I brought up my concern that he might be overreaching here, but the President's longtime assistant, Kenny McDonald, pointed out that our boss was riding the crest of having shown strength in Cuba and Berlin. Thus, the Russians, by responding affirmatively, would be meeting an opponent of equal standing. They wouldn't lose face by agreeing with a strongly regarded president as they would have if he had been a pushover. Signing such an accord would preserve their international standing because to do so would protect the welfare of Mother Russia's children.

As it turned out, the Russian government welcomed this speech as indicating a thaw in the tense atmosphere between our two governments. The Russian papers *Pravda* and *Izvestia* reprinted it in full. Negotiations for a limited test-ban treaty between Great Britain, the U.S.S.R., and the U.S. proceeded.

It suddenly dawned on me that, while Congress could pass on international relations through the ratification of peace and trade agreements, their focus was typically on domestic matters and squabbles. It was up to our Chief Executive and the various diplomats serving by his appointment to monitor and maneuver regarding our nation's place on the international scene. Thus, following Kenny's observations, I realized that this President was not using graduation speeches to merely laud and encourage, but to actually state or redefine policy which his Administration had just formed.

Speaking to the American Legion in the summer of 1964, he stated:

"We must deal with the world as it is. In a time when the desire to be free and to pursue the principles of self-government are becoming widespread, the notions of colonialism are falling by the wayside. Imperfect as their efforts may be, as they struggle to throw off the yoke of foreign rule and assume self-determination, their efforts will be hampered by uncertainty. Their attempts will mirror the burning quest we felt in the 1700's for our drive for independence. Even if the form of government which they choose does not comport with our own ideals, we must support their struggles as reflecting the very heart of our own history: to secure self-government by a nation state.

"Greatness in men often depends on the courage required of them to face the challenges of life. Bravery under fire, courage to risk reputation or friendship, courage to retain deeply-held convictions when all are against you, these are each important attributes. And yet, the rarest form of courage arises when one tries to illuminate the nature of man and the world in which we live. This often must be borne in silence and humility, but since it comes from within, it can withstand the contrary opinions of one's society. Gandhi, Dr. King, the poet Robert Frost each come to mind as embodying such courage. We must heed their example.

"Above all, in times of great pressure, we must not close our minds to the other fellow's position, but must retain open channels of communication, even consultation, to enable us as world leaders to sidestep confrontation and catastrophe. Nevertheless, when it comes to an oppressive form of control such as communism, it is detestable to us. Totalitarian governments suppress rather than nurture their citizens. If their stated objective is expansion to the point of world domination, we must defeat both that purpose as well as ensure that civilization itself is not destroyed in the defense of freedom. This is a vast undertaking in the nuclear age."

During a simpler time back in 1951, Jack and Robert Kennerly had visited Indochina as part of a fact-finding mission. They saw firsthand how inept the French were at combating native forces living in their homeland. This trip had the additional advantage of the two Kennerly brothers sharing observations and discussions; they formed a lifelong bond of trust. Robert would be the fighting tiger and Jack would become known as the likeable diplomat.

During a ride back to Washington from yet another speech, I happened to inquire why Jack had ever considered government service after all his physical suffering while on active duty. His response was not merely revealing; it was riveting as well.

"I was at loose ends after coming out of the navy. Then Jim Curley left office to become mayor of Boston, so the seat in the 11th Congressional District—formerly held by my grandfather Honey Fitz—opened up. I discovered that politics was a very satisfying venue for me. From my readings I knew that the Greeks defined happiness as the opportunity to use one's skills along the lines of excellence in a life affording scope. A man as noteworthy as Win Churchill had once stated that democracy would be the worst form of government in the world were it not for all the other systems that have been tried and found wanting. Democracy is hard on its citizenry because it depends on, indeed demands, their active participation. We all must be willing to give of ourselves to the exacting discipline of self-government. The magic of politics in America is that citizens can participate at any level and thereby make affirmative contributions to our national well-being. We can thereby participate in ensuring that freedom will not only prevail, but also endure.[6]

After being sworn in as our Chief Executive in 1961, Mr. Kennerly inherited from former President Eisenhower a cloak of "advisors" stationed in Vietnam to train the indigenous population in how to protect their section of the country from invasion by Ho Chi Minh's North Vietnamese communists. Vietcong soldiers, as they would become known, were adept at maneuvering and running supply trains during the cover of nightfall. They were so skilled at night attack that they became known as "Zebras" for their ability to approach

American positions in the dark. During daylight hours, they used extensive underground tunneling that permitted surprise attack but then immediate withdrawal, as though their troops had materialized out of thin air and then vanished without a trace.

This was an entirely new way of conducting warfare. No army manual covered such extensive, clandestine tactics. Moreover, the average American soldier was more than ten inches taller than his Vietnamese counterpart. The Vietcong were, for the most part, beyond our reach underground. Even if we found soldiers naturally short enough to negotiate the tunneling, booby traps left in the wake of the burrowing 'Cong would deter pursuit.

Studies by the C.I.A. had determined that conducting war there would result in a slowly escalating stalemate where victory by the South Vietnamese would not even be possible under a regime as corrupt as Diem's. Accordingly, the goal of Mr. Kennerly's administration became helping with materiel and tactics advisors rather than getting drawn into the whirlpool of escalating armed involvement.

The Constitution foresaw the need for a president to have consultative relationships with the senators. This one, with Senator Henry Jackson on the 9th of September 1963, is illustrative:

Jackson: *The criticism we're going to be up against is whether we have the will to use our power, and how far we will do it.*

The President: *In both Berlin and Cuba, we showed that we are ready to use our power in defense of freedom.*

Jackson: *Okay, but what about Laos? If we don't shore that country up, the Vietcong will outflank us and crush South Vietnam.*

JFK: *Absolutely. We will have to remain resolute on that matter. The one important thing I am pushing for is to resolve this mess before the Chinese start testing an atom bomb. They are not part of any treaties on this matter, and they could test in the atmosphere that could lead to the degradation of the planet for both communists and democracies. What we're going to have to focus on is our delivery systems; if the opponent has higher yield, we have to be numerically superior.*

Jackson: *The question is, what will their tests teach them that we don't yet know?*

JFK: *You're right, that is a very big question.*

Even an uninformed outsider could realize that international diplomacy is a labyrinth of convoluted thinking with hidden consequences.

The President had responded to pressure from American businessmen, who wanted to cash in on lucrative contracts for the manufacture of war materiel, by increasing the number of "advisors" who by this time were being targeted by the Vietcong during maneuvers. Abruptly, in 1963, he enlarged our advisor force to some 16,000 men, but shortly thereafter he developed serious misgivings that weighed heavily on his mind as the coming election year approached.

Then Diem allowed the self-immolation of Buddhist monks (the largest religious faction there) to occur in public and thereafter undertook to actively destroy their pagodas in suppression of non-Catholics.

Mr. Kennerly stated his misgivings to McGeorge Bundy of the Central Intelligence Agency as well as to Defense Secretary Robert McNamara: "Unless Diem works out an accommodation with the Buddhists, our country will have to reexamine our entire relationship with this regime. We must come up with a dignified exit strategy because, in the end, this is their war to win or lose."

As my friend Kenny O'Donald was to confide to me later, Jack had changed his mind and intended, after the November election, to make a complete withdrawal of our forces out of Vietnam. The seeds for his gnawing concern had been planted during his first year in office. General MacArthur, and then General De Gaulle, warned him that the Asian mainland was no place to fight a conventional war. No matter how many soldiers we'd commit, we'd be surrounded on all sides by armies that outnumbered our entire population! [7]

Paul Kattenburg, our very own Asian expert at the State Department, who'd known Diem and his family members for ten years, reported to the President that such a regime was incapable of transformation.

He opined, "We're walking into a disaster waiting to happen and ensnare us. South Vietnam is like a drain that gets wider the lower down it goes, swallowing everything dumped into it with increasing rapidity."

Our own expert was thus urging us to quit this escalating program before we got sucked remorselessly into a soulless quagmire.

"There is no solution to the encroaching communists eventually taking over," he said. "Bottom line, we'd be better off learning how to trade with them. We have always maintained a secondary role; after all, it is their country to do with as they wish."

Our President had established himself as a strong foreign policy statesman here at home during the Cuban missile crisis, and then abroad by the delivery of his speech to the throngs in Berlin's Rudolph Wilde Platz. To the enormous crowd of bifurcated Germans incensed over the erection of a barbaric, crude, and repellent wall by the Soviets, he had stated:

"Freedom has many flaws, and democracy is imperfect, but we have never had to put up a wall to keep our people in!" [8]

Of greatest importance, he had agreed with the Soviet Union and Great Britain to sign the nuclear test ban treaty which, importantly, included annual inspections to verify compliance. This pact ended more than a decade of 336 accumulated atmospheric tests together with all the resultant poison of lingering world-wide fall-out. It had also side-stepped our secretly developing the still poorly-understood neutron bomb, a device designed to kill everything within a certain diameter yet leave man-made structures intact. General Taylor had argued that it would be "more precise" but Jerome Wiesner, our science advisor, had pointed out that no one had answers as to what would happen not just to bio-diversity, but to the very basis of life itself: microbes, bacteria, even pathogens that could possibly survive and spread nonstop if the customary controls were eliminated.

This was a unique moment in time—indeed, in the history of the world. Mr. Kennerly possessed the power to decide in favor of economic cooperation while eschewing military domination. The President's decision to steer clear of any sort of large-scale military involvement in Southeast Asia could be viewed by the world as being respectfully even-handed rather than as turning our back on a valued ally.[9]

As a senator, he had stated way back in 1954: "I am frankly of the belief that no amount of American military assistance in Indochina can conquer an enemy which is everywhere and at the same time nowhere. We maintain that the Vietcong are a so-called 'enemy of the people' whereas, in reality, they have the sympathy and covert support of that very same people."

The same year that Kennerly made his trip to Indochina and uttered that statement, President Eisenhower had written a letter to the ruler of South Vietnam, President Diem, and affirmed support for that country with materiel and financial backing, but this was conditional on Diem's instituting reforms guaranteeing his people having a voice in their governance combined with democratic elections. Diem took the aid but ignored Ike's conditions.

Nearly a decade later, when dealing with his national security advisors and the Joint Chiefs of Staff, the now President Kennerly's opinions had not altered one iota. Nevertheless, he realized that the military generals now sought, in concert with the manufacturers of war materiel, a chance to show off their might and, more importantly, to get paid for doing so. What sacrifice was he willing to make should he thwart their strategies?

He recognized that our country was no longer bound by his predecessor's commitments because the conditions of our providing aid had been ignored by Diem. Accordingly, the President held a meeting of the Congressional leaders in the Oval Office in September. In no uncertain terms, he stated:

"I will not pursue a military action that wastes lives and resources merely to perpetuate the continued existence of our armed forces. Nor will I condone a pursuit that manipulates our foreign policy for the profit of defense subcontractors. War in and of itself resolves little, yet wastes much. During the months of my active duty, I witnessed the death of my fellow soldiers on almost a weekly basis; not all were due to enemy fire; some were due to accidental carelessness whether on or off duty. But we were always in the theater of combat.

"Throughout Europe and the entire physical context of the Second World War, we lost over three-quarters of a million young men to a conflict conceived by mankind's pursuit of power and self-aggrandizement at the expense of the many. Those brave Americans who died in the defense of freedom and self-determination might have become the leadership which, following war's end, our country urgently needed."

Pausing to look each of the powerful Congressmen in the eye, he stated flatly:

"During my service in the Pacific Theater, I reviewed in my head all that I had learned writing *While England Slept* and formulated an accurate understanding of the historical genesis of international conflict. Accordingly, it became my life's goal to do everything in my power to help prevent another war that could suck our country irretrievably into such a destructive vortex. Now, as President, I am in a position to do just that. This conflict in which we are presently taking part is of the making of the Vietnamese people; its resolution must be shouldered by them as well."

In conclusion, he affirmed:

"Each of you is present because you have real influence over the future course of our country. It is my fervent hope that all of you will support my changing our course in Southeast Asia. In three wars since 1916, we have lost a <u>preponderance of our youth</u> to someone else's greed and avarice and pride. I ask for your support, should events develop that historically would lead to a fourth declaration of war, to enable me to find a way to avoid such a declaration and to divert heated fervor in favor of finding peaceful solutions. We will furnish aid for the health of the indigenous people, but not troops for their destruction. This goal will be my guiding principal while I occupy this office, and it surely applies to the yawning quagmire facing us in Southeast Asia."

This president was known for being witty, charming, even disarming, but today he had been forceful and persuasive. Grating on Mr. Kennerly was the knowledge that an "advisor" in Vietnam meant that such soldier offered his expertise and training to the leaders of the South Vietnamese forces. This usually required that such serviceman be present during actual battles; therefore, he would be exposed to being shot, yet he carried no weapon. The rules of engagement disallowed his firing on an "enemy" soldier, even if it meant defending himself from being killed. Forty-five rangers had already perished in this far-flung, Pacific Rim country. The President was aware, and deeply perturbed by, the fact that such status meant these American advisors were mere targets in a shooting arcade.

"These men aren't advisors; they're sitting ducks!" I once heard him fume while pacing back and forth beneath the golden symbol of the embossed Seal of the United States in the Oval Office. "What we need is another negotiated settlement like we achieved in Laos where the factions come together under a neutralist coalition government."

Mr. Kennerly was thus at a tipping point, once again walking that fine line between doves and hawks. However, he still couldn't figure out how to execute a respectable withdrawal without undermining the confidence of our allies in the region. Since this was the direction in which he was leaning, he assigned Michael Forrestal to organize an in-depth study of our options: how do we withdraw our support for Diem's corrupt regime, but do so respectably?

Unexpectedly, Tran Le Xuan, the sexually striking but harshly vindictive wife of Diem's brother (known popularly as "Madame Nhu") provided the President with an exit path. Out of the blue in early October, she claimed she had learned that America's Central Intelligence Agency was planning to have her killed.

Her response came savagely over the airwaves for all Americans to hear: "Our soldiers should start killing every Yankee soldier stationed here for not supporting our suppression of widespread dissidence by Buddhists or any other persons we deem hostile to the GVN."

As if that wasn't enough, Diem's brother-in-law, as director of the strategic hamlet program, submitted a formal request to Washington that we withdraw our advisors not merely from that program, but from their country as well.

The Secretary of Defense, as directed by the President, immediately conveyed orders to the commander of our forces in Southeast Asia, General Eastmoreland, to prepare for the withdrawal of all combat troops and military advisors effective on the 30th of November, and to have all support and supply functions shut down by the beginning of February 1964. Robert McNamara then directed the Public Affairs Officer for the Defense Department, Arthur Sylvester, to go public with the news that the United States was folding up shop in South Vietnam. This action was so swift that not even National Security Advisory Memorandum 263, prepared in early October and describing the President's intentions to wind down operations in Vietnam, had envisioned such a fast timetable.

By the following March, the closest American military installation to South Vietnam was located in Japan. Moreover, our Secretary of State for Far Eastern Affairs, Roger Hilsman, was already in Hanoi preparing the groundwork for our sending a trade mission there to establish good working relationships with that country. I don't know the dollar value, but today we are enjoying active trade relations with that communist nation which are mutually profitable.

Samantha Narelle Kirkland

Notes

1. Fay, p. 7.
2. Pitts, p. 109.
3. from Caroline Kennedy, President of the John F. Kennedy Foundation, "Jacqueline Kennedy: The White House Years."
4. Talbot, pp. 47-51.
5. Talbot, p. 82.
6. Widmer, pp. 46, 50.
7. O'Donnell, p. 13.
8. Schlesinger, p. 148.
9. See Dallek, pp. 666-675, 710, for thoroughly detailed insights into the past.

CHAPTER NINETEEN

Quashing Squabbling

I am happy to address something that has been on my mind ever since that horrible day in Dallas. What I am referring to is the improvement in the training of Secret Service agents following the November 1963 incident. When the president is in front of a crowd, the agents are ever watchful for behavior that doesn't fit the moment. If a person is wearing an overcoat on a hot summer day, or just a shirt on a cold one, or he keeps his hands in his pockets as the president nears his position, such aberrations indicate a possible problem.

Anyone who stands out from the crowd will receive particular study. In reacting to a threat, it is vital that we watch the subject's hands; where they go or what they do tells the agent whether there is a threat which must be neutralized, quickly!

In my new role, the "danger" I would watch out for was the wrong word coming out of my President's mouth. Beginning January 2, 1964, I would become a student of a different sort as I undertook to study the administration's false starts and setbacks on domestic policy. Leonard O'Brien would be my prime advisor on matters stateside; I would have to befriend him, for I had much to learn about both electoral strategy and relations with legislators. The difficulty would be in finding my place alongside him without stepping on his elite, erudite toes.

The next day, Ken and I met with Leonard O'Brien, the administration's established whiz kid regarding legislative matters. President Kennerly had implied that if we were to get anything prepared for his signature, we'd have to have Lenny's help first. As I was the new man, Ken took pains to introduce me to ensure that the three of us could work together. It took Len a few days to adjust to my existence; why would a president who is so organized, clear thinking, and steeped in history need a fresh-faced former bodyguard who had never even sat through a session of Congress, much less worked on the preparation of a bill?

I couldn't tell him; I would have to show him.

I settled into my new job eagerly. I was there to keep the President from exposing himself not to physical danger, but to public embarrassment. I would be required to have the names and titles of everyone we encountered on a domestic trip at my fingertips and, where relevant, such man's contributions to the Democratic Party. Although the President was in his mid-forties, he exuded energy that appeared to be barely contained, like an atomic chain reaction just waiting for that one last atom to be added. In fact, he often allowed his young son Jon-Jon to freely crawl over, under, or even through his office furniture because the boy's vitality goaded him to keep striving despite the agony of his ongoing physical pain. Consequently, I soon realized that my main unspoken job, since I was not a longtime pal, would be to spot and then remove temptation. Once my President feasted his eyes on some pretty and became aroused, there'd be no stopping the man. If I could foresee the snake about to offer him the polished red apple, I could snatch it away before he got himself in hot water.

Along the way, I learned to identify on sight the various leaders in the domestic arenas with whom the president dealt almost daily. Detailing their preferences and "hot points" on a clip board, I'd have it ready for the President to scan quickly when he took yet another meeting with corporate, congressional, or self-interested citizens.

When the President was abroad, it would be up to the coruscating and able Sorensen to keep him on the straight and narrow path intellectually, avoiding untoward or insulting phrases during foreign speeches and ensuring that all diplomatic heads were properly complimented with praise. The arena of foreign relations is just another game, after all, though more dangerous.

We all had heard about the famous gaffe which the renowned General George Patton made when giving a speech, in French, to the assembled British, French, and American forces as the surrender of Germany began to look possible. He said we would all go forward united to resurrect the world from its ashes, but he didn't include our ally, Russia. This was a major slight, causing *bouleversement* throughout Eisenhower's staff and, together with his slapping a soldier on the helmet for shirking his duty, caused this skilled and brave general to be put-out-to-pasture until the breakout in the Ardennes led to his being recalled.

I was not about to let my President make any similar slip-ups. Since I was now part of the inside-team, I heard about how Mr. Jensen's nose had been bent out of shape over a seemingly trifling incident. Since he was the Attorney General, Bobby had been asked by the Vice-President to seek the appointment of Sarah Hughes to a Texas federal judgeship; in response, he was told she was, at 65 years old, unacceptable. After returning from a trip abroad, he found out that the appointment had gone through because Speaker of the House Sam Rayburn had used his own influence to see that she was appointed.

"I'm just keeping a seat warm in a thankless office with as much prestige as a pitcher of cold piss," he had lamented.[1]

Fortunately for all of us, and the good of the country as well, the President had plans for Lyndon which would elevate his lofty ego even further, but it is premature to discuss these here.

As the President had so succinctly imparted to me early on, "In my mind, I see the vast potentials of nuclear arms agreements, better race relations, even ending poverty here and abroad, but I can't run this office as though we live in a dream world. I must deal with statistics and realities as they present themselves at the moment; the daily challenges of providing practical solutions take all my time. To assist me, you must focus your energies accordingly."

The one difference the year 1964 bore was that it would be an election year. The President did not have to undertake his prior strategy of getting a head-start on his opponents by campaigning early on. Everyone in the country knew who he was and what he stood for. At some point during his time in office, he had visited the citizens in every continental state and met with the important Democratic Party leaders in each.

We'd enlist Franklin Delano Roosevelt, Jr. again to assist us because he had been such a help in 1960. Our final move would be to fly west to California during the last week of the campaign. With its large Electoral College count, we wanted to make an indelible impression.

Our President's call to follow his lead and support his various initiatives still needed more work, especially in the areas of civil rights and the treatment of miners. He was pleased with the way the tall

Texan had embraced responsibility for the space exploration program. Shouldering such duties had been a natural fit for the man; after all, the main control center was located in Houston. However, what the President really wanted to iron out was how he and Mr. Jensen would campaign as a team in the upcoming election.

They met in the Oval Office, a room designed to inspire even ordinary men to greatness. It has a welcoming fireplace hearth and French windows some twelve feet tall that let in ambient light, as though the entire world was looking in to see what decisions the President of the United States was making. Nearly eight yards wide by twelve yards long, one could almost be inspired to toss around a football in its interior. It is tranquil, luminous, and soundproof.[2]

It almost whispers: "Come, give us your best. This room is made for greatness of spirit and leadership!" The two men, one as leader and the other as standby, sat down facing one another.

"Lyndon, I want to get something straight with you as we start our swings down south this summer."

"Yes, Mr. President?" Mr. Jensen had innocently replied.

"Do you remember what you said to me while the election returns were being reported back in November 1960?"

Mr. Jensen couldn't and thus responded, "Why, no, Jack. What did I say?"

Mr. Kennerly drove his point home. "When I called you, you forthrightly stated that **we** had taken Pennsylvania, but then asked, 'What happened to **me** in Ohio?' We'll have no more of that! We are a team working for our mutual success. We stand together, or we fall. Do I make myself clear?"

"Yes, Mr. President. I am on board. You've got me hog-tied and ready to be branded! You need have no further worries on that score!"

"Good. Thank you, Lyndon. That's all I have for tonight. Get some rest. We'll start early tomorrow."

"Right you are, Mr. President. Sleep well!" With that affirmation, our presidential team retired for the night ready to take on the Coldwater challenge with all guns at the ready.

Almost immediately, it became clear that improvements in civil rights applicable to all Americans would be the single most important domestic goal for the immediate future. If we couldn't work out how to get along with one another nearly 200 years after our Constitution had been drafted, we'd have little influence in the international community when it came to dealing with oppressive regimes and the spread of communism's appeal to the oppressed peasants of the Third World. Already, Jack was being regarded as the savior of peace by having delivered America from being held hostage to nuclear war with the Soviet Union. His heartfelt speeches moved Europeans as no American president had before. Though he was a foreigner, his appeal to loftier principles of human conduct touched their souls; whatever the translation, he made them believe he was speaking truthfully.

The goal of reforming the tax code to encourage investment and reduce the burden on the wage earner had become the most pressing concern. A poll by Lou Harris had shown that Americans were two to one in favor of it, and an even higher ratio believed that it would be good for our economy. "Figures don't lie," Secretary McNamara (nicknamed the-numbers-man) would claim. Unfortunately, the economy in 1963 had performed statistically better than predicted, so a problem had thereby become an asset. Congress staunchly refused to address the idea of reforming the tax code when there was no recession.

True, the Council of Economic Advisors predicted 1964 would see slowdowns without a tax cut, but mere predictions traditionally held little weight with Congress.

Senator Robert Byrd chaired the Finance Committee. His fellow senators refused to countenance tax reductions in the absence of a commitment by the President to adhere to a balanced budget. That seemed logical to me as well, but I didn't run things. Moreover, that senator had not stayed abreast of the times; he had an idea that the budget should settle in at 100 billion dollars, period. Not even an extra million would be countenanced by him.

Unfortunately, this year was 1964, not 1864. That esteemed senator seemed to be living by a set of standards that were far outdated.

As things were to turn out, we would be able to tie the tax reduction bottleneck to the President's drive for equal rights and achieve passage of both despite the hectic schedule of 1964 being an election year. The ace-in-the-hole was, of course, the presidency-as-a-partnership which Jensen and Kennerly had formed in November. Mr. Kennerly's evaluation of Lyndon as a resource of immense skill who, simply by reason of his office, was being wastefully relegated to the sidelines had been correct. Over the coming months, I could be seen sitting behind either of these two great men but, in my mind, I was sitting up high, as though on a lifeguard's chair, looking out for anything that could cause either man to stumble.

Regardless, I spent most of 1964 and thereafter in abject admiration of Mr. Jensen's skill as a "doer," a man who walked the talk.

The primary focus of my job was never supposed to be the repair of interpersonal relations but, during the President's first term, there was one particular problem that was impeding the work of everyone. By 1964, this had become a full-fledged conflagration. I am referring to the intense discord between the President's brother, Robert, and Mr. Jensen as Vice-President.

Going all the way back to 1953, when Mr. Jensen was the preeminent and powerful Senate Majority Leader but young Robert was a fresh-faced staffer for his brother, the then Senator Kennerly, the two men had immediately developed a frosty relationship. Young Bobby had been way out-of-line. He should have behaved himself and deferred completely to the respected leader of the Senate. However, during their exchange arguing over the last remaining turkey sandwich in the cafeteria one day, Bobby's Irish temper got the better of him. He had stuck his neck in a noose by standing up to Mr. Jensen and, worse, calling him a "know-nothing cowpoke."

The lad was fresh out of Harvard University and thought he knew everything there was to know about running this country. Thereafter, their acquaintanceship remained strained until the presidential race of 1960.

Then it became really bad. Things became downright problematical for John Kennerly himself when he decided to ask Mr. Jensen to be his running mate. The night before the Democratic convention opened, his brother Bobby had met with Lyndon to try to get him to excuse himself altogether from the presidential race. As a result of this insult, the two men remained feuding throughout Jack's first term.

Within a few months of Jack's inauguration for his second term, it became clear that Bobby had his sights set on following in his brother's footsteps in 1968. He began throwing his weight around to a degree not warranted even by his status as Attorney General. Lyndon's patience finally ran out completely.

He confronted Mr. Kennerly with his concerns.

"Mr. President, thank you for seeing me today. I know your schedule is busier than a three-legged cat in a sandbox. There are visits by Wally Schirra and your science advisor, Jerome Weisner. Then there's the First Lady's reception for the Vienna Boys Choir later this evening. *Irregardless*, I have something I just have to get off my chest!"

Lyndon's face was so saddened by the serious nature of his complaint that he looked like a droop-eared dachshund whimpering for a bone.

"You know I value our partnership. The number of bills we have seen passed by the Congress since you and I began working together, with you proposing the goal and my shepherding the bill through passage will—I am certain—exceed that of any administration in history, excepting Franklin Roosevelt's terms, of course.

"Nevertheless, Mr. President, we have got to do something about the trouble that the Attorney General creates in our partnership. He keeps wanting to horn in, to be the key advisor to you, and to pick a fight with me at every phase, whether it's denying me credit for what I am able to effect, or simply bad-mouthing me behind my back. When he does, he sits there a-grinnin' just like a possum that's nabbed the coolin' berry pie from the window ledge. You know my staffers are very loyal to me. The majority have been with me for fifteen or twenty years. What they hear gets back to me without delay.

"Jack, I am asking you, face-to-face, for you to muzzle your brother somehow. No doubt you have heard that I referred to him recently as that 'snot-nosed little snob.' I apologize for that; you know me well enough to understand that sometimes my patience can run a little thin, but your brother makes my ass just twitch! I know people tend to fester with impatience as they pass fifty years of age; that occurs to virtually everyone. All of a sudden, a person is confronted with the inexorable march of time. There's no going back to correct your mistakes. If you're ever going to amount to anything, you have to work with what you've accomplished up to that point and go from there. As a result, you tend to become short-tempered with everyone because you can feel the demon, Time, stealing your future day-by-day.

"Accordingly, please accept my regret at having made that off-the-cuff remark. When I see the Attorney General himself, I will state my apology to him. In the meantime, however, Bobby remains a millstone around my neck, especially now that the beans are spilt, meaning I know he plans to follow your presidency and run himself in 1968. To give you a tool you can work with, I will tell you, in no uncertain terms, that I will not seek, nor will I accept, our party's nomination for president in 1968. If you and I successfully complete our terms, what we will have accomplished together will demonstrate that our two terms have been the most productive in the history of our country. We will be remembered as having acted on behalf of all Americans, no matter what their race, creed, or income level. You and I will go down in history as having genuinely improved the lives of our countrymen.

"I can't think of a better legacy. That will be all the satisfaction I need to retire from politics. *Having been good for all of our citizens...* Now, those are words I could roll on my tongue and savor until the day I die! Such an achievement will please Ladybird no end.

"But so long as young Robert makes it difficult for me, at every turn, to proceed as you and I wish, every day in this office will cause me to bear a bad taste in my mouth. I am asking you, man-to-man, to gag that brother of yours until we get past December 1968."

There was a pause as the President collected his thoughts. This was something to which he had given no thought during his years in office. Fractious infighting among his cabinet members did not interest him; after all, each of them was an adult and should be expected to control his personal feelings when it came to managing the country!

When he addressed Lyndon, Mr. Kennerly's voice was most sincere.

"Well, now, your request places me in a difficult position. Everyone knows that I rely on my brother as though he is my right hand. I'm the first to recognize that he has a passionate nature. He's very smart; he understands the ins-and-outs of the system and, perhaps for that very reason, he appears radical to others; however, he's only trying to find a better way. It's all too easy for him to perceive anyone who raises a red flag to that goal as being obstructionist.

"Unfortunately, I put so much thought and effort into campaigning, making speeches both domestically and internationally, as well as daily managing this office, that this friction you have raised has completely escaped my notice. Of course, I would not want such a problem of discord to exist at all, but you have caused me to confront its reality and, looking back over the last few years, I can see your point.

"Between you and me, let's deem this subject closed. I will speak to him; accordingly, you can consider that this matter has ended. Thank you for being so forthcoming, Lyndon."

The President rose from his comforting rocking chair with its aqua-colored arm rests and extended his hand warmly to Mr. Jensen, who likewise rose and held the President's hand in his firm, broad Texas grip.

The next day, the two brothers were scheduled to confer with Secretary of Labor Goldberg (who had replaced Willard Wirtz) and Secretary of the Treasury Douglas Dillon concerning racketeering and the problematic Jimmy Hoffa. The meeting concluded with the President directing the Treasury Department to subpoena Mr. Hoffa regarding unpaid taxes on income which he had failed to report.[3]

Afterwards, Mr. Kennerly took Bobby aside and said:

"Have you a few minutes? I want to talk with you privately."

Robert Kennerly had already packed his papers into his briefcase and was standing, fully prepared to leave, so he was taken a bit by surprise.

"Certainly, Jack. Should I call over to my assistant and let my office know I'll be delayed?"

"Heavens no! You and I can reach an agreement in short order, I suspect. Here, take your seat again."

After Bobby sat back down, Jack leaned forward in his rocking chair so he could speak quietly man-to-man.

"I want this friction between you and Lyndon to end with this conversation. He and I have been working together effectively ever since that attempted assassination in 1963. You and I will continue conferring when I need your advice, but otherwise steer clear of him, make no challenging remarks to his face or behind his back, and instruct your staff to work with members of his staff as professionals should. Do not obstruct, but rather try to facilitate his efforts regarding the Great Society. This is a matter about which he deeply cares. I for one strongly support him in these endeavors.

"In this way, you will not only assure that I leave a legacy of great accomplishment, but you will also be preparing the path if you decide to make your own run for higher office. To ease your mind, I can assure you that he has privately told me that the coming term will be his final in government."

He paused, but seeing that Bobby was still with him, he plunged into the crux of the matter.

"Lyndon plans to retire from politics in January 1969. After all, he'll be sixty years old in 1968; no one can blame him for wanting to enjoy the rest of his life as a private citizen. This is privileged information; you are not to repeat that to anyone, not even your wife Ethel, but you can carry it in your back pocket. You will be unopposed, I'm certain, for the Democratic nomination in November 1968."

The two brothers stood and the older one solemnly stated:

"Let's shake on this. I don't want to have to bother addressing this problem over the next few years. We are now, and must remain into the future, bound by our brotherhood and dedication to the cause of keeping our country safe."

His brother was genuinely moved. Bobby responded from his heart.

"This has been a lot to take in, but you have my word I will live up to your request. As long as you and I can confer as before, more as a sounding board of course rather than as a fellow policymaker, that will be fine with me. I love you, Jack, you know that, and everything I have ever done in politics has been done to facilitate your success."

"Good, I'm glad we are agreed on this. That's the end of it. Now get back over to your office and get to work on that Hoffa fiasco!"

The brothers shook hands warmly, clasping one another's forearms with their left hands, and got on with the day's work.

Ever since prepping at The Choate School, President Kennerly liked to surround himself with a cadre of close friends so he could thrive in the orb of their trust and allegiance. He carried this form of loyalty over to his advisors and associates during his time in Congress and all the way to his gaining the Presidency. The only sacrifice he asked of them was that they get along with one another.

When the Attorney General next encountered the Vice-President, they were both on their way to meet with their President. Bobby immediately seized the opportunity to make good on his promise to his older brother.

"Lyndon, let me take this moment to apologize personally for having referred to you as 'a son-of-a-bitch. It was spoken in the heat of some pressured crisis. I lost my head there for a moment."

"That's okay, son," replied Mr. Jensen. "And, I apologize for being one!"

This brought a chuckle from everyone present. At a stroke, we resumed working as a team.

In my own mind, however, I said, "Phew!" At this point in time, our government embodied two distinct aspects: the "political government" which came-and-went with each election turnover, and the "permanent government," those career employees who made up the bureaucracy and survived each election in place and, all too often, inhibited the impassioned, and thus far too progressive, reforms the "politicos" would try to foist on them. These career employees had neither the need nor the obligation to believe in the policies of the current administration. This was an entirely new factor blocking progressive reform which would exacerbate the Kennerly administration's problems with an already intransigent Congress.[4]

Notes

[1]   McDonald, pp. 8-9.
[2]   Manchester, p. 138.
[3]   Ultimately, he was convicted and sent to jail for conspiring to fix the jury in that tax case. See Caro, p. 577.
[4]   See Schlesinger, *Journals*, p. 164.

CHAPTER TWENTY

Civil Rights Apply Equally to All Americans

These changes were happening around this time:

Sale of Selectric typewriters for professional offices leads to the first MTST computer-driven reproduction of typed pages, thereby enabling fast preparation of legal documents as we become an ever more litigious society.

Postal zip codes are introduced, effecting computer-scanned speedier and more accurate mail delivery.

Johnny Carson hosts "The Tonight Show," making it fun to stay up late.

Weight Watchers helps millions cope with the ready availability of widespread fast food restaurants.

Valium is introduced to make taxes, traffic snarls, air pollution, and divorce bearable.

In order to understand the value of Kennerly's chief-executive partnership, it is important to remember that Vice-President Jensen had been the Majority Whip in the Senate before vying for higher office with John Kennerly. He had started as a page way back in the 1930's. As the sitting Vice-President, he was acquainted with each of the senators on a first-name basis. They had watched as he had effectively been a star performer and, as a result, taken on the top position. He knew them, they knew him, and he knew how they worked. Thus, as he began to collar individual senators in the hall or hold a scheduled conversation in his office, they understood it was only a matter of time before the Senate would end up going along with the tax cut and then the civil rights bill. That was how Jensen wanted it: first the cut, then the rights bill, in that order. Otherwise, the priorities would become mixed, meaning both submissions might go down the tumbler.

Here's how he did it. Initially, he went right to the main man, Senator Byrd, and had lunch with him where he made himself available to do the senator's bidding. Bills have a time deadline; if they are not brought up out of committee and sent to the floor for debate before the end of a two-year Congress, they die as a matter of procedure. Then the process must be renewed all over again when the renewed Congress resumes during the following January.

Jensen wanted to bypass that problem. "These propositions will neither languish as mere hostages to the calendar nor by imprisonment in committee!" he declared to me as we prepared for his meeting with "the power broker" Senator Harry Byrd. His prime focus would now be on that man. This stalwart southerner knew how to use the filibuster to prevent acceptance of a motion to bring a bill to the floor for debate. He could also start a filibuster against ending debate, thereby blocking an actual vote on the bill. Demand for cloture to defeat the filibuster always arose—the citizenry wanted action, not endless delay—but had never been successfully invoked: the votes were never there when needed. Business would be conducted by cries for withdrawal of whatever bill, such as Civil Rights, that was creating the logjam; once its sponsors had withdrawn the objectionable bill, business could proceed in a timely, orderly fashion. Of course, by that time the proposal that had been introduced—with such heartfelt good intentions—would have become mere typeface on some record that would forever be ignored.

That was the process the Congress had used to block most of Mr. Kennerly's domestic agenda submitted during his first term. On the other hand, he was formidable when it came to foreign relations. Indeed, he more or less kept this area as his private preserve. He would be the chief foreign policy maker and deliver the embodiment of his ideals personally through his speech-making and gracious entertaining at the White House. Merely conversing with a few key members and a committee chairman or two would get Congress as a whole aligned to his position.

True, the Bay of Pigs fiasco had been a blunder for which the President forthrightly shouldered the blame. This he did despite his learning that the C.I.A. had withheld its assessment that failure was inevitable. He learned from that mistake. Thereafter, he considered the opinions of military leaders and the C.I.A. as advice, but not dogma. As a result of being tested and formed in the fire of this international crucible, the President came to rely on his innate toughness. He maintained a calm, civil exterior to foster the demeanor of a reasonable statesman yet, beneath the charm, he was hard and steadfast. His father Joe might be known as tyrannical and ever ready to bully, but Jack never allowed himself to resort to such dogmatic posturing.

President Kennerly was passionate about domestic matters, but he was by no means a skilled parliamentarian. His ineffectiveness to win passage of the bills he submitted applied to even innocuous ones, such as federal aid to fund college loans and vocational training. Such had been stalled by a Congress bent on controlling this President. Numerous bills that he had shepherded through passage—classroom construction for all levels of schooling, Equal Pay Act (Senate Bill 1409, finally signed on June 10, 1963), social security increases, a farm bill, minimum wage increases, and manpower training legislation— had nevertheless been so watered-down that the final versions only resembled the original submissions. Sadly, the Area Redevelopment Program had passed, but no funding had been authorized. Programs to help disadvantaged youth combat their descent into delinquency, funds for improvements in urban mass transit, and the preservation of natural resources had all expired in committee without passage.

In frustrated anger, the President had paced the Oval Office after he heard about the latest stone-walling "up on the Hill" to his farm bill.

"Give Mother Nature a helping hand and she can feed a continent. But slit the throat of this golden goose and kiss plentiful crops goodbye," he vented.

These failures doomed many hopeful citizens to living a life in despair. All the motives and suggestions were worthy; there was not a political grab for power in any of them. And yet, it was just that exercise of powerful clout which led to such bills expiring without action. America may be intended to be the example of self-government for the rest of the world to admire and emulate, but we sure seem to have a difficult time getting out of our own way when it comes to providing a helping hand to our own fellow citizens.

President Kennerly himself addressed this issue when he said, "Time and the world do not stand still. Civil disobedience to protest equal civil rights no longer has a place in the America of today. Change is the law of life. And those who look only to the past or to the present are certain to miss the future. I would hate to resort to relying on what Joseph Goebbels observed back in 1942 when he noted: 'If you push an idea widely and frequently enough, people will adopt it as their own in the absence of a contrary viewpoint.' Nonetheless, I will insist on Americans changing their resistance to the concept of equality before the law!"

This explained why the President had so forthrightly partnered with his vice-president on the domestic agenda. Archaic, out-of-step prejudices that had relegated societal improvement bills to the dead-letter drawer were about to get a new lease on life. Enter the hard-driving persona of Lyndon Jensen.

Working primarily with Congressman Halleck, he succeeded in getting the bill out of the Rules Committee where the House passed it on February 10, 1964. When asked about the sudden turn of events, Mr. Jensen quipped that he did not think it appropriate that he, and several members of the House, sit around discussing Abraham Lincoln when the civil rights that Lincoln had held so dear were still locked up in committee.

He had Larry O'Brien alert the Senators that no other legislation would be submitted to them until this particular bill had been passed. This would label them a "do-nothing Congress" if they failed to act. Such a label does not carry well during election time. To obtain passage of the Civil Rights Bill, Jensen worked with Everett Dirksen to win over Republicans; he was so effective that only six opposed it. Interestingly, a future presidential contender, Barry Coldwater, was among those six. It would be necessary to prevent a Senate filibuster and overcome strong Southern resistance to guarantees of equal access to public accommodations and equal employment opportunity. Richard Russell tried to filibuster, but the liberals organized a 2/3 majority vote for cloture, so the bill passed intact. Jensen successfully forged southern congressmen into a partnership with this effort rather than make a stand against the rest of the nation.

He quipped: "100 years on from the Civil War, it is high time that we walk together." Mr. Jensen was not about to sit around waiting for another century to pass before seeing progress enshrined in law. He worked hand-in-hand with Everett Dirksen of Illinois to secure the support of the Republicans. He got Whitney Young and Roy Wilkins on board to rally their support behind Dirksen. It was important that the Republicans know that their support would offer them the best chance of fostering dignity and decency in this country. [1]

It was Abraham Lincoln who struck off the chains of black Americans, but it was Lyndon Jensen who at last led them into voting booths and gave them a handle on their own destiny. They would now be a true part of American political life.[2]

A politician speaks the words his audience wants to hear. A statesman, however, must **deliver** on his promises, aligning his words with his actions. President Kennerly was loved and valued because he acted on what he claimed to believe in was good for America. Jensen spoke of the relief of poverty and educational opportunity as part of a just distribution of rising income. However, having the wisdom to use the nation's burgeoning new wealth to enrich and elevate our standard of living, where leisure would be a welcome chance to build and reflect rather than a feared cause of boredom and ennui, would require some good speechmaking by both men.

Our cities must serve not only the needs of their occupants and the demands of commerce, but also the desire for convenience, the expression of beauty, and the facilitation of community-wide sharing. When citizens are **more concerned with the quality of their goals than with the quantity of their goods**, then the needs of the spirit can be realized. We will enter the new world with the hopes of mankind being consistent with the limitless faith in improving our possibilities. Such impetus has been a desired characteristic since the initial battles at Concord and Lexington.[3]

Around the middle of December of that year, the President gave an interview to several newsmen regarding his concerns over education in our country. With Mr. Sander Vanocur, he spoke unreservedly.

"Mr. President, much of your program still remains to be passed by the Congress. Will you need a second term to get such legislation passed?"

Mr. Kennerly's answer was heartfelt: "I can tell you with assurance that I am pleased with my administration's progress. Regarding improvements in our revised tax structure, the benefits of social security being extended to all those who, frankly, need it the most, changes to our welfare programs, redevelopment of the rundown portions of our cities, raising the minimum wage, and—internationally—the Peace Corps, Food for Peace program, the Alliance for Progress, and the Disarmament Agency, these have all improved the peace and prosperity of our nation.

"We still need to do more regarding our position on trade, but that will come as business leaders perceive the advantages of doing business abroad. What I have let slide, and I admit my failing here, is the matter of education. Secretary Ribicoff and Secretary Wirtz, as well as Secretary Goldberg, have each pointed out to me that, following the conclusion of the Second World War, we are faced with a burgeoning population that is seeing the greatest growth in young Americans in our history. We need more schools built right now than were built in the past century. With all the new demands for scientific knowledge that our endeavors in space will require, we need more doctoral candidates. Those students will need financial support, so scholarship programs must be made available. Our vocational programs need to be expanded in all counties; boys and girls who want to start to work while they are still in their teens must be prepared with technical skills.

The Vice-President listens attentively as the
President addresses reporters.

"The Peace Corps should be made an alternative to induction into the armed services. We especially need to focus attention and provide assistance to agriculture, both with affordable financing for new equipment and rural education opportunities regarding scientific improvements in farming. We are coming to the fore as the world's last resort for grain and corn and soybeans; our farmers must be up to the task, yet large families who stay on and work the land are becoming a thing of the past. We must empower the individual farmer to be more productive.

"I once read that Thomas Jefferson said, 'To expect the people to be ignorant and free is to expect what never was and never will be.' I concur." [4]

He continued. "Let me state clearly how important these considerations are to the future well-being of America. The two most destructive words in America are: 'I want.' This simple phrase can illustrate the rise and downfall of entire civilizations, from the Phoenicians through the Romans, and countless heads of state down the ensuing centuries. For Americans to achieve what each one wants, he or she must have the means to do so in their own manner and to their own ability. Education is the best tool they can wield. I intend to pursue the goal of providing those tools wholeheartedly if I am elected to a second term."

With his closing statement, we—as well as all the assembled reporters—remained silent. There was no arguing with his conclusion:

"There is no sense in having merely a shadow of success rather than substantive progress. We ought to do the best we can, as soon as we can, for our young people!"

As a telling jab at the opposition, Mr. Kennerly pointed out that the Republican Party is the party of Abraham Lincoln; they are proud of that fact, and therefore they must support the right of every citizen to enjoy equality under our Constitution. In his opinion, the members of this party needed to recommit themselves to the objective of equality for all our citizens.

The force of this sentiment erupted in my own household unexpectedly. Jack had wryly observed earlier that day how beauty can convey a sense of peace and tranquility wherever it might be encountered, unless, that is, it was possessed by a woman. So I became firmly in the hot seat when my own comely wife walked in on me hovering over a magazine spread fully across my lap. I was utterly absorbed in the full color layouts before me; I never heard her approach and was so taken by surprise that I couldn't help slapping the pages closed with guilt besmirching my entire mouth.

"Well! What have we here?" came the accusatory query. She would not yield, so I sheepishly opened the tinderbox to reveal a Technicolor spread of the latest Colt AR M-16 assault rifle prototype depicting all its deadly features in cut-a-way view. All the new-fangled operational gizmos were described in proud detail.

"For goodness sake, Clint, why can't you simply look at porn like all the other husbands!" my wife lamented as she turned in a huff, prepared to leave me to my private pleasures. Suddenly, she switched gears and started scolding: "You are aware, I am sure, Clint, that women were severely downtrodden at the turn of the century. We didn't even have the right to vote. We've come a long way since then. However, even today we are paid at a lower wage-tier, we do not have access to top management positions, we are ignored when college scholarships are handed out, and people still say the purpose of our being on this earth is to have babies and stay at home caring for them. The prejudices with which Indian, Negroes, and I suppose even Latinos have to deal are perhaps different in kind from those we women have to deal with, but they're no less important in scope and effect.

"Now, we have been blessed with two sons who are growing up in a loving, stable household. It is my hope that the world will be more cognizant of the rightful place of women when they are old enough to go to work, vote, and choose higher education."

She paused, looking at me haughtily. She had stated her case rather well, she thought, so she relaxed.

Meanwhile, I was flabbergasted. "Ah," was all that escaped my mouth. I'd never thought of discrimination as applying to members of my own household. I pictured my two boys, one with bright green eyes but both with dark hair that would probably match mine as they matured, and I imagined a future where true equality of opportunity would govern their world. Would they get into college? Would there be athletic teams at all, or would such funding evaporate in favor of dress-making and home decorating classes? I then made a big mistake. I opened my mouth to express my thoughts.

"I...I've never considered discrimination as applying to members of my own family..."

"Well, start doing so!"

The full import of reality was now staring me in the face. I had always equated discrimination, prejudice, even the denial of rights as existing in other countries—the Middle East, parts of Africa, even regions such as Burma, but to my own household...? This was a lot to take in.

"Blatant inequality," intoned Gail sashaying down the hall. She had finished my thought.

"Yes, I can see that." I called after her. I rose and followed her into the kitchen and presented myself astride the soiled plates calling out for attention in the sink. I realized I had always assumed that my wife would be the one to make them sparkle with cleanliness again. I started to mumble, "In America; we are founded on the principle of freedom, equally given, to all citizens..."

Gail continued looking at me steadily, waiting for me to stumble toward some point.

Yet there the truth lay, angrily exposed, demanding acknowledgment. Of course, there are places on this earth where the denial of rights is fostered, but such must never be applied here, in America, and certainly not in my own household. As my palpitating heart slowed and I regained my composure, I moved across to where Gail was sitting and raised her from her chair.

Holding her so she could look deeply into my eyes, I confirmed, "I shall always put you before myself. Never let anything slide; if something bothers you, come to me and we'll work it out."

She kissed me but then pulled away.

She murmured, "By the way, you're doing the dishes tonight."

What had I done to myself? If peace was to exist in our home, equal opportunity in our household would have to become the norm. I rolled up my sleeves, tied the apron around my waist, and got to work. Thankfully, after a few minutes, when she was certain I had learned my lesson, my wife came and stood by my side. Together, we finished the washing and drying, content to work, play, and love as a team.[5]

Notes

[1] Kearns, pp. 192-4.
[2] Caro, p. 569.
[3] Kearns, pp. 210-212.
[4] Lieberson, pp. 176-177.
[5] During June, 1963 the President signed the Equal Pay Act into law establishing parity of pay without regard to sex.

CHAPTER TWENTY-ONE

Lyndon in Action

The Vice-President took me aside one day to speak to me privately.

"Clint, you must always keep in mind that in Congress, a member will rise and speak for a half-an-hour without saying anything meaningful; probably, no one will be listening anyway. When the gavel bangs, I'll be dang-burned if they don't all start squabbling amongst themselves. I'd sooner sit on a fence and watch hogs fightin' over slop. Such speech-struttin' simply causes the speaker to open his mouth and insert his foot, causing him to trip and have an embarrassing fall from his perch. One-on-one; that's how you convince people!"

His approach to getting a bill passed was tri-fold. He focused on the various senators who had a stake in the matter, whether through chairmanship or sponsorship. He would bring the pressure of the public to bear; additionally, he would be sure to gain the support of special interest groups because these people would most likely attract the attention of the newspapers. In the 1960's, the force of the media properly manipulated would have much to do with whether a bill got to the floor for debate and ultimate passage. The power of television to convey who was and who wasn't doing their job on behalf of their constituents carried great weight with Congressmen.

As I watched Mr. Jensen perform over the ensuing months, I had to admit he was as good as his word. He was most effective in face-to-face showdowns. However, he also knew that Congressmen do not serve at the pleasure of their President. This independence gives their opinions greater import since there will be no need for them to smooth the ruffled feathers of their president's ego. Nevertheless, their own egos will ever require constant input and soothing to keep them involved and abreast of a bill's progress.

Mr. Jensen pointed out that his decades of experience as a legislator had taught him that guiding a bill from proposal through passage is far from mechanical a process; rather, the process is fluid, dynamic and, most importantly, unpredictable. He was the right man for this job. He was skillful in organizing and maneuvering both the politics and the personalities which, particularly on the matter of civil rights, were complex. As an advisor, I couldn't help admiring his strategies for success.

Some issues resist fading away because they are too vital to the people affected. So it is with civil rights, a fact that was to become all too clear during 1963. Way back on Sept. 27, 1940, Mr. A. Phillip Randolph—representing the Brotherhood of Railway Porters—had argued with Franklin Roosevelt for better treatment of Negroes. He was still pushing this same platform in 1963. The Armed Forces had been integrated and problems in Little Rock resolved by that time, and Jensen had achieved two small improvements during the 1950's, but no one could claim that all citizens were equal either before the law or in educational and employment opportunity. This applied as well to women, native Indians, Mexicans, and people of Far Eastern ancestry. Jew, Catholic, Baptist, Protestant, Mormon, or agnostic were all equal if you were a white male, but that was about as far as our Constitution had been realized in January of 1963, despite its being "color-blind."

As this year dawned, the most vocal of the various deprived minorities in our country had begun to find its voice. The Southerners' solid resistance to Negroes becoming full citizens was long held and aggressively demonstrated through lynching. Robert Kennerly was warning the President of coming violence in the Birmingham community following on the heels of the prior year's riots in Montgomery. To get their point across, the demonstrators were between a rock and a hard place. If they assembled and marched peacefully, a license to do so would be withheld so the group could lawfully be jailed for interfering with commerce. If they rioted, or even merely picketed in the streets, they would be arrested for civil disobedience. They had no one to whom they could go to settle, or indeed even to air, their complaints. The frustration and resulting despair had built over decades. Now, it was a powder keg primed to blow.

The abuse of the Negro had lasted for so long that even the violence advocated by the Black Muslims was gaining appeal. On the other hand, if the government would demonstrate support for their struggle, and friendship in meeting their drive for equality, that would be a strong argument in favor of restraint. Mr. Kennerly decided to send the Assistant Attorney General for Civil Rights, Burke Marshall, down there in person to prove that your Government is not merely listening, but is in fact prepared to oversee change. He would talk to local business leaders about hiring clerks without discriminating.

The President had learned his lesson from a conversation with C. Cheysson, a French diplomat whom Ben Bradlee had introduced. The two men had spoken about Africa, but the point had been made that sending a Negro there as America's ambassador would tend to insult rather than gratify rulers of these emerging nations.

"He listens very well, better than anyone with whom I have ever spoken," remarked Monsieur Cheysson when their friendly chat concluded. He had argued that African leaders would expect to be treated on a par with Italians, etc. regarding our posting ambassadors to that continent.

In the matter of civil rights, it was White America which would have to change, so a member of Kennerly's astute legal circle would be the man assigned to effect such change. C. Douglas Dillon proceeded to contact the various owners of the chain stores with the authority of his being the Secretary of the Treasury. He'd point out that the Federal Government has had race-blind hiring in place for some time. His verbiage would be accompanied by the deployment of federal troops who were prepared to keep order during the long hot summer nights. With this background, change—such as service in public restaurant— could proceed calmly and by the cooler weather in the fall, the chance of angry flare-ups due to deprivations would have become a thing of the past.

This was all well and good, but the President's missions were met with the decision by the store owners to comply so long as someone else took the lead. No one wanted to take the heat of seeming to independently go ahead with such huge changes in their community. Meanwhile, Dr. Martin L. King was preparing more demonstrations.

Dr. King challenged not just residents of Alabama. He challenged the entire nation when he said, "Show me one of my people holding the position of sales clerk, or of produce manager, or even night supervisor of the local theatre. That will be progress. Verbal agreements of compliance are just more of the same empty rhetoric. We Negroes are members of American society and we can do more than push brooms and empty trash baskets. We do not want to hear oral agreements; we want results, and we want them now!"

Mr. Kennerly took Lyndon aside one day and lamented, "I feel like a Wind-talker from the Second World War when I confer with these Dixie leaders. All my exhortations and attempts at shaming them simply evaporate on the breeze without any effect. They act as though they can't comprehend English. See if you can get them to come around!"

With a pat on the broad back of the Texan, the President sent the former Senate Majority Whip on his way. Vice-President Jensen used his vast political wisdom and experiences to approach the civil rights issue as something important upon which to take a moral stand. He would crusade for a value fundamental to the American idea. He lent his considerable influence to the unqualified expression of faith in the righteousness of the cause. Civil rights raised issues of fundamental ethical and moral dilemmas; he was determined to make it America's great moral crusade.

Thereafter, with the atmosphere surrounding the issue of civil rights becoming highly charged, the following men met to finalize plans for an idea that was a stroke of genius:

> Floyd McKissick as chairman of Congress on Racial Equality,
> Whitney Young Jr. as president of the National Urban League,
> John Lewis representing the Southern Negro Christian Conference,
> Mathew Ahmann for the National Catholic Conference for Interracial Justice,
> Rabbi Joachim Prinz as president of the American Jewish Congress,
> Reverend E. C. Blake as president of the National Council of Churches of Christ,
> A. P. Randolph, now president of the Negro American Labor Council, and
> Roy Wilkins and M. L. King, Jr. with the NAACP (founded 1909).

All of these distinguished gentlemen met with the President, Vice-President Jensen, Walter Reuther as president of the UAW, and the Secretary of Labor. They planned the logistics and security for an enormous march on Washington to show solidarity among all races in this country. When it occurred, it showcased one of the greatest comings-together of diverse elements of our society, gave hope that change would now surely take place, and set the stage for effective maneuvering by Mr. Jensen.

Mr. Jensen knew the real solutions lay with changing our laws. Statements of lofty principles were insufficient; our citizens needed enforcement of rules equipped with the teeth to produce equality without further delay. When dealing with telling the citizenry how to conduct themselves, this question always comes up: how far can the federal government go when regulating behavior, especially since many people perceive that *any* governmental action degrades their private lives. It's the great debate between enabling, versus restricting, individual liberties when legislation promoting equal opportunity is put forth.

This was why he had focused on wooing Senator Byrd to get the tax reduction bill passed promptly; once that was a done deal, then attention could be focused on the Civil Rights Bill. True, Richard Russell (D-GA) intended on blocking any sort of progress on a bill extending civil rights to members of the Negro community, but the true "keeper of the flame" was Senator Byrd.

He began by making a telephone call to George Smathers (Fl) with whom Lyndon had worked closely while he was Majority Leader. Smathers could analyze figures as perceptively as Robert McNamara and now held the position of Chairman of the Senate Democratic Campaign Committee. What he relayed to the Vice-President was not good news.

I noted to him later that he had done little more than acknowledge what was said by Senator Smathers. Since he was now in a peeved mood anyway, he turned to me and rasped, "You don't learn nothin' when you're doin' the talking!"

Obviously, his mind was still mulling over the conversation, but there was no point to pursuing further talk without thought.

The key item of which Mr. Jensen took note was Byrd's almost fanatical attachment to a ceiling of $100 billion dollars on the federal budget. A mere $50,000 over that and he would clamp down hard and not allow the bill to proceed to the floor of the Senate for a vote. Then the President had tried an end run around Byrd's committee, which resulted in a major fumble and further increased Harry Byrd's staunch objection. Since he chaired the Senate Finance Committee, what he said or did guided everyone else.

Jensen collared the reporter Walter Heller and confirmed that he was in the middle of a battle between conservatives who opposed deficit spending and governmental expansion into people's lives, and the liberals who saw the tax cut as putting more money in peoples' pockets. This would stimulate the economy and thereby increase tax revenues, making the planned budget deficit a stimulus, rather than a prelude to raising interest rates to stem the resulting inflation.

"I'm a New Dealer aligned with the policies of F.D.R.; if anything, President Kennerly is too conservative for my tastes. So you tell Galbraith and Schlesinger that is actually the case," he growled as he jabbed a long finger into Walter Heller's chest to emphasize his point. "Our administration is not going to give in to the economic bloc. We're going to increase the productive power of this country's industrial might! We're going to turn the ideals of the New Deal into reality!"

Now he could start to deal with the situation as it actually existed on Capitol Hill, not what the President naively imagined it to be. During his first term, Congress had been so successful in blocking legislative action on the many bills Mr. Kennerly had submitted to improve society that they now felt emboldened to contest anything the President might send their way for approval.

"They've got the bit in their teeth and are ready to pull for all they're worth," observed the Vice-President to me. "And they won't be pulling in the direction we want to go!"

Therefore, he had to confront the problem piecemeal, get a little bit here, a little bit there, so the entire tax-cut pie would eventually be available for a vote. Mr. Jensen latched onto the sale of wheat that had come up as the Mundt Bill. Mr. Jensen saw that the vote on this matter would have larger implications. He allowed Leonard O'Brien to attend to other matters and proceeded to handle this situation himself. He knew that the bill had many supporters, but the leaders did not know what the count was or which senators had to be turned around; however, knowing such information and conversing with these men in a manner to sway them to his position was something Mr. Jensen excelled at. He possessed a gift for sensing the moment when debate in the Senate could be turned in the direction he wanted; moreover, he had the fortitude to seize on that moment to launch the maneuvers that would turn them to his point of view.

After all, the President had paid him just this compliment during their heart-to-heart talk following the assassination attempt back in November 1963.

Another asset he possessed was his collegiality with many of the country's governors, such as William Scranton of Pennsylvania, John Reynolds of Wisconsin, Karl Rolvaag of Minnesota, and Pat Brown of California. Relishing a moment of epiphany, he decided to put pressure on them to turn their individual state's senators around. He made sure reporters were present so his remarks would be part of the nation's news the next morning. That would alert all the nation's governors to start pressuring their own Congressmen.

He used the same basic message for each of the senators he collared:

> "We live under a system of checks and balances. However, Congress has improperly exercised its power to prevent this President's programs from moving forward right from the get-go. Even as we sit talking this November, we are mere weeks away from adjourning for the holidays, yet we still do not have approval of those appropriations bills that are necessary to keep our government running! The space program is growing and needing more funding than it got last year, and you **know** our defense budget has to keep pace in order to contain the threat of communism. So your chief executive has simply got to have some cooperation regarding the budget. Each of you is a great patriot! No single party has an exclusive hold on patriotism!

> "We have to meet the problems of inequality, of poverty, and the resulting unemployment. These failures are far too prevalent in this great land of opportunity. I want each of you to confer with your congressional delegations and get them on board. The best way to address these problems is something the Congress is holding up: passage of the tax bill introduced by the President eight months ago! It will stimulate more investment and raise the level of employment and put money in the pockets of our citizens as never before, and that will produce more revenue for your national government. This has become a matter of serious urgency!

"Do not let me hear you say down the line, 'All we have would we gladly have given in order to improve the lives of our fellow citizens, but we let the chance slip by.' Act now: the time is ripe for the full realization of civil rights for all Americans."

He left us listeners breathless. The feeling in the room was that our country was unusually blessed. We had two men who shared the highest office in the land, one adept at foreign relations, the other at domestic problems; our nation could only benefit from this serendipitous partnership.

Mr. Jensen then tackled what he knew would be a tough nut to crack. He got cozy with Ted Sorensen.

"I know you are Mr. Kennerly's right-hand man when it comes to writing speeches. Since he and I are working together on domestic issues, I surely would appreciate your helping me draw the threads together on these programs. With my Southern approach to speech-making, your input would surely improve my chances of reaching people when I give a speech."

This required some soul-searching by Mr. Sorensen. I couldn't help him; Ted had to thrash this matter through for himself. It was well known that he despised Mr. Jensen.

"He's a man of hyperbole and hypocrisy," he'd state with conviction from time to time, as though to assure us that he had not changed his opinion.

In contrast, Mr. Kennerly was the living embodiment of the precepts and tenets espoused in the speeches drafted by Mr. Sorensen. After talking over Mr. Jensen's request with the President, a man for whom he had been writing speeches since Mr. Kennerly's days in the Senate, he acquiesced. At this time of great need, his making himself available to Mr. Jensen would be the right thing to do for the good of the country.

At this point, Mr. Jensen had his mission, his strategy, and someone who could express in words what he was thinking. He would take on Richard Russell by appealing to his patriotism. As staunch a segregationist as there could ever be, Senator Russell was nevertheless a loyal American whom other southern senators followed wherever he led. He reminded Mr. Russell that his support had made Mr. Jensen effective as a young senator and such skill had landed him the Vice-Presidency. He needed his mentor to now follow where he was leading.

Then he evoked this thunderclap: "Mr. Senator, you never turned your country down before today. Let's not fall out over ensuring every American has the full use and access to those rights guaranteed him under our Constitution."

With a sigh, the famous man said he would do as Mr. Jensen asked when it came time to vote on the Civil Rights Bill.

In a conversation with the Secretary of Agriculture, Orville Freeman, a few days later, he opined, "Lyndon will twist your arm off at the socket without you being aware he even has a grip on you, and then, once he's holding your arm in the air, will beat you about the head with it until you come around to his position."

Now Mr. Jensen was ready to take on Senator Byrd. He would start with tax reduction. The key would be to soften that man's staunch resistance to everything Mr. Jensen was going to say; therefore, the Vice-President would let the senator do all the talking. At first, that is. He would begin with his classic handshake: firmly hold the "mark's" hand beyond the customary time while smiling and telling Mr. Byrd that he had come to do the man's bidding. He would establish rapport with the physical connection of this prolonged handshake.

Mr. Jensen was a parliamentary tactician to his core. Among his bag of tricks and treats, there rested a cunning and resolve that lent his argumentative skills a special magic. His opponents could sense that he would be a dangerous man to cross. As he entered Senator Byrd's office, he wanted to work into the conversation a paraphrase of Churchill's commentary on the British Air Force during the opening years of the Battle of Britain.

"No men have ever done so much for so many in such a short period."

Taking hold of Harry Byrd's wrist, Mr. Jensen looked him in the eyes and affirmed, "Harry, by God, those words can apply to you. It's high time you stood up for what is right here in America and bury the hatchet of segregation forever."

Mr. Jensen was not going to let his reputation as "the greatest salesman one-on-one to have ever come down the pike" stop with this single exhortation. He was skilled at getting a person to do something that he was in fact determined not to do. He pressed his case. He would have one of his polite aides ask around to see how the various senators were going to vote and then relay the information to Mr. Byrd without being asked. He knew that the senator had passed 70 years of age and was no doubt being bothered by a sense of being out of touch. A deteriorating performance would lead to a deeply feared sense of humiliation. Jensen offered Gerry Siegel as an assistant to prepare drafts asking for the senator's suggestions. He would personally ask for Mr. Byrd's advice on some problem. This made the man feel useful as an elder statesman of high value.

Lyndon understood one key truth: older men enjoy deference. The more powerful a senator is, the greater his enjoyment of a person who is respectful and expresses gratitude for the wisdom he dispenses.

Gradually, Mr. Jensen swayed the Senator. When Mr. Byrd was eating out of his hand, he arranged for a luncheon during the first week of December. A personal tour of the White House was followed by his favorite sort of lunch: potato soup with a simple Southern salad. As they both leaned back wiping their mouths with satisfaction after the meal, the Vice-President leaned over and handed him a written budget that came in under $100 billion. Lyndon took great pains to ensure that this Senator felt well-respected, both as a man of distinctive lineage and as the locus of power in the Senate. He also pointed out that the federal government had taken the lead in economizing; their total payroll would hold fewer people than had last year's budget. He added that he had worked especially hard on the Secretary of Agriculture, who wanted large increases in personnel to handle the increasing workload, and Postmaster General Gronouski, who had likewise perilously inflated his personnel requests.

"I made these sacrifices, so you can rest easy with the proposed budget. You can be certain that we have fulfilled one of your most dearly held objectives: to keep government spending under control." Lyndon had sat back and watched as Mr. Byrd's eyebrows had risen. He had heard the compliment and Mr. Jensen's words had indeed gratified him.

The Senator had replied, "We can do some business." While this was somewhat vague, Mr. Jensen took it as a sign of progress and, indeed, within a few days the senator disposed of some thirty amendments and released the tax bill from his committee. Doing so required close attention by Secretary of the Treasury Dillon and the other Democratic members of the Finance Committee to shoot down entangling amendments, but success was in hand.

In fact, Senator Byrd had appended a message when the bill reached the Senate floor and was approved on March 29: "To John and Lyndon—I was happy to cooperate."

In the main, the Vice-President had persuaded the Senator to subordinate his desire to stall the tax cut bill in favor of realizing the grand aim of his public life: to control governmental profligacy. Later, behind the scenes, various appropriations were made to cover the many administrative departments that were howling over their constrained finances. Senator Byrd was not brought into the loop when these were doled out, but committee heads such as Hale Boggs, Carl Albert, Wilbur Mills, and even John McCormack were.

The Vice-President had observed, "You have to spread the largess around a little so that everyone feels they contributed something important to the thing."

It was now time to bring the civil rights fray to a conclusion. Due to the December break, hearings on this matter would await the January reconvening. Here the Vice-President displayed his mastery of procedure. Passage of this landmark legislation would surely be blocked by the gaggle of southern politicians except for a procedure little used. A Discharge Petition would be a resolution signed by a majority of Representatives to discharge the Rules Committee from its control of this bill and send it directly to the floor for debate. Mr. Jensen skillfully couched a vote against the petition not just as a matter of procedure, but as a vote against civil rights for all Americans, something that would not sit well politically.

"Let's do this now because it is the correct thing to do!" stated the Vice-President authoritatively.

Even Mr. Kennerly weighed in, making a television appearance during which he called for all men of good conscience to step up and extend civil liberties guaranteed under our Constitution to all Americans. These were matters of basic principles, principles of fair dealing upon which our very Constitution was founded, after all.

Mr. Kennerly and Dr. King saw eye-to-eye and had done so for some time. Way back when Jack was still a senator and coping with extremely close polling vis-à-vis Richard Nixy, the Rev. M. L. King, Jr. was jailed by a judge in Georgia for attempting to get service at the Magnolia Room in Rich's Department Store. Jack called Coretta and expressed his concern and to console her, especially since she was pregnant, and volunteered his help. His brother Bobby telephoned the judge who had ordered King jailed, and that very night King was released on bail. This American would not die martyred in prison.

Negro political leaders everywhere began removing their Nixy buttons in favor of ones that said: "Let's lick Dick!"

Jack's aides seized the moment and got two black ministers to write a pamphlet extolling how the affair was handled. The "Case of Martin Luther King" quickly reached black churches in the South. This publication moved sufficient numbers from the party of Lincoln to that of Kennerly to enable him to squeak by and become president with a plurality of less than 120,000 votes.

Jack and Martin each owed the other their loyalty for life. This fealty moved Jack as President to state:

> "At present, and for some two hundred years prior, we have been the disappointed hope of the world. Each of our citizens is entitled to be treated as he would wish for himself as well as for members of his family. In this decade, we have undertaken to land men on the moon, but right here at home, it is time for every American to be able to enjoy the privileges of being a citizen. It is time we righted our grievous mistake and acted according to the tenets of our Bill of Rights; thereby, we will be restored to being the envy of the world!

"I call upon every citizen to consummate this ideal for the nation as his solemn duty," stated President Kennerly with great dignity. Then he added the sentence that could be singled out as having motivated his entire conduct while in office: "This country values and cherishes its citizens; therefore, **there is no difference between the person and the principle**."

He admired Dr. King's extraordinary forbearance in the face of violence and challenges to peaceful assembly.

"Justice delayed is better than no justice at all," Dr. King would quip in response to being jested for his promotion of peaceful protest with sit-ins.

As these men brandished the saber of civil rights as being applicable to everyone, they devised fresh, bold ideas likely to advance the national well-being, focusing their speechmaking on the shortcomings of our constitutional society more clearly than anyone had done before.

Mr. Jensen stated: "The Democratic Party has always emphasized human values and ideals. The time is right for a great moral crusade; indeed, our country is uniquely suited to lead the charge. What we do here today should be evident to all that it is morally the right thing to do for our citizens."

Even as Mr. Jensen won over senators, Mr. Kennerly was thinking beyond our borders with the intent to lead our country forward as an exemplification to the world of the value of our principles. He'd meet with foreign ministers and ambassadors from all over the globe promoting our values.

Privately, he'd quip, "The world is like a checkerboard, with all the various countries positioned as black or white squares sitting there, just waiting to be won over by our example."

Looking back, I suddenly realized that the President was now simply restating what he had seen so presciently back in 1960. He had pointed out that the world was in a state of uneasiness, where despite the conclusion of two horrifying wars, there remained much undone that still needed doing. He saw that our influence as a nation was slipping beneath the overwhelming weight of hard-driving communism, but he was ready to undertake the challenge to reverse the decline and rally us to his shining prospective causes.

What drove him was at heart a very simple affirmation: "If God has a place for me to fill in this world, I believe I am ready to fulfill His faith in me."

That stated the challenge pretty well, but it would be up to Mr. Jensen to effect passage of any sort of bill advocating civil rights. The two proposed in 1957 and 1960 had been merely *pro forma* rather than effecting substantive change. By this time, however, the man had proved himself canny enough to transform passion into passage. He assembled the Negro men of distinction earlier listed and told them the Discharge Petition still lacked sufficient signatures to pass, and then he listed the legislators in their various districts who had not yet signed. Those men could see that Mr. Jensen was "committed to their struggle with an inner fire that welled up from deep within him," as one observer noted.

"We could all see that only the successful enactment of the Civil Rights bill into law during 1964 would quench the heat of his inner drive," stated Mr. Young, a man who bore his own set of convictions on his sleeve.

Mr. Wilkins, while saying goodbye to the Vice-President, said, "Sir, please have a Merry Christmas, and take care of yourself."

"I'm going to, don't you worry none," came the fervent reply.

Then Mr. Wilkins stated, "Please provide for yourself, Mr. Vice-President. Attend to your own health. We need you. You are a doer!"

Lyndon smiled quietly to himself. No one could have given him a better Christmas present than this accolade. On the other hand, no one needed to remind him that he had already suffered, but then recovered from, a serious heart attack while serving in the Senate.

As a former majority leader of the Senate, Mr. Jensen knew full well that compromise had always been a key strategy in southern bloc strategies. Besides, the Senate by its very nature was a deliberative body; the very rules by which they governed themselves fostered delay as a defense tactic. Time had always been their ally. Working out amendments and resulting compromises required lengthy debate, either on the floor or behind the scene in private rooms, bars, or an occasional street corner late into the night.

The men who by seniority or deferment were in control liked to call their strategy not merely time-consuming, but month-consuming as well! The typical bill failed because discussion on it had come up against Christmas or some such break, which meant the discourse would have to start all over again when Congress reconvened. Prior to 1964, bills other than Congressional pay increases and war declarations were hard to pass. Thereafter, the wise and experienced approach of Lyndon Jensen would help win the day.

Challenges in formulating equal opportunity for our own citizens had the unique pressure of living up to our Constitution while doing so in the glass house of countries around the world watching our struggle. Trying to alter our nation's viewpoint on civil rights would be tough in the House, but that challenge would be dwarfed by our trying to get changes passed by the Senate. In that body, the procedural rules allowed a sitting member to filibuster any attempt to transform the "status quo."

The President wanted to end discrimination in public places, whether for serving food or lodging. That would follow in the footprints of the Fair Employment Practices Commission which had been set up in 1961. The business communities in the South were in an uproar as to both; no northern lackey was going to show them how to run things when they'd been doing it successfully long before the Constitution had ever been enacted.

Ensuring that all citizens enjoyed full civil rights had seen insignificant progress during the late 1950's. What made things different now included the successful peaceful demonstrations being led by the Congress on Racial Equality and the eloquent words, both written and spoken, of Dr. Martin Luther King, Jr., head of the Southern Christian Leadership Conference. The unique attribute of the demonstrations promoted by these groups was not merely that they were conducted in a peaceful, respectable nature; they also displayed assurance that this country held the world's best hope of equality for the individual. Respecting a man for his potential to contribute to society, rather than be relegated to some secondary status by reason of creed or color, was for them the fundamental premise of America's founding.

A further iron in the smoldering cauldron of civil unrest came via, by then, a widespread medium. The crude and cruel handling of peaceful marches by Southern governors had been displayed on national television, arousing otherwise apathetic Americans to the ongoing injustices in their own country.

As the President noted, "Bull Connor's police dogs did more to bring the plight of the Negroes' inequality to the fore than any other event in our history. Those dogs awakened our collective conscience."

He capitalized on this new-found concern in a television address on June 11, 1963.

"We all recognize that not every child has either equal ability or equal motivation, but they should each have the equal chance to develop their talent and ability in concert with their motivation to make something of themselves. The Negro community must be responsible and follow the law, but they have the right to expect that the law will be fair, that the Constitution will be color-blind. This is a matter which concerns this country and what it stands for. I ask for the support of all our citizenry in righting this wrong."

Other moves for progress included the Negro Robert C. Weaver being appointed as administrator of the Housing and Home Finance Agency with the acquiescence of southern Democrats. Discrimination in public housing could begin to end. The Supreme Court had mandated desegregation in public schools and the integration of municipal bus systems in several southern states. Lyndon Jensen had been the Senate majority leader prior to being elected as Vice-President, and his effect on his former colleagues was still palpable; he proved to be a capable ally to our President. These factors cumulatively made changes in co-existence among our different races not merely desirable, but also mutually beneficial.

Nevertheless, congressmen who called themselves Southerners still held fast to the long-held prejudices of the districts they represented. It became the job of Leonard and me to soften them up so the gentle urging by the President and the more aggressive arm-twisting of the vice-president would have an effect. Mr. Kennerly opened the campaign by pointing out his early commitment to equal opportunity for all. The establishment, in March 1961, of the Committee on Equal Employment Opportunity now endorsed equal consideration standards for hiring federal workers. It was also empowered to deny federal contracts to businesses that denied equal hiring consideration regarding Native Americans and Negroes.

Georgia Senators Russell and Herman Tallmadge saw this proposal—to bring all Americans to the same level regarding the exercise of their civil rights—as just another in a long line of compromise-delay-filibuster-further-compromise-and-debate but defeat by virtue of recess. At the very least, amendments sufficient to weaken the bill to acceptability by the staunchly anti-change Southern bloc would work in their favor.

Mr. Jensen understood all this, of course. After conferring with Mr. Kennerly, the duo launched a new method of promoting a bill.

"There will be no compromises. This time, there will be no wheels and no deals."

Lyndon eloquently expressed their position. He also knew that the men in this body guarded their prerogatives jealously, almost to the point of denying a beneficial law's passage if their egotistical boundaries would be infringed. Thus, the hand of the President or Vice-President could not be too visible. The task fell to the Assistant Leader of the Democrats in the Senate: Hubert Humphrey, a man of gifted oratorical skills. Humphrey sallied forth with the full backing of the chief executive's office. He'd even referred to the towering intensity of LBJ as motivation. He could manage debate so that all parties remained congenial and respective of the other person's point of view.

There was a peculiar quirk to the US Senate. Each senator on any particular day was allowed two, and only two, opportunities to address his colleagues. Business could be conducted only if a quorum of fifty-one or more senators was actually present. Thus, opponents of a bill could speak twice against it, counting on the session being adjourned for lack of a quorum, and then when the new legislative day reconvened, they'd get their two chances anew. Debate could go on seemingly until adjournment was required by the holiday season.

When actual business was conducted with sufficient members present, Humphrey organized proponents into five man teams which would address each attack on the segments of the bill effectively. This gave them exposure highlighting their support for civil rights.

Jensen had figured out that of the sixty-seven Democrats holding office, those from the Border States would be unalterably opposed to desegregation, so 44 had to combine with 23 more to effect cloture. The man to round up the traditionally conservative Midwestern Republicans was Everett Dirksen.

"Give him a piece of the action to make him look good on TV," Jensen urged. "He has a strong sense of the importance of history. By George, he will want his name to find its place in it! He thinks of his country before his career. He's our man to effect a rallying point for the others."

It thus came about that this senator became historically important in the most significant struggle for civil rights this nation had known since 1865. Humphrey put it eloquently. "He was to become the master builder of a legislative edifice that would last as long as Mankind has breath. He puts statesmanship above partisanship." With Mr. Jensen pushing the concept that this was going to be a strong bill for change, Dirksen understood that, this time around, there would be neither compromise nor delay to enactment.

By mid-summer, large union organizations such as the UAW and the AFL-CIO had weighed in demanding action by their representatives. The pressure was making opposition by those in office untenable. Since he was more familiar with the legislative process, Mr. Jensen had revised the language in Mr. Kennerly's initial bill to cause its being referred to the more receptive Commerce Committee for consideration. Doing so was prescient on his part. Now it thereby became a bill which sought to invoke the power of the federal government to regulate interstate commerce. In this way, it sidestepped the philosophical and contentious debate over equal treatment before the law. Granting the Interstate Commerce Commission the power to prohibit discrimination in public restaurants and motel chains that crossed state lines now became readily acceptable. Segregationists were left with the rug being pulled from under their stubborn feet.

All the Republicans who had initially opposed the Petition, but who were in fact men of the party of Abraham Lincoln, rallied round. The Petition had gone forward, the debate on the legislation had been held, stymied by filibuster, then resumed, concluded, and on July 2, the Civil Rights Act of 1964 became law. *Life Magazine* published a photograph of Mr. Jensen leaning over his desk with his arms extended and looking "tall in the saddle."

After almost two hundred years of existence, our country now afforded equal treatment for all citizens in public facilities, guaranteed the right of every citizen to vote, and outlawed discrimination on the basis of race, color, religion, sex, or national origin.

One of our Congressmen penned a passage marking the occasion: "Our system of government has succeeded in large measure because, over the long term, it has both promoted the dynamic forces within our society and provided a means of keeping them in balance. From its very beginning, our form of government has defined and promoted the rights and liberties which individual citizens could exercise and provided the security—military, judicial, and social—that would allow citizens to pursue their ambitions and take advantage of the opportunities afforded them by the equal application of our laws of the land." [1]

Mr. Kennerly had turned the office of the vice-president around from a stand-by, do-nothing cubicle to an office of action where its occupant stood in the forefront of bettering lives for all Americans. Jack and Lyndon joined for a celebratory luncheon that included only the two of them. They had become a solid, synergistic team, able to elicit and listen to all sides of an issue, build consensus by accommodating differing viewpoints, and find acceptable solutions through compromise that resolved differences.

"Accommodation will lead to action" couldn't be used as a campaign slogan, but it sure made sense as a formula for successfully running our country.

The congressional logjam had finally been breached.

Now all our government officials had to do was to enforce the act. That would take some arm-bending because the governor of Mississippi, Ross Barnett, immediately began giving speeches staunchly protecting "home rule" in his state. The issue came to a head when a well-groomed, immaculately dressed James Meredith sought to be educated at 'Ole Miss.

"It's the best college in my state," affirmed Mr. Meredith when interviewed by the press. "That is why I want to go there."

With the governor threatening to close the college if Meredith persisted in being registered, the students showed what was important to them. They stated to the news reporters on camera that, regardless of what was happening in the admissions office, the football games would have to continue being played against their arch-rivals.

One of them quipped on television, "After all, we have a standard of excellence to uphold." He wasn't referring to the student body's tolerance.

Both Assistant Attorney General Katzenbach and his colleague Burke Marshall were apoplectic. "This is squirrel hunting season, and every single pickup coming onto the campus today has a rifle slung from its rear window brackets. This situation could easily get out of hand!"

The first step had been a failure. The local National Guard, being as prejudiced as Governor Ross Barnett, had proved utterly useless. Thereupon, the President deemed it advisable to federalize the army reserve units in the State of Mississippi and to send them onto the grounds to keep the peace on the college campus proper.

The troops had been slow to deploy and had even shown disorganization in their ranks, but their presence demonstrated the federal government's commitment to enforcing the laws of the land. As the line of troops formed and moved forward to confront a wall of rowdy students and their supporters, one of the troops suddenly removed his gas mask, dropped his bayonet-festooned rifle, and held his arms open wide as though for an embrace.

There was a momentary stunned pause within the ranks of the all-white demonstrators. Son-of-a-gun, the trooper behind that gas mask is a Negro! But that was the least of it. Very quickly, two white protesters rushed forward into those very arms and the three men together danced a short jig.

Roy Chesboro had been reunited with his buddies-for-life, Jim Root and Harry Ruskin!

Neither side then knew quite what to do. Gradually, the various protestors laid down their signs as they each in turn became riveted by the sight of a Negro rejoicing in the arms of a Caucasian. The soldiers removed their masks as though bidden by an unspoken command and brought their weapons to Order Arms. There seemed to be a new sort of allegiance being formed, that of American with American, irrespective of color or creed. As soon as he heard about this, President Kennerly sought a firm political solution. When Governor Barnett invoked the Doctrine of Interposition denying the federal government's power to enforce registration by Meredith, President Kennerly simply brushed this aside and stated:

"The citizens of this country are free to disagree with, but not to disobey, the laws of the land," he affirmed. "The governor can invoke all the doctrines he wants; however, they will be of no effect where federal policy supersedes state law."

Then, pausing for effect, the President concluded his televised address with this affirmation:

> "Be aware that the eyes of this nation, as well as those of the world, are upon you. You cannot sidestep responsibility for your actions in this matter. Americans are free to disagree with, but not to disobey the law. In a government of laws and not of men, neither a citizen nor a mob is entitled to defy a court of law. This is as it should be. Our nation is founded on the principle that observance of the law is the eternal safeguard of liberty, whereas defiance of the law is the surest road to tyranny. The laws which we obey include the final ruling of the courts as well as the enactments of our legislative bodies. Few of these will be universally loved, but they must be uniformly respected in American society. For the honor of yourselves, as well as for your university, have the courage to accept those laws with which you disagree, and not just those which you support. You have here today a unique opportunity to show that you are men and women of patriotism and courageous integrity. Honor this tradition of your nation."

Later, the Attorney General himself would observe to Larry and me: "It was damaging to the President to do this, but political considerations were not, and could not be, a factor in upholding the rule of law there.[2] Besides, it doesn't matter if you break down a barrier for a single individual; there must be others ready to benefit from the change for our actions to be significant."

Surely, millions will follow in the footsteps of Mr. Meredith's courage and determination. Once Mr. Meredith registered peacefully, the rest—as they say—became history.

Notes

[1]   Hamilton, Nigel, p. 24.
[2]   See Lieberson, p. 163.

CHAPTER TWENTY-TWO

An Intimate Evening

By February, I was sufficiently abreast of the challenges facing the President's reelection in November that I began to work side-by-side with O'Brien. We had to devise new slogans for this campaign, some of which really hit the nail on the head regarding emotional accuracy. Slogans would be geared to getting the voters' blood boiling mad, or to give them the satisfaction that their leader was doing a good job and, with their continuing support, would accomplish even more in 1964.

So, obviously, this became our prime saying: *Let's do more in sixty-four*! Another favorite was: *Be ecstatic: vote Democratic to keep America great!*

The man impressed me with his sensitivity when he remarked: "We've got to create jobs for our kids. They'll never make a living off our memories, regardless of how much we have already accomplished."

Such a slogan would play well if the next year did result in a slower economy, rising inflation, and widespread job losses. This would make a viable environment in which to pursue a tax cut. Politically, tying it to a war on poverty would make good sense. Jensen was a cattle farmer who thrived in a cosmopolitan environment. His War on Poverty similarly combined a dual-pronged approach addressing both those living in the ghettos as well as the hills of the back country of Kentucky and West Virginia. Called the "permanently invisible poor" by such authors as Dwight Macdonald and the esteemed John Kenneth Galbraith, our elderly, Indian, and Negro populations lived in cyclic poverty that called stridently for relief. But any such effort would have to be tied to benefits for the middle-class as well; after all, they constituted the backbone of America's economic production and would thus have to be included in any social program that was intended to relieve poverty. Reporters such as Walter Heller of the *New York Times* would have to understand that patience was required if results were to be lasting.

This, of course, would be where I would come in and act as a sort of explanatory buffer, as Mrs. Kennerly had so adroitly dubbed my role. After all, she herself had once worked for a newspaper.

Just as in the prior election when the candidate outlined what states to focus on, Mr. Kennerly called a meeting of his top strategists including—naturally—Lyndon, Bobby, Ted, Larry, Kenny, and his brother-in-law Steve Smith, but also top experts John Bailey as party chairman, Richard McGuire as treasurer, and Richard Scammon as Director of the Census Bureau. This latter would know where Democrats lived. I took note of these many names in order to make up organizational charts to help keep our campaigning efforts on track.

The strategy would use a three-pronged approach: (1) the party leaders and state office-holders controlling the convention delegations (2) the county commissioners and regional party leaders; and (3) the everyday Democratic voter who could influence the aforementioned officials.

"Leave nothing to chance!" was our President's organizational byword. For example, Mr. Scammon was tasked with determining the income point at which a voter was likely to change his loyalty and become a Republican. These citizens would require more attention.

As events came to pass, I had less time to spend with my wife Gail than had been the case as a Secret Service agent. I hoped she was finding enjoyable activities in which to immerse herself in addition to raising our third child, Ellie, named for her grandmother. I wasn't simply on call for duty during a trip: I was now fully involved in the planning, logistics, and organization as well.

The weeks progressed, drawing me ever more tightly into the close-knit group of presidential advisors. The president would often speak to us in subtext.

McDonald, O'Brien, and Bobby and me would hear something like, "I think we ought to pay the good people of Sarasota and Miami a visit to remind them what I stand for, and to pay our respects to Cape Canaveral and the fine people there who are sending our astronauts on dangerous missions in unfamiliar environments."

What our leader would actually mean was more succinct: "Let's go to Florida and show those Republicans a better choice!"

We all knew what he meant when he spoke in such short, concise sentences. He was not one to be cryptic; rather, he preferred being explicit. His fecund mind would perceive all the snafus that might occur. Such a man is easy to follow because he has explained himself before he acts.

As the seasons slipped toward the warmth of summertime, I was surprised when the President stopped me as we passed in the hallway one morning. He invited my wife and me for dinner to be shared with Jacquelean and the McDonalds. I accepted on the spot. The date, hour, reason—none of that mattered. Gail would simply be thrilled to have the chance to meet and converse personally with Jacquelean, I knew. My parents would be so jealous!

There was one thing in particular that, by this time, I had become well acquainted with regarding John Kennerly: women. It wasn't simply that they found him irresistibly attractive; he, well, he needed their attention and, apparently, needed it desperately. Having a stream of ladies parade through his daily affairs was almost like white blood corpuscles fighting off disease for him. Their presence diverted his attention from the endless pain with which he battled every day. Some days were so bad that he had to be hospitalized. Along with Addison's disease, his bad back, and intestinal woes, incipient Leukemia fought for his attention as well. His Dr. Feel-good, Admiral Burke, would never go into detail about some of his ailments. This patient was particular about the good doctor remaining mum. While Mr. Kennerly's physical torment was real and oftentimes ever-present, he did not want to advertise his suffering to others.

This fabulous man, who radiated confidence, verve for life, and tanned vitality, had a back door that hid ongoing, severe suffering. Women provided a conduit of pleasure which made it possible for him to tolerate his daily pain.

None of these ladies ever confided in me, of course, but I heard through the grapevine that Jack didn't want warmth or cuddly reassurance from his women. Apparently, the challenge of having to pursue to make a conquest was what drove him; he sought conquests as though he was trying to place notches on an ever widening kaleidoscope as he rotated endlessly from bed to bed. He gave off such light—erudition, wit, status—that none of these women seemed to mind being a mere fling. They simply enjoyed sharing the incandescence of his aura, albeit for only a moment. I knew this to be true: everywhere we traveled in motorcades and speaking engagements, everyone, especially women, impulsively sought to be physically touched by him. In this way, the appeal of his words would have lasting, tangible imprint which would stay with them for the rest of their lives.

The important thing is this: this man *wanted* to live. Pain might be his daily fare, but this curse became the engine that drove him to pursue improvements for others. He might shy away from sharing intimacy, but he wanted to be in a position to lead others to a better life. His doing so—while he was still on this earth—would provide him with salvation.

In the five years I worked at Mr. Kennerly's side, I saw him attend Mass often, but never once did I see him take confession. I gently inquired about this with McDonald. The retort was immediate.

"For heaven's sake, don't be an idiot! No one has suffered here on earth, whether for his humanity or his sins, more than John Kennerly. Taking confession would be redundant to the daily sacrifice of his personal self. Besides, he knows he's not going to stop his behavior, in any of its forms. There's nothing God or the medical professionals can do to end his physical suffering. Just as significant, there is no point to being granted forgiveness when you know full well that you will continue the same behavior as soon as you leave the confessional. He's going to die young; he knows that, so he's got to pack all his life in a few fore-shortened years! Listen Clint, I'm serious when I tell you to never raise this matter again, with anyone! Is that clear?"

I'd heard him through and through, so I nodded my acquiescence. There are some things in life that a person simply can't pursue, no matter how curious he may be.

I'd been taught by the nuns at BAH, and subsequently had the lessons reinforced by Lloyd and Ellie, that a wise person avoids extremes of behavior. Everything is done in moderation, including moderation. This approach allows for the occasional overindulgence when circumstances suggest doing so would be pleasurable. Thus, for the entire world to see, Mr. Kennerly behaved like a loving husband, father, and dutiful son, but he made this bearable by allowing himself the appropriate amount of overindulgence. For him, this meant women. He didn't want to be restricted to merely donning a new tie or hat as a form of diversion. He wanted—no, he *needed* to have his outlook refreshed, regularly! Rather than be limited to the same old familiar faces every day, he wanted to sprinkle his daily regimen with a new body, enjoy it, and then go on to the next stimulus, whether it be political or governmental or personal, with zeal and confidence.

I conveyed all this to my wife. She merely looked at me as though I might be crazy. "He's a very good man, Clint," she stated. "Let's enjoy being in his company without trying to delve into the inner recesses of his mind." Without more being said, I immediately understood that my curiosity on this matter was over.

The appointed day arrived for Gail and my having dinner with Jacquelean and Jack as well as the McDonalds. It was a pleasant, almost balmy evening in June, so we came in shorts and open neck shirts or sleeveless buttoned blouses. We enjoyed a cookout astride the sandbox in which the Kennerly children played, swapped tall tales, and laughed while savoring grilled lamb chops with rice pilaf, sliced tomatoes, and corn-on-the-cob. With hardly any room left, the six of us managed to swallow slices of strawberry shortcake for dessert. The supper could not have been more agreeable.

The experience was so heady that, as I look back on that evening, the only conversation I can recall was an after-dinner exchange between my wife, Jacquelean, and the President. She was commenting on the vicissitudes of daily living that often came unbidden, yet had to be dealt with.

Mr. Kennerly remarked, "Well, Gail, I would much prefer to sidestep the vicissitudes such as King Lear endured and simply embrace his little-known predecessor, King Leir, for whom everything had a happy ending."

"I've never heard of such a man, Mr. President." My wife had little problem being direct and concise. "Who was he, an actual person whom William knew?"

The President, who of course was a brilliant man in his own right, replied, "He was someone on whom the esteemed playwright based his tragedy following the death of the beloved Queen Elizabeth. However, he completely turned the plot of that other writer around to evoke one of the greatest of Shakespearean tragedies; that is, until *Macbeth* came out later that same year. Like all playwrights, this great writer based his stories on what he knew or had observed."

"Not so for my dear husband," interjected Jacquelean. "He sees things as they ought to be and asks 'why not?' rather than accepting the status quo."

"That sounds like something Sir Winston Churchill would say, Jacquelean," I observed.

She replied in that musically velvet voice of hers. "Why, yes! That could well be so. My husband is a steadfast admirer of that great man."

Ken now leaned forward to ask, "Jacquelean, this may be personal, but I'd like to know what struck you most about Jack here when the two of you first met? I've known him for a long time, so now I'm interested to learn whether I sized him up correctly."

A light chuckle skittered around our group lounging in the soft chairs and crashed with an embarrassing *plop* onto the glass tabletop holding our now-empty plates. After a pause, Jack himself broke the tension and said, "I'm sure I told her my chief characteristic is 'curiosity.' She interviewed me for the Washington Times-Herald and wanted to know the answer to that very same question. I'm afraid I also revealed that my chief failing is impatience with mediocrity. Fortunately for me, I have married a lady who pursues the best in whatever she undertakes and, more importantly, satisfies my unending curiosity about how happy she can make me!"

Jack deserved, and received, a poke-in-the-rib for that from Jacquelean. This time, our laughter was robust and real. Then he added as an after-thought:

"If anybody ever thought to inquire as to what trait I wanted in abundance, I would respond with: 'Energy.' When I watch little Jon-Jon tear around the office after luncheon, just when I'm feeling the need for a short doze, my own son makes me jealous; if I had his energy, I could do anything!"

Then he sighed, knowing his workday was far too jam-packed with tension and consequence for such to ever be possible.

Bringing him back down-to-earth, I probed whether religion would be an issue during the 1964 campaign, but Mr. Kennerly just laughed, tilting his head back as he enjoyed remembering the sleepless nights this mountain-out-of-a-molehill issue had caused him in 1960.

"You know, actually my religion was a great help. If I had been a Choate graduate and Harvard alumna who hailed from a wealthy family, I might have never gone anywhere. But being Catholic caused me to stand out as being different, and this led people to ask questions and debate my qualifications. In other words, it helped me to become known, and thus to be elected!"

Then, with a smile crinkling his mouth and his eyes shining with the memory, he added, "Do you realize that, at the time, I was the only thing standing in the way of Richard Nixy entering the White House? That was a very heavy burden to bear, but I'm glad I was up to the task!"

"Frankly, I'm relieved that religion is an issue we can lay to rest," I observed. "Looking back, what are some of the things that stand out in your tenure so far that mark points of real enjoyment for you? I'm not talking about great achievements, such as the space program, or events such as the March on Washington resulting in passage of the Civil Rights Act. I mean, what's been the most fun of being in office."

My wife looked over at me with a dark glance as if to ask, "What are you doing?" but I could see that I had struck a responsive chord with the President.

He leaned back, rolling an unlighted fat cigar between his right-hand fingers as he obviously relived some hilarious moments, probably some that couldn't be shared with tonight's mixed company. But he then leaned forward and broadly smiled.

"Certainly the day that young Jon-Jon popped out of the hidden access door beneath my desk in front of those anxious cabinet officers gave each of us a great laugh. Here we all were sitting around pondering the threats to the very survival of civilization that Soviet duplicity in Cuba had created, and my son showed us in one stroke why our making a correct decision was so vitally important.

"On the lighter side, there was a time I was way up north in New Hampshire with Bernie Boutin campaigning. A dog sled race was on. When a team ran right alongside our car, we stopped one of the teams and the musher showed me how to ride on the back as he ran alongside. With the dogs all excited and straining at the harness and the sled bouncing up, down, even sideways, I got one of the deepest feelings of freedom of my life. Only being out on the ocean and sailing before the wind, controlling your own course despite the vagaries of the currents, beats the pleasure I experienced while gliding across the snow that day!"

We were all impressed. "Different strokes for different folks," the saying goes, but this man had obviously been places and done things that, collectively, would have made even Earnest Hemingway jealous.

At this point, my wife turned to our hosts to mention that this evening had been very pleasant. "I'm sorry it has to end but, like

Michelangelo said of his paintings, a work of art is never finished; it is merely abandoned for yet another project."

"And how can you tell when an Andy Warhol work of art is finished?" inquired the ever quick-thinking Jacquelean.

Even I knew that one. "When the check clears!" I responded. It was one of the few times I was able to keep pace with this nimble-minded couple.

Amidst the ensuing laughter, Jack announced, "Well, that's enough erudition for this night. Gail, Clint, go straight home. Early day tomorrow!"

The McDonalds followed us out. As Jacquelean and Jack waved their good-byes, they affectionately stood arm-in-arm on their doorstep and tilted their heads together, resting against one another. Even after five pregnancies, Jacquelean was as slim as the day she married, and Jack with his full tousle of brown hair was as sexy as ever. What a couple to have in the White House!

"Thanks, Jack. We enjoyed sharing such a fun evening with you!" My wife's eyes were shining brightly. She turned and took my hand as we strolled to our car together.

"Golly, Clint, to think we've had dinner with Jacquelean! I was enthralled listening to her softly refined voice describe the art collection at the Museum of Modern Art. We've just got to tour that someday. And she knows so much about the lives of the French Impressionists and Paul Gauguin's lifelong experiments in expressing the vivid colors in his mind. I just loved being with them tonight. I'm a lucky wife!"

"You can't one-up me tonight," I stated firmly. "I'm a lucky husband to have a wife who is so at ease in the midst of greatness. You captivated everyone with your in-depth conversation about topics each of our hosts held to be important. You impressed me tonight, Gail!" I affirmed while squeezing her hand for emphasis.

In short order, I had parked our tan Ford station-wagon in our driveway and scooted around the bumper to open Gail's door. When she lightly stepped out, I took her in my arms and held her for a moment. I was so pleased with myself: I had married a sweet and intelligent lady who was still devoted to me despite having been married to me going-on six years. I still felt that, whenever I went somewhere with her beside me, I was the better for it.

We walked up the short, bricked path and I opened the front door to our treasured Colonial Revival house in Barnaby Woods. The evening was softly warm, and the clear black sky set off the glow of millions of stars. A few months before, we had gutted a portion of the second floor of this Georgetown house and installed a bedroom-cum-sitting room facing the north side, and then we'd glassed in the porch terrace so we could lie in bed while admiring the Milky Way or watching white snowflakes drift down in January. This is where I guided Gail tonight; we would sleep beneath the stars and awake to an organdy sunrise reflecting off the painted sides of the house across the street from us.

She entered the bedroom and promptly stretched luxuriously across the bed. Her face was filled with rapture from the fun-filled evening we had just enjoyed, then she kicked off her pumps and began to fiddle with the buttons on her smooth muslin blouse. I watched as her eyes came to rest squarely on my belt buckle.

"Here, let me do that for you," I suggested eagerly, brushing her hands to her sides. Keeping my fingers light, I slowly undid each button and then gently slipped the folds of her top from off her shoulders. I studied the smooth, fragrant skin and the subtle mounds of her breasts as they were gradually revealed. The town had settled for the night. A few night birds chirped from their perches atop the roof gable, and some katydids stirred the air with their pulsating buzz. That's how quiet the room had become as I bent toward her mouth. She offered up her lips to me in welcome surrender. Our caresses and finger stroking were gentle, even languorous; we wanted this bliss to extend the pleasant comfort that we had felt at dinner with Jacquelean and Jack Kennerly. Who knew whether we'd ever be given the chance to relive those delights?

Resisting the urge to rush things, I kept my shorts on while hovering astride her pristine body. After a moment of anticipation, I slid my forefinger along her clitoris until she began moving against my steady finger on her own. As her body became more demanding, I leaned down and flicked with my tongue, bringing my beloved wife to shrieks of delight while she tried to tug my normally groomed hair out by the roots. A final gentle flick made her hips arch as her body gave in to the pulsating delights of coming.

As her thrilling spasms subsided and her body relaxed amidst the soft folds of the now rumpled bed sheets, she turned to me with her eyes all aglow with giving. "Now it's your turn," she breathed while gently cupping my bullocks, thereby taking control of my body. I could resist no longer. She helped me find her entrance and my penis probed, found the path to heaven, and proceeded to control my brain from there on. My body and mind surrendered to achieving ecstasy. As my climax came, I tingled all the way down to my toes; my entire being was enjoined in this pursuit. Her welcoming warmth put me into ecstatic whirls of delight as her body quivered beneath my hot thighs. Her hips rose to meet my searching fingers and arched with desire as I thrust myself home. We each moaned deeply, and then I could feel Gail grow rigid once more. Lightly I touched her clitoris. She began to shake as spasms of joyous release took control of her. I had little trouble joining her. It was all we could do to catch a breath as our bodies pressed together in consummation of our mutual affection.

Our lovemaking had held urgency tonight, as though we each silently knew this one time would be particularly important.

With thankful tenderness in my eyes, I rolled to my left and lay astride my wondrous wife, and then wrapped her in my arms. As our breathing subsided and our racing hearts slowed to normal rhythm, I cradled her head in the crook of my arm and whispered, "That was unusually good, wasn't it? It was more than wanting you; there was a force that seemed to propel my being more penetrating than usual."

"You felt it too? Your touch always arouses me, but tonight was more like we needed to express how we felt about one another rather than simply satisfy our sexual desires. If my instincts are right, I think we've made a good one tonight, Clint." My wife lay peacefully within my protective embrace, softly breathing as she held my hand.

"Are you saying we've made a child tonight, Gail?"

"I wouldn't be surprised. I'll be able to tell you better around the start of the school year, perhaps Labor Day or a week later. I'll keep you posted."

"You better! I've never given much thought to there being more than the four of us. When I was on protective detail, I didn't want to contemplate the consequences if I had to step in front of the President to prevent his being injured. Now that I've done just that, I realize I want to have lots of children very much, just in case…"

"That being so, shouldn't I be made aware of your preference regarding the sex of our child, if you have indeed made me pregnant tonight? Boy or girl?"

I paused, but only for a second. She'd asked a relevant, important question, but very quickly I knew my own feelings. I answered honestly as I looked into her eyes.

"Gail, I want whatever we have. If the baby is healthy and, of course, smart, then I'll be happy. Just tell me, okay, if you have any difficulty along the way. I want this to be our joy child, so you are not permitted to suffer along the way, do you understand?"

"Oh, you big hero, you! Don't you know we women are built to handle pain better than you men? My mom was fine when she was pregnant. I've got good genes. I'm confident that we—you, me, and this baby—will do just fine." She snuggled a little bit closer, and her soft, rhythmic breathing lulled me. Gradually, a feeling of complete contentment percolated through my entire body. All my daily trials and mental tensions seemed to ebb away. My breathing became slow and deep, and I rolled toward my wife and held her gently, but very close. My body was at peace with itself. I felt as though I had been born for this very moment and had thereby fulfilled God's purpose for me. As my wife and I fell asleep beneath the warm covers, I took one last look at the broad firmament far above with all its many twinkling points of bright light. I knew I had done well; this night would mark the beginning of an entirely new dimension to our lives. Our having this child would complete not just Gail, but me as well.

Isn't it surprising how, sometimes, the most treasured events in life can occur without you having given them even an iota of forethought? Only by their happening do you come to realize how important such events are to you.

CHAPTER TWENTY-THREE

Chief-Executive Partnership

President Kennerly rather curtly summoned Ken McDonald and me to the Oval Office the day after our delightful supper together. This room is made for both thorough thinking and wise decision-making. It may be termed the boiler room of our ship of state, formed into an oval shape crowned by a gently arching ceiling.[1] The windows looking out on the Rose Garden are taller than a man stands while its French doors allow sunlight to pour through the numerous panes, thereby seeming to fill the room with warm inspiration. The Presidential Seal prominently overlooks the action in bossed relief on the ceiling while the American eagle holds justice and peace in its talons above the door lintels. The impression is one of serenity and tastefulness, with a stuffed couch and President Kennerly's rocking chair gracing the richly embroidered floor rug. Upon entering, one can't help but feel that here is a place where leaders of men and nations make consequential policies. Even the doors are flush with the walls so as not to intrude on the important matters occurring there. The courses of action agreed upon herein have often proved not merely memorable, but magnificently prescient as well. [2]

As we entered, we saw our leader with deeply furrowed brow leaning heavily on the front edge of his desk. It had been constructed in the Victorian style from mahogany planking taken off the *H.M.S. Resolute.* Uniquely, it sported a secret door in the leg cavity. Oftentimes, his son or daughter could be found lurking within; they would squeal with delight when discovered by the President. Obviously, today would not be about childish games.

"This is the day," he began with a tone of foreboding, "when I largely hand over my control of our domestic affairs. Lyndon is due here in ten minutes. I'm going to lay it on the line with him, so don't be surprised if you hear some crude language. Red Fay previously confided to me that Lyndon has grumbled to him about being useless. Apparently, he claimed that no one cared whether he came to work or not. He feels that everyone around here is doing something important for the country, but he simply sits around in his brass-studded leather chair and thinks about his ranch. He feels like he's a do-nothing blob of corpuscles.[3]

"Well, I'm about to give him something to do that will probably blow his tooled-hide boots clear off! Therefore, it's important that you witness our talk because what he and I decide here will mark a new format for the conduct of this administration. What we agree on today may even alter the perception of future president/vice-president relationships."

He paused, looking at us both for any sign of objection. We merely remained mute. Just then, Lynne Lincoln, the boss' secretary, entered to announce the arrival of the Vice-President. Mr. Kennerly strode confidently forward, thanked Lynne and, upon spotting Mr. Jensen, extended his hand to the Texan. Both men displayed wide smiles on their faces as though they were attending fund-raisers for their alma maters: one in the north, the other southern.

"Good morning, Lyndon, it's so good of you to come today. I have some ideas of how we can better serve our country, and I would highly value your input. Have a seat over here and make yourself comfortable."

After smiling a greeting, Mr. Jensen's grin faded from his face. As he settled into the soft cushions, he wore the look of a hound dog that was about to be scolded. For just a moment, I imagined that I saw his prominent ears droop a bit. Our President started right in on the man.

"Look, Lyndon, let's lay it on the line here and now. You were Assistant Secretary of the Navy for Intelligence the first time you met my father. I know that he returned in disgrace from having mismanaged his ambassadorship to England.[4]

"You probably have opinions about this, as well as my family's background. Frankly, in many respects, I would be in agreement with you there, but I'll thank you to keep them to yourself. Personally, I find you uncouth and unpleasant to be around in social settings. Politically, you have always struck me as a man more concerned with his ego and public image than with what works for the country. I've heard reports from various staffers that you can be not merely overbearing, but bitterly nasty to subordinates as well. Shortness of temper can never be productive in our form of government. The fact that you suffered, and then recovered from, a heart attack 8 or 9 years ago does not give you the right to act like a bully, especially with your subordinates and aides, when you're an elected official in this democracy."

The President paused as a small smile crossed his lips. He could see, and appreciate, the lighter side of even the most searing situation.

He noted, "One of your daughters was chatting with Jacquelean at some party and, somewhat in jest, mentioned that she believes you have an alarm clock embedded in your brain that goes off every hour, telling you that it is time for you to stand up and go chew someone out. This form of dominance, by letting off steam to belittle some staffer, ends with our conversation here today."

It was obvious from the way he was sitting forward that Mr. Jensen was all ears.

Our President continued: "None of this is important to the matters at hand. What either of us thinks about the other or what we've heard as whining complaints is unimportant. Starting now, I propose that we work as a team on domestic affairs. You have an extraordinary gift for bringing men with large egos around to your point of view. Thus, you enjoy a reputation for handling senators and congressmen adroitly, regardless of their party affiliation. I am inviting you to work closely with me. I envision our cooperation more as a partnership rather than as a chief and a reserve executive. On domestic affairs, we'll team up to secure the passage of legislation for the betterment of our fellow citizens."

The vice-president sat back, arching his eyebrows at this remark. "Well, I..." he began in response. He was cut short.

"No, listen to me. This is not a time for recriminations or self-defense. I've a bit more than four years left in which to right grievous wrongs and imbalances in our diverse society, and I can't think of a man better positioned than you are to undertake, even to lead, a domestic agenda. I assume that when our mutual term ends, you will want to retire from politics."

As Lyndon opened his mouth to reply, the President stopped him yet again by raising his hand.

"Actually, your personal ambitions do not interest me, nor are they relevant to this conversation. What I'm saying to you, if you'll open those large, flapping ears of yours, is that right now is the time for us to start to work together as no two chief executives ever have before. The world political situation and threats to the safety and well-being of all Mankind have never been under greater duress. I have got to focus on the international scene. The peoples of the world, particularly in the developing nations, need vision, inspiration, and financial aid. I can help with all of that. Additionally, I must strive to keep the people of the world safe while enabling them to achieve self-direction and national pride rather than suffer under the boots of colonialism or communism."

Then, placing a hand on Jensen's shoulder, the president continued, lowering his voice to emphasize the urgency of his demand for cooperation.

"Before my efforts can be successful, I've got to know that our government has a capable person handling our domestic affairs. Of course, equality before the law and the enjoyment of civil rights by all citizens should improve markedly what with your recent successes with Congress. Nevertheless, we still have to resolve the wide disparities extant among our citizens even as we speak. That work must be ongoing, but no less important are the problems faced by mine workers laboring in dangerous conditions and forced to live in hovels facetiously dubbed 'company towns.' We must address the failure of our government to provide opportunities for our native Indian populations by laying the groundwork to enable members of the diverse tribes to believe they are capable of actively contributing to our society. Such concerns must be given high priority, but attention to them is not meant to sweep problems such as industrial pollution and incursions across our southern borders under the rug. As I see it, if we don't address all these problem areas now, they will soon blow up in our faces and we'll lose the chance to correct historic errors.

"What I have just stated forms the underlay for my foreign policy approaches. An effective foreign policy depends on our country having a strong economy with which to produce the materiel and instruments for leadership in outer space, ocean transport, and powering up remote areas with electricity, and that means we must have social cohesion amongst our peoples. If this administration fails to make domestic proposals that are universally applicable, we may not have a united country with which to take on the international challenges of Soviet communism. I am asking you to stop playing the truckle role. From here on I want you to be at the center of domestic events. You are particularly skilled at shepherding items on our domestic agenda because your legislative acumen allows you to understand how the senate works and on whom to focus the necessary placating compromise, while I am effective with heads of state and relish international brinksmanship.

"The long and short of it is that we will work better as a team rather than backups because, Lyndon, the time has come for you to make use of your highly reputed skill as a persuader of individuals. We may be in office because our combination won a plurality politically, but now that we are here, I believe our fellow Americans have anointed us with a consummate opportunity to effect good in this country. I fervently hope you can see it that way."

He paused, allowing the vice-president the opportunity to absorb the import of his message. He waited a moment, watching Lyndon's brain working, and just when the man appeared ready to respond, President Kennerly resumed.

"We are blessed with one new advantage that no other administration has enjoyed: the extensive paved road network which our predecessor instituted. Our society is more mobile than at any other time in our nation's history. We can put that to work for us by shifting disadvantaged people to places where they are needed to fill employment vacancies, transporting goods whether perishable, frozen, or static for the improvement of every family's living conditions, and improving our strategic military response initiatives by locating missiles in relatively uninhabited regions to gird our shores with a semi-circle of protective response.

"Lyndon, if you will join with me in this great quest, we can ensure both the nation's safety as well as its economic stability. Acting as only you yourself can, you can bring about the Great Society and pull together the CORE, Panthers, SNCC, and NAACP movements to bring all peoples together living in harmony. Together, you and I can make America a far stronger, more egalitarian, and thus effective nation. We can then spotlight our exemplary form of government to disprove the claims of the communist world which seek to dupe the emerging countries with deceitful and false lures.

"I am asking you to henceforth put aside all grudges and dislikes. Rally your prodigious talents to persuade and gain cooperation. Devise a schedule and plan for bringing each of our Congressmen into the fold, and make yourself available to civilian leaders whom we can sway to this single great cause: to renew our nation by enabling each member within our society to realize his or her potential."

Jensen stood up and extended his hand. With feeling, he stated:

"Mr. President, you have kick-started this quest in one phrase: we will move forward and make our nation anew as 'The Great Society.'

"There is no doubt in my mind that your eloquence and humane aspirations inspire us all to become involved in improving our daily lives. To effectively move proposed legislation through a Congress that, admittedly, seems committed to impeding your every move, you need my skills as a parliamentarian. Therefore, I gladly accept your partnership proposal and pledge to do my utmost to achieve these goals for the good of our country."

The President curtly motioned for him to resume his seat. Looking him squarely in the eye, Kennerly stated in no uncertain terms.

"This means that you'll have to curb that famous public temper of yours. Even if you have to cut back on your love of liquor, you must, whether or not you are in the public eye, be the charismatic, assured, and warm-hearted leader whom so many love. No more calling someone on the carpet if they fail to meet your goals. Encouragement and enabling must be your watchwords, not castigation or humiliation."

Jensen huffed, even choked back a lump in his throat. "Well, Mr. President, if that is what will be required, I shall do it. As you say, I will probably retire from public life come 1968. Thereafter, I can take in as much liquor as I want!"

"That would be just fine, Lyndon. As they say in the navy, whatever you want to do with your free time is your own choice. However, there is one further mode of behavior which I simply must discuss. You and I both like chasing women; that's not the problem. What has everyone buzzing is your habit of disrobing, often completely, when on Air Force-Two. What you are accustomed to doing in the privacy of your home with your family is not my concern. However, I cannot have you displaying yourself in a venue that is associated with our government, the Democratic Party, or indeed any public or private facility.

"Freedom to disregard your responsibility regarding the public's perception must apply at all times now that we have undertaken to retain the public's trust. If we are to work successfully as a team rather than mere back-ups, we must present an image that is both unified and tasteful. When you prance around like a cowboy in your Stetson and little else, such behavior reflects badly on your position as a Democrat and as an elected official charged with responsibility for the United States. So even at your ranch, if you are entertaining domestic dignitaries or are otherwise on official business, you must conduct yourself with decorum as though you were right here in the White House. Hold in the forefront of your daily thoughts that photograph published by *Life Magazine* of you sitting astride that sleek chestnut bay of yours evincing a man able to lead but who retains his roots in the soil of his country. You are a highly esteemed public figure; I don't want you to ever tarnish that status."

He coughed, and then asked, "Am I getting through to you?" as he jabbed a finger on the armrest.

By this point, Mr. Jensen was squirming a bit and curling his long frame as though he was a snail trying to disappear into its shell. He felt small, just like when he lived with his father long, long ago when they were poor and he would be scolded for having skipped school for the day.

Nevertheless, Mr. Kennerly was not finished and continued forcefully.

"Regardless of how impressive your bullocks may be, they are not relevant to your performance as an elected official. If you want to impress me, get those important agenda items resolved within our mutual terms of office. If we are successful, we may rate the same esteem enjoyed by FDR, George Washington, and Thomas Jefferson. I can't think of any higher reward for public service than that!"

He was abruptly interrupted by his newly-anointed "partner."

"Jesus, Jack! You have screwed just about every female in America who is over the age of 18. That's not just gossip. I have that from Hoover himself! He keeps taped conversations of you and your many paramours locked in his desk. Don't get high and mighty with me!"

Jensen didn't like being corrected by anyone, and certainly not by a man who was his junior in age.

The President remained calm and said simply, "You have a point, certainly. I already agreed that our sexual escapades are our private business. The difference in our behavior is that I pursue my activities with all the discretion that my position permits, and certainly I never cavort around in front of the First Lady. You have simply got to curb this need to flaunt; people will doubt your common sense if you keep such behavior up. We cannot throw the rules of decorous behavior out the window simply because we have large egos, and most definitely not while we are holding public office. I'm firm on this point, Lyndon. If we stand indivisible, we will stand invincible! No slip ups, none at all from here on. Can we shake on this?"

The President stood up and extended his hand as he looked straight at his Vice-President. Lyndon realized that a unique partnership was in the offing, his to embrace or irrevocably toss aside. On the spot, he decided he wanted to be a part of this wider frontier. What the President was proposing would be good not only for his countrymen, but also for his legacy.

Jensen likewise stood and forthrightly gripped Kennerly's right hand in his own. The two men forged a strong bond that went well beyond party fealty; theirs would be a partnership for the good of the country.

Thus began a symbiotic spirit of pursuing mutual goals for the immediate benefit of the nation. It was none too late to do so. If they had waited a mere two years, the spread of poverty and the resulting unrest among our diverse populations would have deteriorated so broadly and deeply that the nation would have become mired in rioting. These two men had to act now.

One was the thinker, the dreamer who saw that making our nation more fully participative was a goal worth achieving. The other was the doer, the one who could get the laws passed and then implemented. As a team, they could help some fifteen million citizens, who had been too long neglected, but who now needed to take center stage.

James Reston of the *New York Times* was to write: "Jack and Lyndon are two very different men. The former used vivid language, a sense of humor, and a deep understanding of the lessons history can teach while the latter was disinclined to retreat from an adversary standing up to him; in fact, he would grant nothing to his opponent, not even time for rebuttal. He would size a person up to determine his weak point, what would make him vulnerable if Lyndon failed to grant his wish. His guide when dealing with people was not Jesus' well-known adage: *Do unto others as you would have them do unto you*, but rather: *What have you done for me lately?*" [5]

In essence, what these two leaders were saying was that everyone in our country must be accorded an equal opportunity to learn, earn and turn their life around; in short, to offer them **the chance to**

contribute to the society of which they are a cohesive part. Life, liberty, and the pursuit of happiness are written as guiding tenets of our form of government. The executive branch rules for the people, as well as by the people. There is nothing therein that seeks to exclude one class or group from the chance to better themselves.

There is immense power in the office of the president to effect transformative change for the better in our nation. There is even greater power when the two men holding the highest offices in the land agree to work closely together in coordinated efforts for change rather than maintain one man out front while the other is merely waiting in the wings. These two executives would hereafter effect a symbiotic presidency whereby they would take pride in their mutual accomplishments. This would transform their relationship into one of genuine warmth.[6]

When O'Brien commented on this astonishing improvement, Jack sagely responded, "I can't afford to have a member of my team simply sitting around with nothing to motivate him. We have fundamental disparities—color, wealth versus poverty, capital versus labor, place of birth—which are presently being maintained for the advantage of the few. We need to draw on the nation's greatest resource—our diversity—to make our society the most viable in the world. Everyone has a job to do, and everyone must get to it!"

Looking one another in the eye, they exclaimed: "To the *Great Society*!"

Thereupon, Ken and I stood up.

I asked the question relevant to our positions. "Mr. Vice-President, whom do you think you will select to coordinate with Kenny and me as your plans develop?"

The Vice-president caught my eye and huffed, "Let me get back to you on that." Immediately, he was gone in a swirl of Texas dust.

Mr. Kennerly looked over at us, which caused all of us to burst out laughing. "Give him time, guys; surely, my proposal has set his spurs to spinning."

The president had a twinkle of mischief in his eyes as he recounted the story about one of his young aides during the 1959 campaign. This eager, well-groomed man had stopped by Mr. Jensen's home to deliver the itinerary of prospective stopovers for that day. He had located Mr. Jensen by the sound his water was making as he pissed off the back porch of his house.

The three of us looked out one of the Oval Office windows and watched Lyndon get into his chauffeured car. I could see that Mr. Kennerly was stroking his chin thoughtfully. He turned to McDonald and me, then stated succinctly: "Don't ever let me be killed while I'm holding this office. I doubt our country would be able to handle Lyndon Jensen as president; he'd surely embarrass all of you."

Despite our levity, we both understood that we had just witnessed an historic transformation in governmental policy. From this day forward, the mantra would not be "What's in it for me?" but rather "Together we strive for the good of all!"

Kennerly and Jensen quickly set about putting their program overhauls into action. They had mutually agreed that campaigning for the November election would be downplayed until August or so. They would let Rockefeller or that strong-faced man in the black glasses have their go. In the interim, they would see how fully they could improve the lives of their countrymen with speech-making that translated immediately into the creation of youth councils, the appointment of industry and financial leaders as chairmen of neighborhood improvement committees, and inviting the various religions to pitch in. Though Government was forbidden to force matters of state on the church, there was no prohibition in asking the leaders of the various denominations for help with programs which bettered Americans.

Their aims were not an expansion of the dole; rather, somewhat akin to FDR's CCC, where men were given the opportunity to pull themselves up by the bootstraps and regain pride in self, Jensen and Kennerly would partner to roll through Congress programs for the betterment of all members of our society. Men would finally have the chance to pursue their education, to labor at work which paid a remunerative wage, and use their talents and energy to their benefit. Strength would beget even greater strength. These leaders would seek to enable and empower. The chief goal was to render the pernicious compression of societal strata to be but a mistake of the past that had, at last, been corrected. Customs that relegate people to the status of noncitizens in their own country were to be rooted out and abrogated. This partnership would relegate the denial of the rights of citizenship as merely an old concept that was forever consigned to the misguided history of America.

The foundation for all these bootstrap programs is this: <u>our nation does not provide help to numb the needy to get, and remain, on the dole. Rather, it seeks to enable, indeed, to ennoble each citizen to possess the chance to realize his and her own potential to contribute to our society by becoming self-reliant Americans.</u>

To foreigners, Kennerly was genuinely focused on making the world peaceful and its inhabitants secure. He recognized that maintaining stockpiles of nuclear weapons was necessary in a world of suspicion and distrust; regardless, such indiscriminate weapons were also the most inefficient means of keeping the peace.

"They can destroy, but never create," his speeches would lament at various times. One day, in fact, while we were idly enjoying his son Jon-Jon and Carolyn cavorting on the lawn with some local schoolchildren, he observed: "It would be so much simpler to get along in the world, indeed, in our own nation, if we could all act more like kids having fun. Look at them. Skin color or nationality makes no difference on the playground. The nations of the world could get along so much more readily if we had an international language of play!" We both broke up with laughter, but was this really such a puerile goal?

It was Secretary McNamara who voiced the problem of nuclear confrontation succinctly: "A credible deterrent cannot be based on an incredible act. We shall defend Berlin using conventional weapons and tactics, but our reliance on this form of deterrence must not weaken the readiness of our nuclear arsenal."

In an address to American University's graduating class in 1963, the President had stated: "The pursuit of peace is not as dramatic as the pursuit of war, but we have no more daunting a task before us. The pursuit of peace is not filled with impossibilities. Our problems are man-made—therefore, they can be solved by man."[7]

He affirmed this to me one day by likening the different cultures in the world to that of pet dogs.

He told me: "It doesn't matter what breed a dog is, Clint. Each animal wants to feel safe. They fear abuse and will respond to such threat with bared fangs and growls, displaying their defenses aggressively. At heart, however, they want to be handled and controlled and prized in such a way that the uncertainty of life is removed. To the person who is willing to do that, they will forever-after earn the dog's loyalty and affection. You have only to place the right dog in the right environment for happiness to reign. Match its temperament with the owner's personality."

"People look for certainty in their own security in much the same way," he concluded.

Notes

1.   Widmer, p. 8.
2.   Caro, pp. 438-439.
3.   See O'Donnell, pp. 7-10 for a fuller discussion.
4.   This is a widely-held perception, albeit somewhat misleading. At the time of his being posted as our representative to Great Britain, the ambassador had four sons whom he desired to see grown and successful. "I don't want them to be killed in a foreign war," he had stated privately. He polled American theater-goers regarding their views and a preponderance subscribed to isolationism. More importantly, he feared another market crash that would lead to national chaos and bankruptcy, thereby threatening his ability to provide for his family. "An unemployed man is hungry whether a swastika or some other flag flies over his head," he had observed. Like Neville Chamberlain, he viewed the sharpening international differences in Europe more as economic imbalances rather than self-aggrandizing power grabs. "I have sent reports which were my best judgment about the forces that were moving, the developments that were likely, and the course best suited to protect America. I have a great stake in this country and the kind of America that my children will inherit." He thus separated himself from his president, seeking to prevent America's involvement whereas Mr. Roosevelt thought intervention, evincing strong American purpose, would become a necessity. However, this former ambassador went on to nominate F.D.R. for a third term as President so, while they had disagreed, they had not fallen out. For additional in-depth detail, refer to: Beschloss, pp. 162-3, 183, and 220.
5.   Refer to Caro, p. 594.
6.   See Schlesinger, *A Thousand Days*, p. 707 for a contrarian view of reality.
7.   Dallek, p. 619-620.

CHAPTER TWENTY-FOUR

Principle versus Popularity

Lyndon, who sincerely believed in equal justice for all Americans, led the challenge in blunting southern opposition. It was during one of these exchanges when the famous picture of his towering over a senator who was reeling from the onslaught of Jensen's close-in "cajoling" splashed across the papers. He meant business; the good-old-boy days were still a part of his relationship with the sitting senators but, nevertheless, he was devoted to moving bills along. Obstructionist senators would—from here on—have to come around to his points of view.

The President was equally as committed. Continuing his drive for equality among all citizens, he pointed out how he had begun doing so early in his tenure. During his first inauguration, he noticed there were no Negroes in the ranks of the Coast Guard parading before the reviewing stand. There soon were. He had asked each of his cabinet secretaries to consider Negroes when job openings arose in their departments. The State Department began assigning ambassadorships without regard to a person's pedigree or color, regardless of the race that predominated in the country of assignment.

The following exchange was not amusing; rather, it was more an indication that the President had to balance important goals according to their current importance rather than their future attainment. When one of the members of his Civil Rights Commission noted the absence of any Negroes in the Alabama National Guard, Jack held up his hand to call for patience. It was extraordinary to see how this man could maintain an equable manner when everyone around him was losing their mind.

"Given the situation in Germany, I may have to order that unit to Berlin to assist in the crisis developing there. I don't want to have to do that and deal with a revolution going on here at home. Let's take things in order, and you will see that everything will resolve in its own time."

This was similar to his handling of the Cuban Missile Crisis during 1962. He had vision that far exceeded that of even august senators or cabinet members. His Secretary of State Dean Rusk, who was so skilled at intelligently defining the inherent risks of international confrontation that you'd think he could save the world, lacked the ability to figure out how to handle such challenges. His fear of making the wrong decision overcame his ability to act. This inability placed great strain on President Kennerly. He plucked the Harvard Dean of Faculty, McGeorge Bundy, from that post and elevated him to be his in-house, full-time National Security Advisor. When coping with a crisis, he would make the final decision as to how to react, but he didn't want to be forced to make decisions off-the-cuff when faced with a severe threat to mankind.

With conditions at their most tense, I remember well how he showed us, and the world, that he was in command of both emotion and judgment.

Toward the end of October 1962, he had dramatically stated:

"The Soviet Union has pursued a course in which it aims to be superior to our country both militarily and politically. We do not see it that way. Whether or not Premier Crushchev intended on firing missiles from Cuba is irrelevant. In this situation, as in all political confrontations, appearances matter the most because they foster everyone's perception of reality. Therefore, our allowing those missiles to remain would have altered the balance of power between our two nations as well as our position of influence throughout the world. Mr. Crushchev will have to realize that his actions in Cuba placed the future of the world on a precarious brink of no return.

"While it is true that our two nations could not be more diametrically opposed both as to our goals and the welfare of our citizens, at heart, we are in the same boat. We are geographically separated by only a narrow peninsula of land, but one that is so forbiddingly cold that no one wants to go there for any reason. We place and protect completely different interpretations on the value of individual liberty, yet we enjoy the most basic common link of all, and that is simply this: we all inhabit this planet. We all breathe the same air. We all cherish our children's future. And, we are all mortal. We must not, indeed, we cannot act in such a way that would endanger all life existing on this earth."

Nonetheless, he couldn't resist taking me aside one day and remarking, "Clint, you will soon come to understand that politics often presents the politician with a choice between two blunders."

I laughed as I stated, "Why, Mr. President, that's a line from your book, *Profiles in Courage!*"

The President smiled my way as he laid a hand on my shoulder and affirmed, "So it is, Clint, so it is, but I've never forgotten to heed my own advice." Still smiling, he then winked my way.

Dire predictions for his reelection campaign began to trickle in because he was taking such a firm stance on controversial issues. The President held a press conference and declared to the entire world:

> "The question is, whether ensuring civil rights for all citizens is worth losing an election? Today, in our country civil rights, and the withholding of same from large numbers of our population, represents a national crisis. At such a moment, whoever is the President must meet his responsibilities by advancing the rights of all our citizens equally. If we were a nation of laws differing from our Constitution, there might be room for debate. However, this is America. What we stand for—and it is at the very core of our national identity—is freedom for all men and women who hold citizenship in this great land. There is no debating what that means; the words speak for themselves. And yet we have spent two centuries, as well as waged and settled a war between brothers, arguing the meaning of these words. The words are self-evident: freedom applies equally to all our citizens and, more importantly, it applies now!"

He paused, letting the photographers take their photos in order to make their deadlines, then he concluded with this sobering thought:

> "I would rather be right on the significant issues, even if I stumbled along the way as I searched for my footing, than to never make mistakes because I ignored those challenges which our citizens face on a daily basis."

"I see no further need for embellishment, Mr. President." Kenneth offered, somewhat unsure of himself.

"We shall soon see if such thoughts are convincing not just to our electorate, but to our distinguished lawmakers as well!" Kennerly smiled that smile which made his face fairly glow with magnanimity, and then added: "We would do well to get Howard K. Smith of Virginia on our side; of course, that would be like getting the fox to grow feathers and start cackling."

We all laughed, but the import of his thought was clear.

CHAPTER TWENTY-FIVE

Reelection Platform

In the faint pewter light of an Irish dawn, a young man riding bareback on an old gray draft horse emerged from the opaque mists blanketing the fields bordering a river port south of Dublin. A summer shower pelted the sides of his horse, as well as his exposed cheeks beneath his broad-brimmed fedora. The fog roiled up from the warm soil and condensed within the tree branches, concealing the road ahead. A stranger might have hesitated to proceed any further for fear of getting lost, but the young man knew this countryside like the back of his hand. The sum total of his life's experience had, along with the memory and bones of his ancestors, been encompassed within a fifteen-mile radius of this town. That was soon to change, however. Shortly, he would board a ship bound for America where he would settle in the state of Massachusetts.[1]

The son of this man was named Honey Fitzhugh. Mr. Fitzhugh became a lifelong politician but, during his many years as Mayor of Boston, had earned the nickname "Fitzblarney" for his excessive talkativeness. His greatest contribution would be to marry and thus to provide his family name to the children of his son, Joseph Kennerly: Joe Jr. and John and Robert and Edward.

Our 35th president was the second grandson and appears to have been born to lead this nation. Yes, his judgment could err; he was human, after all. However, he held fast to the premise that, by everyone working together, each of us would improve our lives. In short, he reignited our belief in the American Ideal of achieving—by our own hand—all that we can be.

People listened to his cultured, educated words. He was readily understood, whether he was giving a speech to a packed Democratic convention or a living room of fascinated women. He knew how to couch his phrases in the luculent language that everyone would find welcoming.

By the time he gained the presidency, Kennerly appealed to every color, class, and age group in the country. Only those whom his party's rise to leadership had dispossessed of power or self-enrichment viewed his success with scorn.

Subsequent to his consultation with the Vice-President, Mr. Kennerly faced the international challenges which were brewing and about to become "boil-overs," as he liked to refer to the myriad unsettled regions in the world.

He had laid solid groundwork for the pursuit of a better world during his inaugural address way back in January 1961:

> "To those old allies whose cultural and spiritual origins we share, we pledge the loyalty of faithful friends. United, there is little we cannot do in a host of cooperative ventures. Divided, there is little we can do. We dare not meet a powerful challenge when we are split asunder. To those nations who would make themselves our adversary, we offer not a pledge, nor a threat, but rather a request. We should both begin anew from this day forward in a quest for peace, before the dark dangers of destruction that is unleashed by science or stupidity engulf all humanity in planned or accidental self-destruction."

He had concluded this magnificently synergistic offer with this affirmation:

> "I welcome the responsibility of protecting freedom in its hour of maximum danger. The energy and faith which we bring to this endeavor will lift our country to new heights of discovery and accomplishment. To all my fellow countrymen, I assure you that there is little quality to life if you are free but live constantly in the shadow of fear. Accordingly, I extend the olive branch of cooperation so that all who live here can discover how best to serve her. Our mutual efforts as citizens will ignite flames of achievement, tolerance, and respect. The glow from such fires can truly light the world."

It's a well-known facet of oratory that, once you begin to speak, causing everyone nearby to turn your way in order to hear your words, the whole course of your day and how your listeners feel about you will be directed by how you finish. The structure of an address can give the words a momentum of their own. In this way, their import may go beyond the literal meaning they convey. A love of language may not guarantee happiness, but it allows you to express your goals eloquently, and that is worth everything. There was no question in anyone's mind that, even for a politician, the eloquence of Jack Kennerly's form of expression was extraordinarily clear, incisive, and motivating.

Consider this opening from his speech at Rice University in Houston. It addressed our country's pursuit of space exploration in the fall of 1962. After honoring his host and the esteemed faculty members, Mr. Kennerly said:

> "We meet today at a college noted for knowledge, in a city noted for progress, in a state noted for strength. We need all three because we live in a time of accelerating change and challenge. We live in an age where the greater our knowledge becomes, the greater our ignorance unfolds. Despite Mankind's rapid rise from learning how to make fire to sending men into outer space, the vast stretches of the unknown and the unanswered and the unfinished still far outstrip our collective comprehension. If history teaches us anything, however, it is that Man will pursue his quest for knowledge and progress with a determination that cannot be deterred. The exploration of space will proceed, whether we join in it or not, because it is one of the greatest adventures of all time. No nation which expects to be the leader of other nations can afford to be left behind in this race. For these reasons, my administration is proud of the many men and women training to work for NASA here in Houston. I extend our Nation's thanks to each and every one of you." [2]

Embracing the race for dominance in space was a necessity in the 20th Century, but the President's holding forth and joking with each of the astronauts in turn after they made their mark orbiting the earth made for enthusiastic camaraderie. The President liked both the glamour that surrounded these men and their wives, and also admired the courage and skill required for them to perform successfully. He observed: "They are personality boys; if they didn't know how to enjoy a joke and laugh at adversity, they'd die up there, alone and bored to death!"

Internationally, people have different customs and religions and forms of government, but there are no foreign cultures, only different ways of pursuing universal desires—the transition from rags to rugs.

The President would stand up to state something that needed to be done, and then he would stride out the door and see that it was done. In times of crisis, whether of morality or security, he was not going to sit on the sidelines and remain neutral. He would stride right into the thick of things because that was where a man had to be if he was going to change the course of society.

The job of getting his speeches transmuted into action on the ground would be up to men like O'Brien, McDonald, McNamara, and—most importantly—Mr. Jensen. The latter didn't want to offend those longtime friends of the President who had become his advisors, but he pointed out to me one salient fact about Mr. Kennerly's first term. Yes, he had effectively dealt with international situations such as developing the Peace Corps, saving the world from nuclear annihilation, extracting our nation from the quagmire of Southeast Asia conflict, and maintaining the tenuous balance in Berlin. However, here in his own country, the Southern coalition, made up of conservative Congressman from both sides of the aisle, had essentially blocked all his domestic proposals.

It didn't matter to them that the guarantees of civil rights to all Americans would be tied to a tax reduction bill aimed at economic expansion. These southerners were firm in their united front of blocking equality for the Negro race. We had dealt with the native Indians by overrunning their civilizations, had used the Chinese as coolies to sweat out railway construction but then forced them to be third-class members of society, and had denied Mexicans any standing at all after killing many of them on the frontiers of Texas. In the future, much the same fate would befall the Inuit when we began to pay attention to Alaska, and the Seminole Indians once we finally ventured into the dark swamps of Florida.

Our nation may have been the first in the world to promulgate a document guaranteeing equal rights to all our citizens, but we sure have been slow to actually follow the tenets of that Constitution when it came to living with persons of different beliefs or ethnicity within our borders.

For this campaign, Mr. Kennerly would not have to go from town to town and community center or public plazas shaking hands for the purpose of making himself known. His first term had made him a world-wide figure of prominence. The days of connecting via a handshake in saloons, post offices, on the docks, and firehouses and homes during teas were not necessary. Those who had perceived his religion as an obstacle had been wrong or simply prejudiced.

However, we still needed to curry the favor of those political bosses who ran things in the various halls of power. As Ken would note, their egos were outsized to begin with; otherwise, they would not have sought the sort of limelight they enjoyed. Each person had feathers that needed preening in one way or another. The big difference was that this time the President would not have to prove himself. What he stood for—the betterment of jobs, education, and standard of living for every American, as well as peace throughout the world—were distinctive planks in his platform. True, much of what he had sought and promised domestically had been thus far blocked in Congress. That was actually the idea behind Mr. Kennerly forming a partnership with Mr. Jensen. Using the slogan, "Let's Back Jack," Vice-President Jensen expected that Congress would fall in line to support them as the year closed on the November elections.

The usual tactic of meeting a voter who volunteers to work for the campaign would be to position such person in a job right away, thereby committing him to the success of the organization. Thus, he'd feel connected with the candidate. His feelings and concerns would be felt by the candidate in this closeness. "Give them something to do to bind them to the team" was Jack's mantra. Together, we'd make the difference. Even if they were too young to cast a vote, teenage girls could be part of a telephone bank to call around a district to determine who was registered as a Democrat. Such cold calling had the benefit of enlisting the support of the person being called simply because he'd been noticed, and asked.

We continued to tap that great underused resource—female power. Mr. Kennerly would take his winning smile and penchant for repartee to junior colleges where his visit would include impromptu talks to the students or meetings at church or community functions. Sometimes he'd do so with Frank Sinatra at his side: the girls would go just crazy!

He had become an identifiable political figure the world over.

As the campaign whorls of 1964 began, Messrs. Kennerly and Jensen could point to various accomplishments that had been achieved or were finally bearing fruit:

1. The Peace Corps under Sargent Shriver was oversubscribed, having passed 7,000 volunteers, despite a commitment of two years in developing countries providing education, environmental preservation, and communication infrastructure development. Medical help would be available when possible. These programs would be available in 139 countries in the future.

2. Navy SEALs are training for unconventional warfare. Green Berets have been instituted as the U.S. Army Special Forces designed for unconventional warfare, hostage rescue, and/or counterterrorism.

3. The goal of reaching and then landing on the moon was proceeding with dual capsules now circling the earth. Gordon Cooper had solo orbited some two dozen times. Two-man missions would soon be successful.

4. The Civil Rights Act had passed all its hurdles and was gradually bringing equal opportunity to the vast majority of Americans.

5. Stopping nuclear war via a surprise attack from Cuba.

6. America and Great Britain initially joined with Crushchev, and thereafter Brezhnev, to sign the July 1963 Nuclear Test Ban Treaty prohibiting tests in space, underwater, and the atmosphere. Averell Harriman negotiated it, and Congress passed it on October 7, 1963.

7. Crop harvests exceeded expectations.

8. Televised press conferences are ongoing, air live without editing, and are immensely popular. The President and Vice-President are not walled off from the public but communicate in person twice a month with their citizens. Television proves to be a revolutionary means for communicating with the citizenry.

These became the Kennerly & Jensen team's domestic goals:

1. America is an open society, welcoming to immigrants, but managed for the general welfare. Safeguards against abusing such a system include preventing abuses of our tax code. There is a big difference between becoming rich, as President Kennerly's father was, but quite another to be grossly wealthy at the expense of corporate minions and industrial wage earners. The President's eye was focused not only on the coal mine owners here, but also on the top auto manufacturing, communications, and pharmaceutical executives. Corporate leaders are to be encouraged to have their workforce participate in their company's wealth, rather than limit distribution to upper management. If a firm should decide to make a class of salaried personnel able to participate in profit sharing, such plans should be made available to all employees by rules laid out by the Internal Revenue Service. The President made these supporting remarks when he submitted the bill to Congress: "We will not stand by and permit the diminution of the working man nor the devaluation of the union member simply because he does not wear a tie to work."

2. Great diligence must be used to eliminate poverty and to promote a living wage that is tailored to fit the regional cost-of-living environment. As an example, the towns in Logan County in West Virginia and the surrounding areas should be considered below the level at which Americans at the bottom tier should be required to live. The owners of the coal companies must stop enslaving their workers and pay each of them a livable wage, utilize the highest standards to ensure safety, and do away with the company store and its script. The mine and production owners should step forward and pay wages that ensure that the workers have pride and purpose in their toil. Such increases can be made up from their substantial profits without raising the price of their coal.

3. Price controls on both basic materials as well as finished goods to prevent inflation undermining the everyday citizen's purchasing power will be closely enforced. Whether raw materials or executive bonuses, any increase would have to

pass strict, uniformly applied standards. Price decreases would be encouraged through national recognition for executive responsibility. The basic tenet of running a corporation for the benefit of stockholders must be tempered by the same preferences as bond-preferred-common stock designations. Those who take the greatest risk are first in line, then those who enable earnings through their sweat and skill are next, and then those who foster its expansion and competitive position follow. Last on the ladder are those who provide ongoing maintenance. America is a free and competitive society, but the days of a Morgan or a Ford, or even a cartel raking in incomes hundreds of times greater than wages paid to corporate employees or farm harvesters, must be discouraged. Incentive-based pay rather than disparity through rank stratification must be the motto of our work-for-reward society.

4. The interest rate for bank passbook savings would fluctuate with the Prime Rate, but the Federal Reserve should be strongly encouraged to support a minimum of 4%; otherwise, such accounts will be subordinated to the rate of inflation too readily. Men do not work for the benefit of chief executives, but to secure a livelihood and stable family life of their own. Our government should foster this precept. The Federal Reserve is tasked not just to soften business cycles, but primarily to **retain the power of the dollar's purchasing power from decade to decade.**

5. Regarding schools, a program will be started whereby astronauts who are not currently training for a mission are tasked to speak to sixth through college-aged students. They are to be paid their salary as well as travel expenses. The host school will take care of their accommodations and reception. This program would be intended to educate youngsters about the opportunities for space exploration, whether as a pilot or an assembler or designer of the equipment.

6. Changes to the tax structure are long overdue and held as too sacrosanct by an entrenched Congress. Our nation has expanded to fill all its borders. Farming no longer requires 7

or 8 in a family to shoulder the daily tasks. Therefore, every wage or salary or self-employed worker is entitled to one personal tax deduction. A second deduction is available for his or her spouse. A third and fourth deduction is allowed for two dependents, whether young, disabled, or elderly. Thereafter, any additional dependents would incur a head tax equal to one exemption. Thus, a family boasting eight dependents would zero-out their personal exemptions. If a married couple wants a family bigger than four, they must be prepared to support these additions themselves.

There will be no income or local taxes on military personnel serving on active duty in combat arms. Support military personnel or construction workers on federal projects are freed from paying federal tax during these periods of employment. Local, inheritance, and death taxes will still apply to these citizens. Sales and use taxes will apply to every service, commodity, and staple item to provide revenue for individual states.

Income taxes are to be steeply tiered. Earnings for the lowest tier are taxed at 1%, but the highest tier, over $4,000,000, is assessed at 70%. If a corporation can afford to pay salaries and bonus packages in that range, they are charging too much for their service or their product. Compensation packages for professional athletes and entertainers must be tied to their annual performance rather than flat contract amounts; this should allow ticket prices for ordinary seating to be held to what is affordable by wage earners.

Off-shore tax havens and dodges of fiscal responsibility are to be closely defined and thereby restricted. The guiding mantra for every American individual or corporation must be that **every citizen shall participate in the financial support of this nation** according to their ability. There will be no further ducking a citizen's national fealty. The more you earn, the greater the percentage you will pay. America is the land of opportunity, but every citizen must contribute according to financial status to support the nation's inherent financial strength.

The goal of a corporation's management should be to share with those on whom the generation of the company's profits depends. Charging lower prices for services or goods must be encouraged as a viable competitive option. Partnerships maintain their legal status, but each partner is treated as an individual regarding payment of income taxes.

A minimum floor is to be established whereby corporate dividend payments amount to at least 15% of profits, regardless of the legal form or amount of gross income. Retained earnings must come from management's take, not investor capital.

Any business, including a public utility, which violates environmental laws must pay assessed penalties from the salaries of management; it is their responsibility to conduct operations without harm to the air, water table, or health. Off-loading such burden onto customers must not be tolerated by the federal government.

7. When a veteran returns from a war zone and wants to purchase a home, he may be offered a preferential mortgage by the Veteran's Administration or receive a ten year exemption from real estate taxes, as he chooses.

8. To encourage the preservation of open land now and into the future, anyone wishing to buy or build a home will be granted a substantial tax credit if a vacant lot within municipal boundaries is selected on which to build, or if a derelict property is renovated or torn down and rebuilt. On the contrary, razing tracts of standing timber or virgin/cultivate fields and installing housing via tract or single homes will be roundly discouraged via heavy taxation and "open land-destruction" penalties. The preservation of open spaces and wild places in their natural setting is to be our mantra. Keeping wide areas of our country free of mankind's spoilage is a goal that we Americans are duty-bound to pass down through succeeding generations.

9. The Second Amendment will be strongly observed. The right of citizens to have and carry a gun is fundamental to the creation and preservation of our form of government. Gun ownership is not the problem. Overcrowding is. We are too often at one another's throats simply because we have run

out of space to expand; we are painting ourselves into a room with insufficient elbow-room. Educating families to limit their production of children as well as monitoring our borders to prevent unskilled immigration will be embraced in support of No. 6 above. Emphasis on the quality of an individual's contribution is far more important to our nation's success than enabling sheer numbers.

What went unsaid in these tenets, but was clearly understood, was that we must undertake to do these things now; we may not have a second chance. Thereby, these Chief Executives served notice that our seemingly endless, even reckless pursuit of growth as an end in itself must finally be tempered.

Despite their being independently wealthy themselves, these leaders recognized that it is more effective to give $5000 to a poor family than to a rich one. The utility of such tax-break money is far greater to the family that has little. Greater happiness attaches to them because their well-being, and accordingly their productivity, is increased. Accommodating this disparity is the mark of a Great Society, as Mr. Jensen would put it.

Cats, dogs, songbirds, and gardens all have a similar attribute; they bring happiness to the person who values such stimuli. As for Nature herself, compare the Japanese ideal of serenity versus the English desire for lushness and mystery with the French drive for symmetry. Recognizing that there are different strokes for different folks is a fact of life, but tolerance can make our world better for all. As the land of the free—where personal industry is encouraged and personal success rewarded—our system of compensation must not be abused by tax laws that promote financial wealth accumulation for the benefit of only a very narrow segment. Such a society dooms its long-term survival.

Notes

[1] This beautifully imaged passage is from Klein, p. 121. Perhaps these evocative lines will inspire my esteemed readers to enjoy reading his entire book, *The Kennedy Curse*.

[2] Weiner, pp. 157-158.

CHAPTER TWENTY-SIX

Resurrection

As the agreed upon delay-date for campaigning expired in August, Lyndon and Mr. Kennerly mapped out their political strategy leading up to Election Day. This would be much simpler than their prior struggles to gain political office. This time around, Jack Kennerly was already the sitting president. He had toured and visited most states in the union; Florida's exposure to drug running and predicted rising sea levels, as well as Kentucky with its mining woes, would require additional attention. Then, of course, there was Texas and California with their large Electoral College blocs, but Vice-President Jensen could tackle those states. Both he and Lyndon would have to take the heat for turning the southern states' world of segregation upside down. Should there be time, given world events, the President could stop up north with a focus on New England, New York and the rust-belt around the auto and steel industries.

Despite his own singular advantages, the President enlisted the assistance of the tried-and-true team of his brother Bobby and brother-in-law Steve Smith to serve as campaign strategists, Sorensen for speeches, McDonald for tracking appointments, Lynne for coordinating the schedules, my legislative guru Leonard O'Brien for meetings with state and Congressional political leaders, me at his side to identify people as he shook their hands and prompt him with points to cover for regional speeches ("touch points" he called them), Gerald A. Bean to run the White House Secret Service detail and organize security for motorcades or speaking engagements and, finally, Jacquelean Kennerly's secretary Caroline (Tish's replacement) to keep track of the First Lady's commitments.

The sitting President could now truthfully state: "This time around, of course, I enjoy a supreme advantage that provides entrée to hitherto shuttered doors. Not only are Lyndon and I recognizable personalities, we are proven as well. We can list successful endeavors that are now in place, either as laws or as self-help measures, to resurrect disadvantaged citizens from the 'cellars of constant constraint.' Nevertheless, doing the right thing by Americans is more important than my being reelected."

There was no doubt that all the members of his Cabinet knew how the President worked and what he expected of them. I must relate this incident, however, because it proved to be so amusing that it swept the gossip halls in the Big House. When the movie *Spartacus,* starring Tony Curtis, came to the screen, President Kennerly advised me that he would like to go see it. I conferred with Red Fay, and together we bought tickets without revealing who they were for. As the time for the show arrived, we entered the theatre a bit late in order not to make any sort of hoopla with the other movie-goers, but the manager had heard that a special patron was coming and he had delayed the start of the film until the President's party was seated. Thus, the house lights were still up when Mr. Kennerly spotted Orville Freeman and his wife in the row just ahead. Reaching over and tapping his Secretary of Agriculture on the shoulder, he remarked:

"Haven't the leaders of the New Frontier anything better to do with their time than spend it going to a movie?"

With quick wit, but proper respect, Orville replied: "I just wanted to be immediately available should my President need me!"

Everyone within hearing enjoyed a big laugh.

Jack had personal, even quirky habits the same as everybody, but they would be noticeable in a movie theatre due to the forced constraints of the seats. Jack would raise his knees and press forward on the back of the chair to relieve the strain on his back, he'd tap his teeth with his finger, and he'd even brush his forelock back with his whole hand. All these were signs that, while he was deeply absorbed in the historical scenes which he knew well from all his reading, his body was protesting its prolonged deprivation of comfort.

Undergoing some discomfort is often the price one has to pay to experience substantial pleasures. Obviously, as much as we admired the judgment and ability to inspire which our leader possessed, he was just a normal human being at his core. When we returned to the Oval

Office, Red returned to his job as Undersecretary for Naval Affairs and the President took up the business of the current campaign.

The key element to winning his first election as a Congressman had been the use of informal tea parties hosted under the direction of Rose. Both her daughters and her sons' wives had been utilized. However, these were not ordinary teas conducted in a small den. These parties might include as few as 200, but they might well comprise 2000 women. Larry O'Brien had estimated that some 70,000 potential voters had been reached with the Kennerly message. These gatherings allowed him to discuss the issues important to everyone there, but to subsequently broaden the message when he addressed very large crowds.

Obviously, such a method would not work when a candidate is trying to reach 20 million voters. However, television had now become not merely an accepted medium in politics—due to the success of on-screen debates—but also its reach dwarfed even that of broadcasting. By 1964, TV sets were considered to be a household necessity. Few people would even bother to turn on their radio set if they could **see** who was talking or singing. The initial wallop of purchasing a television would be gradually offset by finding entertainment right in your living room rather than spending money downtown at the theater or stage palace.

When a candidate is already occupying the office of President, he thereby enjoys an enormous advantage without spending a cent. His appearance at weekly press conferences provided both image exposure as well as a chance to show what he was accomplishing on behalf of the citizenry. Jack's photogenic face, together with what he said, provided such good copy that no television news station could afford to miss one of these sessions.

As he had finished one broadcast in September 1964, our President had quipped: "Holding a microphone sure beats holding a teacup!"

As summer waned, it seemed like we were well ahead of Mr. Coldwater's fierce posturing with the electorate. We had also left behind men like Rockefeller and Romney whom the President had considered more potent challengers. I learned from McDonald that Mr. Kennerly had predicted at a November 13 staff meeting, just prior to his trip to Texas: "Give me Barry to run against, and I won't even have to leave the Oval Office during the campaign." The issues from his first campaign as a "Catholic candidate," as well as his inexperience and bad judgment regarding the fiasco over invading Cuba seemed to have largely evaporated. In fact, there was a palpable feeling in the air—the sitting president was going to win regardless of what the other side did, so "come on everybody, let's get on the bandwagon and vote Democratic!"

I never ceased to be amazed by the unpredictability of a threatening situation. As we prepared for a visit to San Francisco as part of our fall campaign run, the agents scoping out the venues and neighboring buildings reported everything secure in the Presidio, a military complex boasting impressive overlooks of the Golden Gate Bridge. Even I imagined this site would be safe with little risk. Since it would be comfortably cool in San Francisco, I expected the venue would be packed with people taking the air as much as listening to their President.

While our President was speaking to the assembled servicemen and their spouses, he reached forward to drink from a glass of water. Merely shifting his weight caused the rostrum to topple forward over the edge of the platform. Two Secret Service agents posted to his front in the crowd reached up and caught their man before he received injury.

With typical composure and quick wit, Mr. Kennerly turned the moment of shock to his advantage by quipping, "We flew down from Los Angeles earlier today; I guess I thought I was still wearing my seatbelt!" This brought widespread chuckles from everyone present. Nevertheless, thereafter I made sure that if a rostrum was to be used, it was always screwed down to the platform on which it rested.

He once turned to me on our way to a speaking engagement and stated, "Politics is the art of understanding the possible. It involves conciliation, balancing, and interpreting the forces and factions of public opinion. Knowing how big a step, and when to take it, is a fine art. My brushes are my speaking engagements and my medium the conversations I inspire our citizens to engage in."

What the hell was that he just said? I just looked at him, glad that he, and not me, was president.

On the other hand, he had achieved what would probably be called the most important agreement of the 20th Century when the Nuclear Proliferation Pact was signed with the Soviet Union and Great Britain on October 10. The Test Ban Treaty prohibited testing in space, the seas, or the atmosphere. Testing could still proceed underground, armies would continue to assert their acquisitive goals, wars could still erupt, and China had yet to be included in such intelligent pacts, but this treaty was a significant step in de-escalating world conflict. The alternative would have led irresistibly toward world annihilation.

While we were stewing over the coming election and the effect the president's stance on civil rights would have in pushing voters into the Republican camp, Lou Harris, the pollster, approached him with some reassuring news.

"Mr. President, it is time you ignored the accepted wisdom regarding Southern traditions. States' rights and segregation are of course major concerns, but the outstanding developments in this region, such as the burgeoning space exploration industry, military base construction, the new highway system drawing disparate regions closer together, and television giving everyone greater contact with diverse thinking from other parts of the country have each worked to dilute the strength of the anti-equality block. We have a "New South" in the making, Mr. President. Business is booming. Moderation in dealing with diverse populations by civic-minded governors rather than red-necks predominates. Pay attention to satisfying the "southern development" councils which are springing up all over as Southerners become better educated. You will thereby encourage the new industrial and educational explosion, and this will win you votes. The fact that you are ensuring the reliability of Medicare and Social Security, as well as your backing of unemployment insurance, will win still more hearts over."

"Thank you, Lou. You have managed to resurrect a fine day from the ashes of impending disappointment. Please stop by anytime." The two men smiled at one another as they shook hands.

Sometimes, the right person comes along to say just the right thing when it's most needed.

Nevertheless, the President wanted to go to Florida to speak with local politicians, labor leaders, and the Inter-American Press Association members about the domestic economy and how American companies could interact with Latin America for their mutual benefit.

CHAPTER TWENTY-SEVEN

Reelection

This trip south would be followed by another trip over to Texas. Given our experience in Dallas last year, we chose his speaking engagements and facility visits with far more care. Motorcades would be put on hold until a bulletproof Plexiglas dome was perfected. That was the thing about Texas; the state was so big that a person could fly, rather than motor, and no one would raise an eyebrow. At this point, the Space program was so successful that the President could really claim that in return for further federal largesse regarding construction of facilities and grants to educational institutions, he would require a far better showing from their residents in the election. He knew he could win over the average voter, but the political bosses and those who controlled campaign contributions would also need to be brought on board.

About the only time he had ever been at a loss for words occurred last year during a swing through Oklahoma. On this trip, he had wanted to stop off at a dusty cowpoke sort of town where there were few cars but lots of horse-drawn wagons. The streets, however, were laid out wide enough to accommodate four cars abreast, yet on this particular day, nary a one was in sight except those of the presidential party. He had stopped his limousine and was sitting up on the rear of the back seat chatting with a few folk when he inquired as to why, in a relatively small town, this street was so wide.

"Well, hell, Mr. President," the mayor had drawled, "that's so's a buckboard and its horses can turn around without having to do any backin' up! Makes sense to all of us here. How wide are them there streets back your way in Bosstown, anyhow?"

Our man in the White House had simply smiled. His advance men had neglected to fill him in properly regarding this local custom, but thereafter he never forgot it.

The President had also come to understand the saying that residents of that state held true: *We may live far apart, but we stay close to*gether. Anything one family believed would likely be held as true by his neighbor. That's why adherence to the tenets of Republicanism had been so hard to penetrate by Democrats. If that didn't make this year hard enough already, this campaign would entail dealing with voters' reactions to the recent passage of the Civil Rights Bill. "Equal rights go hand-in-hand with equal opportunity" the President had wistfully observed when thoughts about a Voting Rights bill had first surfaced, but he could have also cracked that "equal rights raise an equal amount of resentment." Penetrating southerners' resistance would surely be a tough nut to crack.

Once again, Mr. Kennerly wanted to rely on using the best weapon in his arsenal: his wife.

Jacquelean, as Jack had noted succinctly, has her own ideas about what she will and—more significantly—will not do. For her, nothing was ever carved in stone, least of all a schedule. She preferred her day to be unstructured. That way, she could visit somewhere politically important simply by dropping in without forewarning. When she did that, she liked the way people would be more natural in her presence. No formal lunches or afternoon teas for this First Lady. And, as everyone by this time knew, she did not like campaigning of any sort.

There was one distinct advantage that had gradually become evident to everyone associated with the First Couple. The longer they were resident in the White House, the more comfortable they seemed to be with each other. Mrs. Kennerly had explained to Ken and me that Jack was indulgent; when she was feeling that the pressures of service to the nation were growing too intense, her husband would send her off to visit a sister or even take a cruise to the Greek Isles. When she returned, refreshed and eager to embrace life with her husband as President, their marriage would have become that much stronger. She could then be cheerful and supportive when his workday ended, enabling him to find solace upstairs. Their marriage thrived because brief separations, taken when needed, enriched their affection.

In response to our probing, Jack replied, "Well, this is our own private way of keeping the love in our marriage. She likes it, she then makes me happy; thus, it works for us."

And that was that.

So, there we were, stuck with the personal whims of Kennerly's best political asset while Messrs. Coldwater, Rockefeller, and perhaps even Romney had maneuvered to give the President a run for his money. I'm not boasting, mind you, but the tactic I came up with was to bear fruit. We would use the television networks for debates and broadcasts of our message, of course. It had worked in 1960 during the campaign against then Vice-President Nixy. Mr. Kennerly had looked sunny, healthy, fully informed, and happy to be taking on the challenge of leading the people. Mr. Nixy's appearance was somber, skittish, and perhaps even a little unkempt; he had used make-up to hide his 5:00 shadow, but both had been visible under the hot TV lights!

My idea for this go-round did not involve my President submitting to a heavy roster of televised debates. Holding the office as he did, Mr. Kennerly could get television time to discuss any issue or concern he wanted to present to the American public. He could then use this opportunity to direct their attention so they would support whatever he was proposing. The key byproduct of this would be that voters would retain his face fresh in their minds all the way to the polls. This would be so even if he had never made a single whistle-stop in their town during the campaign.

The Democrats would thereby have wider dissemination of our party's message but with far less expenditure of either effort or money: this was an all-American deal if ever there was one!

Ken McDonald and Len O'Brien and I set about contacting the three prime television companies and scheduling air time that matched Mr. Kennerly's schedule of meetings with foreign ministers, pitches to Congress, or attendance at ribbon-cuttings for federal construction projects. His main tactic would be to open a dialogue with his political opponent, asking how that man would handle such and such a situation, and after the candidate had stumbled around a bit with his answer, the President could relate succinctly how he had in fact already effectively handled that very same situation. Obviously, the removal of missiles from Cuba had been his most important triumph. In those circumstances, he used restraint and rational thought rather than allow emotions and war-like responses to rule his thinking. Nowadays, there were matters of less significance to the world, but nevertheless these were very important to the individuals involved.

For example, just like Bobby produced an outstanding assistant when he had, years ago, introduced his Harvard roommate Kenny McDonald to his brother, who was then serving as the Representative from Brookline, he now put forth the name of his prep school roommate from Milton Academy. David Hackett had played ice hockey at the Olympic level, so his appointment as the executive director of the President's Committee on Juvenile Delinquency and Youth Crime was a natural choice. He had a good head for first impressions, so the first thing he did upon taking a seat behind his desk was to put through a phone call to the stationer. He wanted all the letterhead for his department recalled and the name "Juveniles against Crime" substituted. JAC was a far sexier name.

Two areas in which the President had demonstrated real foresight and leadership were the exploration of outer space but, more significantly, the need to control the arms race.

On October 28, 1962, in the wake of the Cuban crisis, Premier Nikita Crushchev had stated: "We should continue the exchange of views on the prohibition of atomic and thermonuclear weapons, general disarmament, and other problems relating to the relaxation of international tension."

Knowing full well that the Russians could not be relied on to be consistent with their pronouncements, our President seized on this opening and proceeded to pursue the prevention of testing in the atmosphere, underwater, and in space. With this attitude publicly expressed, he was able to meet the Chairman's concerns and finalize the Nuclear Test Ban Treaty. Time alone was creating real pressure to do so. He foresaw over a dozen nations having nuclear bomb capability in the future, so the U.S.S.R., Great Britain, and the U.S. met on August 5, 1963 to sign the Limited Nuclear Test Ban Treaty. This was ratified by Congress on September 24.

This led Mr. Kennerly to state at a talk before the University of Maine:

"The Russian Bear favors bluster, posturing, and the rattle of sabers to bend countries to its will. We will not be cowed by such hysterics. Let us never fear to negotiate, but we must never negotiate out of fear. The Russian bear may rant, but underneath the teeth and claws is a mind that is aching for conciliation. While Russia and the United States have never been in openly declared conflict, that vast country has been invaded, subjugated, and rent asunder numerous times over the last 1000 years; we cannot blame her leaders for being intent on protecting her standing among other nations. The wave of the future is not the conquest of the world by a single dogmatic creed but, rather, the liberation of the diverse energies of free nations and free men.

"Just like a man trying to survive a prison camp torture, you have to have something to focus your mind on in order to provide the will to stay alive. Let us today resolve to be the masters, not the victims, of our history. We must ensure peace not merely for Americans, but for all men and women around the world; peace not just for our time, but for all time. Through concerted, voluntary action, the nuclear nations must control the destructive power of the weapons of war before they destroy us. Working and trusting together, we shall save our planet or together we shall perish in its flames." [1]

Naturally, none of the politicians opposing him occupied positions which would allow them access to developing expertise in the frontier of outer space. He had told Jim Webb, as Director of NASA, and Dr. Weisner as an influential scientist to cooperate with the Vice-President. Noting that no one could manage such a huge undertaking better than a Texan, he had asked Mr. Jensen to oversee the budgetary and objective goals of the space program. He had also stated what should be the prime objective of our country's becoming involved in the space race.

"We want to focus on the moon. Finding out about all the properties of space and how we could survive in this new frontier are important, but our focus must be beating the Soviets to a landing on the moon, pure and simple. Part of the prize will be to show how we started behind and lagged for a bit, but then caught up and technologically surpassed them at their own game. In this day and age, we need such a dramatic result to stunt the communist claims that they have the better political system. Developing countries will turn over their raw materials and provide foreign bases to the country that appears to be the leader in world technology. I will not allow the Russians to supersede our primacy in this area.

"Moreover, this program will devour huge amounts of our national GNP, thereby eating into many of the worthy domestic programs we have, and need to have in the future, so we need a highly defined goal which, once met, will allow us to pull back and resume our important domestic work."

As for Cuba itself, by the time the 1964 campaign got underway, his position toward that imprisoned island had become one of offering peace overtures. The message proffered through Bill Atwood, a WWII paratrooper veteran turned journalist who had known Fidel while he was still a hill fighter, was that if revolution was no longer exported to South American countries, then trade relations between the two neighbors could be normalized.

At a speech before the inter-American Press Association in Miami, the President addressed the presence of problems in our Southern Hemisphere by countering with a policy of social idealism whereby liberty and progress could function hand-in-hand. As for the threat of revolution, he declared that, "This, and this alone, divides us. As long as this is true, nothing is possible. Without it, everything is possible."

For a few days afterward, Art Schlesinger proudly strutted around his fellow journalists. He had written these lines. Sadly, he never relished the move to position Mr. Jensen prominently in Kennerly's administration. By 1964, he no longer covered the goings-on at the White House. He had been a good friend but, for some men, the rancor of disdain proves stronger than the bonds of loyalty.

Mr. Kennerly theorized that once America recognized Cuba as a sovereign nation, the desire of her citizens to "buy American" would prove overwhelming and the dictator would have to put up with imports from the United States. Physical commodities would win out over political maxims. Clearly, the President held no rancor toward the Cuban people; it was only their dominance by a dictator who was in the thrall of Russia that he abhorred. In this case, we would have to simply wait for that dictator to die before relations really improved.

A problem which apparently had not gone away despite the President's now evident ability to serve the nation was the issue of his religion. In 1964, it dogged his campaign once more. Finally, Mr. Kennerly had had enough of the slanted slights and innuendo contained in the questioning by reporters who preferred to ambush him on the campaign trail.

One night we made a stop at some high school in Wheeling, West Virginia. The President stood before the assembled crowd of citizens and newsmen with their film crews. He spoke in no uncertain terms.

> "It has come to my attention that you are still questioning what kind of church I believe in. That is not the relevant question. The sort of religion I follow is important only to me and my family. What **is** important is: what kind of America do I believe in? In America, the separation of church and state is absolute. It is clearly demanded by our Constitution. I am not governed by any Catholic prelate any more than Protestants are told by their ministers for whom to vote. Each citizen has the right to choose what religion to follow, and he also has the right to select the right man for the job of President. I hope I will get each of your votes!"

Thereupon, the president immediately did what he does so well: he strode into the group of assembled reporters and camera technicians even before he met with the local residents. He began shaking everyone's hand as he smiled broadly their way. He was very effective at this.

As the campaign came to a close, Lou Harris and even the national press were claiming that the Kennerly/Jensen team was going to make mincemeat of the Barry Coldwater/William Miller challengers. The Democratic duo did just that. Thus, even before November rolled around, we were confidently working on making the next year a resounding success for the average American family and, except for Mr. Kennerly's appearances on television and at the National Democratic Convention, ignored further whistle-stopping along the campaign trail.

Knowing how Mr. Kennerly liked to get away from the pressure cooker of the capital every so often, especially during political campaigns, it came as no surprise when he suddenly announced that he was taking the weekend off to spend it with Jacquelean at the home they had bought in Wexford. These attractive grounds were located in the rolling hill country of Middleburg, Virginia. Jacquelean loved going to this retreat because she could freely ride with her children Carolyn and Jon-Jon for hours in the sparsely-settled region.

As for himself, the President didn't much care whether he relaxed there or down in Florida or up at the Hyannis family compound. Even a house on the Chesapeake would have been nice. All he needed was a complete change of scene, freedom from reporters, and a phone that would ring only for emergencies.

Naturally, the couple could never be absolutely alone. In addition to the Secret Service agents and various administrative assistants, Captain Tazewell Shepard (code-named, interestingly, *Witness*) had to go wherever the President went. This naval aide carried the codes required to launch nuclear retaliation in the event of a surprise attack. These had to be immediately available to our Commander in Chief at all times. Thus, no matter where the presidential party might journey for a weekend respite, the presence of this tall, darkly-brooding man carrying a black briefcase reminded us that we were in the company of no ordinary man. This fun host, who laughed so heartily, was the leader, and therefore guardian, of the free world. "Bagman" was a constant reminder of how important it was for us to keep our host healthy and relaxed, but also vigilant.

When possible, Jack enjoyed the ubiquitous presence of his longtime friend Kirk Billings or, less frequently, the rousing intellect of Ben and his wife Antoinette (Tony) Bradlee. Neither of them worked in government, but they could hold their own when it came to the President's curiosity and inquisitive mind. Joshing with these friends rather than with foreign potentates was relaxing.

Mr. Bradlee had served in the Navy during the war, graduated from Harvard University, and been raised in Boston. These attributes, along with his nimble brain and ever-ready wit, complemented Jack Kennerly well. The Bradlees were social associates who could provide levity over a weekend. Their presence put Jack at ease and thereby permitted the President to escape the thorny pressures of the Oval Office for brief periods. [2]

Despite the relaxed ambiance these friends fostered, Jack could manage to get himself in trouble because he would become so unperturbed that he could momentarily lose touch with reality. One lazy evening, the Kennerlys and Bradlees were sitting around trading tall tales; Ken, Larry, and I would be allowed to participate whenever there was a lull in the conversation. During a break, I happened to mention that Ben had married a very svelte, alluring woman. To my mind, the compliment was well-deserved, and since Gail was not present, I thought it *a propos* to state the obvious.

Jacquelean riding with Carolyn and Jon-Jon

Jack, however, immediately thought I was baiting a hook and stated, "Well, now, what makes you say that, Clint?"

Jacquelean quickly intervened: "Oh, come now, Jack! You know you are always saying that Tony is your ideal."

"Yes, that's true," he said, not thinking, but promptly caught himself from going over the precipice by adding, "However, you know you are my real ideal, Jacquelean!"

She turned and smiled knowingly my way. When he was in front of the television cameras or holding forth at some political function, the President could be sharp as a tack, but here in the country, with not a reporter within twenty miles and the secret service agents unobtrusively patrolling the perimeter, he could be just a regular guy and say not-so-smart things. All of us loved him for that.

"Getting into an argument over points during a game of backgammon gives him respite from the grueling pressures of the presidency," Kirk would observe. "In fact, I don't remember a single instance where I didn't feel lucky to be in a room with him, even if it was at a ward in some Washington convalescent hospital. After he rescued his PT boat crew, and islanders rescued them, the Navy hospitalized him. For the remainder of his tour, he was in physical pain nearly every day, but not once did he complain. He simply loved being alive and embracing all that life had to offer!" [3]

For his spouse, however, Wexford was everything. There were no pressures from ever-present relatives to "get in the game" and participate in an endless variety of family contests.

Most importantly, there was space in which she could mount Bit o' Irish and roam freely amidst fields and forests. Jacquelean was not merely an expert rider. She had been a show competitor while in school, true, but she simply loved being a part of such large, powerful, and fleet-of-foot animals. Atop her mount, she could be as athletic as any runner or swimmer. Holding her heels down in the stirrups and her shapely fanny tucked under her spine, she could post for hours with a feeling of complete release and independence. Even her artful dinner parties couldn't provide the same sort of release and sense of freedom.

"This is where I truly feel *joie de vivre*!" she exclaimed to her husband one sunny day as he watched horse-and-rider seamlessly glide across the countryside.

For the President, relaxing at this home in the company of his German Shepherd Skipper meant good cooking and a laid-back atmosphere of easy-going relaxation. The chef and his staff at the White House were—under the First Lady's tasteful guidance—superlative in their ability to provide sumptuous, even exotic fare for state dinners but, for Jack, a simple down-home meal was his favorite kind of cooking. He wasn't sure, in fact, whether it was their cook, or the ambiance, that made Wexford so appealing.

"Good morning, Mr. President!" said Jeremy as his boss descended the stairs for breakfast on a particular Saturday. His broad smile beamed as his thick, black eyebrows rose in pleasure at Mr. Kennerly's arrival at the table.

"Well, now, Jeremy, what have you got laid on for us today? Scrambled eggs, I hope. You know how I like your whipped eggs!"

"Yes sir, just the way you likes them. And Southern pork sausage with French toast swaddled in butter and syrup. There's plump strawberry jam on the side should you like a little diversion." Jeremy rocked back on his heels, displaying his prominent stomach as though it served as the vault which contained all the secrets to his delicious cooking.

"Now tell me, Jeremy," the President began, "You've been taking care of my wife, son, and daughter as well as a host of visitors during your time here at Wexford, yet you've never revealed even a few of your secrets. How is it that you can make these scrambled eggs so fluffy and tasty? I've never found any better and, as you know, I've been round the world a few times!"

"Why shucks, Mr. President, there ain't no big secret. I'm just careful to get the pan evenly hot, melt a little butter to prepare the surface, and then pour in my mix of eggs, half-and-half, and a little vanilla, and then use a spatula to ensure the edges don't brown as I stir them eggs around. That's real important: don't neglect them while they're in the pan, and they'll do right by you!"

A long-held secret of his had been exposed, but since it was his President who sat alone at the table while thoroughly engrossed in devouring those delicious yellow creations, the cook felt privileged to have something to share that was important to the leader of the free world.

"God Bless Almighty, these **are** delicious!" exclaimed Mr. Kennerly as he hoisted another forkful into his hungry mouth. He spread some of the richly red berry jam across the fresh faces of French toast gleaming with melted butter, and then savored a slice as it silently disappeared between his lips.

Just then Carolyn sauntered into the room, pouting wisely with some profound secret yet to be revealed. She sidled up to her father's leg, so he reached around her and held her close by his side.

"Look what Jeremy has for us today," said her father, pointing to his half-empty plate.

Her eyes went wide and she rushed over to wrap her arms around Jeremy, saying "Oh thank you, thank you! Jeremy. You make our trips out here so much fun!"

Jeremy couldn't help smiling at this adoring child's angelic honesty. He loved making the members of this family happy.

As he turned to head back to the kitchen, Mr. Kennerly asked, "By the way, did my wife skip breakfast?"

"Yes, sir, that she did! She had all her gear on and simply licked right outta here, saying she couldn't wait to get on Bit o' Irish fast enough. I reckon she'll be right hungry when she comes back in time for lunch, however."

As he exited to the kitchen, the paneled pantry door—large enough to slide a food-laden cart through—swung behind him with a hushed *whish.*

Carolyn had sat down and was carving her sausages into small pieces when her father leaned over and asked about Jon-Jon.

"Oh, he's still upstairs. He made another wee-wee in his bed last night and Miss Shaw was just super mad at him, so they're washing the sheets together before she'll allow him to come down."

"Oh, I see," The President of the United States observed, smiling to himself. He loved his job. He not only felt comfortable in the position, but also believed himself qualified to run the daily affairs of state. It was as though he had prepared for this post during his entire life and could now bring all his knowledge and rational thinking to it. True, he could speed-read documents while clearly comprehending what he had just read. More startlingly, he could raise some point that had been stated within a treatise that he had read even months earlier. This capacity, to reach back into what was obviously a library's worth of retained knowledge, and to then trot out some fact at the opportune moment, just wowed his friends, governmental associates, and even his wife.

He was the right man in the right job at the right time but, above all, he relished the antics and fun—even the arguments—that his kids got themselves into.

"Well, eat up, Carolyn. I want you to grow up to be just as tall and beautiful as Mommy, okay?" He smiled her way as his daughter looked up at him with her shining, intelligent eyes.

"Daddy, don't rush me; I like teasing little Jon-Jon too much to act grown-up."

Jack smiled and sat back in his chair, enjoying himself. This was family life as it should be. He wanted to enjoy many such slices—not just of French toast, but also vignettes of American family life, despite his holding such a responsible position in government.

This weekend made him so happy that he told me all about it when we met in his office the following Monday. The President's family escapades made me glad that Gail and I had made Chris and Corey. We wanted to have happy laughs with our own kids as the boys grew up: if only I could stop working such long hours virtually every day!

I still hadn't learned to be careful about what I wished for.

Notes

[1] Schlesinger, *A Thousand Days*, pp. 619 and 689-690, and see Dallek, p. 621.

[2] Ben Bradlee would later be named as Editor of the *Washington Post*.

[3] Pitts, p. 148.

CHAPTER TWENTY-EIGHT

Second Inaugural

After celebrating the New Year in 1965, the pressure mounted as the date for the Inaugural Address drew near.

"Well, Ken, we better get Sorensen in here to stitch together my upcoming Second Inaugural Address," the President lectured. "The leader must always walk the fine line between the approval of those he governs and the control he must exert over them. If I'm to stand before the Congress and the American people for a second time, I want to assure them that I understand their concerns and that I intend to address these problems. Being dignified, educated, and a gentlemen will no longer suffice. If they don't believe I understand their personal problems, they won't think me worthy of either their attention or support. This is the daily burden which I carry around; it's a concomitant of being able to bask publicly in the glory of this office."

I nodded in agreement, but he was not done with this train of thought. One of Mr. Kennerly's distinguishing traits was the ability to learn from his mistakes so that he did not repeat them. He could admit he was wrong, but you'd never see him repeat an error of judgment. This allowed him to use level-headed restraint in times of crisis.

"In politics, as in governance, you always want to sell your strengths while diverting attention away from your weaknesses. The key to my success thus far has been the feeling I instill in listeners. As I enumerate goals or list key facts supporting my presumptions, the members of my audience realize that they *want* to believe in me," he affirmed to Ken, Leonard, and me as we prepared for January 4th.

"As far as Conservatives are concerned, I'm one of them; but Liberals identify with my proposals as well. I present a unique set of values and capacities not found in other presidents. You won't find my sort of appeal on the ingredients of a soup can. I have tried, throughout my life, to be self-reliant in a world where everyone is constantly attempting to pigeonhole me as being this or that. For all I know, I may be a bifurcated, and thereby a one-of-a-kind, politician."

He chuckled after revealing this tidbit of self-indulgent thinking.

He had demonstrated even-handed judgment during the steel crisis created by industry executives, such as Roger Blough, almost three years ago. He had parlayed a promise to the labor unions to keep inflation under control into an agreement not to strike for increased wages, but then a cartel of steel companies had gone behind his back to raise their prices without giving Labor a share of the increased revenues. President Kennerly promptly had the attorney general threaten a grand jury investigation of their expense account deductions for vacations, phone calls, and entertainment. The mere prospect of the Internal Revenue Service nosing around did the trick but, as an assurance, the Pentagon was directed to purchase its steel from companies which had left their prices unchanged.[1]

Appearing on television, the President had chastised this cartel with: "The American people will find it hard, as I do, to accept a situation in which a handful of steel executives pursue private power and profit while disdaining their sense of public responsibility. They have shown utter contempt for the interests of 185 million Americans. Monopoly naturally appears to him who enjoys it as the best possible system, but such is not the case here."

He had never confronted the executives directly; rather, he used round-about maneuvering to outfox them. He asserted to William Martin, who headed up the Federal Reserve Bank: "What these men believe is not accurate. We must assure them of the soundness of the dollar and that inflation will be curtailed. They are acting as though ongoing problems cannot be corrected!"

Of course, if he hadn't successfully gotten the price increases rescinded, he would have permanently lost the confidence of Labor. Fortunately, he was capable of working the points of pressure from both ends. We couldn't have had a better man for the job.

This triumph had indeed been significant, but the *Boston Globe* became so enthused when reporting it that the newspaper had mistakenly referred to him as "Saint John Kennerly." We were able to kid him about that for around two days, if I recall, whereupon some different crisis arose, causing this merely mortal man to return to earth in order to deal with yet another "rift in our nation's serenity" as we were now referring to such problems.

He had become known as a man who not only believed in the line between right and wrong, but acted on this belief as well (so long as it didn't involve the privacy of one's bedroom). Such forthright behavior could not be said of every governmental employee. For example, the Justice Department had recently pursued the indictment and subsequent imprisonment of George Chacharis for conspiracy and tax evasion while serving as mayor of the steel town, Gary, Indiana.

"Easygoing on the surface but ruthlessly dedicated to honesty," wrote Pierre Salinger as an aside about Mr. Kennerly in his column summarizing the Chacharis case.

These characteristics had been formed during his terms in Congress and had now become characteristic components of his personality.

By this time, I had been close to the Kennerly political train long enough to know that the candidate was a serious student of political reality. He studied ethnic and religious patterns of voting with systematic depth and then applied his deep knowledge of history and political necessity and national need to craft his platforms and flesh out the "Sorensen structure" of his speeches. After carefully studying the political terrain, he'd tour the country giving speeches at conventions and rallies. His support team would ensure that the wide-circulation magazines, such as *LIFE* and the *Saturday Evening Post* and *McCall's*, were publishing articles about Jacquelean and Jack and their family so the public would want to reach out and touch them during their public appearances. While making himself available to his public, he'd also meet with local political leaders, who were raising funds through dinners and rallies, to gain the support of their delegations at the convention.

Larry O'Brien had, of course, heard much of this posturing many times before, so he simply suggested, "Sure, Mr. Kennerly. As your longtime friend, I accept your thoughts. Meantime, what do you think of these rough drafts which Ted has prepared for your Second Inaugural Address?"

After some tweaking, these became his wonderfully inspiring words:

<u>Second Inaugural Address delivered January 4, 1965:</u>

"My fellow Americans, today we come together for the second time, but there is no passage of power, no immensely different challenges for me to spread before you. Our meeting today marks the continuation of our mutual pursuit, a quest in which the citizens of our country are made safe from want, fear, or destruction.

"Ours is the land of the free. We have the right to choose our leaders in government, to applaud or criticize them as they deserve, to select the type of schooling and work we wish to pursue, and to decide on whether to marry and raise a family. In the past, whether due to war, famine, or the challenges of the frontier, it was governmental policy to encourage our population to grow. Our country is blessed with national parks of unfathomable beauty, yet there is not a corner of our great land which we do not now occupy in some form. Even the farthest tip of northern Alaska has permanent human settlements.

"In the not too distant past, producing large numbers of offspring was important to work a farm and bring the harvest in, or to fill the ranks of vast armies which could overwhelm by massing on the field of battle. In the nuclear age, such demands are outmoded. It is appropriate, therefore, to tackle head-on the menace which our burgeoning population poses to our individual, and collective, happiness. I am not suggesting rules of restraint; I am merely stating that there is no longer an imperative to multiply in order to function well as a nation. Our population is predicted to more than double its 160 million by the turn of the century. No longer is there a pressing need to multiply in order to function on the farm or in the factory. We have ample numbers in our nation. It is still important to foster improvement in the quality of our everyday lives even as we pursue our constitutional right to happiness. But for your government to encourage large families as a bulwark against attack or famine is no longer necessary. A married couple should produce offspring according to their desires, not as the means to their survival.

"I am therefore today directing the Internal Revenue Service to revise the rules regarding personal income taxes to allow a standard deduction for a taxpayer, spouse, and two dependents, whether offspring or grandparent; neutral for the third dependent; and then each dependent thereafter is to be taxed at an amount equivalent to the standard deduction offset.

"In this manner, we will be able to accumulate, and thereafter maintain, the funds necessary for new schools and public recreation facilities that the overall level of our population requires. Those of you who think rationally will see immediately that this does not infringe on any ethnic, nor indeed on even my own religion's beliefs. It is purely secular and, most importantly, goes to the core of our tenets: to value each individual's quality of contribution, rather than sheer numerical multiplication. There will be those who will disagree, but these proposals are put forth not as my personal agenda, but for the good of the country's future well-being.

"Vince Lombardi once remarked: 'It's not whether you are knocked down that's important; it's whether you get up afterward.' He was a great football coach, but his observation applies to our tax structure as well. If we do not favor our citizens shouldering the burden of their procreation, we shall create a welfare state that fails inwardly due to the weight of its own demands.

"Civility is not a sign of weakness. We cannot expect that every person seeking high office will speak forthrightly to the American people. Unfortunately, sincerity must always be proved. But we can hope that fewer people will listen to nonsense. The notion that we are headed for defeat through uncontrolled deficits, or that our being strong is a matter of slogans, is simply nonsense. But the ability of a population to continue to be civil to one another can be threatened by overcrowding. Too much of a good thing can not only make you a candidate for diabetes and heart disease; it can lead to great stress on one's family, as well. We must, as a people of diverse cultures and beliefs, come together in the realization that our continued expansion has reached its zenith. Should we press on without reigning in our ambitions, we will pay the price in discourteous disregard of our fellow man. This, eventually, will erupt in open conflict, not just civil disobedience.

"As an adjunct of civility, it is time that we stop burdening society by incarcerating those who ignore respect for the rules of a functioning, respectful society. Let us invoke a national policy wherein any of us are capable of making a mistake that merits forgiveness. Do one crime, serve the time. But, do another, and it's goodbye brother.

"If we always give our best at whatever we undertake in this great nation of ours, if we look at conditions as they are without the obfuscation of party loyalties and positions, we can get past the persistent myths of prejudice and embrace meaningful dialogue and exchange. Thereby, we will be amazed at what we can accomplish by working together in harmony."

Our President paused a moment while he looked over the assembled well-wishers. Then, taking hold of the corners of the lectern, he resumed fervently:

"When the sanctity of our country, or that of another sovereign nation or, indeed, even a city of such country, is threatened by acquisitive aggression from outside its borders, resolution must be in favor of freedom. Let us never negotiate out of fear, but let us never fear to negotiate. You have only to ask the people residing in West Berlin to understand the truth of this. Let both sides explore what problems unite us instead of belaboring those problems which divide us. Let both sides formulate precise proposals for the inspection and regulation of arms so that we may bring the absolute power to destroy other nations under the absolute control of all nations. If a beachhead of cooperation can push back the jungle of suspicion, let both sides join in creating a new endeavor—a new world of law where the strong are just and the weak secure and the peace preserved. America's strength must be the instrument whereby peace in our world is assured."

For a moment, the President paused, wiping his handkerchief across his nose. He scanned his audience, and then he resumed at a slowed cadence.

"Now I am going to speak to you in a manner unusual for presidents. The office of President of the United States should not be limited to shaping public opinion, but indeed to leading the nation forward, even if the objective initially appears to be distasteful. It is important to understand the personality of one's country. In Japan, harmony is achieved for the greater good of the society; no individual is rewarded for sticking out above the rest. This is the character of their collective culture. In African villages, everyone works toward the health and welfare of the entire community. In communist nations, no one is allowed to project themselves in importance except those who rule from a position of power. On the other hand, in America, sticking out above the rest is promoted as being a valuable part of the fabric of our society. Individuals are rewarded for being individualistic. People here can afford to be generous owing to the incredible bounty and natural riches lying within our soil. If you order fish or meat in a restaurant, condiments and spices are free. Paying for the first cup of coffee opens the door to free refills. Not so for tea in Britain; each cup comes with a price.

"Quest has been the dominant note of our history, whether for independence, personal liberty and economic opportunity, more dignity, or more effective democracy. What makes us able to achieve these lofty goals is our sense of destiny, our optimism about the future possibilities, and our willingness to experiment. We did not come to this land burdened with the baggage of centuries of caste and feudalism; we came with the sense that new frontiers would be unfolding with

279

each new generation, and we flourished immersed in the bold challenges we faced. Here, the pace of change has been faster than elsewhere in the world. That is because, in the main, we believe in progress by evolution, not by revolution. Our resourcefulness and ability to organize will permit us to lead the world by our making progressive improvements both in our productive output as well as to our societal structure. It is time for us to move beyond the chains and bonds of enslaved thinking and treat all men and women as equal before the laws of the land. A person having a sense of his own self-worth is the very kernel of being happy. With the Civil Rights and Voting Rights Acts as a part of our fabric, we shall stride onward in this regard.

"Accordingly, I call on each of you to come forward, to be active, to be a part of something larger than yourselves, and in this way help our nation recognize, and then correct, its problems.

"In this regard, I will now address a matter that has never been proposed in our country before today, but the importance of which should no longer be shunted aside. To begin with, those young men and women who are soldiers or sailors or airmen in our military branches, or who serve in the Coast Guard, are the public servants of the people. It follows that if we, through Congressional declaration, send them into harm's way, we must back them up in full, provide the most up-to-date materiel they need, and empower their commanders with the authority to execute their assigned missions full-bore. If political exigencies call for merely tiptoeing around, then such a mission must not be undertaken. Perhaps more importantly, after backing them to the hilt, we must be ready to care for them when they return home as veterans. Some will have given of themselves in full, and their memories must be honored; others may have left a part of their physical, or psychic, being on the battlefield. They too must be honored, and I call upon our state and federal legislators to commit us as a people to caring for our returning troops to whatever extent they are in need. This includes benefits for the restoration of health and ambulation, the pursuit of higher education, and even intercession when monitoring their progress reveals that someone is falling by the wayside.

"And now I come to what some will perceive as overreaching by our federal government, but which I believe will empower us as a nation as we pursue improvements to our lives. I am addressing here the need for universal service. This would not be like a wartime draft; rather, it would be a responsibility applicable to every citizen without regard to sex, color, creed, education, income or claimed familial hardship. Every person who, by birth or naturalization, reaches the age of 17 but before becoming 35, will be required to give of self to our country's preservation and enhancement. In this way will every young citizen become bonded to our success as a people in this ever-shrinking world. Service in the branches of the military will be but one option out of many. Expanding on the current role of enlisting citizens to help other nations through the Peace Corps, we will offer fields such as electronics, communications and information processing, medical service in the field or at hospitals, maintenance of clean waterways, farming and food production that promote natural yields while minimizing the use of pesticides, transport and logistics, preparation of manuals and cartography to include surveying, development of lighter yet stronger structural materials or less expensive compounds, and the expansion of knowledge and understanding of the world's diverse cultures are but a few of the options envisioned in the proposed "Citizens Serving America" program.

"This new approach—taking on the responsibility of citizenship as opposed to merely sponging off the largess of our success—will enhance our ability to cooperate, rather than quarrel, with one another. We need to be fully united as a nation in the face of ever-increasing threats of extremism on this planet. NASA has postulated to me that once we orbit a spaceship around our moon, the photographs of earth as a solitary blue planet rotating in the black emptiness of outer space will demonstrate how we must depend on one another.

This is everyone's home, Mother Earth is all we have for the conceivable future, so it is imperative that we learn to live together in peace.

"Happiness is sublime because it is the zenith of what we as humans can attain, feel, and desire. We as a people can be happy when we believe in something or someone because such belief gives us hope for improvements to our future well-being. Thomas Jefferson's vision and words capitalized on this human trait. Americans would be fulfilled if only they would act on his example of leadership: to study, listen, explore, and learn.

"Time and the events of everyday life do not stand still. There is nothing in life as constant as change. Those who look only to the past or the present are sure to miss the future.[2] We must prepare ourselves. The youth of the current generation will be urged to take on responsibilities far greater than any that have come before. They must be made ready to shoulder the burdens placed on us as exploration proceeds in outer space or beneath the ocean waves or—perhaps most daunting of all—within the dimensions of human interaction. An ever shrinking world will force the nations of diverse cultures and languages to become interdependent.

"The Constitution of this great nation of ours provides for the pursuit of happiness; it is up to each one of us to go out and ensure it for ourselves, and to do so in the world in which we find ourselves. Moving from one place to another to find happiness will cause it to elude you forever. This is true because we always bring our original selves to the new place, rather than allowing ourselves to be molded by site. Doing so would permit adaptation without being torn by countervailing temptations. Nowadays, we seek out external forms of adventure and excitement rather than simply creating such for ourselves right where we are. We even go so far as to pay money for such diversions. No place has benefits without corresponding downsides. For example, California is warm and favorable for active lifestyles, but it has traffic jams and wildfires, not to mention fault lines.

"In America, we float rather than put down roots. In our perpetual pursuit for contentment, we may be fairly happy today, but there's always tomorrow beckoning us toward the prospect of something better. We thus never fully commit, but rather leave alternative options on the table for future inspection and reference. To really love the space you're in, you have to commit to it, to put both feet fully on its floor and form bonds and relationships within its boundaries. And so, my fellow Americans, I repeat the enjoinder I uttered four years ago: it is time for you to stand up, to be counted, and to ask what you can do for your country!

"Being happy because you are pleased with your circumstances is an end in itself. If you order a cup of specialty coffee, cappuccino for example, and its aroma is savory and its taste captivating, you may say nothing, but—you come back again! If it's bad, you complain loudly and, if the problem is not sorted out, you never again darken the door. Pleasure is gained when your needs are met, albeit tastefully, and multiple experiences such as this will make you happy to return to that establishment; that is, until some new management takes over and changes everything. This, unfortunately, happens often during corporate takeovers of competitors.

"On the other hand, our country and its geography are sources of unique happiness. Nowhere else is such beauty combined with spaciousness, where the form of government permits enjoyment of, and enrichment by, those places which we hold to be national treasures. Over the centuries, the world has witnessed a handful of Golden Ages. Athens before the Romans; Elizabethan London; Renaissance Florence with its sculptors and painters; Asheville, North Carolina even as this speech is delivered, but each such flowering is like francium: fleeting in the blossoming of creativity and thoughtful expression.

"The new era that we have begun will provide us with endless opportunities, both domestically and internationally. I urge each of you individually to eschew any guilt of what has gone before; instead, seize the opportunity to make history by embracing the responsibilities of citizenship in this country. Most significantly, this will require each of us to support equal opportunity for every American citizen. Look beyond cultural, physical, ethnic, or religious differences to see the true worth of the person at his or her core. We must enable all our citizens to be in a position to take advantage of their potential to pursue these new frontiers. Only in this way will we discover and nurture the skills, energies, and ingenuity extant in our population.

"As Americans, we often have the financial power to make our dreams come true, buying the house we think will satisfy our need for happiness, only to wallow in disappointment when our decision produces unforeseen expense, worry over theft, high taxes, flood or earthquake. Simply having more money often makes us turn inward rather than reaching out to other people in our community to form those human bonds which are the true source of a worthwhile existence. Connections that fray with others isolate and produce unhappiness with a fragmented life. Visiting family, friends, and participating in community groups adds to involvement, caring, a sense of self-worth. These nourish the kernel of happiness residing within ourselves. Familiar places and faces ensure contentment, but these require your continued attention to retain them as valued connections.

"When I took the oath of this great office four years ago, I pledged to faithfully execute its tenets and, to the best of my ability, to preserve, protect, and defend our cherished principles of self-government embodied in our Constitution. In our trade relations with Europe, those nations should strive for interdependent relationships where decisions are equally shared, thereby ensuring benefits along with attendant burdens. Here at home, strong economic growth **must** result in quantitative abundance for all citizens, not merely a privileged few. Such sharing is how the quality of our cherished society is measured. Modern technological society demands that human initiative be integrated with diversity of independent thinking, but the benefits accruing to our society must percolate down to everyone. I pledge today to continue to do so for the good of all Americans. With you at my side, we shall succeed together!

"And so, in closing, take to your hearts this maxim: Happiness is having few wants. Hold fast to the ideal that it is better to help your neighbor achieve something, rather than focus narrowly on amassing more for yourself. If we all do so, we shall improve our lives together as a unified nation. In this way, we shall ensure our national well-being far into our future. Thank you very much."

The President left his top hat off his head as he took his seat. His blood had been up while he talked, but even with the butterfly pressures gone after delivering this erudite message, he continued to feel warm all over. He scanned the amazingly quiet throng; his speech was concluded, but the crowd remained silent. A lump closed on his throat; had he been too long-winded? Abruptly, his hands began to feel the chilled January cold, so he turned to his wife and asked her to hand him his gloves. Mrs. Kennerly was seated a few feet away from the lectern, so she had to stand and reach the gloves over to him. As she did so, her lovely face caught the attention of the assembled audience. Immediately, the steps and veranda and entire plaza area filled with deafening applause. It was as though they had been transfixed by the words of the President, but the sight of the First Lady's movement broke their reverie and returned them to the moment.

Sitting where I could keep an eye on the First Lady, I imagined she was amply warmed by the praise which the crowd was now showering on her husband. Who knows? Perhaps their thundering approval was as much for her.

With the close of this great speech, President Kennerly and Vice-President Jensen felt energized. They were in their second term, a term in which—traditionally—real progress is made because there is no worry about electioneering. All that mattered now was providing solid benefits for the citizenry. Momentum was with the Kennerly-Jensen team. They must act to get bills submitted to and passed by Congress before this energetic but fleeting force dissipated.

The President and Vice-President standing together as they observe
the parade following their inauguration on January 4, 1965.

As January melted seamlessly into February and then March, Mr.
Jensen made this telling point when summarizing the purpose behind
the array of education bills and programs which he and the President
were submitting to, and getting passed by, the Congress:

"Genius does not have a color line any more than does social
justice. Education from kindergarten up through graduate and
professional schooling should be available to all Americans without
regard to ability to pay, race, age, or gender. Demonstrating talent,
understanding of principles, mastery of facts, and eagerness to know
more should be determinative. The only sort of hunger we want to
witness throughout this great land is an ongoing hunger to learn! Such
are the goals we will strive to attain during this administration's term
of office."

Young Bill Moyers had come aboard to assist Mr. Jensen as he
pumped vitality and wisdom into his Vice-Presidency. Moyers was
a former seminarian who was well liked by the men in Kennerly's
circle of close associates. He was intelligent and was serving at Sargent
Shriver's side in the Peace Corps when Jensen tapped him to be his

special assistant. In fact, he mirrored my duties with Mr. Kennerly, thereby lightening my double load so I could stay more focused on the President. It was he who largely drafted Lyndon's lines for a speech before the Knights of Columbus:

"Regarding earning money and having a sense of personal dignity, I say this: If a fellow can buy something with money that he has earned through his own work and mental effort, he becomes proud. He has demonstrated his ability to care for himself as well as his family. This makes him proud to live in this country. Further, it makes him proud to be an American! Franklin D. Roosevelt proved the value of this sense of self-worth after initiating the successful public works projects during the 1930's. The benefits to society's orderly functioning are invaluable. We must open the doors to every person bettering himself through his own muscle and motivation. Engendering a sense of self-worth in our citizens justifies the very purpose behind the programs for the Great Society!

"I know that some of you will feel we are making too great a change and doing so too quickly. In actuality, it is no change at all, but merely a recommitment to those precepts our forefathers established nearly 200 years ago in Philadelphia. We have talked long enough in this country about equal rights. Not just this administration, but every individual citizen as well, needs—no, requires—adherence to the Civil Rights Bill. Words are not enough: we must embrace equality before the law in our everyday lives!"

No wonder Moyers was valued: he was very skilled at conveying ideas.

As their second term proceeded and domestic bills began to pass successfully, the President/Vice-President team would choose the site for signing a bill according to what would have the most public significance. A small rural schoolhouse was chosen for the education bill; the NASA guidance center in Houston was best for signing a bill funding our outer space programs, but the White House itself was selected for signing civil rights legislation. The picture of Mr. Jensen's pen poised above the bill as dignitaries as well as ordinary citizens stood behind him, such as Dr. King and young Negro children, is an image many of our fellow citizens will remember to their demise.

During 1965, Medicare was appropriately signed in Independence, Missouri where the elderly Harry Truman lived. "I want him to know that his country has not forgotten him. After all, he will probably go down in history as the man who had to make the single most difficult decision anyone in the White House will ever have to decide," Lyndon observed when reporters questioned him about this relatively remote site.

The Vice-President capably embraced responsibility for the space exploration program, assuring the public that regardless of its costs, it will provide a solid investment return in terms of security, prestige internationally, scientific knowledge, and new products for the everyday consumer. Jobs created in a wide array of our cities would be spread throughout all regions of the country.

"The boon to our educational institutions and the broadening of interest in science among the young will serve us well into the 21st Century," he had affirmed during one speech delivered at Cape Canaveral in Florida.

Kennerly was to come to Vice-President Jensen's support when he appeared at a rally for the Democratic Party. He strode into the assembly hall tall, tanned, and trim: in short, looking like a million bucks in his statesmanlike, dark navy tailored suit and conservatively striped tie set against a white shirt and buttoned-down collar. Now just shy of forty-eight years young, his hair remained full and naturally brown, his eyes reflected the wisdom of having been at the nation's helm for over four years, and his demeanor exuded confidence in his ability to lead. His aura was so bright, it fairly gleamed!

The confidence in his bearing was sufficiently powerful that he didn't have to say, "I'm in charge. Stick with me and our party will carry the day! Your countrymen have the sense that their success is tied to our success." He had once remarked that "image is reality in the eyes of the public" and, I must say, he embodied the best that a leader of men could be today. Everyone there already felt it as soon as he entered the room. Obviously, he had learned from prior mistakes, such as his handling of the Bay of Pigs invasion, to hear and evaluate advice from his advisors and then perform his own sort of triangulation, looking at what has been presented from different perspectives, in order to finally decide on the course he wished to follow. He knew that, while he took the defense of this country, and the assurance of equal opportunity within its borders, seriously, he didn't need to take himself seriously. He still spoke to the citizenry with clarity in straightforward sentences.

"These programs are an energetic continuation of our space-exploration effort. They represent not merely a determination to put a man on the moon; they are a means to stimulate all the advances in technology, in understanding, and in experience which can move us forward toward man's mastery of space. Understanding how to weather the long-term confines of the voyage, or cope with the demands of an emergency in space, will be the opening endeavor for us to explore Mankind's most distant and greatest frontier."

He paused for a moment, as though making an off-the-cuff decision to do so, then said:

"Speaking of space exploration, I want to reveal that we have made progress in reaching an agreement with the Soviet Union regarding our cooperation in space. This entente will permit the construction of a permanently orbiting platform which can support astronauts as they live and work some 200 miles above the earth's surface.

"Back here on earth, we are moving ahead with consummating several trade agreements between our two countries. We have come to an understanding regarding civil air protocols. True, Berlin remains a thorn in the sides of each nation, but we are making progress toward overcoming mutual distrust, and such a move forward will allow the citizens of both countries to breathe a little easier. Creating ties that bind our different approaches to governance will foster better trust and certainty as we come increasingly to rely on one another.

"Ties that bind our two nations together economically will be far better than pointing missiles at one another."

After this talk, Jacquelean had held onto her husband's forearm and observed: "Jack! You are rushing around as though there is no tomorrow. What's gotten into you?"

He turned and kissed her lightly on the cheek while whispering, "I don't have much time. My term will be up before you know it, yet there is still so much to be done! Each day is like a strong beacon from a lighthouse, beckoning me to seize the opportunity to help my countrymen today. Tomorrow, the beam may be obscured by fog or burned out entirely. The chance to make a difference may vanish if not seized when first it's presented. In that sense, I feel like time is running out for me and I must learn, understand, and then act with urgency. The hopes of our citizenry for a more vital existence are centered on this office, and therefore on me. I must exercise the power I possess to secure freedom and fulfill the hopes of my countrymen for a better life. In this regard, change effected now is not merely desirable, it is mandatory." [3]

His wife stared at her husband. What with all the campaigning and speeches and international travel, she hadn't noticed what was so clear to her now. Jacquelean may have been adored by the American public, but she suddenly realized that, far more importantly, she was married to a champion of the people.

Notes

[1]   *The Turbulent years: the 60's*, p. 101.
[2]   Pitts, p. 105.
[3]   More fully denoted in Pitts, pp. 155-157.

CHAPTER TWENTY-NINE

Lyndon in His Element

Mr. Jensen sought instinctively to identify himself with the sources and objects of presidential power even though he was the Vice-President. He could talk with governors, members of Congress, send along orders to the executive branch with the JFK imprimatur, and meet with businessmen, labor leaders, civil servants, and civic leaders. He had an encyclopedic memory that gave him command of the details of matters significant to his power and its exercise that was prodigious. In one sitting he would deal with issues of education, finance, poverty, and housing. His mind remained resilient even when his body was fatigued. He tended to rest from one kind of activity by engaging in another.

Jensen's main agenda goals: effectuate the Civil Rights Bill, enhance federal aid to education, and pursue executive action to improve life in the cities, medical care for the aged, poverty elimination program, and tax reduction for individuals. What he needed most was political support to mobilize behind him. He had to prioritize and organize the introduction of the various pieces of legislation so they could be readily swallowed and digested by a Congress that, up to this point, had been obstructive to most of Mr. Kennerly's bills.

Worried that the man was boxing himself in by these positions, I gingerly suggested that he might not want to spend so much time on what everyone was referring to as "lost causes."

He turned to face me and said, "Hell, what is the office of the chief executive for if not to help people with their lost causes?"

"Yes, sir" I responded. "Enough said."

His forte was meeting one-on-one with whoever was trying to promote some pending bill that was contrary to his values. The challenge would be to learn what it was that mattered to such man, understand which issues were critical to whom, and why. Knowing the leaders and understanding their organizational needs let him shape proposed legislation to fit both their needs and those of the country. His *modus operandi* was to seek out what was most important, the thing he most needed—in other words, what his hot button was—and knowing what was desired, or dreaded, allowed Jensen to control him by withholding or bestowing the solution.

One device was for him to remain noncommittal, or even forbiddingly silent, on issues critical to an adversary if they were not immediately important to him as Vice-President. He wanted each of the Congressmen who opposed a position he favored to participate in the administration of government in a dozen different ways. The key was to get men from diverse groups so involved with each other, on so many committees and delegations, and covering so many issues that no one Congressman could afford to be staunchly uncompromising on any one issue alone. This would engender a cooperative, mutually supportive spirit among Congressional leaders and, *voila!* Bills would get passed rather than tied up in committee or debate hearings.[1]

When a Congressman or Senator is weighing which way to vote, he may consider his conscience, or the wishes of the majority of his constituents, or simply follow the lead of his or her party and congressional faction. However, there's the matter of the future: if he votes a certain way today, will that engender or alienate his colleagues on some issue down the road? If an associate pleads, "I really need you on this one," that carries great weight, for the future will always provide opportunities for payback. Thus, a congressman is always calculating; he or she never makes a thoughtless press of the "yea" or "nay" button during the vote roll-call.

In February 1965, Mr. Jensen inspired us all when he delivered the following speech to a packed house at the Boston Convention Center celebrating the landing of the Pilgrims on Plymouth Rock back in 1620.

"We must provide for our own happiness, education, health, and protection of our environment. This will require us to restrain our appetites. If we avoid greed, we will never be short on the wherewithal to meet our needs and to solve our conflicts. Accordingly, you will find that my actions will conform to your desires.

"We retain a dream that this great country of ours provides every citizen the opportunity to build for himself and his children a better life. A president does not shape a new and personal vision of America. He collects his vision **from the scattered hopes** of the men and women who have lived in its past. It existed when the first pilgrims saw the coast of Massachusetts as a new world, and as our pioneers moved westward, it has guided us every step of the way. It sustains me, as it does our president. Every person must be allowed to share in the progress and the responsibilities of being a citizen. No one should be deprived of the essentials of a decent life. An equal chance must be ensured by your government.

"Thus, the Great Society will offer something for everyone. Medicare for the elderly, educational assistance for those who seek it, subsidies for farmers' stock and crops, housing for the homeless, finding meaningful jobs for the poor, safer highways for commuters, legal protection for the indigent, schooling for Indians, retraining for the unemployed, auto-safety courses, livable pensions and social security for the retired, fair labeling on products, conservation for hikers and campers, and a higher minimum wage balanced by executive compensation ceilings. [2]

"The reason we are pushing for Americans to pick themselves up by their bootstraps is the dignity inherent in hard work. A person who has a job can sustain his family with pride, and pride-of-citizenship makes him a willing contributor to our society. **We don't want to deepen a man's dependency; rather, we want to energize his success!**

"Mr. Kennerly and I want to urge each of you to be a participant, not merely an admirer or critic, of your government. Our country is set up with the executive branch to propose laws and lead us in worthy directions, a Congress to help the executive implement laws which it deems worthy, and a judiciary to ensure that such laws, when passed, conform to the guidelines of our Constitution. We all have a stake in this process, so it makes sense that we come forward to discuss and debate and, when necessary, sue to question the validity of a law. Sitting on the sidelines and merely watching as our country progresses is certainly legal, but those who do nothing but watch or complain are not taking advantage of the greatest political advantage our country enjoys, and that is having the ability to enter the ring and get involved.

"*Participative government*, my fellow citizens, is what this country enables and, indeed, requires from each of you in order to function properly. Only by participating will you exercise those powers the Constitution guarantees as your right to representative government. Working together, rather than by fiat or dismissive noninvolvement, whereby we all have a stake in the outcome, will ensure that our ability to work, live, and laugh together is preserved.

"It may not be the norm for a politician to go around the country stating principled utterances, but when he is crusading, as I am, for principled goals, he will state his position forthrightly at every opportunity which presents itself. We have many Americans living on the outskirts of hope. Our task must be to replace their despair with opportunity. This administration today, here and now, declares unconditional war on poverty in America.

"Our weapons of choice will be better schools and vocational facilities, better health care and diagnostic testing to stem the spread of disease, and better housing for all. In the end, our goal will be to both relieve the symptoms of poverty and to correct the causes so as to prevent its future occurrence in any population group.

"This great leap forward to promote social justice will result in a widespread societal transformation. We, by living and working together in harmony, will bend the arc of our morality toward justice for all.

"In closing, I will remind you that the job of your President is the ultimate office, but such office is conferred by the voters upon an individual who is otherwise an ordinary citizen. Any one of you standing here before me today, or your relative or neighbor, could be the person on whom that tribute, and heavy responsibility, is placed in years hence. Therefore, it behooves you to get an education and pursue honorable work so you're ready to accept whatever post or job comes your way. At its heart, the goal of your government providing equal opportunity for education in our great land is to ensure that **the ability to make intelligent decisions is distributed** throughout our land.

"The Pilgrims came to these shores in pursuit of religious freedom and the right to express themselves without retribution. If they could be with us here today and see how far our nation has come, I believe they would be proud to call themselves Americans! May God bless this great country!"

At the conclusion of this address, we all sat back and realized that here-in-waiting was a real leader who could grasp the essentials of a problem and wade right into solving it.

Mr. Jensen had shown that he knew how to contact and control the resources that could be brought to bear to do so. Publicly, he was still the same affable person we knew as the Vice-President, but after many months in office, he had become confident in his ability to command. Whether Democrat or Republican, whether serving as a governor or as an aide to a congressman, any citizen could feel that they would do well to place their faith in this man, i.e., should anything happen to President Kennerly.

In short, we citizens were lucky to have such a capable team at the head of our government. One was a dynamic, inspiring public speaker; the other was convincingly unstoppable one-on-one. Both men possessed an inner fire to express himself with dignity as well as clarity. Their listeners could readily grasp the concepts they were espousing and, more importantly, be roused to action by their words.

Jensen believed that all legislators were influenced by two emotions: the desire for recognition contrasted with the fear of losing their grip on power. Desire opened the door to the exercise of presidential power; fear closed it. Receiving acknowledgment for supporting change was counterbalanced by the fear of losing, which would immobilize a Congressman, causing him to stand pat. Jensen's solution was to get Congress to merely initiate a bill's passage, and then he would personally step in to oversee its implementation.

Gaining confidence as his partnership with the President progressed, Mr. Jensen loftily intoned: "My trick is to crack the wall of separation enough to give the Congress a feeling of participation in creating a bill without exposing me or my plans to congressional opposition. In truth, legislative drafting is a political art. The president is continually faced with a number of tough choices between balancing the bill he really wants and the bill he's likely to get. He must consider whether to make it a single-purpose or omnibus bill, how to package its presentation, even when to send it up to the Hill."

Jensen would seek congressional advice for all these choices. He pointed out to us that if a legislator had a hand in shaping a proposal, such bill would become easier to support than if it was simply handed down from the top.[3]

Conversely, he could never transfix audiences as the President did instinctively. His part was to do the background work, whereupon Mr. Kennerly would stand on the solid foundation which the Vice-President had laid and state the course to which the administration would be committed. The Senate, in particular, was a cloakroom operation where the front erected by speeches would mask the real goings-on behind the scenes. The members of that esteemed chamber balanced conviviality and glad-handing amongst themselves with the daily pressures of satisfying their constituencies.

Now, each senator had to remain loyal to irreversible commitments which defined the course of action already set by President Kennerly's first term.[4]

He had his eye on the business community as well. He knew how much they valued fiscal responsibility. The tax reduction bill had been difficult to get through the Senate. The Senate Finance Committee would act favorably only if members of the business community were behind the President. To facilitate their doing so, Mr. Jensen had met with the members of the Business Council, a large and influential body made up of 100 corporate and financial executives chaired by Frederick Kappel of American Telephone & Telegraph.

Mr. Jensen marshaled arguments that forestalled objections so well that he astounded the businessmen. He began by demonstrating that, with the stimulus provided by the proposed tax cut, there would be a general increase in resources, which in turn would significantly reduce the possibility of class conflict. So long as the economic pie continued to grow, there would be few disputes about its distribution among labor, business, and the underprivileged. The latter were people whose mental state he understood well from his early days as a teacher at Cotulla, but now he was in a position to support poverty programs through the Department of Labor.

He met with the Daughters of the American Revolution and the AFL-CIO members as well as the Business Council to enlarge the poverty issue so it would become a matter of public concern. He followed his speeches of exhortation with personal visits to Huntington, West Virginia and Chicago, Illinois in April. The cities of South Bend, Indiana and subsequently Pittsburgh, Pennsylvania were toured over the course of successive days. Both these regions were being hard pressed by the low-priced but high-quality steel that Japan was introducing world-wide. At the conclusion of World War II, Japan had been forbidden from maintaining a military force, so they had set about sending all their young university students over here to study. Upon returning to their island home, they improved on what we Americans were doing. Their mills were now leaving us in the turbulent economic wake of their superior products.

The solution was to bring not just the mill owners, but also the labor unions and the producers of raw materials and the transport shippers to the table with the same message: We Americans are pricing our steel out of the market. Jobs, even our very prosperity, were at stake. Either we had to find new production alternatives that cost less than the Bessemer process, compensation of top executives had to be tied to productivity, or the making of American steel had to develop some superior annealing process that was as yet undiscovered.

He had a significant weapon on his side. All the steel owners could remember how President Kennerly had persuaded them to hold the lid on prices in exchange for labor not raising demands for higher wages back in 1961. Walter Heller had advised him that America was pricing itself out of the world markets now that Japan was free to produce high-quality steel but at low prices.

Then, one of the companies independently raised prices, and seven others had jumped on the bandwagon. Immediately, the attorney general threatened them with a lawsuit charging antitrust violations. Vacation expense records and entertainment bills suddenly became fair game for IRS investigators, whereupon the increases had been quietly rescinded.

No business executive wanted to be embarrassed like that again. These exhortations would have to be embraced by area universities and chemical companies as well. Mr. Jensen was addressing long-range problems that required immediate solutions: he would not abide prima donnas who sought to preserve their long-held niches.

We needed an improved way of doing things, and we needed it *yesterday*!

Currently, the coal mining regions of eastern Kentucky were considered the most economically depressed area in our country, so he would begin the war on poverty there so that people would see him as compassionate in spite of his calling himself a staunch cattleman. As the result of Mr. Jensen's travels and televised addresses, what had formerly been the concern of some liberal intellectuals and government bureaucrats became a national disgrace. It shattered the complacency of a people who had always considered their country to be the land of equal opportunity. It would not be sufficient for mine owners to simply recognize unions as the bargaining agent for their laborers; they had to reorient their approach to the mine workers and move their operations into the more participative 20th Century.

Meeting with Congress, Mr. Jensen declared:

> "This is an unconditional war on poverty that is to be a total commitment by this Administration and this Congress and this nation to pursue victory over this most ancient of mankind's enemies. This domestic enemy threatens the strength of our nation and the welfare of our people. If we contain this enemy, we will win a secure and honorable place in the history of the nation and the enduring gratitude of generations of Americans to come." [5]

Mr. Jensen would conduct briefing sessions for Congressmen and Senators which would give them an opportunity to get an advance look at presidential submissions and documents. Thereby, they could confront the relevant cabinet members with concerns and questions before a bill came to the floor for debate. A legislator who is not blind-sided tends to be more receptive.

Charts, tables, even supporting arguments—they got it all. They'd each get an advance copy so they could appear to be well-informed the next day in front of reporters and photographers. By that time, they would have "gotten their ducks in a row" so they wouldn't be embarrassed on television. This made them more disposed to support a bill. [6]

Congress has the power to decide which bills to consider and in what sequence. But the president can shape this by the order and pace of the messages he sends to the Hill. The right moment to send a bill up depends on momentum (how hot the issue is) which depends on preparation, the availability of sponsors in the right spot at the right time, and the opportunities for neutralizing the opposition. Correct timing of sending a bill up thus becomes essential.

Consider the Elementary and Secondary Education Act. This passed in 1965 because Mr. Jensen obtained an agreement by which assistance would go not to the school, but to the impoverished child, so whether they attended public or parochial school became their choice rather than a source of conflict.

Cajoling congressmen might involve carrots such as an invitation to walk the grounds with the Vice-President. The privileged guest would realize that photo ops would make him famous; his hometown newspaper would be informed by White House sources that the man was highly valued and was frequently asked for advice. Appointments to a special presidential delegation or commission or designation as a bill's sponsor would give him status. Direct rewards would include public works projects or military bases or scientific/medical research facilities in his district.

Mr. Jensen avoided formal press conferences, eschewing them in favor of the President so the news would be dispensed as Mr. Kennerly wished rather than as a journalist might want.[7] Jack used them to advance his ideas for programs, whereas the Vice-President would take up half the allotted time with long prepared statements which left little time for repartee or questions. One trick he learned to use with great success, however, was to announce them with ample notice. This allowed thoughtful questions to be submitted prior to the event, so then his answers on TV could show him to be well informed and in control.

"Never ignore them or leave them in the dark; they will create their own light which may not reflect well on you or your programs," he'd admonish before adding, "Many of them are frozen in time in their department, as though hidden in an iceberg without anyone being aware until the heat of their indignation melts their fortress and out they come clamoring for my head!"

Notes

[1]   Broder, p. 71.
[2]   See Kearns-Goodwin, pp. 217-219.
[3]   Kearns, p. 222.
[4]   Kearns, pp. 186-7.
[5]   Lyndon Johnson, "Total Victory over Poverty," March 16, 1964, Senate Document No. 86, Washington, D.C., 1964: The *War on Poverty: The Economic Opportunity Act of 1964.*
[6]   Kearns, p. 224.
[7]   Kearns, p. 248.

CHAPTER THIRTY

Jack and I Get a Surprise

Mr. Jensen differed from the graceful, witty, incandescent personality of Kennerly. He rarely retained, even if he clearly understood, what he'd been told. His power revolved around assessing a man's weakness and dangling lures. He had never had to evaluate the merits of policy, as Kennerly had done on a daily basis ever since he'd left the Navy and run for Congress.

Jack, for his part, needed to be surrounded by not just Bobby or Ted, but also by longtime personal friends such as Red Fay, as the token Republican, and several other "buddies-from-the-war-days," as he called them, such as Bill Battle and Jim Reed, or his Choate roommates or colleagues from Harvard and Stanford. In one way or another, or at some time or other, each of these diverse people served as a life-saving ring that rescued Jack Kennerly from ever being alone. I suppose his need to be surrounded by friends was a result of his growing up in a very large family where there was activity all around, all the time, in which every member—whether by blood or marriage—was expected to participate.

This need made for an unusual characteristic, and one day it struck me full on: once you made friends with Jack Kennerly, such bond would last a lifetime.

Red had met him during the war in the Pacific when his own PT boat put into Tulagi for repairs. Lt. Kennerly was in the hospital there recovering from his ordeal with the Japanese destroyer. With a bunch of educated, intelligent naval officers standing around waiting for new assignments, a discussion group formed, with Jack at the center, regarding foreign policy and strategic military decisions. Their discursive conversations proceeded to accepted conclusions through the use of reason rather than emotion and prejudice.

On the spot, Lt. Fay made a bet with Jim Reed that this thin, unhealthy officer who spoke so eloquently and intelligibly would one day become President of the United States. The importance of a citizen committing himself to local or, even better, national politics seemed to be of paramount concern to their new friend. Of course, first he would have to live through the war; fortunately, he did.[1]

During his terms as a member of the House of Representatives, the usual form of conferencing with young Kennerly had to be dispensed with after the man became a senator. What was affectionately referred to as "the tub sanctum sanctorum" was used by Jack so he could relax in a steaming bath while whatever hotel suite he was occupying filled with perspiring aides and advisers. By the time I joined him, the soothing balm of soaking in a container of water had largely been replaced by Jacquelean herself. This switch was a good idea, from my perspective. Otherwise, some feisty reporter would doubtless have accused Jack of acting like a Roman Emperor who was dominating his vassals rather than absorbing their wise counsel.

Unfortunately, this need to "always be in the midst of a group" had a severe downside: if you bored him, Jack could be quickly dismissive. He needed his friends to rotate throughout the day. Novelty and the stimulus of a fresh face were as much a part of his psyche as immersing himself in the heroic history found in biographies or diaries. That was probably why the presidency appealed to him. In that office, something different would be happening every half hour or so, and thus Mr. Kennerly could address it with his vigor refreshed.

It was interesting for me to watch this daily rotation through the various enclaves of friends and advisors: no one was ever put out by being dismissed to go off and deal with whatever The Boss had assigned him. As the result of having their own area of expertise that was valued by the President, they were all made to feel like "you're part of my team, and hence very important to me!" When a person fell into orbit around Jack Kennerly, he became a participant rather than a mere onlooker. Even reporters were made to feel that they were intimate accomplices.

I privately hypothesized that this trait had been handed down from his father as a result of the family touch-football games at Hyannis Port, not from playing sports at Choate or Harvard. He was a lucky American to have grown up in such an active family enclave!

Mr. Jensen was not skilled at concentrating on substance, but he was unsurpassed when applying pressure to gain him victory on the legislative front. The Vice-President was far more formal with his advisors, but he adapted to the frenetic pace of Kennerly's administration because different problems required shifting his focus, and this sort of mental activity refreshed him. In this way, he was kinder to his associates. He could use crude, perhaps vulgar language, and he had a whale of a temper in him, but following that "partnership talk" with President Kennerly, rarely did I witness him being coldly dismissive.

This constant, rushing sort of activity had put Jacquelean off somewhat. She could enjoy a game of softball or badminton—for as much as an hour, perhaps—but then she'd want to enjoy a discussion about Renoir or the latest equestrian stud from Arabia, or to see some historical or archaeological site without having to change into football togs or sailing sneakers.

Jack, of course, grew up with this kind of pressure around him all the time. Even when he was sitting quietly with his father stretched out on lounge chairs as they watched the sun go down over the Hyannis Port shores, they had to be discussing or reviewing *something*. Time could not be spent in light idle chatter; it was too precious to fritter away. More importantly, doing so meant one was not striving forward in order to achieve some goal or status.

Thus, unless he was engaged in reading Churchill or some author of major distinction, Jack could get bored quickly and easily, but his friends could prevent that happening. Men like Kirk Billings and Torbert MacDonald, who had formed a bond with the President at The Choate School, remained fast friends for his entire life. Through them, Jack was always exposed to fresh ideas or pursuits; these men prevented Jack from stagnating. Perhaps that was why the President could exhibit such a wide smile of genuine warmth and greeting. He absolutely loved being immersed in activity, whether a prank, a party, or a political speech.

This ability to make a friend an intimate who would then be part of the joking and kidding extended to foreign leaders with whom he became close. Harold MacMillan was such a man. As Prime Minister of Great Britain, he held a job as pressured as that of Kennerly, but when Nikita Crushchev profanely pounded his shoe to show disapproval of Macmillan's speech to the United Nations, Harold asked, "May I have that translated, please?"

Mr. Kennerly always enjoyed someone who possessed a quick wit. His British counterpart showed sensitivity, however when the Kennerly's lost their youngest, Patrick, only two days after his birth. Harold cabled: The burdens of public affairs are more or less tolerable, but private grief is poignant, cruel, and often totally undeserved." [2]

With such a strong need to always be in the company of others, I found it odd that Jack Kennerly did not like being physically touched. A handshake was fine, but don't try to hug him. That kind of physical communication made him as jumpy as the north pole of a magnet brought up close to the north pole of another magnet.

One evening, he asked Kenny to come join Larry and me in the Oval office. He sat rocking in that comfortably favorite chair of his as we three strung out on the couches. We all watched the fire burn with ever-changing colors while it warmed the chill of this fall twilight.

"This evening reminds me of the great stress we were all under two years ago. Every time I think back on how close we came to the destruction of Mankind, with Lemay all bellicose calling for air strikes and the Army ready to jump in and invade that Cuban island while, silently hidden over the horizon, rested the vast arsenal of the Soviets' rockets, well, I just thank God that the Premier was level-headed enough to accept a reasonable way out."

"I think he surmised that he had you over a barrel, Mr. President," observed Kenny. "Based on your meeting in Vienna and the Bay of Pigs fiasco, he was betting that we'd simply roll over and do nothing. Then Adlai brought this gamble to the attention of the whole world, and the Russian duplicity was exposed for all to see. Bobby was smart to suggest using the bases in Turkey as a trade-off so Crushchev could save face and agree to a way out."

"Yes, you're right," the President responded, but then he changed pace and inquired, "By the way, what do you think of this new man Brezhnev who seems to be rising in power in the Kremlin? Larry, contact Bobby at the Attorney General's office and make sure the C.I.A. has prepared a full dossier on him so we know who we'll be dealing with should he take over for Nikita in some power struggle."

Pausing, he expressed something that he was mulling over in his mind.

"Isn't it interesting how, down through the ages, rulers keep popping up who desire nothing more than unassailable power to wield over their fellow countrymen? Occasionally, there are good monarchs, such as Charlemagne and King Arthur, but almost all of them are in it for their own self-aggrandizement. Since the days of the Roman emperors and pharaohs of Egypt, all the way down to our friend King Saud in Saudi Arabia, their approach is an all-for-me and nothing-for-the-people gambit.

"In this vein, we are lucky that such men typically embody the gene for their own self-destruction. After Adolf Hitler had taken over the Balkans, Austria, and completely quashed France, he could have rested easy. Germany was allied with Italy, Spain was embroiled in civil war and Franco's dictatorial policies, and there was ready access to Crimean oil fields through his treaty with Russia. He even felt a kinship for the British.

"Then, personal ambition led to his own destruction as he sought first to subdue England, and then turned in frustration on his ally to the east. Just think what a different place the world would be today if he had simply stayed put, holding all of Western Europe and being satisfied with that? The Germans are an industrious people possessing great ingenuity, but the arts and culture embodied in France and a free middle Europe would have been ground to dust."

We four ruminated on these dark possibilities for a bit and then adjourned to be with our families for dinner.

For me, once my work was done for the day, I loved sitting down and simply watching or listening to some football game or quiz show. I never felt the restless drive to be engaged in an activity or a discussion. One day, however, I got far more than I had bargained for when my wife Gail showed me a side of her of which I knew nothing.

One week-end, the two of us had stopped over at Jack and Jacquelean's home, "Wexford," in Middleburg, Virginia. Mrs. Kennerly had designed it and proudly named it after a county in Ireland where her husband's great-grandfather had been born.[3]

As we followed Jacquelean into the family room, with its 9-foot ceilings, parquet floors, and comfy couches facing French doors opening onto a sloping lawn of pristine grass, Gail and I exchanged glances; we were glad we had stopped by. The other assembled guests would make for a convivial group. Today, the Kennerlys were in rare form.

When a momentary lull in the general level of conversation provided a moment of quiet, we could all hear an insistent knock at the front door.

Jack paused, looked around the room, and then used his finger to count heads.

"Well, everyone who is supposed to be here is here. Who could that be?"

Jacquelean turned those wonderfully large brown eyes of hers toward him and, with a nod of her head, subtly indicated that he should go to the door and open it.

I could hear the President mumbling as he rose and headed for the door: "I wonder why the Secret Service didn't open it?"

When he turned the knob, the unadorned and heavy oaken door was pushed aside and an athletic-looking, attractive girl slipped past the President. Sprawled outside were the incapacitated bodies of several secret service men writhing on the ground.

Prancing into the living room, this woman announced: "Well, ladies and gentlemen, are you ready for your entertainment this evening?"

When everyone, including me, remained puzzled by her presence, she strutted over to my wife and pulled her out of her chair. As Gail rose, she looked over at me with a mischievous smile on her lips. All of us there were about to be fascinated by an enthralling faux-karate combat performed by these two females. With guttural yelps and fast-swinging limbs, they leapt and scooted around the chairs and couches, even momentarily "flying" across the walls of the room. Each of us in the now dumbfounded audience sat immobile as the two women cart-wheeled and executed balletic high-leg kicks; it would not be good for our health to get in their way. As the moves were performed, we could feel the wind from the speed of a hand chop or leg swing.

We remained glued to our seats. The realism was so genuine but, except for those unfortunate men guarding the door, no one sustained an injury during this balletic show.

As the entertainment ended, Gail collapsed into a chair and sat panting next to me, but the dark-haired slip of a girl said, "Good night, ladies and gentlemen. It has been our privilege to entertain you. If you need my services, contact the CIA."

As we sat there stunned, she glided out the door, causing the now recovering guards to arch backward to avoid her exit. Jack thought he better alert them that it had all been for show, so he headed straight for the door to calm the agents. Meanwhile, Jacquelean turned to face her friend-turned-acrobat and breathed:

"Good gracious! As a show-jumper, I thought I knew balance and body-control, but you, Gail, have out-shown me completely! If you ever want to take riding lessons and join me for an outing, please do let me know!"

At that, the President returned and sat down with a cushioned-wheeze as the pillows absorbed the weight of his now fuller frame. "Whew!" he sighed. "Clint, you've got a secret weapon here! I've never seen two gals provide such excitement without at least one of them touching me." Then, glancing over at his wife, he mumbled, "You know what I mean, don't you, Jacquelean!"

This got a big laugh which allowed most of the men to stand and head over to the bar, but I remained seated and, turning to my wife, I asked quizzically, "Who was that?"

"That was Connie Connors. Your father introduced us during one of your extended absences on the President's detail. She gave me lessons and, over time, we became friends. We thought this would be an unusual form of entertainment for everybody. What did you think?"

"**That** was Connie Connors! Oh boy, she was something!"

Then, realizing my goof, I quickly added, "You were so impressive! You never told me you had an interest in that sport. Have you taught our son Chris as well?"

My wife smiled demurely and asked me to pour her a drink. I walked toward the bar, leaving my question hanging. I wasn't about to pursue the answer. It was suddenly clear to me that my career, my happiness, my family, even my very life, were now complete. My wife had made it so. There was no need to be nosing about like a curious cat. The close calls in my life had probably already used up most of my nine lives already—I wanted to stick around for the remaining ones.

However, in the future, I would be very careful to avoid arguing with my wife.

Notes

1   Fay, p. 130.
2   See Pitts, p. 236.
3   The Kennerlys had occasionally retreated to Glen Ora, a residence owned by Mrs. Raymond Tartière and generously made available for the Kennerly's use during the President's first two years in office. That arrangement came to an end in 1962; thereafter, Wexford was purchased to serve as their new retreat.

CHAPTER THIRTY-ONE

Crisis South of the Border

Congressman Lee Hamilton (IN) to this day remembers voting in favor of the Voting Rights Act of 1965, the creation of Medicare and Medicaid, the first general aid to elementary and secondary schools, and its offspring—student aid for undergraduate study. These embodied social benefits applicable to all subsequent generations of Americans. No wonder he remembers their passage! He was living through the decade when our government enacted laws for the genuine betterment of society rather than narrow, heavily-financed private interests.

It was a heady time to be alive. Our President kept the federal budget close to $100 billion and held inflation to 3.5% while the stock market and the various economic indices increased steadily. Mortgages were at or close to 5%, unemployment below 6%, and factory workers were earning more than ever before. He doubled food rations for poor citizens as soon as the second term began and launched Medicare for the elderly.[1]

In a move that generated grumbling among the wealthy, he strengthened the continued existence of the Social Security fund by altogether eliminating any cut-off on earnings subject to this beneficial tax. FICA would now apply to the <u>entire</u> amount the highest paid executives in the country were earning.

He stemmed complaint by saying, "The more you earn, the less is the imposition of this tax on the taxpayer's lifestyle. The greater your income, the less of an imposition it is for you to be required to share with those less fortunate."

He realized that such a uniform regulation might be viewed as a restriction on a wealthy person's freedom to spend. But social security checks are like accident insurance: they are there just when needed the most! Within a few months, all the uproar had died down as everyone came to understand the wisdom in this tax-law revision.

One of Mr. Jensen's lasting domestic achievements was ensuring that every individual citizen had an opportunity to share in America's abundance. Working together with Stuart Udall, the President's appointee as Secretary of the Interior, Lyndon established protective measures to preserve America's pristine natural areas. With the passage of the Wilderness Act in 1964, the Appalachian Trail was assured protection as a recreational and restorative resource.

"There ought to be places left in America the way God made them!" he affirmed while signing this historic measure. "We must learn to respect the land rather than greedily exploit it for economic gain. We must embrace our wild spaces as a treasure-house of wonders!"

As more and more people from around the country, and indeed the world, began to find pleasure, exercise, and fulfillment from walking this 2,160 or so mile-long-route, some would elucidate their experience in log books left at the various trailside shelters.

"To experience the Appalachian Trial is to get to know the soul of our country and what we value deeply, to experience the locations we have chosen to protect and preserve in perpetuity. Americans have a longing for wildness and nostalgia for the landscape of our forefathers when the mountains were forested, farms dotted the valleys, and signs of modernity had not yet been paved. An ordinary person can spend six months immersed in nature. This is long enough to foster a life-altering experience. One learns how few material goods one needs to survive and be happy, and yet how much we humans are social creatures bound to each other." [2]

Eventually, a hiker named (coincidentally) David Brill would get around to extolling his memories of time on the trail as moments of sublime happiness when he felt himself becoming immersed by the forested, mountainous environs. In his book, *As Far as the Eye Can See,* he wrote about *Images of lush, green mountains, of gray clouds of mist wafting thru virgin stands of hemlock and oak, of bald-tipped mountains with views that roll out across miles and miles of blue hazed hills, of hawks swirling above sun-drenched granite ledges, of springs that run so cold they make my teeth ache. The views choke me with emotion and fill me with pride to be an American.*

In this land of pioneers, cowboys, and inventors, we tend to float rather than put down roots. In our perpetual pursuit of happiness, we may be fairly contented today, but there's always tomorrow and the prospect of a happier locale and life. We thus never fully commit, but rather leave alternative options on the table for future inspection and reference.

As I opined previously, to really love the space you're in, you have to commit, to place both your feet fully on its earth and form bonds and relationships within its boundaries. The Vice-President exemplified this, both in his tenure in the Senate and as a life-long resident of Texas.

When a crisis arises, our Constitution puts ultimate authority for its solution in the hands of a civilian elected by the people of this country. He can make a mistake, but he does so with his citizenry united behind him as our president rather than swayed by manic hotheads or bellicose knee-jaggers. Considered, reasoned action is the name of the sane game. The decision to commit our nation to war is too important to be left in the hands of the generals.

In the case of Jack Kennerly, he had learned an all-important lesson from the Bay of Pigs failure: when everyone is railing at you to decide in their favor, the decision is ultimately yours to make. As President, he must rely on what he thinks is right at the time. In this respect, his characteristic trait of allowing himself to become detached from the conversation allowed him to suppress emotional reaction and use a reasoned approach that would—significantly— comport with his concerns for the safety of his fellow citizens.

God may have provided the fiasco of the Bay of Pigs to test President Kennerly's mettle and thereby steel his resolve when, a mere year later, the genuine crisis with Russian missiles being deployed in Cuba appeared. The world's worst nightmare had suddenly become real. By this time, he had gained confidence in his leadership role. He would listen to and evaluate the advice of his military advisors, but not be overwhelmed by them. His goof regarding the Bay of Pigs had given him the strength to save the world. In short, he had gained entelechy, or the capacity to realize his potential, as opposed to having potential but producing no benefits.

Using all his gifts and skills, he had seen world tensions ease as the dynamic changed from dominance by a single dogmatic creed to one of liberating the diverse energies of free nations and free men around the world.

Now as the following crisis suddenly mushroomed, would the men in the Situation Room wisely counsel our President? More importantly, would that man take appropriate action and handle it to preserve the safety of peoples throughout the world?

His justification for initiating the Peace Corps was to help targeted countries develop their industrial and agricultural base and to facilitate education, thereby improving their living standards. Bottom line, the goal was to pressure the leaders of such lands into acting on behalf of their people rather than purely in their own interests. Doing so would enable such society to be strong enough to resist internal power struggles or outside invasion. If residents are zealous about preserving and valuing their way of life, then it can be defended against despots.

In short, the United States had the opportunity to help not just backward regions but also our own neighbors to the South. Our agricultural harvests of food and the education of talented technicians practically obliged us to enable the developing countries to better the living conditions within their borders. Eventually, the rationale went, better nourished and educated residents would seek freedom for themselves. President Kennerly had seen the importance of doing just that in 1941 after traveling to Argentina, Peru, Colombia, Ecuador, and Brazil prior to enlisting in the U.S. Navy. He wrote to his friend Cam Newberry that, "Our country is by no means as popular, nor are its commercial interests as secure, as people back home—including my older brother—are led to believe. The influence of the Nazi party line is very appealing to these people." [3]

The need to "look after our own" had never left the deep recesses of his brain. As President, he was in a position to assure the success of neighboring countries.

The idea for a Peace Corps had sprung from Jack's imagination when Vice-President Nixy had collared then President Eisenhower to stump for him. As the 1960 campaign had neared Election Day, Mr. Kennerly proposed relieving nations from the twin-prongs of ignorance and the burden of poverty. The idea of a Peace Corps, possibly as an alternative to conscription, rejuvenated the candidate for the closing week and made him enthusiastic about reaching for the highest post in the land.

Once he held the office, he had performed exceptionally well, despite initial growing pains, but each year brought something new to handle and, possibly, to trip over.

As the calendar passed the middle of March 1965, our government was burdened with a crisis from south of the border rather than from across an ocean. Venezuela was now a world-class producer of prime beef for export. The quality rivaled the best which our own Wyoming or Texas ranchers could produce. Appetite for steaks was an all-American tradition, so producers were thriving in 1965. Despite her huge reserves of oil, beef was where Venezuela had placed her bets for financial independence. For most of the prior decade, this emphasis worked well for the people of Venezuela. Each night, bats sojourning in Peruvian caves would cross the border and suck blood from the Venezuelan cattle as they grazed placidly overnight. Their fangs were so sharp that piercing the tough hides of cows was easy. In fact, the same bat can not only find the same steer in the dark, but also settle upon the exact wound it had made during earlier raids. Bat saliva prevented the blood coagulating, so the creatures were feasting heartily.

The sharpness of the scoundrels' fangs allowed the blood-sucking to continue without bothering the cows; that is, until one of the bats became rabid and quickly spread this dreaded malady throughout the bat warrens. Steers and cows either started dying where they grazed or turned up contaminated when butchered.

Almost overnight, one of the most stable and financially healthy countries in the western hemisphere was about to turn belly up. Their leaders began screaming, "Secour, secour!" in near panic both on televisions and in the newspapers. The problem reached crisis proportions during the early part of 1965 because South American countries enjoy the warm part of their grazing season when we are just emerging from the chill of winter. The bats were in full nibbling mode just when the cattle were at their fattest. As meat, and incomes, became scarce, riots in the cities began disrupting what food could be distributed. The U.S. Ambassador, Allen Stewart, warned that anarchy and revolt threatened to destabilize this important southern ally. With Fidel Casstra threatening to export the sabers of revolution so openly, weakness in this oil-rich domain warranted a fast response and an even quicker solution.

President Kennerly consulted with Secretary of Agriculture Orville Freeman and thereafter sent down Secretary of Commerce Luther Hodges on a fact-finding mission. Our government's concern was that the possible revolution would establish yet another dictatorship whereby alien forces would take over to repress freedom and place control of the land in the hands of a puppet such as Fidel Casstra. The American people would not support such an event, despite our own freedoms being founded in revolution.

Secretary Hodges met with the in-country diplomatic staff. Working together, they devised a plan to stave off the looming disaster by importing foodstuffs at below-market cost from Brazil and America. More to the point, Secretary Freeman dispatched teams of trained men to assist in the eradication of the bat warrens.

The *quid quo pro* would be barrels of oil being exported to the United States at a substantial discount to the then market price. Crisis resolved, we Americans got on with our frenetic motoring and consumption of gasoline as though there was no tomorrow.

Afterward, our President sagely noted: "Like poker, politics and the art of statesmanship requires not the skill to bluff, but the ability to calculate the odds vis-à-vis the costs of misjudgment."

Notes

[1]   See generally Hamilton, Lee H., *How Congress Works*.
[2]   Laurie H. Potteiger, 1987 Appalachian Trail thru hiker, writing in the Trail Log after surviving the constant rocks along the Pennsylvania section. At the first shelter in New Jersey, she had stopped to recover and had added in that journal: "The AT provides you with a feeling of being surrounded by all the good things, like love and peace and joy. It seems like a protective surrounding, once you've gotten past all those rocks!"
[3]   Hamilton, Nigel, pp. 402-4.

CHAPTER THIRTY-TWO

A Parent's Worst Nightmare

On Friday the 2nd of April, a crisis occurred at the very heart of our government that changed the tenor of the current presidency. What President Kennerly had done for every individual citizen's faith in the future, as well as for foreign leaders' confidence in our leadership, was severely damaged. Even my job was put at risk.

A permanent *bouleversement*, as the French would say, was about to upset everything. All the grandly eloquent oratory which had so inspired us thus far was about to be stifled. There would be no going back to the familiar. To my deep regret, not even skilled medical practitioners would be able to restore the status quo.

On that Friday, our President had his pen poised in mid-air, ready to sign yet another social welfare bill greased through the skids of Congress by his vice-president, when Evelyn stuck her head through the office door.

"Mr. President, Agent Montrose from the Secret Service is here and has asked to speak with you as soon as you are available!"

Kenneth and I had already been summoned so we were standing astride Agent Montrose when our President motioned us to enter. Surprise and curiosity lined his forehead, but nothing could have prepared him for the shock which this agent was about to deliver.

"Thank you for seeing me so promptly, Mr. President," Mike Montrose urgently stated as he went straight to the heart of the situation. "Something has happened about which we are unclear at present, but your son Jon-Jon may be in danger. Mrs. Kennerly notified us about an hour ago that he had gone missing and his nanny, Mrs. Shaw, is mystified as to where he might have gotten to."

At this point, Mr. Kennerly rose from behind the desk and strode forward to confront the agent face-on.

"What are you talking about? He was here in this office only three hours ago cavorting about and hiding in my desk's secret compartment. He should be asleep and taking a nap at this hour."

He looked down at his watch to confirm that it was after 2:00 PM.

The agent shifted uneasily from one foot to the other before he spoke.

"Yes, sir, that should be the case. However, when Mrs. Shaw poked her head into the Kidde Room, he wasn't there, and when she checked with Mrs. Kennerly, she confirmed, just as you did, that he should have been down for his nap. Now, I am here because no one has been able to find him anywhere. He may be hiding, playing another game possibly, but the only thing we have noticed—and we don't yet know if this is a clue—is that the cabinet door on the rear of the bar in the Green Room, where you do so much informal entertaining, is ajar. That compartment is where a keg is kept to tap when serving beer. It's just the right size to serve as a cubbyhole for a little adventurous youngster intent on finding a secret hiding place. The position of the knob would be easy to reach for a boy of four-and-a-half-years. I focused on this because Mrs. Kennerly flatly stated that it is always kept closed when not in use."

President Kennerly was visibly shocked and called out to Evelyn, "Cancel my appointments for the rest of the day. We're going to get to the bottom of this right away!"

It was at this point that Mrs. Kennerly entered. Her face was contorted and her shoulders sagging with worry. She had none of the poise and equanimity for which she is famous. She saw her husband standing in the center of our group and immediately collapsed into his reassuring arms.

"Oh, Jack!" she cried, sobbing. "I can't believe this has happened, and in the White House! When Mrs. Shaw came to me stating our son was not in his usual hiding places, we looked in every nook and closet where we'd seen him play-hide before, but when we couldn't find him, I called the housekeeper and the doorman as well. None of us located him, so then we called in the Secret Service, but we have not yet found him!"

The President turned and, with some fury in his voice, asked, "Aren't Agents Landis and Jenkins supposed to be assigned to his detail? Where were they?"

"I'm sorry, Mr. President," came the belated reply. Agent Landis stepped forward and explained, "We were down the hall. Jon-Jon was supposed to be napping and in Mrs. Shaw's care."

As these excuses were being cranked out, Agent Montrose found himself still shifting uneasily from foot-to-foot. Secret Service Agent Landis was being called on the carpet but, there was no denying it: he had screwed-up, big-time! Mike silently resolved to himself to solve this disappearance, and to do so promptly!

He admired both Mr. and Mrs. Kennerly—greatly, in fact! But today, these two were merely typical American parents who have suffered a heavy blow to their family. The President's arms, which were capable of leading and inspiring millions of people, even entire nations, were now so numbed by fear that he could barely hold Jacquelean erect. They sagged as one toward the brass-studded, dark green leather couch that had offered reassurance and security to so many distinguished foreign leaders during the last few years. Once seated, they collapsed against each other. Though Jacquelean immediately began to sob, Jack remained more manfully stalwart. The single most important man in the world—and one of the most elegant women to have ever walked the planet—were at that moment as mortal as any two human beings can be.

I turned to Evelyn and called, "Would you please locate Carolyn and make sure she is brought down to the Oval Office to be at the side of her parents."

Then I addressed Mike Montrose. After all, I had been detailed to an agency similar to his only two years earlier, so I was sure that he and I would think the same way.

"Why don't I assemble the entire staff of the White House, explain that we believe the lad has been kidnapped rather than become lost, and ask for their help. What I suggest is a focus right from the start on the tour-guides; those groups prowling through this place on a daily basis are, to me, the most obvious weak link in our security. The kitchen staff and the various secret service agents may possibly have something to contribute, but that would be like bowling a perfect score twice in one day. The tour-guides would most likely be the ones who might have seen something suspicious!"

I didn't fold my arms across my chest and assume a confident air, but I was pretty sure of myself.

"Good idea!" was all Montrose said as he rushed off to confer with his higher-ups. I got busy notifying the various section-staff directors, so it wasn't long before each member of their units was trooping into the Red Room and learning the bad news. Nothing much came to light until one of the doormen, Chester Noonan, and Madeline Stone, a longtime tour-guide for the Kennerlys (with her college degree in Louis XIV French furnishings, she had proved invaluable during the First Lady's preparation for the televised tour of the White House back in February 1962) stood before Agent Montrose, Kenny, and me. They weren't sure, but they thought they might have a lead to suggest to everyone.

"This is only supposition on our part, but we have discussed it and we think we have something that might help," Chester said hesitantly. Agent Montrose, sitting Sphinx-like behind a utilitarian metal desk, immediately told him to proceed.

"Well, as it happened, I worked an extra shift this week, so I was on-duty all five days. It's my job to speak with every member of the public who comes through the White House. As you know, Mrs. Stone here works every other day in order to give her feet a rest. She worked Monday, Wednesday, and Friday of this week. We don't ask visitors to sign in because we meet and greet every single one who comes for a tour and, well, you take over now, Madeline…"

"Thanks, Chester," she politely said as she stepped forward. After months of dealing with inquisitive and curious tourists, she had no trouble holding our concentration as she looked from one to the other of us. She postulated: "There was one particular female guest that caught our attention. She was part of our Monday group and very pleasant. She came again on Tuesday, according to Chester, and then she showed up again on Wednesday. She was easy to note because the majority of guests consider visiting the White House to be something special, so they dress in their best Sunday clothes, or at least something close. In contrast, this woman was very casual, wearing blue jeans with a colorfully patterned hem on the cuffs and a gauzy over-blouse. A bit impolite, I surmised, but she might still be in college where informality is often the norm, so I really didn't ascribe any significance to her attire.

"Once the Wednesday tour got underway, however, she seemed jumpy, even anxious. She kept peering into rooms which we typically bypass. Even when I addressed her directly, asking that she keep up with my group, she continued to lag behind, as though she wanted to poke around rather than simply admire. And, the thing that struck me as being truly odd, she wore sunglasses during the tour. Indoors!"

Madeline paused, as though she was trying to put some mental image into words. "At the time, I thought it a bit odd, but I noticed that on this day, she seemed more intent on listening, as though she was trying to hear some sound that the rest of us were basically ignoring. When I mentioned it to Chester, he joked that she was simply listening to the furniture and walls spill their secrets. We both laughed. I took no further notice; that is, until today."

"When she came again yesterday," interjected Chester, "I recognized her instantly because, once again, she was wearing dark glasses—for an indoor tour! I even mentioned to my partner Robin that we could set our watches by her arrival times." He smiled my way at his little joke, but I remained stone-faced. These two employees might be on to something. What Mrs. Stone said next raised the hairs on the back of my neck, so I looked down at the seated Montrose. He was leaning forward, resting his chin on his fists as he listened intently to her story.

Madeline proceeded to relate her observations: "Well, when I came to work on this Friday, I recognized this same woman, but today she was wearing a fulsome coat, the kind of Parisian design with big buttons down the front that Jacquelean had made famous. It sports a billowy hem that gives a woman a lot of freedom to move. You can easily carry your handbag beneath it so it stays safe while your hands come through side slits so you can balance and maneuver. I was a bit surprised by her getup; she's somewhat willowy and mousy, so this sort of outfit was a bit bold for her. But, being a woman in her mid-twenties, a sporty getup would not be unusual."

Mrs. Stone bowed her head down to study the floor for a bit, and then she raised her eyes to look us men squarely in the face. She had dark circles around her sunken eyes, and her mouth trembled as though she was about to burst into tears. "I'm so sorry to say this, because I may lose my job for it. Nevertheless, I feel honor-bound to tell you that I was startled to see this person again today. As I stated, Chester confirmed that she came *every* day this week. Occasionally our tours include a repeat visitor, but never has anyone shown up every single day in a week before. And, today she was wearing a fancy sort of coat which contrasted significantly with her relatively informal attire earlier in the week. I just thought that she was finally trying to be a bit more respectful of the Executive Mansion and all, but I should have said something to one of the house ushers, or maybe even to the Secret Service. Her behavior was so out of the norm that, well, I should have said something, but I just couldn't bring myself to do it. In my job, I'm supposed to be shepherding folks, more like a mother hen than a tattle-tale. I'm so sorry."

Kenny, Mike, and I exchanged brief glances. I then postulated, "Mrs. Stone, Chester, these are unusual facts, no doubt about it, but I don't see any fault on your part. We have to welcome people as they present themselves; you can't be expected to delve into why citizens dress the way they do. Moreover, I cannot see any connection between what you're telling me and Jon-Jon, the President's missing child."

Frankly, I was a little discouraged. What had seemed like a promising lead had seemed to fizzle as a figment of my wishful imagination. I was mentally preparing for the next person to interview when the pair hit me with their bombshell.

"Please, Mr. Brill, Mr. McDonald, consider what I saw."

At this point, Madeline almost began to plead for us to take her seriously.

"At some point in my tour this afternoon, this woman left my group. I didn't notice it until everyone in my group was assembling at the exit. Chester happened to mention that he had seen this woman leave alone, and walking rather purposefully, he thought, a half-hour before my group finished at 3:30 PM."

Her last word was interrupted by Agent Montrose slamming his fist down on the table. He looked up at Kenny and me. "I think we've got ourselves a lead!" was all he said as he rose and dashed for the nearest phone. He wanted to issue an all-points bulletin immediately and try to find whether this "visitor" drove a car that had parked in the lot across the street from the White House. Someone might have spotted her acting suspiciously. He posited that this person was probably delusional, even desperate. Perhaps she had seen Jon-Jon's face on one of the many tabloids and decided to risk taking him. Whether for ransom or to keep, he couldn't fathom; regardless, he doubted that she would have a criminal record, so there would be no mug shot. If only a rule was in place where each tour group would be photographed before beginning their visit...

His method would be to search for the **boy**'s face. Such would be well-known by everyone living in the capital district. But, he had to act fast! If this woman boarded a train and left the District of Columbia, then canvassing a much larger circle would be just that much more difficult. Surely he was faced with a case of kidnapping; consequently, time to locate the missing Kennerly child might run out all too soon. He was hoping for a ransom demand, either today or tomorrow, because that would suggest that the child was still alive.

CHAPTER THIRTY-THREE

Tears of Rejoicing

Dari Delft had been the youngest of a passel of children growing up in Iowa. That's what her mother had called all her brothers and sisters. Being at the bottom of the hierarchy, she was often kidded and teased by her siblings but, as she learned early-on, they also truly loved her. Her parents reinforced the "mothering" instinct natural to most women by showing affection for their children. Even when the middle-aged couple had perished in an automobile accident when she was only twelve-years-old, Dari had never felt deprived or lonely; her siblings had all rallied round to look after her.

Now that she was past twenty-five but living alone in the glitzy city of Washington, D.C., she felt the absence of her treasured siblings and parents deeply. She was missing something, but she didn't know what, much less how to get it. When she was growing up, she had become skilled at conniving in order to safe-keep things for herself. In such a large family, where rank was based merely on age, there was very little that she could call her own. Even the clothes she wore were hand-me-downs. As a result, all the boyfriends who dated her were eventually put off by her seemingly endless need for something to possess.

Then one day, she got in line for a tour at the White House. After a lovely time experiencing all the beautiful and famous artwork treasured by the President and his wife, she happened to purchase a copy of *McCall's* at the newsstand for her nighttime reading. Within that issue was a spread detailing the latest Kennerly saga. In a previous issue, she had laughed out loud when she saw one of Jacques Lowe's pictures of the President being nudged over by Carolyn's pony. But in this issue, when she turned a page and saw Jon-Jon peeping out from the secret door of the President's mahogany desk, she absolutely fell in love with this little boy.

"I'm going to make that angel mine!" she thought to herself. She even found herself fantasizing about how he'd be better off with her: "He's always alone, his parents never seem to have time for him, and his only diversion is a snotty older sister. Who wants an old nanny for a playmate? Why not a young, athletic, winsome mommy such as myself? I can devote my entire existence to him!"

She began to set her plan in motion. Now that she knew the layout of the interior of the Executive Mansion, she figured she could anonymously join the tour each day until an opportunity arose for her to discover the young child-in-hiding and then whisk him away to her own apartment.

She found the perfect means when she passed Pearson's Department Store the next morning. Its display window boasted a knock-off of Jacquelean Kennerly's picturesque, wool Melton coat designed by Oleg Cassini. She went inside and bought a size-too-big, took it back to her apartment, and got ready for the morrow. When her big day dawned, she took no personal items with her except her car keys, a silk scarf, and slim black gloves. Her license could be left in the glove compartment. Donning the voluminous coat, she motored to the designated parking lot which, by this time, she knew well. Joining the tour on a Friday would allow her to be lost in a larger-than-usual group since many out-of-towners came to spend long weekends in the capital.

At one point about mid-afternoon, Madeline had halted her group outside the Blue Room and, after gaining everyone's attention, had announced that they would now have the chance to study photographs of the many foreign dignitaries who had visited the President over the last few years. Everyone had stopped talking at the thought of such a privilege. In that moment of silence, Dari had heard a soft *thunk*, such as a small shoe hitting the side of wood might make. As the other visitors ambled out of sight, she entered a room obviously designed for parties and spotted an imposing, leather-topped bar. Stepping behind it, she found a small door cracked open just a hair. Opening it, she saw her dream angel asleep, scrunched up as if hiding from a parent but bored by not being discovered. She scooped him beneath her coat and proceeded, without display, to leave the building. The doorman even tipped his hand to his forehead, as though in a little salute, as she left.

"She probably is rushing to do some last-minute marketing," Chester had briefly thought to himself as she slipped past him.

He had heard nothing untoward. The silk scarf tightly bound over the child's mouth gagged any outcry.

She made her way to her light-blue Volkswagen bug and then untied the silk bond. Enticing him with the prospect of a car trip, she sat the little boy on her lap, saying, "Look, honey, see what fun it is to be driving a real car!"

She had her own child at last, but how could she get him to her apartment without the neighbors gossiping? Somehow, she managed to do so, but by the very next morning, word of the kidnapping had been splashed across all the newspapers in the Washington, D.C. area, together with a picture of Jon-Jon's smiling face for the entire world to see. His signature hair-cut showed his locks falling forward over his forehead. These, of course, had been shorn by Dari the night before. Nevertheless, she was afraid he was still too identifiable as Jacquelean's son, so she retained him in her apartment and occupied him with storybooks and yummy snacks. After a couple of days, she took her new son to the playground. On a Monday morning, most mothers would either be working or seeing their kids off on the school bus. Very likely, few people would be using it.

Just to be sure, she bought a coonskin cap and, as she settled it on the child's head, she stated gleefully: "There. Now you look just like Davy Crockett! Everyone will think we are going exploring together!"

To herself, Dari excitedly fantasized: "This will be the first time we share an outdoor excursion!"

Little Jon-Jon didn't know what this reference to "Davee-Cockit" meant. He was still too young to understand Walt Disney's televised sagas about the legendary frontiersman, but since The New Lady kept offering him cookies and lemonade, he accepted her attentions with delight. He was sitting innocently in the front seat as Dari pulled into a playground. When he saw the sandbox, he recognized it as a source of pleasure and raised his arms with glee, shouting "Hooray!"

The little boy's excitement caught the attention of Mabel Greenleaf as she was chatting with Sybil Hornsby. The two friends were monitoring their own children as they climbed all over the jungle-gym. Something about this boy caught her attention. She had never seen the woman here before, but the son she was holding close by her side looked vaguely familiar. As she watched mother-and-child head for the sandbox, the kid tripped; spellbound, she watched as his hat fell off. Even as his mother stooped to pick up the cap and replace it, Mabel's hand went to her mouth to cover a shriek.

Stifling the rush of her excitement, she managed to extend her hand to grip Sybil's arm, causing her friend to turn and face her at once.

"Heavens, Mabel, what's gotten into you?" she started to ask, but even as she did so, her eyes looked at her friend's wide-open mouth and followed her stare. "Oh-my-God! That's the little Kennerly boy!" she wanted to yell, but Mrs. Greenleaf was already standing erect in front of her and waving her hands for her to be silent. The two women stood together for a moment, held hands briefly, and then both turned to seek out the park's horse-mounted policeman they had noticed outside the entrance.

Patrolman Leon Saxby had thought this would be an easy day. The air was balmy and visitation light, so he was sitting on his horse reviewing yesterday's log reports when two women breathlessly rushed up to him.

"Officer, you've got to help us, now!"

"Yes!" Mabel screeched even louder than Sybil. "We think we've spotted Jon-Jon Kennerly!"

The officer held up his hand, "Whoa there, ladies. Talk one at a time. Now, what's the problem?"

Ignoring his request, the women were obviously beside themselves and couldn't stop jabbering at the same time.

Despite the women's garbled statements, he began to understand the importance of what they were saying. He lifted his walkie-talkie from its holster and contacted headquarters. "Hey, O' Toole, we've got a lead on that Kennerly kid."

While talking to O'Toole, he used his binoculars to spot the boy in the sandbox and immediately addressed the women. "Now, ladies, which of those cars parked over there is yours?"

The two women pointed out their cars, whereupon Officer Saxby addressed O'Toole again, stating: "I believe the perp is driving a blue VW bug, license plate: bravo—delta—eight—two—three."

Dispatcher O'Toole put the phone right down. He could hardly believe what Patrolman Saxby had just told him. He rallied and, picking up the handset again, dialed straight over to the White House. His brother was one of the gate guards, and Dennis O'Toole rang through to the Secret Service's duty-phone. The agent who answered wasted no time in notifying the F.B.I., and when Montrose was reached, he telephoned Evelyn over at the White House.

Meanwhile, the local police were surrounding the park without sounding any approach sirens, and they brought up a van to block the parking area's exit. When everyone was positioned, their lieutenant blew his whistle and the cordon of police rushed Dari. Startled, she took one look at the oncoming wall of blue uniforms, stood up, and promptly fainted. The last thought she had was only this: how fleeting happiness can be!

Little Jon-Jon was methodically building bucket-castles; thus, he protested rather loudly when someone suddenly picked him up and bundled him straight into a police car. When it went streaking down the street, the just-rescued boy was thrilled; he never got to see the whirling red beacons or hear the sirens when confined in the Kiddie Room, so he was happily smiling when the car pulled up to what he recognized as his home. The car had only just braked to a stop when his daddy and mommy came rushing out to scoop him up into their arms.

Under the portico of the White House, everyone was exuberant, hugging and kissing the little, lost lad. Meanwhile, when Dari revived, she found herself locked in a van and lying on a cold, very hard steel floor. Two policewomen sat near what looked to be a locked double-door. As the van careened along some avenue, she was bounced around more than if she had been on a roller-coaster, but where she was headed would not be fun.

* * *

As the direct result of all his worry and anger prior to his son being returned, President Kennerly's Addison disease suddenly worsened to the point where he became almost totally debilitated by acute adrenal failure. While there was much speculation in the medical literature that such a disease was survivable if contracted later in life, Mr. Kennerly's condition had presented while in his early teens; thus, the sickness would surely be fatal if the President continued to undergo his customary levels of mental and physical stress.

The instant Admiral George Burkley walked into the bedroom of his longtime friend, he knew this beloved leader was at a point-of-no-return. One look at his patient's skin-coloring, as well as the weakness in his normally sagacious, uplifting voice, and the doctor could tell that the condition induced by the Addison's disease had finally become all-consuming. Gently, he asked the President whether he would be willing to turn over the duties of his office to Vice-President Jensen while undergoing the treatment that would now be required. Mr. Kennerly had no choice but to agree. Mr. Jensen was immediately summoned.

Then the admiral took Jacquelean into an anteroom and told her in no uncertain terms: "This is it. If you don't have your husband step aside and forego all duties of his office immediately, he may not be alive next week. Only staying comfortable and eschewing all pressures to perform, even something as ordinary as answering a telephone, must be stopped at once. I am so very sorry to be so direct, Mrs. Kennerly, but we have known all along that this day might come. Well, here it is. If we act at once, Jack may hang on for another two years or so, but he can no longer be the inspiring, ennobling leader we have come to cherish over the last five years."

While Mrs. Kennerly stood silently for a moment, stricken by this ultimatum, I turned at the sound of some scuffling feet. There stood Vice-President Jensen. He took one look at the face of President Kennerly's wife and he instantly understood that, whether he was ready or not, the helm of the nation was about to be placed in his hands. His first reaction, however, was to be completely attentive to Jacquelean. As he wrapped her in those long Texan arms, his tone was most soothing, but he also looked over her shoulder straight at me.

With a start, I suddenly realized what he was silently asking me to do.

According to the rules of succession contained in Article 2, Section 1, Clause 6 of the Constitution, when the then vice-president is to assume the role of president due to incapacity, as opposed to the death, of a president, then the Chief Justice of the Supreme Court is to be summoned to administer the oath of office, but only after due notice has been furnished to the members of Congress as to what is about to happen. Informing the Chief Justice would be my assignment, while Larry O'Brien would be tasked to tell the Congress. Kenneth would have Pierre Salinger hold a press conference to announce the impending change of leadership.

CHAPTER THIRTY-FOUR

Departure

Due to his physical incapacity, the President
watches his replacement being sworn in

For such a momentous turn of events, I must say that the wheels of
our government worked smoothly. By Tuesday, the 13th of April 1965,
Mr. Jensen was President of the United States. Leading our country
successfully and inspiring all citizens to become better people would
now be up to him.

After the trauma of the transition ceremony and the hubbub had died down, it dawned on me that no one had asked me to continue on. With mixed emotions, I realized that I was about to have the opportunity of seeing my Gail a great deal more from here on.

Following the new president's inauguration, the now former President and Mrs. Kennerly made a trip on the evening of April 15 to Cambridge, Massachusetts. They intended to make this their farewell "thank-you" to the people who had first endowed Mr. Kennerly with their trust as one of Massachusetts' Representatives in Congress. As the entourage wound its way into the center of town in the late winter twilight, suddenly—on both sides of the road for some twenty blocks—throngs of chilled but cheering New Englanders turned on flashlights. Every one of them was roaring welcoming good wishes and waving hats and mufflers while fire engines trilled their horns or whirled their sirens and nearby churches chimed their bells.

I was privileged to have been asked to accompany the team of Secret Service shadowing the former Chief Executive this evening. I was thus in the middle of this uniquely exciting, yet tearful, evening.

The couple, snuggling together in the open four-in-hand carriage thoughtfully provided by a rich Boston lawyer-friend, David H. Morse, made this a unique home-coming. They were clearly moved by the unabashed fervor of everyone. Upon reaching the hotel where they were to spend their first night as ordinary citizens once again, Mr. and Mrs. Kennerly appeared on a balcony. No one had left for home; the citizenry was still wildly cheering their voluble thanks. In the depths of the chill of this freezing east coast night, everyone expressed joyous praise. The onlookers felt a warmth and sense of kinship with this former First Couple that would be cherished by them for the rest of their lives.

Turning to face the well-wishers bundled against the chill, our former President spoke only briefly, but from his heart.

"I leave you with this principal that must be ongoing: I believe in an America where every family can live in a decent home in a decent neighborhood, where children can gleefully and safely play in parks and playgrounds, rather than in a street, where no home is unsafe or unsanitary, where a capable doctor and good hospital are neither too far away nor too expensive, and where the water is clean and the air is pure for the health of everyone. I trust that you perceive that my, and now President Jensen's, administrations have been ones of fulfillment along these lines, not mere promise. Focus on what we share as a commonality rather than on differences that can work to divide us. You should be thrilled by all that you have to look forward to as our country's government forges ahead to provide a more even and just distribution of the benefits of being an American!"

President Kennerly, having worked closely with a domestically-minded Vice-President, had passed the many constructive improvements which would enable the now President Lyndon B. Jensen to dub America as "the Great Society." Jack could leave office proud that he had done so much for his countrymen.

Smiling, he waved to the well-wishers and then turned to Jacquelean to observe: "My years in public office have flown by as if in a dream, but they have allowed me to make the dreams of countless citizens come true. We've fulfilled so many hopeful yearnings. I listened to them, understood what they needed, and they perceived that I cared.

"It's as though we, as a nation, thrived for a while in peace, happiness, accord, and, finally, equality before the law. In short, let there ne'er be forgot that, for a treasured moment in time, all of us shared a spot known as *Camelot*."

In this medical transfer of power, there had been no interregnum. Thus, after bidding a goodnight to the adoring crowd, it was in keeping with the rules of decorum that Mr. Kennerly place a phone call to incoming President Jensen.

During this call, he stated simply: "Be forthright, and give it your all. I did."

With that final, simple act, he acknowledged that he was a plain citizen again, but a citizen who could not be considered ordinary in any sense of the word. He had given us his very best, and thereby he had encouraged the same from his fellow Americans. Great administrations have, like exquisite French restaurants, an ambiance all their own. Mr. Kennerly's had been zestful, devoted to bettering the life of his countrymen, and elegant. His ringing oratory would inspire us for decades to come. He had opened his arms wide and we had all rushed to be within the welcoming embrace. Every day, he made us feel good to be Americans. Establishing human contact had always been his most endearing attribute.

In response to some reporter's parting question about his legacy once he left office, Mr. Kennerly had smiled and then spoken from his heart: "I don't want to be known as a great president. I want people to remember that the events we experienced together formed a great period in America's history."

After hearing this, the clutch of reporters surrounding the President at the time had remained motionless for a moment, and then they had all clapped together as a token of their huge esteem for this former leader among men. Their united accolade expressed the feeling of the entire country.

The former President's last act was not an official one, but it was surely soulful. He summoned Bobby via telephone and expressed this hope:

"We have done well working to maximize the success and well-being of our fellow citizens. Those of us in my administration had many good days together but, as it turned out, not enough good years. It may very well be that I am not around to counsel you, as our Dad counseled me when I started out, but if Lyndon decides not to seek this job on his own in 1968, can you follow me and finish what we have begun? Surround yourself with good advisors, but think clearly. The decisions you make must be your own because you will have to live with the results."

That would prove to be a question that would have no answer. Sadly, violent death would retain its hold on members of the zestful, erudite Kennerly clan for years to come.

* * *

Much, much later, my wife Gail and I attended a reunion with some of my former colleagues from the Secret Service. At this point in 1972, no matter our ages, we were all members of the same family. We saw Joyce and Jerry Blaine, Art and Betty Godfrey, Win and Barb Lawson as well as many others. Since we were meeting in Dallas, Texas, I became curious after a bit of partying and found myself walking over to the TSBD building. Looking at it up close, feelings of long-dormant panic and worry rippled through the length of my spine.

Bravely, I squared my shoulders and took the elevator to the 6th floor. It was now known as the "Dallas County Administration Building." Despite its new use, the county had turned the 6th floor into an exhibit of the events of November 22, 1963. Some of the photos showed me at full tilt rushing to mount the president's car bumper.

There was one enlarged photo which singled me out—my covering the President with my torso as the bullet intended for the Chief Executive's head struck me in the back.

Obviously, someone in the crowd had been very alert and quick-acting to get these action shots. The Secret Service should have sought him out and offered him a job.

Choosing me for protective detail to the motorcade on that day had been a minor decision by Chief Rowland—something small—but it had saved us all because I kept the "People's President" alive.

On exhibit also was the sniper's "nest" constructed of various boxes on the floor. I looked out the window at the view the assassin would have had. Doing so made me exhale sharply: this would have been a turkey-shoot for someone with military training, particularly if he had the assistance of a scope. The would-be killer had enjoyed all the advantages that day. The fact that he'd been thwarted was most definitely God's hand at work.

I leaned against the window ledge and murmured a prayer of gratitude: "Thank you, Lord, for calling upon me at the moment I was needed."

I heard a soft swish of shoes on the wood flooring. When I turned, there was my wife. She had been standing close enough to overhear my prayer of thanksgiving. She looked up into my face, a face tested by experience and lined from years of pressured service, but one that still believed in the good that resided in the everyday American Citizen.

Gail murmured her own expression of gratitude: "Thank you for being you, a person who remained ever true to his calling."

Hand-in-hand, we turned together and took the elevator down to the street. We then left through the swinging glassed doors, thankful we would never have to relive that hateful November day of 1963.

Human beings cannot yet travel back to the past, but we can return to a place that transcends the erosion of time and thereby retain, even re-experience, a memory that ever remains immortal for us. Next stop: our return to the Costa Bravo to relive our honeymoon! After all, a promise is a promise, and I intended on keeping the one I'd made to myself way back in 1956. The hardest decision I'd be forced to make would be whether to take our various children, several of whom were now teenagers, with us.

If faced with the chance to relive your own honeymoon, what would you do?

ODE WRITTEN AS THE BELL TOLLS

The Lord lent him for only a day,
Then the Lord took him away.
Mankind needed the lad to stay,
Hope was lost when he went away.

Camelot was once ours, but now is gone.

The champion with the handsome head,
In whom dwelt such resolve
To achieve happiness for those
Who live in toil upon this earth,
That gallant leader is now dead.
Alas, he can lead us no more.
His wise eyes have closed,
His warm smile has gone cold.
We glowed for but a moment in the
Brilliance of his shining light;
Each of us is now the better for it.
Can the likes of him come forth again?
This hope shall burn ever so bright.

Words penned long ago by Sam N. Kirkland, a freshman at Yale College, while listening to the Harkness Tower bell sadly, so very sadly, toll the death of our stalwart President. The time was 2:30 p.m. on November 22, 1963. Over fifty years later, the pain of his loss still cuts so very deeply.

EPILOGUE

It is a shame that the foregoing are wishful imaginings regarding an event that altered history in a few seconds one November day in 1963. Very likely, what actually happened was kept secret by Mr. Hoover. As the head of the F.B.I. since the 1920's, this man had not only carved out a solid niche for himself (he referred to his agency as "the seat of government") but he also bore an intense dislike of Jack Kennedy as well as his younger brother Robert who was serving as the Attorney General. When Jack was running for the nomination as his party's candidate for president in 1960, Bobby had approached Mr. Hoover and asked him if he would step down should Jack win the election. This affront was neither forgotten nor ever forgiven by J. Edgar Hoover, and from that moment forward he maintained secret files on both brothers, placing particular emphasis on their sexcapades.

During the investigation into the events of November 22, 1963, this man's suppression, and outright denial, of any evidence contrary to the theory that there was a lone shooter during the assassination of the President was compounded by then President Lyndon Johnson's intense pressure on the Warren Commission to come up with a single-shooter theory in order to close the matter and sidestep any international entanglements of complicity.

From that time forward, Mr. Hoover sought to conceal, contain, and to wholly deny matters that could cast suspicion on what really occurred that awful day. His approach backfired, with the result that this singularly tragic, life-changing event is still being written about more than five decades later. This stupidly narrow-minded assassination tragically emasculated the improvement in the lives of everyday citizens, not just in this nation but throughout the world as well. The tragedy therefore remains a jack-in-the-box that keeps popping up even today. Separating fact from speculation and fantasy has obfuscated the truth. While *Something Small that Saved Us All* expresses one viewpoint of what we Americans soulfully wished had happened, the actual event on November 22 could well have transpired in this manner:

For years after the October assassination attempt, many ballistics experts and news editors speculated that the attack in Dallas had been orchestrated by a small, secret sect that sought to wrest power from a leader who eschewed armed conflict and thus stood to deny them the chance to profit from manufacturing goods for a foreign war. They reputedly found the perfect patsy in a wannabe who was willing to attempt an assassination simply because his victim was already so famous; killing a president would thereby project the pawn into becoming famous himself. The flunky fired twice: the first bullet was deflected by an intervening tree limb and struck the curb near the underpass, causing several bystanders to suffer small wounds from flying cement particles; the second penetrated the president's right shoulder blade adjacent to his windpipe and then passed on into the governor's chest and rib cage. He had been instructed to leave three shells on the floor. Unknown to this puppet, however, was the clandestine group's plan to have a second shooter stationed at a window at the opposite end of the TSBD building to fire at the president. This man missed; it was his shot that hit the governor in the wrist and leg. His escape through the rear exit was witnessed by several people. More likely, and most regrettably, some skilled assassin was stationed in the area of "the grassy knoll" who could have fired frontally into the president's forehead, thereby blowing the skull apart.

Due to the sound dynamics and echo effects of the plazas astride Elm Street, there would be intense confusion by bystanders about the noise from multiple rifle reports as well as the motorcycle motors, the nearby highway, and the adjacent switching yard. The professional shooter could have quickly disassembled his weapon and handed it over to a confederate who was dressed as a yard worker and could thus disappear into the rail complex. The lethal assassin, dressed in a dark navy business suit, could then melt into the general crowd of onlookers and, if confronted, use counterfeit identification papers to show he was functioning as a secret service agent. In all the terrible confusion, no one bothered to record his name or to question his presence.[1]

With Kennedy now dead and a more pliable man occupying the chief executive's seat, the clandestine group's goal of arms production funded by gargantuan government outlays would make their companies extremely wealthy on into the 1970's. Having achieved this goal, there would be no need to crow and boast about having shot the man standing in their way—which is often the downfall of a typical murderer—because they would be luxuriating in soft beds of billions of dollar bills.

They would justify their actions by stating: "This is America. In this country, we are permitted to earn money in any way we can!"

The loss to our country, however, is incalculable. His longtime buddy, Charlie Bartlett, remembered Jack Kennedy this way:

"We had a hero for a friend. We mourn his loss. Anyone—and fortunately there were so many—who knew him briefly or over a long period, felt that a bright and quickening impulse had come into their life. He had uncommon courage, unfailing humor, a penetrating, ever-curious intelligence, and a matchless grace. His life was our best moment. His loss is our worst. We will remember him always with love and, as the years pass and the story is retold, *with ever increasing wonder.*"[2] (emphasis supplied)

Jacqueline's stepfather was impressed by the freshman senator when Jack came-a-courting the then Jackie Bouvier (Auchincloss): "He always asked questions, but as you answered, he'd sit back and listen, treating you as if you knew more about the subject than you actually did. He was a wonderful friend as well as a husband for my step-daughter."[3]

Our country was the better for this man having lived among us. As his brother Robert intoned: "What happens to our country, and thereby to the world, depends on what we do with what my brother has left us."[4]

Similarly, Adam Walinsky, a graduate of Yale Law School and former assistant to Attorney General Kennedy, wrote that the question following JFK's shooting should not be: "What if he had lived?" but rather, "Going forward, what do we do with what is left us? It's up to those of us who remain to carry on."

Ted Sorensen said this of John Fitzgerald Kennedy in remembrance: "This man, commander in chief of the world's greatest military power, who during his presidency did not send one combat troop division abroad or drop one bomb, who used his presidency to break down the barriers of religious and racial equality and harmony in this country and to reach out to the victims of poverty and repression, who encouraged Americans to serve their communities and to love their neighbors regardless of the color of their skin, who waged war not on smaller nations but on poverty and illiteracy and mental illness in his own country, who gave his annual salary away to help crippled children, and who restored the appeal of politics for the young and sent Peace Corps volunteers overseas to work with the poor and untrained in other countries, such a man was a [magnificent] president." [5]

A further trenchant analysis is found in the writings of William Manchester: *A series of terrible "ifs" had accumulated. If there had been no Bay of Pigs fiasco, Khrushchev would not have concluded that Kennedy was a weakling and would not have risked creating the crisis in Berlin. "Brinksmanship with a vengeance" some have called it.[6] If he hadn't been the surprise loser there, the Russian leader would not have tried to regain prestige by installing missiles in Cuba, which resulted in an even bigger loss of face for him, depriving him of any influence in Southeast Asia.*

Khrushchev's actions caused Chairman Mao Tse-Tung to dismiss him as an insignificant leader, and thus China proceeded to encourage the North Vietcong to proceed with their long-drawn-out war of conquest in the south. [7]

People, while they are alive, can only provide a good example of how to live; it's up to each individual in his or her own life to actually go about doing so. The Kennedy years remain an important touchstone, a reminder of how great a man can be. More than any other actually elected president, John F. Kennedy's inspired oratory formed a pact with the youth of our country. It made us ebullient about beginning anew and throwing off the bonds of prudish, puritanical conservatism. He gave citizens the conviction that everyone could share in and be personally rewarded for the fruits of their effort and toil. He set so much in motion in the short time he was our President, but then vanished so quickly, that we never had the chance to possess the fruits of his leadership.

Despite the brevity of his tenure, he inspired us to subordinate our selfish impulses to higher ideals. His ambassador to the United Nations, Adlai Stevenson, remembered him as a contemporary man, involved in our world and immersed in our times, yet responsive to its challenges rather than engulfed by them. He embodied the essence of the vitality and exuberance of being alive. "Today we mourn him, but tomorrow we will miss him. His blazing talent and drive to labor on the unfinished agenda of peace and progress for all remains for another wholly unique and caring person to carry forward." [8]

Perhaps his own brother, Bobby, or a Eugene McCarthy or even a spirited and sage Bernard Sanders could have been as appealing to younger Americans, but each of these great men failed to attain the goal of actually being president. They could thus never experience the intensely conflicting pressures embodied in that office. It is one thing to **talk** about what you would do if you were elected, but it's quite another to actually **effect** those goals once you occupy the highest seat in American government.

Some might consider the following as the best summation of our nation's loss. It was written by a former member of JFK's staff, Harvard Law School graduate Richard Goodwin:

"There is no curse upon the Kennedy family. The brothers Jack and Bobby sought to change history, and some people cannot abide that. They lived heroic lives, but Joe Kennedy's family was not cursed. Since their deaths, time has shown that the curse is on our nation. Five decades have passed since their murders, but no new leaders have appeared to lead the country to the same heights. We've been on an endless cycle of retreat ever since the Kennedys passed into history. We no longer have the sense of excited involvement in, nor commitment to, our own country. These men made us feel that we were better than we ever thought we could be. They liberated the youth of America to pursue ends beyond their own individual gain, inspiring us to respond to the call to improve the lives of both ourselves and our fellow citizens." [9]

For his part, Lyndon Baines Johnson achieved great success domestically riding on the tails of Kennedy's tenure. These measures were part of a frothy period of social justice passed following Kennedy's death during which President Johnson intoned: "We have to value the natural landscape more than even our GNP because it is so very finite!"

1964: Civil Rights Act to ensure social justice before the law
Wilderness Act: preserving 9 million acres in a road-less natural condition

1965: Voting Rights Act
     Medicare/Medicaid
     Head Start
     Model Cities Act
     Numerous education and public housing laws which fulfilled our government's responsibility to those citizens who were "caught in the tentacles of circumstance," a phrase coined by his own father when he was a legislator

1964-1968: War on Poverty. President Johnson embraced this as his lifetime endeavor:
     "This is my kind of program. I'll find money for it one way or another. If I have to, I'll take money away **from things** to get money **for people**." [10]

Despite this whirlwind of achievement (Schlesinger called it *motion without movement*), he could not inspire everyday citizens to work for the good of society in the way his predecessor had. To inspire in others the exhilaration of pursuing idealism in America was not his forté.[11]

Robert McNamara is said to have stated simply: "There is no one on the horizon to compare with JFK's leadership."

Both the middle Kennedy brothers lived their political lives as though their broad smiles, clear eyes, and hand gestures were inviting us to: "Come, my friends, let us lead you to building a better America for all our peoples. Genuine pleasure will be found in the pursuit of excellence, so give your country your best, and we will give you ours."

The esteemed journalist James Reston added:

What was killed in Dallas was not only the President but, almost more importantly, his promise. The heart of the Kennedy legend is what might have been. [12]

As his devoted advisor Kenneth O'Donnell noted, President Kennedy was a most skillful politician who was fascinated by the give-and-take of political intrigue, winning of a reluctant leader's support, and the whole business of getting votes, no matter what the level of election. JFK was committed to politics because, "If we do not take an interest in our political life, we can easily lose at home what so many young men have so bravely, and bloodily, won abroad." [13]

He pursued his calling to lead our nation, and he did so nobly. [14]

It has been written by many about the power of coincidence, where seemingly insignificant events come together to set the stage for a truly significant result. A few call this Fate. Any one of the following decisions could have spared the life of this unique leader:

1. Using the bubbletop or a car similar to the Pope's protective vehicle
2. Stationing agents on the rear stand or walking astride the President's car
3. Using a driver skilled in reacting to an unexpected crisis
4. Selecting a different exit route as the cavalcade wound down
5. Positioning agents and policemen on the ground or on roofs along the route
6. Choosing a different city to visit
7. Being more guarded about allowing a defector, who traded national secrets (U-2 specs, etc.) in exchange for residency in the U.S.S.R., to ever return to America.

Alas, as Clint remarked earlier in *Something Small*, "life is a game we play which each of us must lose some day." For Jack Kennedy, that day was November 22, 1963. He probably suffered pain for fewer than six seconds, but for those of us who survive to this day, the pain has lasted a lifetime. We must not let his death negate the purpose of his having lived: a better world for all peoples.

Years later, Jacqueline said of her husband: "As President, Jack enjoyed solving everything that came his way. He derived satisfaction when dealing with some intractable problem. He'd smile at me and say, 'Someone has to do it!' Then he would relax by surrounding himself with friends with whom he could joke and kid and parry wits. He could even read while keeping alert to intense joshing going on around him. For him, doing so was like taking a swig of Coca-Cola: refreshingly bright!" [15]

An Englishman, David Pitts, who later immigrated to the U.S. and became a citizen, wrote of Jack's era as: *The last decade in which liberalism dominated American life. That may be why the man remains vivid in our memories. We have lost what we were and are uncomfortable with what we have now become.* [16]

Will we ever be able to govern ourselves for the good of all, and thereby reach the reality of a better life, rather than simply dream the dream?

Mr. Pitts quoted Jack as saying: *If, by a liberal, they mean someone who looks ahead and not behind, someone who welcomes new ideas without rigid reactions, someone who cares about the health, housing, education, civil rights, and jobs of the people, and someone who believes that we can break through the stalemate of international differences, then I am proud to say I am a liberal.* [17]

At his funeral, private grief mixed with widespread public sorrow. The person who grieved more than any of us was, of course, Jacqueline. In the November issue of *Look Magazine*, she said in 1964: "There is no consolation to my husband's death. What was lost cannot be replaced. He was magic, but I should have known that it would be asking too much to dream that I might have grown old with him and, together, watched our children grow up. So, now he is a legend when he would prefer to have been a man." [18]

His legendary wit was always at-the-ready to reduce his friends to fits of laughter. After the intense campaign and the narrow victory over Richard Nixon in 1960, he had noticed his very pregnant wife and their equally expectant friend, Antoinette Bradlee, descending a set of stairs together and eager to learn the election outcome. Spreading his hands expansively, the president-elect quipped, "It's okay, girls, you can take out the pillows now. We Won!" [19]

Jack and Bobby will be remembered as an inspiration to successive generations of young Americans, urging us to reach for ideals and to use our talents wisely in service to our fellow man. In fact, Jack Kennedy could very well have joked, "I know that history will treat me kindly because I intend to be the writer!" Other than Ronald Reagan ("It's good I ducked!" or "I hope everyone in here is a Republican..."), such ability to laugh at oneself or in difficult circumstances has never been supplanted.

This former man-for-the-people president could well have written:

In my memoirs, I will affirm that those who question the use of power are to be lauded. Protest helps determine whether those of us in government are abusing power or whether power is abusing us. I was lucky to have been born when I was: as your President, I fit my era. I hope that I have inspired many to give back to the country which has given us so much. And, I trust that everyone knows that I gave my all to the office of President of the United States!

As younger brother Ted Kennedy famously said at the 1980 Democratic Convention: "The work goes on, the cause endures, the hope still lives, and the dream shall never die."

His friend Ben Bradlee wrote of him some ten years later: "His brief time in power seems to me now to have been filled more with hope and promise than performance. But the hope and the promise that he held for America were real. Regrettably, they have not been approached since his death."[20] Bugliosi's penultimate analysis of November 22 noted that Kennedy's oratorical eloquence displayed the power of exemplary words, sprinkling the air with idealism which inspired so many to rally around the goals of changing our country, and the world, for the better.[21]

It is high time we located—and elected—an ineffable leader like him who can, once again, inspire us to be better than we thought possible.

Are you such a person?

I realize that, in your heart, dear reader, you have needed to sit and consider the great good which the presidency of John Francis Fitzgerald Kennedy could have achieved if he had been unharmed during his trip to Dallas, Texas. Yes, he had style and charm and good looks. Schlesinger noted that he quickened the hearts and minds of the nation. These attributes made him a charismatic leader. Of far greater importance was his vision for a better, safer world, and the drive he possessed to reach just such a world without prevarication. [22]

This great former President could have paraphrased the much-admired Robert Frost with:

I have miles to go before I sleep,
For I have many promises yet to keep.

They say the good die young, but our country died a little with him that November day. I hope that *Something Small that Saved Us All* has provided gentle solace for such a wide abyss which JFK's untimely death created in our national well-being. We have come to laugh again but, will we ever again know such verve?

Our former president always relished a good story. This one's been for you, Jack.

Notes

1. See Tague, p. 278 and following.
2. Matthews, p. 404.
3. Pitts, pp. 134-135.
4. Lieberson, p. vii.
5. Matthews, p. 389.
6. Schlesinger, *Journals*, p. 134.
7. Manchester, p. 215.
8. See Pitts, p. 248 for more detail.
9. Talbot, p. 375.
10. Caro, p. 540.
11. Schlesinger, *Journals*, pp. 223, 295.
12. O'Donnell, p. 414.
13. O'Donnell, p. 413.
14. Schlesinger, *Journals*, p. 204.
15. Schlesinger, *Journals*, p. 147.
16. Pitts, p. xix.
17. Pitts, p. 163.
18. Pitts, p. 249/*Look Magazine*.
19. from Bradlee, p. 32.
20. See Bradlee, p. 12 ascribing a litany of adjectives to his personality, such as "interesting, and interested!"
21. Bugliosi, p. xii.
22. See Schlesinger, *A Thousand Days,* p. xi, and p. 713 for a listing of proposals successfully passed by Congress.

WITH GRATITUDE

A skilled hunter thrills with the freedom of relying on instincts and experience to survive. The more elusive and experienced the quarry, the greater the satisfaction of success.

The same goes for me as a writer. According to the Internet, some 5,000 articles have sought resolution to the enormous psychic load that befell us Americans on November 22, 1963. In addition, 600 or so books have been written by erudite historians, skilled theorists, and savvy lawmen. The content of *Something Small that Saved Us All* sidestepped the speculation and controversy. It pursued a kinder event. The goal was to offer salve for the still-painful sore that dwells in the hearts of those of us who experienced the incandescent leadership and oratory of that exemplary American leader, John (Francis) Fitzgerald Kennedy. I trust its fundamental premise—that JFK was a very good man—was objectively presented and, most importantly, comported with the facts.

If a hunter is smart, she ignores the temptation to go-it-alone and partners with others in the field. I was fortunate to join forces with Pamela Kuulei Keyser for imaginatively spirited dialogue and accurate grammar. She is a published author (*The Red Glass*, Ex Libris Publishing, 2009) and is soon to publish a second book even as I pay her this heartfelt compliment. I have relished our partnership and warmly thank her for her commitment to good writing.

In closing, I thank you, dear reader, for coming along. It is often said that the journey can be more pleasurable than the goal, and so it has been.

Samantha Narelle Kirkland

BIBLIOGRAPHY

Andrew, Christopher. *For the President's Eyes Only.* New York: Harper Collins, Inc., 1995.

Beschloss, Michael R. *Kennedy & Roosevelt.* New York: Harper & Row, Publishers, 1980/1987.

Bishop, James. *The Day Kennedy Was Shot.* New York: Funk & Wagnall's, 1968.

Blaine, Gerald. *The Kennedy Detail.* New York: Gallery Books, 2010.

Blakey, G. Robert. *The Plot to Kill the President.* New York: Times Books, 1981.

Bradlee, Benjamin C. *Conversations with Kennedy.* New York: W.W. Norton & Co., Inc., 1975.

Broder, David. *The Party's Over: The Failure of Politics in America.* New York: Harper & Row, 1972.

Bugliosi, Vincent, Esq. *Reclaiming History.* New York: W.W. Norton & Co., 2007 (penultimate authoritative analysis of the events on November 23, 1963).

Caro, Robert A. *The Years of Lyndon Johnson: The Passage of Power.* New York: Alfred A. Knopf, 2012.

Churchill, Winston. *Their Finest Hour.* Boston: Houghton Mifflin Co. & Cambridge: The Riverside Press, 1949.

Dallek, Robert. *An Unfinished Life*. Boston, New York, London: Little, Brown and Co., 2003.

Fay, Paul (Red). *The Pleasure of His Company (i.e., Journal of a Friendship)*. New York: Harper & Row, 1966.

Giangreco, D.M. *War in Korea*. Novato, CA: Presidio Press, 1990.

Hamilton, Lee H. *How Congress Works*. Bloomington, IN: Indiana Univ. Press, 2004.

Hamilton, Nigel. *JFK: Reckless Youth*. New York: Random House, 1992.

Hill, Clint & McCubbin, Lisa. *Five Days in November*. New York: Simon & Schuster, Inc. (Gallery Books), 2013.

_____. *Mrs. Kennedy and Me*. New York: Simon & Schuster, Inc. (Gallery Books), 2012.

Kearns-Goodwin, Doris. *Lyndon Johnson & the American Dream*. New York: Harper & Row, 1976.

Kennedy, Caroline: President of the John F. Kennedy Foundation, "Jacqueline Kennedy: The White House Years" (Hamish Bowles, Ed.), The Metropolitan Museum of Art, New York, 2001.

Kessler, Ronald. *In the President's Secret Service*. New York: Random House, 2009.

_____. *Inside Congress*. New York: Simon & Schuster, Inc., 1997.

King, Stephen. *11/22/63*. New York: Scribner, 2011.

Klein, Edward. *The Kennedy Curse: Why Tragedy Has Haunted America's First Family for 150 Years*. New York: St. Martin's Press, 2003.

Kunhardt, Philip B., Jr. *LIFE in Camelot – the Kennedy Years*. New York: Time, Inc., 1988.

Lieberson, Goddard. *John Fitzgerald Kennedy: As We Remember Him*. New York: Atheneum Press/ Columbia Records Legacy, 1965.

Manchester, William. *Remembering Kennedy: One Brief, Shining Moment*. Boston: Little, Brown & Co., 1983.

Matthews, Chris J. *Jack Kennedy – Elusive Hero*. New York: Simon & Shuster, 2011.

McClellan, Barr. *Blood, Money & Power: How LBJ Killed JFK*. New York: Sky Horse Publishing, 2003.

Means, David. *Hystopia*. New York: Farrar, Straus and Giroux, 2016.

Mikaelian, Allen (with commentary by Mike Wallace). *Medal of Honor*. New York: Hyperion Publishing, 2002.

Neustadt, Richard. *"Afterward" in Presidential Power: The Politics of Leadership*. New York: Wiley, 1960.

O'Donnell, Kenneth P. & Powers, David F. *Johnny, We Hardly Knew Ye*. Canada: Little Brown & Co., 1972.

O'Reilly, William. *Kennedy's Last Days*. New York: Macmillan & Sons, 2013.

Pitts, David. *Jack and Lem*. New York: Carroll & Graf Publishers, 2007 (containing a very complete reference bibliography).

Posner, Gerald. *Case Closed*. New York: Random House, 1993.

Reeves, Thomas C. *A Question of Character: A Life of John F. Kennedy*. New York: The Free Press, 1991.

Schlesinger, Arthur M. Jr. *Jacqueline Kennedy*. New York: Hyperion Press, 2011.

_____. *Journals: 1952-2000*. New York: the Penguin Press, 2007.

_____. A Thousand Days. Boston: Houghton Mifflin Company, 1965.

Stone, Oliver. *JFK* (film starring Kevin Costner). Hollywood, CA: Time/Warner Bros., 1991.

Tague, James T. *LBJ and the Kennedy Killing.* Waterville, OR: Trine Day LLC, 2013.

Talbot, David. *Brothers.* New York: Free Press, Simon & Schuster, Inc., 2007.

Time-Life Books Editors. *Turbulent Years: the Sixties.* Alexandria, VA: Time-Life Books, 1998.

Weiner, Eric. *The Geography of Bliss.* New York: Hachette Book Group, USA, 2008.

Widmer, Ted. *Listening In – the Secret White House Recordings of JFK*. New York: Hyperion Press, 2012.

PHOTOGRAPHIC CREDITS

Page 89: No. PX65-108-1(also as: KN-C21922, and from the Internet Public Domain: http://www.weheartvintage.co/2013/03/13/60s-style-icons-Jacqueline-kennedy). Jacqueline Kennedy attending a dinner for the President of the Ivory Coast on 22 May, 1962. Photographed by Robert Knudsen. Used by permission of The John Fitzgerald Kennedy Presidential Library and Museum, Boston MA.

Page 111: Agent Clint Hill mounting the trunk immediately following the fatal shot to the President's head. From the Internet Public Domain: https://en.wikipedia.org/wiki/Clint_Hill_(Secret_Service) #/media/File: Clint-Hill-on-the-limousine.jpg.

Page 191: No. KN-26090. President John F. Kennedy delivers remarks at a signing ceremony for the Plans for Progress while standing below the portrait of Lincoln; sitting on his left side is Vice President Lyndon B. Johnson. Photo taken by Robert Knudsen. White House Photographs. Used by permission of the John F. Kennedy Presidential Library and Museum, Boston, MA.

Page 268: No. PX65-108-SCS 78990 and ST-498-1-62, and from the Internet Public Domain: http://www.apartmenttherapy.com/Jacqueline-kenn-123041). Mrs. Kennedy and John, Jr. riding Sardar while Carolyn rides her pony Tex at Glen Ora in Middleburg, Virginia on November 19, 1962. Photo by Cecil Stoughton. Used by permission of The John F. Kennedy Presidential Library and Museum, Boston, MA.

Page 286: No. PX65-108-SC578990. Viewing the parade following the inauguration of John F. Kennedy as the 35th President of the United States and his Vice President, Lyndon B. Johnson. Photo credit: United

States Signal Corps Photographic Collection. Used by permission of The John F. Kennedy Presidential Library and Museum, Boston, MA.

Page 327: No. PX65-108:1. Lyndon B. Johnson is sworn in as the Vice President of the United States during the inauguration of President John F. Kennedy in January 1961. Photo credit: United States Army Signal Corps Photographic Collection. Used by permission of The John F. Kennedy Presidential Library and Museum, Boston, MA.

Page 346: S.N. Kirkland family collection; taken by David Lorenz Winston in front of the Philadelphia Ethical Society building.

Chair with view on page 344, Cover, and End-flap are from the author's personal work.

LASTING LEGACY

Our former president, known and loved as JFK, will live on in the immortal words and works that he left behind. He will live on in the mind and memories of mankind because he will remain in the hearts of his countrymen.

Lyndon Baines Johnson as he addressed Congress, November, 1963

Few will have the greatness to bend history itself, but each of us can work to change a small portion, whether through events or rhetoric; taken together, such numberless acts can shape human history. My brother Jack could effect such change all by himself: he had the vision and force of personality to do it. He stood up for his ideals and acted to improve the lots of his countrymen and strike out against injustice. For all of us left behind, let us send forth our own tiny ripples of hope and, crossing each other from a million different centers of energy and daring, such ripples will build a current that can sweep down the mightiest walls of subjugation and oppression.

Robert Kennedy, 1966

Printed in the United States
By Bookmasters